THE DARK
CAILING

ALSO IN THE ARCANA CHRONICLES

Poison Princess

Endless Knight

Dead of Winter

Day Zero

Arcana Rising

KRESLEY COLE

THE DARK CALLING

THE ARCANA CHRONICLES

VALKYRIE PRESS

NEW YORK   BASIN TOWN   STERLING   REQUIEM   FORT ARCANA

Valkyrie Press
228 Park Ave S #11599
New York, NY 10003

This book is a work of fiction. Any references to historical events, real people, or real places are used fictitiously. Other names, characters, places, and events are products of the author's imagination, and any resemblance to actual events or places or persons, living or dead, is entirely coincidental.

Copyright © 2018 by Kresley Cole

ISBN 978-0-9981414-1-1
ISBN 978-0-9981414-0-4 (ebook)

Published in the United States of America.

—THE MAJOR ARCANA—

0. The Fool, Gamekeeper of Old (Matthew)
I. The Magician, Master of Illusions (Finneas)
II. The Priestess, Ruler of the Deep (Circe)
III. The Empress, Our Lady of Thorns (Evie)
IV. The Emperor, Stone Overlord (Richter)
~~V. The Hierophant, He of the Dark Rites (Guthrie)~~
~~VI. The Lovers, Duke & Duchess Most Perverse (Vincent & Violet)~~
VII. The Centurion, Wicked Champion (Kentarch)
VIII. Strength, Mistress of Fauna (Lark)
~~IX. The Hermit, Master of Alchemy (Arthur)~~
X. Fortune, Lady Luck (Zara)
~~XI. The Fury, She Who Harrows (Spite)~~
XII. The Hanged Man, Our Lord Uncanny (??)
XIII. Death, the Endless Knight (Aric)
~~XIV. Temperance, Collectress of Sins (Calanthe)~~
~~XV. The Devil, Foul Desecrator (Ogen)~~
XVI. The Tower, Lord of Lightning (Joules)
~~XVII. The Star, Arcane Navigator (Stellan)~~
~~XVIII. The Moon, Bringer of Doubt (Selena)~~
XIX. The Sun, Hail the Glorious Illuminator (Sol)
XX. Judgment, the Archangel (Gabriel)
~~XXI. The World, This Unearthly One (Tess)~~

THE FIELD OF BATTLE

During the Flash, a cataclysmic flare, the surface of the earth was scorched to ash, and bodies of water evaporated. Virtually all plant life was killed, most animals as well. The majority of humans perished, with women hardest hit. After months of total drought, rain began at last—then fell constantly, until the first flurries of snow. The sun has ceased to rise, leaving the world in endless night. Plague spreads. Famine is sweeping the land.

OBSTACLES

Militias unify, consolidating power. Slavers and cannibals hunt for new victims. All are bent on capturing females. The Bagmen (Baggers)—contagious zombies created by the Flash—roam the wastelands (the Ash), wailing for blood.

FOES

The Arcana. In every dark age, twenty-two players with supernatural powers are destined to fight in a life-or-death game. The winner will live as an immortal until the next game, when the fallen reincarnate. Our stories are depicted on the Major Arcana cards of a Tarot deck. I'm the Empress; we play again now. Death, my enemy through the ages, is now my staunchest ally. In our sights: Richter, the Emperor Card, who massacred an army, murdering my friend Selena and possibly Jack, my first love.

ARSENAL

Knowledge of the game will help me survive it. My grandmother was a Tarasova, a wisewoman of the Tarot. Before she died, she helped me to better understand my Empress powers: regenerative healing, the ability to control anything that roots or blooms, thorn tornadoes, and poison.

Though Death trains me, my powers have been muted by some unknown force, right when I'll need them most. Can I, along with my alliance of killers—rogues, witches, and warriors—defend against Richter's fiery wrath?

1

Do you not know you're pregnant?

Do you not know?

Do you not know?

I sputtered, "I-I . . . what?" *Tick-tock.*

Tick freaking tock. I'd been struggling to wrap my head around Jack's possible survival, trying to decide if Matthew was bent on driving me crazy.

Now this?

Aric's blond brows drew together. "You're carrying our child." Though he sat beside me on the edge of the bed, he sounded miles distant. "I was wondering why you hadn't told me. Clearly you had no idea."

This. Could. Not. Be.

I was seventeen, riding out an apocalypse and counting on a one-way trip against Richter. I clutched the sheets as the bed seemed to spin. "I didn't know—because it can't have happened. I'm on something. There's no way."

"There must have been. Paul tested your blood."

"You let him take my blood when I was passed out?" The idea of the two of them administering a pregnancy test on me rankled.

My reaction seemed to surprise Aric. "Yes. After my wife lost

1

consciousness, I bade our medic to determine what ailed her." When he put it like that, I sounded ridiculous to question his actions. "You were out for an entire day."

"That long?" I glanced out the window. A blizzard raged in the never-ending night. Lightning flashed as brightly as daylight, illuminating the dense shower.

Last I knew, we'd been hightailing it away from Richter and Zara's attack after meeting up with Finn. Then Matthew had contacted me, giving me a blinding headache and a nosebleed, but *letting me hear Jack.*

Matthew could have pulled up an old memory of Jack's voice, fooling me into believing he lived. But why?

"*Sievā*, when you lost consciousness, I was frantic."

I turned back to Aric. Silvery rays of light shot through the blinds, accentuating how tired he looked. He obviously hadn't slept. "Something else must be wrong. I can sense a seed deep in the ground—wouldn't I be able to tell if something was growing inside of me?"

He frowned. "Not necessarily."

"So how far along does Paul think I am?" For weeks, I'd had that ominous countdown feeling in my head. Had I been sensing *this?*

"His test could only confirm positive or negative. I was so stunned that I asked him to run it twice."

Of course Aric would be stunned. He'd longed for a kid. Yet even when he'd wanted to try to start a family with me, he'd doubted Death could help create life.

My heart twisted for him. When he found out he'd been duped . . . "Paul's lying to you. I took a shot. Remember? You and I talked about it." Aric had been delighted that I'd premeditated sleeping with him.

"We did. But I have to wonder how you're pregnant if a contraceptive was administered."

"He must've faked the test results." I knew how insane this sounded, but I still expected Aric to trust my word. "You believe his story? That he tried to get me on birth control and I refused? Why would I do such a thing?"

Seeming to choose his words very carefully, Aric asked, "Why would he lie?"

"I don't know." Paul had always been the most helpful person in this household. He'd taken such great care of my grandmother that I could've nominated him for sainthood.

"During that time, you were going through intense stress. And you admitted that things had gotten confused in your mind."

Before the Flash, I'd been programmed by Gran, then deprogrammed in a psych ward. After our reunion, she'd nearly programmed me again. In her last days, I recalled thinking that my brain felt like Swiss cheese.

Or a bloody battlefield.

"Perhaps they have again?" Aric offered gently. "Are you so certain of your own memories?"

Ugh! I wished I hadn't admitted my memory issues to him. "I remember the prick of the needle. I remember counting the shots Paul had left, figuring that Lark might want some once she found Finn."

What if Paul had given me a dummy shot? No! I refused to believe that. Because it would mean . . . *Nope. Not going there.*

God, I didn't need this right now; I needed to find out if Jack was alive. What if I'd . . . imagined Matthew's call?

Aric said, "I think you have been through too much trauma and tragedy. How could it not affect you? Especially during a pregnancy?"

I could kill Paul for this! Not because I believed I was knocked up, but because Aric did. This would crush the knight.

Though he'd adored his parents, Aric had accidentally killed them—and their unborn child—with his touch. Through one of Matthew's visions, I'd experienced Aric's harrowing grief. Even after two millennia had passed, he still carried it. "You told me that you trusted my judgment. I helped save our asses against Richter, but you're taking Paul's word over mine? He's lying, which means he's dangerous. Yet you're letting him walk around free!"

"When I realized his version of events was vastly different from what you told me two months ago, I asked Lark to monitor his movements with a creature."

Which only worked when she was awake. "I'm going to confront him." I leapt from the bed.

Aric swiftly rose to assist me. "In time. You need rest."

I grabbed my robe, pulling it over my nightgown. "Because of my alleged 'condition'? I feel fine."

"Can we not discuss this first? I am asking you to wait. Can you do that for me?" When I hesitated, he said, "Let me draw you a bath. We can talk. You can relax and contemplate things."

"A bath?" Not a murder?

"You can confront him later; he isn't going anywhere. Come, love."

If I was pregnant, I would definitely eviscerate Paul, and the red witch—my homicidal alter ego—would want to savor the kill. Maybe I should wait for my powers to recharge a bit. As my adrenaline waned, my weakness increased. "Fine." For now, I would cooperate with Aric.

I allowed him to lead me from the bedroom, shuffling along docilely—just as I had whenever the nurses had steered me around the mental ward.

As Aric filled the tub, the winds roared outside.

"What's going on with this weather?"

"A blizzard blew in not long after we arrived back here. We've had nothing but snow and lightning."

"What happened with Joules and Gabriel after I passed out? I'm sure you were all politeness when you kicked them out of the truck." A stray thought: *Where's the wedding ring I had in my pocket?* I'd vowed to give it to Aric after we'd returned home with Finn.

"Alas, I managed zero politeness when I ejected them." He added my favorite bath crystals to the water, bubbles forming. "In my haste to get you medical care, I drove directly here, taking no pains to elude them. I have little doubt that they followed us. Circe confirmed that she saw something land on the next mountain over, just in advance of this blizzard."

I tied my hair into a knot above my head. "Will they attack?" Had we bonded with them enough when all of us had worked together to survive?

At the edge of the tub, Aric helped me undress. "If they get hungry enough, they will. But should they somehow make it past Lark and Circe, they'd be thwarted by our home's defenses. Not even the Flash could overcome our blast-proof doors and bulletproof windows. We'll keep the castle on lockdown." He took my hand and assisted me into the water. "In you go. Is the temperature acceptable?"

No. I wanted to scour my skin. I reached for the hot water lever, but he stayed my hand.

"Too warm isn't good right now." He rose to switch on the bathroom heater, then returned to sit beside the tub.

"What are you talking about?"

"While you were unconscious, I did some reading. I have few books on the subject of pregnancy, but I scanned them all. Excessively hot baths aren't recommended."

Oh, yeah. That. "I'm not knocked up."

"Then why do *you* think you lost consciousness?" He dipped a cloth into the water. As he ran it over my back, my lids went heavy. "Why do you think your nose bled? I read that both can be symptoms of pregnancy."

Should I confess to him that Matthew had communicated with me? That *Jack* might have? Or would Aric take that as proof that I was mental?

I had more than one reason for confronting Paul. *I* needed to know if my mind was right. *Chain of logic, Evie.* If Paul convinced me that he was telling the truth about the shot, then I'd know I was whackadoodle enough to imagine other things—like Jack's voice. If I decided that Paul was lying, then why should I not trust my own mind? Why should I not believe Jack lived?

Reason told me that I'd gotten everything confused. History told me I'd had problems before, and I'd heaped tons of stress on myself. But I needed to believe.

I told Aric, "That truck window exploding in my face might've had something to do with my symptoms. Or anxiety. Even Paul said I probably had PTSD." That asshole. I dunked my hands under the bubbles, hiding my purple thorn claws. "Have you spoken with Lark or Circe about this?"

"They've both heard you're with child, of course. There's little they do not hear." Lark spied through her creatures, Circe through water.

We didn't have a lot of secrets here at Castle Lethe, a.k.a. the castle of lost time. "Then they might've picked up on my conversation with Paul."

He shook his head. "Regrettably, no."

"You asked them? Why couldn't you simply accept what I'd told you?"

"Can you say without any doubt whatsoever that he lied?"

After a hesitation, I said, "No. But I don't trust him." Unfortunately, I didn't trust myself completely either.

Aric washed one of my arms, then the other. "Until you have decided with absolute certainty, I will lock Paul in his rooms. Will that make you feel better?"

"Why are you being so understanding with him?"

"Not everything is black and white in this situation." He paused with the cloth. "This pregnancy does not strike me as lamentable. Nor worthy of a murderous rage. Yet your hair was turning red earlier."

"So, Paul will be acquitted because you don't think this is *lamentable*? He's screwing with our lives." With my mind.

"He has been a loyal servant to me since not long after the Flash." Aric had once told me that the medic had grown up in this area. After the apocalypse, he'd found Paul in the nearest town, treating others' injuries, sharing his supplies with them.

Aric had hired him, inviting him back here to do anything and everything—castle maintenance, vehicle repairs, cooking, cleaning.

"Well, he hasn't been loyal to me." I pulled my knees up to my chest. "And where's *your* loyalty? I told you that I wasn't ready to have kids, that I didn't want to bring a child into a world like this." For a split second, I wondered if Aric had conspired with Paul. My resentment simmered hotter and hotter. I understood why the Fury Card spat acid. I wished I could right now. "You can't truly want a kid."

Seeming to tread carefully again, Aric said, "I don't *not* want it. Maybe your pregnancy was inevitable. After all, a fertility goddess imbued you with powers. For ages, the Empress Card has been associated with motherhood."

And with wrath; I'd been imbued by the goddess Demeter as well. When she'd gotten enraged enough, she'd laid a curse on the entire earth.

I remembered the red witch saying, "Demeter withholds viciously—and gives lavishly. GIVE," right before I'd euthanized a colony of plague victims. Matthew had told me, "Power is your burden."

Not lately.

Aric continued, "When you wanted to use contraception, I agreed. But for whatever reason, this is our situation now. And I, for one, welcome it. After all the death I've caused—"

"I'm seventeen!"

"Your current incarnation has lived that long, but over your lifetimes, you're much older." Equal frustration showed in his expression, but he stifled it. "Can you not see why this could be a good thing, *sievā*? We will change history. Overturn the game. Perhaps even end it."

That prospect called to me. Before I'd lost Jack, I'd wanted to end the game more than anything. But the fact remained: I wasn't pregnant.

Aric cupped my cheek. "Talk to me. I need to know all the thoughts in your beautiful mind."

Jack's possible survival. Paul's lies. Aric's coming disappointment. Claws. Poison. Punishment. "I'm done." With my bath. With waiting to vent this rage.

I stood in the tub, glaring when Aric used his speed to lift me and wrap a robe around me. "I can walk."

"As you wish." He slowly set me on my feet. Back in our room, I passed the full-length mirror, pausing to take in my appearance. My eyes were glassy, my cheeks pale. I didn't *look* pregnant.

In the reflection, I spied the white bloom in a vase beside my bed, the rose plant Aric had grown from a seed after we'd had sex for the first time.

Over the millennia, he'd always carried a white rose on his standard. I'd painted one on the wall that overlooked our bed.

Was that budding rose one of those memory waypoints my grandmother had told me about? If so, what else did it signify?

Aric stood behind me and put his hands on my shoulders. For everyone else who'd ever lived, contact with his skin was lethal. For me, his touch was warm and pleasurable. Together we were different.

If Paul had given me a dummy shot, why *wouldn't* I have gotten pregnant? After all the times Aric and I had had sex?

Potentially unprotected sex.

I swallowed thickly, then closed my eyes to take a mental inventory of myself, using the same power I'd used to find seeds deep in the earth. *Sensing, sensing . . .*

I opened my eyes, staring into my own hollow-eyed gaze. *Oh, dear God.* Something felt fundamentally off with me.

Another glance at the white bloom. Aric had planted more than a rose seed two months ago.

I was . . . pregnant.

"You perceive something, do you not?"

Life and Death had gotten together—how could I think there'd be no repercussions? Realization struck: I was always going to get pregnant by him. He was right; it did feel inevitable.

Didn't mean Paul would escape my wrath.

Over the last several months, we'd been puzzled why my powers had grown weaker. Aside from the global destruction of plants, I'd blamed the Bagman bites I'd sustained or the weather—cold and lack of sunlight in the endless night. Aric had blamed my bottled-up grief over Jack.

Whatever the cause, a pregnancy couldn't be *helping* things.

How would I contribute in the battle against Richter like this? I was now effectively benched—and would be for months to come.

Aric caught my gaze in the mirror. "Love, all will be well if you trust me."

Paul had garnered my trust. The doctors in the mental ward had wanted me to trust them. Gran had. Matthew had. The Hermit had. *Just tell me your story.*

I was tired of trusting, could barely bite back that acid rage. The Empress didn't get caged or contained.

Or *compromised.*

Aric had seen me as a bloodthirsty red witch in the past and must fear I'd return to form. *He should.*

If Paul had screwed with me, he'd die.

I told Aric, "I *am* pregnant."

His eyes glittered with emotion. "So you are, little wife."

I smiled into the mirror. "Which means I'm going to kill Paul."

2

"This can't be undone," Aric told me as I laced up my boots. "If you're wrong, you will have murdered an unarmed mortal who's been of great service to everyone here. Guilt for things in the past already eats at you."

"Paul gave me a shot and told me it was a contraceptive. This happened." *Almost positive about that.* I finished with my boots. "I believe it's a woman's choice when to start a family. Paul has robbed me of my choice. I'm going to punish him for it."

"Who will deliver our child? After working as an EMT, he attended two years of medical school. He's the only one with medical experience. When I prepared this castle for any foreseeable future, I never imagined that you and I would have a baby—I have no other doctor for you."

"That's a problem I shouldn't even have to consider." More blame going to Paul.

"If not for your sake, then think of the Magician." Finn had gotten his leg mangled in a cannibal's bear trap. Then he'd rebroken it fighting the Lovers. The bone had never healed properly. "Paul believes he can reset the boy's leg."

I tensed. "He won't *touch* Finn." My happy-go-lucky friend might be a trickster, but the Magician was no match for Paul's scheming.

Aric looked taken aback by my tone. Changing tack, he said, "For two thousand years, I've rewarded faithful service from the mortals I employ, providing protection and guidance. Do we not owe Paul some consideration after his care of your grandmother?"

I recalled the medic's gentle expression as he'd tugged up Gran's cover, and a nagging doubt surfaced. I quashed it.

"Paul saved your life," Aric pointed out. "He dug bullets out of your heart."

"I can regenerate."

"Not when you had a contagion in your veins. His quick work could have been the difference between your surviving or not. I owe him my eternal gratitude for that alone."

"You think that contagion ran its course?" I tapped my chin. "Or maybe this spawn of ours will be part Bagger." After all, it'd only been a few months since four Bagmen had bitten me, per Sol's orders. *With friends like that . . .*

"I'm confident it ran its course. Remember how hard you were able to push yourself dancing? You were blooming with health." Except for my powers. "But that brings to mind an important point: You somehow found a way to trust the Sun Card after his betrayal, and he redeemed himself. I fear that if you suspend your trust of Paul, you'll hate yourself. Especially if he's innocent of malice."

"He's not. For whatever reason, he's lied to you about me. You told me you don't let vipers slither around in your home. Either he goes, or I go." *Go. Out into the wastelands.* Was the game calling me forth?

At that moment, I yearned to leave. To find out if Jack lived. To forgive Matthew if he did.

Maybe I wasn't hearing anything more from them because I was too deep in this castle, too far behind Circe's watery boundary. Out in the Ash, I might have a better chance of getting to the bottom of Matthew's message.

But Aric would never let me go. Especially not now. Yet more blame to lay at Paul's feet.

"Don't be ridiculous," Aric said, right on cue. "You're not going anywhere."

He hadn't said that Paul would be leaving instead. With a roll of my eyes, I headed toward the door.

Aric followed. We started for the east wing, wending our way among the numerous animals tromping, waddling, and skittering through the castle hallways. He scowled when a family of porcupines simply gazed at us, refusing to budge.

As we edged around them, I said, "It's freezing in here." My breaths smoked. The vines and roses I'd grown along the ceilings were already withering.

"I've started conserving fuel. Only our wing and the occupied rooms will be heated from now on."

"You told Jack we had fifty years of fuel."

"That was before I knew we would have a child. Resources must be managed differently now."

"What else has changed?" I slowed to a stop. "Maybe our plan to go out in a blaze of glory together?" He and I had agreed on a one-way ticket to fight Richter and save mankind. "I know you, Aric. I know you've already been puzzling out these new moving pieces...." Suddenly I couldn't get enough air. "One of us will have to live to raise a kid. You're going to make me win the game!"

I'd be forced to endure his demise, then later our child's. I'd have to endure life alone as an immortal for centuries.

In the meantime, I'd be separated from all the fighting, helpless to have a say.

"No," he said firmly. "Lark informed me she has no interest in immortality without the Magician, so I spoke to Circe." About being our Arcana patsy? "She has agreed to win the game, at a time in the far distant future. For now, we will defeat Richter and survive the battle. We will fight hard to live. Both of us."

"How? What's different?"

"I wish I had a specific answer for you, but I don't just yet. I learned that we're having a child less than a day ago. For eons, I'd envisioned a certain existence, then I altered my plans to have a life with you. Now everything is in flux once more." He took a step closer. "But I do know that we must be stronger, smarter, and more adaptable. We'll call on allies as never before. We'll do whatever it takes to survive long enough to raise our child *together*."

I must've looked unconvinced, because he said, "I have prevailed against the Emperor before." By using Richter's rage—his strength and his weakness—against him. "We can do it again."

"And if we fail? If we die?"

"With your consent, Circe will be our child's godmother."

Though our options were slim, I probably would've chosen her above anyone. She adored children. In a rare moment of trust, she'd once confided to me that she and her fiancé had planned on three of them. "I agree. She's a good choice."

"I also entreated her to do that memory spell for us." In future games, we'd be able to remember our shared past—so we didn't kill each other. "She said it is demanding to perform, but she will try."

Then he wasn't planning to crown me the victor. My relief was short-lived. I still had Paul to deal with.

Aric reached forward and cupped my nape. "I know what I want in the future. I know what I will work toward. And step one is making my wife believe me when I tell her this baby is a good thing."

I wanted to be more understanding with him. Yet I couldn't manage it at all. "Step one is getting rid of the man who betrayed me." I shrugged out from under Aric's grip and continued down the hall.

As we neared the den, I heard Lark and Finn laughing at some movie. The scent of buttery popcorn hit me, and my stomach lurched.

Aric said, "The Magician's appetite is equaled only by his use of incomprehensible slang. While you slept, he must have eaten a year's worth of rations."

Rations. I'd never heard Aric speak about food in those terms. So we were conserving everything? He'd been prepared to feed *Ogen*; I had to believe Finn would eat less than a demon/troll.

We reached the den entrance. Inside, the lovebirds were snuggled up on the couch.

Lark paused the flick. "Look! It's the mama bear, up from her nap!"

Between mouthfuls of popcorn, Finn said, "Blondie's baking a bun!"

I grated, "Apparently."

Lark scanned my face. "Uh, where're you headed?"

"To confront Paul. Seems he gave me a mock contraceptive shot. Then he lied and told Aric I refused to get one."

Finn set aside his jumbo bowl of popcorn. "Uncool! What gives?"

Good question. "I'm trying to figure that out myself."

Lark sat up straighter. "What happens if he did screw you over?" *If?* "Are we talking exile?" She waved at the window. Snow fell in a torrent of white. "'Cause that'd pretty much mean killing him. You ready to do that?"

"That, and so much more." Could she not comprehend what he'd done *to me?*

"Finn needs that leg operation." She pointed a claw-tipped finger at the Magician. "He tries to hide the pain he's in, but you can't hide things from a girl who can see through an insect's eyes."

"I'm chill, babe." Finn took her hand. "All in all, I'm not stoked to get my leg cracked again. And if Paul dicked Evie over, then he's got to vacate."

Again with the *if.*

Lark murmured, "You're just saying that because I told you Evie got you in here." I'd talked Aric into letting Finn live in the castle.

Gazing into her eyes, he said, "That's a pretty good reason, huh?"

Looking unconvinced, she turned to me. "I heard some of the stuff your grandmother said in those last few weeks. She was 5150 crazy, and you just sat there listening to it, hour after hour. How could it not affect you? You'd already been through a lot. Maybe you got confused about some things."

When Gran died, Aric had said much the same thing—that I was too shocked to grieve. Wasn't *too shocked* a way of saying *messed up mentally?* I shook my head. "I remember going to Paul for contraception, and I remember talking to *you* about it. I told you there were a few extra doses, and you said you'd leave the breeding to the animals."

Her blank look gave me chills.

"You *do* remember that, right?"

She stared at her animalistic claws. "I remember girl-talking with you, but not that specifically."

Perfect. A potential witness for me was casting doubt on my story. "Well, half of your brain was in a falcon at the time." When she'd been relentlessly searching for Finn out in the Ash. "You weren't tracking great yourself."

"Before you do anything to Paul, think about the fallout, Evie. This castle will collapse without him. We might have frozen food, but there're no staples. He prepares everything. Fixes everything. Cooks all the meals. Scrubs the entire place."

Her words only convinced me that we were far too vulnerable to him. "You've listed things he can *do* for us. Not reasons why he should be trusted." I continued down the hall, leaving Lark and Finn with worried expressions.

She called after me, "He fixed *you* when you showed up with three bullets in your heart and no legs to speak of!"

Aric caught up to me as I neared Paul's door. The medic occupied a large bedroom connected to a spacious study that had been converted into an examination area. When we entered, he was seated at his desk, making notes.

For my patient file?

He glanced back at us with a toothy smile, but his wide blue eyes held concern for me. "I'm not sure you should be up so soon. And I would've come to you." As accommodating as ever.

Doubts arose. *Maybe you've just lost it, Eves. Maybe Richter's attack was the final mental straw.*

Paul laid down his pen and twirled his chair to face us. "What can I help you with? I'm sure you've got a ton of questions. This is exciting, right? I know the boss is beside himself." He waved at Aric.

Before more uncertainty gripped me, I said, "You gave me a shot. Why wasn't there a contraceptive in it?"

He blinked, then said cautiously, "Because you told me you didn't want one?"

I clenched my fists. "You're lying. A little more than two months ago on the night all that snow fell, I'd been crying, and you asked me how you could help."

Paul scrubbed a hand over his buzz-cut black hair. "I did. I'd been worried about your mental health. You were cooped up inside, listless and not eating."

As if he hadn't spoken, I said, "As you injected my arm, you told me the contraceptive would last for three months, and I told you the idea of living that long seemed far-fetched. Your response: 'Better safe than sorry.'"

Paul's lips parted. "I don't know what to say. I don't remember things the same way." His voice was kind, his demeanor baffled. "I recall giving you a B$_{12}$ shot. You can look at your file. It's all right there."

"That's not what happened!" My claws budded.

"Evie, it *is*."

Aric watched this interchange with his muscles tensed, as if he expected he might have to step in—to save Paul. Aric was believing him over me.

I rubbed my temples. Maybe *I* should believe them over me?

No. Paul was lying to my face! For what malicious reason?

Gaze on my hideous claws, he held up his palms. "Ah, let's just take it easy. Hey, this is A.F." After the Flash. "Maybe I, uh, got everything wrong."

Why did he have to roll over? If he'd continued his denial, I would have skewered him.

"I don't want to do anything to cause a patient distress. Regardless of what happened in the past, you are pregnant now, and you don't look so great. Please let me check your vitals again."

"No need. You know how resilient I am." My claws *ached*. "Do you think a single medic and his lies can slow me down?"

When my hair began to turn red again, Aric stepped closer to me. A warning not to use my powers? As if I could! Though my claws had sharpened, my vines still seemed to be dormant.

Paul exhaled a breath. "Lies? You think I would purposely withhold birth control from you? Why would I do such a thing?"

"You know I don't want a child, and you know Aric does." Paul glanced at him with a nervous look. Again, I wondered if they'd plotted this thing. Gran would believe they had. *No, Aric could never do that to me.* "You're trying to drive a wedge between us."

"You're making me out to be evil. I'm not. I can only imagine the horror you've seen out in the Ash, but I'm not like the villains you've encountered. I'm not a cannibal or a mad scientist. I'm not a torturer living in a house of horrors."

"That's what makes you even more dangerous."

"All my life, I've tried to look out for others. To help." Paul's blue eyes were guileless, his tone willing me to understand and be rational. "That's my job, my calling."

Calling. Gran had mentioned the *dark calling.* Had she been talking about Paul? I remembered her words: *You have to kill Death. He will turn on you—they all will. Death is poisoning me!*

What if Paul had hurt her, and she'd thought Aric was responsible? What if *Paul* was crazy?

He must have lost loved ones in the Flash. Had the apocalypse twisted him as it had every other survivor I'd met? "What exactly did my grandmother die from?" I would go back and study each word she'd written in the back of my chronicles. I would compile all she'd told me—even what I'd considered to be mad rantings.

"Your grandmother was sick, had been suffering from strokes." In a tone that would rival a mental ward doctor's, Paul added, "Evie, do you not *remember* that?"

"Of course I do. I want to know why she took such a turn for the worse on the one night I left the castle."

"She'd been steadily declining." He turned to Aric. "You recall her condition when she first came here. You told me you'd feared she wouldn't survive the journey. I kept her alive for months more. When she passed, it was a mercy."

Though Aric had in fact found her in dire straits, I demanded of Paul, "Did *you* show her mercy?"

Meeting my eyes, he solemnly said, "I would never hurt anyone under my care. Never."

He was so freaking believable. So why didn't I buy any of this?

Aric gazed down at my face. "Let us leave and discuss things."

Paul stood, addressing him: "Sir, you've always been fair to me. What do you want me to do? How can I make this right? I need to make this right."

God, he was good. Aric looked sympathetic. Not me. The tiny hairs on my nape rose. *This is all an act.*

"My wife and I will consider the situation at length. In the meantime, you'll be confined to your quarters."

My head whipped around. "What?" Not good enough. Aric had said he'd keep Paul locked up until I decided his fate. I'd decided.

Paul told me, "You've been through so much, Evie. If you need me to stay sequestered to feel comfortable, then I'll gladly do it."

Baring my claws, I said, "I need you out of our lives—"

Aric took my arm and squired me outside, then shut the door behind him. "I'll install a lock on this after I escort you back."

"Locking him up won't be enough! If he'll do this, what else is he capable of?"

"*Sievā*, I cannot fathom any motive for his actions."

"What if *he* is crazy?"

"What do you wish me to do? Execute someone for mental illness? After the apocalypse?"

I didn't want Aric to kill someone he believed was innocent or sick, but . . . "I know he's acting. I sense malice in him."

After a moment, Aric gave me a grave nod. "Then I will exile him. Once the blizzard passes."

I ground my molars. "You expect me to wait for the weather to break?"

"It would be a death sentence otherwise. How dangerous can he be, jailed in his room? What will a couple of days hurt?"

"What will they help? If you believed me, you would cut him down!" Inhaling for calm, I said, "I can't wrap my head around this. My husband, the one who applauded my judgment, is doubting me." I turned back toward our wing.

In the den, Lark and Finn both sat up. "Well?"

I put my hands on my hips. "Don't you already know, Lark?"

She shrugged without shame. Naturally, she'd used one of her creatures to spy on my confrontation. "What if Paul did get everything mixed up back then? This Arcana stuff would be a lot for any mortal to take in. Just a few months ago, he was in a coal bin, hiding from a rampaging troll." Ogen.

"You want someone that messed-up to do surgery on your boyfriend?"

"Paul sounds good now," she said. "Good enough to fix Finn's leg."

I stared the Magician down. "Don't let him touch you. Please don't."

Eyes wide, he shook his head. "Wasn't gonna."

I looked from him to Lark. "Tell me you aren't trusting one of Paul's shots for protection."

Finn's face turned red. Lark glared.

Clearing his throat, Aric said, "Paul will be exiled once the weather clears. In the meantime, do not speak to him. Lark, you'll bring him meals and take over his duties."

She opened her mouth to argue, then closed it. Her gaze landed on me, her eyes tinged red.

Like a warning light.

Later that night, Aric and I lay side by side, staring at the ceiling in silence. The blizzard had strengthened, winds howling over the castle. Lightning flashed every couple of seconds.

Inside, flames crackled in the fireplace and warmth emanated from his skin. I gazed over at his flawless profile.

Before we'd gone to bed, I'd found the wedding ring I'd made him, still in my coat pocket. A startling thought had arisen: *I'm glad I didn't give this to him.* I'd hidden it in a drawer beside the red ribbon Jack had saved from before the Flash. That keepsake had survived even my run-in with Sol and Zara.

Aric turned to face me and rasped, "Talk to me." As I struggled to marshal all the thoughts swirling in my head, he said, "We agreed that if either of us needed something out of this relationship, we should talk about it."

"Can you not understand how trapped I feel right now? Not only have I had this pregnancy forced on me—against my will—I have to live in the same place with the asshole who betrayed me."

In addition to wanting revenge against Richter, I'd come up with four new missions: to find out if Jack lived, to somehow strengthen my powers, to uncover proof that Paul had harmed my grandmother, and to get him gone.

"I'm trying to protect you."

"How?"

"By making sure nothing is done that cannot be undone. You've never been pregnant before—all of this is new to us—so let's proceed with caution."

Was he hinting that my judgment might be off because I was knocked up? When would my judgment ever be considered *on*? "Why won't you even look at the notes I made?" Earlier, I'd written down everything I could remember Gran saying. To be fair, I didn't understand the majority of it, but some fragments were beginning to make an eerie kind of sense.

Aric hadn't even glanced at them. "Because I recall her vehemently accusing *me* of killing her. In light of that, I must discount her other statements."

"Maybe she confused Paul's actions with yours, or thought you'd ordered him to harm her." On the day she died, she'd told me, "He's murdering your last blood relative. A rat! The agent of Death. A salamander. Noon serpents in the shadow. Midnight takes my life!" What if she'd considered Paul to be Death's *agent*?

"Are you accusing Paul of cold-blooded murder?" Aric asked. "Even though he's never demonstrated a hint of anything sinister?

Again and again, he's behaved with compassion and loyalty. Malice on his part isn't logical. It doesn't make sense."

"But confusion on my part does?"

Changing the subject, Aric said, "Are we not to talk about our baby?"

"The li'l Bagger I'm carrying?" Sol had told me that his zombies transmitted a 'radiation-based mutation.' That couldn't be good.

"Our child will be mortal or Arcana. No more, no less. I've lived a long time, and I feel that all will be well." He reached for my belly. "I am asking you to trust me."

I brushed his hand away. "You have lived a long time. You've garnered a lot of experience. But not in this area." My head started to hurt. When would Matthew contact me again? *Where are you?*

For the hundredth time, I replayed my last exchange with him. Through our spotty telepathic link, he'd whispered in my mind. . . .

—*Have a secret. He doesn't want me to tell you.*—

My nose had been bleeding, my temples pounding. I'd mentally shouted, *Get out of my head, Fool!* He'd killed me in the first game, and he'd let Jack die. How dare he contact me!

He'd told me to listen. Then I'd heard Jack's voice: —"*What kind of danger is she in? Damn it, tell me! What's coming, coo-yôn?*"—

I'd whimpered. *Jack??? Is that you?* He'd sounded so close. Though I'd called for them, no one had answered, and I'd blacked out.

Aric narrowed his amber eyes. "There's something you're not telling me."

Until he trusted me *and* my memories, I wouldn't tell him about the message. "You, Lark, and Paul keep talking about how mixed-up I was when Gran was dying, that my head must not have been right."

"You'd suffered through so much, love."

"During that exact time, I made a big decision—to be with you. To be your wife. Maybe I really was mixed-up. Maybe I shouldn't have made any far-reaching decisions in that frame of mind."

His lips parted. "*Sievā* . . ."

"We either trust both my memory *and* my judgment, or we *dist*rust both. What will it be?" When he didn't answer, I turned over on my side, giving him my back. "Jack would believe me."

I could feel Aric's gaze lingering on me. His troubled sigh made my chest tighten.

3

DAY 514 A.F.

"A baby on the way—how delightful." A stream of water had just slicked across the ceiling of the (plant) nursery, then descended in front of my face as a plume of liquid.

Circe.

I sat in a corner with greenery all around me. In my lap were my chronicles and the list of Gran's statements. "Is nowhere off-limits to you?"

"Irrigation is my friend," she all but purred from the water. "Such a week you've had, Evie Greene. In your bid to save the Magician, you were attacked by the Emperor and Lady Luck, then aided by the Sun. Upon your return, you discovered you'd been impregnated by Death. Yet there is contraceptive drama. . . . Did I miss anything?"

"I am *not* in the mood." The breakfast I'd helped Lark prepare sat badly in my stomach. My cooking skills hadn't improved with disuse.

For the past two days, I'd come down here to search for clues, practice with my powers—and get a break from Aric. This morning, he'd tried to ply me with vitamins.

Even with the sunlamps on high, I'd barely managed to germinate seeds. As my chaotic emotions all battled each other, fury and misery took the lead.

I was furious at Paul for being a devious liar—and at myself for getting played. I was furious that Aric didn't trust me enough.

I was miserable not knowing whether Jack was alive. What if he'd somehow survived but he and Matthew were now in trouble? Had the Fool's message to me been a garbled plea for help?

Before that contact, I hadn't spoken to him in weeks, not since I'd read about his betrayal in the first game.

According to my chronicles, in the second game, he'd vowed never to win again if I would forgive him. I'd spared him, allying with him, while planning to poison him at a later date—just as I'd done with my other allies: Aric, Lark and Finn, the Lovers, and even Circe.

If my current allies could get over my vicious past, how could I hold Matthew's against him? Apparently, I could forgive him for *my* murder—but not Jack's.

Matthew, are you there? Answer me! Jack? Are you . . . alive?

Tears welled, so I turned away from the water plume. It slinked around to my other side. "Ugh! You're like a spider dangling from a web."

"If I'm Charlotte, that makes you Wilbur." When I didn't remark on that, she said, "Come now, chin up. This isn't the end of the world. That already happened." Though she sounded playful, a strain of fatigue marked her voice.

"You truly didn't hear me talking about that shot with Paul?"

"No." At my irritated look, she said, "I do have to sleep every now and then. And I monitor other bodies of water all over the world."

"Have you seen Matthew or anyone else out in the Ash?" I was tempted to reveal that I'd heard them, but my same hesitation arose. Something told me that in the very near future I'd need all the credibility I could muster.

"I've seen no one. I would've told Death if I had."

"But not me?"

The plume seemed to shrug. "We're still not allies, even if I'm your child's godmother."

A gust rocked the castle. Boards groaned, and grit dusted down from the ceiling. Were we headed into an ice age? "Is it cold in the abyss?" Circe had once told me she lived at the bottom of the sea in the Bermuda

Triangle. She'd shown me her torchlit temple through a water window.

"Yes, compared to the sultry breezes and bright rays I was always used to. To the north of the castle, the temperature has dropped even more sharply. No matter how much I churn my rivers and streams, they're icing over. Without them, I can't see or hear Richter's approach. Without flowing water around the castle, I won't be able to ward him off."

If the Emperor found our home, we would be under fire. Literally. "Wouldn't Richter melt any ice?"

"I'll be able to put out the flames, but I won't be able to prevent them. By then the damage would be done. Without advance warning, well, as Fauna would say: you're all sitting ducks."

"Maybe the temperature is weakening him as well."

"Yes, now he'll have the impact of one atomic bomb instead of two. All of the players who defeated him in the past did so before he grew too strong."

Like Death. Two games ago, he'd strategized to get the enraged Emperor to blow all his power before striking him down.

Aric had said he would teach me how to fight an Arcana like Richter as soon as I'd reclaimed my powers and invoked the red witch as never before.

I didn't see that happening anytime soon.

Circe murmured, "I should have drowned the Emperor before this cold came."

"Why didn't you?"

"After the Flash, I thought I wasn't yet strong enough, was greedy for the rain." She sighed. "Perhaps I was never meant to flourish in this game. Certain catastrophes affect some cards more. This seems designed to harm me—and you."

Because I needed sun? I'd perked right up when bathed in Sol's light. "When do you think Richter will come for us?"

"Sooner, now that we have company in the neighborhood. His high-value targets are the Centurion, the Tower, the Angel. The latter two have set up camp on the next mountain over, just beyond your line of thorn trees and my diminishing reach." I'd noticed that her river had receded since we'd left to retrieve Finn.

Yesterday, Lark had said, "Finally, she's not breathing down my neck. What to do with all this elbow room? Maybe practice my faunagenesis?" That's what she called her animal regeneration.

In theory, her blood could reanimate all creatures, not just her three wolves and falcon familiars. She'd never tried it before.

I asked Circe, "Richter wants to take down those three Arcana even more than me?"

"All of them can strike from afar. After Fortune's encounter with you, I doubt he considers you a threat."

Zara had sneered to me, "The great Empress? You're just a weak little girl." Without my powers, I *wasn't* a threat. No wonder Aric hesitated to teach me about the Emperor. If I ever faced Richter, I'd get myself killed.

I scowled at my stomach. *Not helping things, kid.*

"Soon the Tower and the Angel will no longer be a worry for anyone either," Circe said. "They're starving. I suppose you could say they're at Death's door."

I couldn't stand the thought of them going hungry. "There's got to be food out there somewhere."

"Such as Olympus, the Sun's bountiful lair? The last I saw, the prisoners you freed were rioting. Chaos was the only thing you left growing there."

Not my best moment. "What about the Lovers' shrine?"

"Raided by the other half of the hunter's army." Jack's Azey army. "Without leadership, they've scattered to the winds. There were government facilities and stocked bomb shelters, but Richter keeps sending lava underground, incinerating them."

Hell on earth. We were going to need every Arcana to fight against him. I would talk to Aric about giving my friends food. Maybe I could pay Gabe and Joules to do a search for Jack and Matthew! As soon as the storm broke, I'd contact them. "Are *you* going hungry, Circe? What do you even eat?" I'd never asked her before.

"Whatever I can drag down."

"Like a tiger?" Lark had suspected the witch of tiger theft.

"What? Me? I would never!"

If Circe's rivers froze over, what could she drag down? "Do you need us to send you food? We could try to waterproof a barrel or something."

"It's much easier if I come to land in my true form and eat."

"Not the water-girl form you use to sneak through the castle?" I'd seen her liquid body skulking around before the snow had come. We'd found wet footprints in the pool house.

"Such aspersions!" she cried, but I could hear the humor in her tone. "You're not the only one struggling with powers these days. My water form is difficult to maintain. Materializing is simpler."

"I thought we all agreed that your body wasn't coming to land as long as the game continued." Or until Aric and I died, and she came to claim our kid.

"It's awfully quiet down here in this lonely abyss. You four sat together this morning to share breakfast." Her voice grew absent as she admitted, "I felt a scalding envy."

"I'm sorry."

Making her tone brisk, she said, "While you were unconscious, I officially met Lark and Finn."

Apparently, the lovebirds had been bonding like crazy, whenever Lark had time off. The blizzard meant she was getting a break from her Richter-watch duties. Even if her falcon could negotiate the arctic wind gusts, visibility was nil.

"Finn wanted to share magic secrets with me." Circe chuckled. "How adorable. He's only an illusionist, able to create lifelike scenes and fool the senses, but not much more. An *entertainer* versus a *practitioner.*" At my raised eyebrows, she said, "He can't seal blood invocations to stretch over centuries or brew esoteric potions. He doesn't control a spell book that's as old as the oceans. While Finn can mimic the look of a tide, I can steer them. I explained all this to him." Circe wasn't one to sugarcoat.

"What was Lark's reaction?"

"Sharpened fangs and claws. Even her ears seemed to point. In her mind, he's one of the greats. They're already so in love, picking up right where they left off in the last game. Just before you murdered them."

I can deny nothing. But her comment made me wonder what my relationship with Aric would be like if we'd had no animosity between us in the past. Maybe he would believe me about Paul.

Earlier, Aric had told me, "I informed him that he will be exiled once the weather breaks. *Sievā*, I will not reverse myself on this." His gaze had gone distant. "We're giving him no mercy with this course. Exile equals execution."

True. I'd often pictured the castle as a spaceship on a barren moon, with the only life support around: crops and livestock, clean water, sunlamps, and tankers of fuel. But I still wasn't satisfied with only a banishment, much less a belated one.

I asked Circe, "Have you noticed anything off with Paul? Ever heard him say something suspicious?"

"Not a single time. In light of current events, I suppose you no longer want to set me up with him?"

I might have once mentioned that. "I got conned. We all did." But Lark and Aric still seemed to be under the influence. The jury was out on Finn. "What would you do about Paul if you were me?"

"In the past, you would already have stabbed him with your poisonous claws, then desecrated his corpse with your plants. In this life, you've agreed to wait for an exile, with the added mercy of a storm break. Perhaps you are different from before."

That was about the nicest thing Circe had ever said to me. Great. Now I'd have to go along with the exile plan just to stay in her favor. *Don't want to piss off the watery godmother.* "So, speaking of sealing blood invocations across centuries . . ."

"I told Death that I would look into a memory spell as a gift to honor my alliance—with him." Was I never to be forgiven for betraying her in the past? I'd keep working on her. "Such a spell would tax me greatly."

Making my tone light, I teased, "Ah, but you're a *great practitioner.* Unless you think I should ask Finn to do it?"

"You push your luck, Evie Greene." But she sounded amused.

"So you're freezing, and I'm knocked up. Ain't we a pair?"

"Worse things could have happened."

"Really?" I was having a difficult time seeing this pregnancy as anything other than a parasitic invasion—probably not a tidbit I should share with the kid-loving Ruler of the Deep. "One of the last entries my grandmother made in my chronicles was *She can never be with him. She has no idea what Life and Death become.* Sounds pretty dire to me."

"Perhaps you two become the End *and* the Beginning. The end of the game and the beginning of a new era."

"Gran said the earth won't come back until there's an Arcana victor." Until all were dead but one.

"Though that was true in the past, do you not feel as if destiny had a hand in this pregnancy? Life and Death uniting for the first time? Maybe the arrival of your baby will bring about the rejuvenation of the earth. I told you the Fool's powers were unfathomable, but Mother Earth also has powers of birth and rebirth that we can't know."

"Mother Earth, huh? So I pop out a kid, and the sun rises?"

In a wistful tone, she said, "I can imagine an infant's cry clearing the skies for the sun to shine. I see tiny balled fists flailing in time with grass poking up from the soil."

I blinked at the water plume. And everyone thought *I* was loopy? "When Aric and I first slept together, the weather freaked out. Apocalyptic hail, winds, and lightning. We both had the feeling we were crossing a line that maybe we shouldn't."

"Hmm. Do you think the gods were protesting?"

"Sounds insane when you put it that way. But Matthew specifically told Finn that the gods mark us all."

"Perhaps he meant that they were *listening* to us. A pregnancy like this would be a huge statement, a message that we Arcana won't be defined by our histories."

Yet all the other cards kept defining me by mine. *Everyone knows the Empress breaks her vows each game.... The Empress is a treacherous betrayer.... Creature, you folded first....*

"In short, I believe this is a good thing," Circe said. "It's in our best interest to protect you and your child."

At least I'd no longer fall asleep wondering if she would turn against Aric and me. "What happens if I have this baby, and nothing changes?"

"The game trudges on." The plume suddenly perked up. "Do you hear that?"

"What?" All I heard were assorted animal grunts in the castle above.

"A ringing sound. It seems Death is getting a call."

4

I ran to Aric's study. Only one person would be calling him. The Centurion.

When I sped through the doorway, Aric was sitting at his desk, phone to his ear. He gestured for me to join him. I took a seat and dropped my chronicles onto his desk. Scattered over the surface were papers that looked like inventories. Of our *rations?*

"Then we're in agreement," Aric said into the phone. "You have our coordinates. When can we expect you?" Pause. "Very good." He disconnected the call.

"Was that Kentarch?"

Aric cast me one of his unguarded smiles. "Indeed. He is journeying to the castle as we speak." He sounded almost jubilant.

"What was the agreement?"

"His months-long search for his wife, Issa, has reached a dead end." Aric had told me that Kentarch was obsessed with finding her. "He needs Fauna's tracking skills. In exchange, he will join us here and help protect the castle and those within."

"What if Issa's not alive?"

"The odds are against her survival, but he refuses to accept she might be gone."

Sounded familiar. "If you're so concerned about rations—and about the convergence of cards—why would you invite another Arcana here?"

I knew Kentarch wasn't a friend of his. Just a few nights ago, Aric had told me, "Jack was the closest thing I've had to a friend since my father died."

Aric stacked papers on his desk. "I invited him because his teleportation ability makes him a crucial ally. Aside from that, he is a decorated soldier with an impeccable military record and advanced technical skills. He told me his truck is a weapon in itself, stocked with guns, a winch, and hi-tech electronics."

"If he can teleport, why does he need a truck?"

"As with all Arcana, he must conserve his power." According to my chronicles, I'd been able to defeat him in a past game because he'd been wiped out. "And his dire food situation has weakened him. Once he's here and rested, he will be an invaluable safeguard, able to evacuate this castle's inhabitants, should the need arise. His presence will help me sleep better at night."

I thought of Circe's "sitting ducks" comment. She wasn't the only one worried about that. "Evacuate all of us? Not just me and a kid?"

He inclined his head. "All of us."

"What's Kentarch like?" When Aric's gaze slid to a folder on his desk, I teased, "Do you have, like, a dossier on him?"

"Yes." He handed it to me.

Brows raised, I opened the folder. The photo on the first page was of a young man dressed in a military uniform and beret. *Whoa.* Kentarch was hot, with smooth, dark skin, intense brown eyes, and sigh-worthy cheekbones. He looked to be in his mid-twenties.

I thumbed through his basic information. *Born into the Maasai tribe in Kenya . . . raised to be a lion hunter . . . nearly killed by a lion . . . still bears scars over his torso.*

Before the Flash, he'd been assigned to train conservation officers. He'd gone from hunting lions to protecting them against deadly poachers. Talk about a change of heart.

I knew from my chronicles that he'd also been called the Chariot. His title was the Wicked Champion, his card all about duality and victory. His Arcana call was *Woe to the bloody vanquished,* and he'd always allied with Death and Circe.

I closed the folder. "Do you have one of these on me?"

After a slight hesitation, Aric went to a cabinet and retrieved another dossier. Why had he never divulged this to me?

Another pause before he handed it over. Mine was much thicker than Kentarch's. On the first page was a glossy picture of me from some social media account or another.

My smiling face had clearly been stabbed with a blade.

I ran my fingers over the serrated edges. *So much rage.* It reminded me of our early days in this game when I'd been his prisoner; the nights he'd tormented me, making me walk barefoot over punishing terrain; how he'd forced that barbed cilice onto my arm to curtail my powers.

I peered up at him. "You really despised me."

"I did." Honest as ever. "Your actions warranted it."

"The Lovers were shaped by their deranged father—and my history with them. I'm pretty sure the Hermit was abused by his father as well. Maybe those Arcana wouldn't have become murderers if their parents had treated them decently. If taught a better path, *I* might not have become a murderer."

But no matter what, the heat of battle would still have called to me. My mind touched on memories of what I'd done to the Lovers in a previous game before I recoiled from those grisly scenes. "Or maybe *killer* is my default. Aric, what if I'm . . . evil to the bone?"

He didn't answer, his gaze growing unfocused.

"Aric?"

"My apologies. These errant thoughts keep hitting me. Strange." Seeming to shake himself, he murmured, "You were saying?"

"Forget it." I glanced at the folder again. The picture of me was pre-Flash. "How did you know I was the Empress in this game?"

"Your home has always been called Haven. You were the right age. I sensed it."

Just as I sensed Paul was a dangerous liar. I flipped through more pages, coming across aerial maps of the sugar cane farm. Aric had known right where I was. "You could have struck before the Flash."

Nod. "I think some part of me hoped you would perish."

"And spare you the confusion? What a great foundation we have." I quashed the urge to cheerily ask him, *What color shall we paint the nursery, darling?* "And now I'm carrying the spawn of a bloodthirsty Empress and Death—seasoned with zombie juice. What could possibly go wrong?"

Aric shook his head. "Do you not understand how monumental this is? We are changing history. You wanted to end the game; this child might do just that. Our destiny feels fated. It feels *right.*"

"For you!" I cried, slamming the folder onto his desk. "Of course it does to you. You're the Grim Reaper, and all of a sudden you believe you're going to have a line to come after you. But I'm the one bearing this burden. The real reason you hesitate to punish Paul is because of *what he's done for you.* Because of his actions, you're getting what you want most—a child."

Bitter laugh. "Do you think that's what I want most?"

"Then what?"

Aric stood. "I wonder if you know me at all."

I watched him walk out the door. He'd left me with my folder. Part of me clamored to read the rest of the contents, but I feared to as well.

Our strained relationship couldn't take the weight of a feather right now.

5

DAY 528 A.F.

I tossed and turned in bed as the blizzard-without-end raged on. When I finally drifted off to sleep, a nightmare scene arose.

Richter and Zara, the deadly Fortune Card, were in a locked warehouse full of their ragtag prisoners—men, a few children, and even a couple of women. Ropes bound their captives' wrists.

Zara reached out a bare hand to touch one man's face. As soon as their skin made contact, her eyes and veins turned purple. She'd just stolen his luck!

She moved on to the man beside him, and then the next. She even knelt to brush one child's tears away.

When she'd harvested from all of them, Richter motioned for her to leave. They shared a look as he locked the door behind them.

Outside, Zara handed him a knife. As she gazed on with sick fascination, Richter sliced his palm. Blood welled, beginning to glow and heat, turning into lava. It pooled out of his skin, spreading over the ground, nearing the warehouse.

Then he began to slowly cook those people. . . .

I shot upright, their agonized screams still ringing in my ears.

Had that been a dream, or had Matthew sent me a vision of Zara building up her luck reserves through survivors?

I rubbed my eyes, glancing at Aric's empty side of the bed. He rarely slept these days. With a troubled sigh, I rose, anxiety like a noose around my neck.

Despite this, my stomach growled. I glared at my belly, then bundled up in a thick robe and slippers. Maybe if I could keep some food down, it'd help me sleep. As tension mounted within the castle, so had my nausea.

I started for the kitchen, my breaths beginning to smoke in the stairwell. The winter storm continued, the temperature dropping. Paul remained.

After mulling over what Gran had said and written in her last days, I'd grown more convinced that he'd harmed her. Yet I'd lived under the same roof with her killer for an additional two weeks.

I passed a frosted window and glowered at the falling snow. Nature wasn't cooperating with me—or Circe. Whenever she slept, ice would creep over the moat. To break up the frozen surface, she would strain her powers.

We often heard ice cracking down at the river shore, then the SLOSH as a huge block plunged into the water.

If the weather didn't change, she waged a losing battle. When I'd spoken to her a couple of days ago, she'd sounded increasingly weak and harried: "The ice choking my rivers is like giant earmuffs. The thicker the ice, the more isolated I feel." She'd added in a whisper, "My coffin of ice . . ."

Downstairs, I shuffled through the withered leaves covering the floor. All my vines had died. My powers showed no signs of rebounding; my red witch seemed to be taking a long winter's nap.

The light in the kitchen was on. I wasn't the only one making a food run at this late hour. Could it be Aric?

He and I seemed to have reached a standstill. When he wasn't training to an obsessive degree, he was staring out the window, awaiting Kentarch's arrival.

I'd once felt like the castle of lost time was a powder keg. Now it seemed to be a warhead. Just when I was ready to go nuclear on Aric, he would come to bed and we'd lose ourselves in sex. He was gentle, even worshipful.

Last night, I'd again tried to reach him.

"*You keep saying this is my home, but it doesn't feel like it. It won't as long as Paul's here.*"

In a distracted tone, he answered, "*I've made my decision. The rest is up to nature.*"

"*You told me I could decide his fate.*"

"*And you have. But I have chosen the timeline: after the blizzard.*"

That comment still set my teeth on edge.

I found the Magician in flannel pj's, raiding the fridge. "Blondie!" His brown eyes lit up. Since he'd arrived, he'd put on weight, thriving here—except for his leg.

I often heard Lark and him laughing as they explored the castle. I envied the simplicity of their relationship. They had no baggage, and they didn't take a single second for granted.

He asked me, "You making another attempt at dinner?"

Earlier, I'd bolted from the table to vomit up good food. *Thanks, kid.* Jack had once called Matthew a resource-suck; I was currently saddled with one. "Maybe I should."

Finn held up his triple-decker sandwich. "Here. Take mine." A dollop of mayonnaise oozed to his plate. *Plop.*

Ugh. "No thanks. I'll just grab some toast."

"Suit yourself, chica." Balancing his plate, Finn maneuvered his crutch to hobble over to the kitchen table. Without a hint of bitterness, he said, "When you have a crutch, you're always one hand short." And a Magician would need both of his. Finn's Arcana call was *Don't look at this hand, look at that one.*

I popped a frozen piece of bread into the toaster, then poured a glass of milk. Now that Lark had taken over cooking duties, I helped her as much as possible. Mainly, I cut up things while trying not to puke.

She'd prepared meals for her dad before the Flash, so she could put together a decent spread. But she couldn't recreate Paul's staples—like hot-out-of-the-oven pastries and succulent, freshly butchered game; our frozen supplies continued to dwindle.

When Finn dropped down into a seat, he banged his bad leg, gritting his teeth. He lived with that pain every day, had only one hope of ever getting it fixed.

Yet I was standing in the way, which hadn't improved my relationship with Lark.

Her single-minded pursuit had fixated on one goal. We'd had another clash earlier:

"Just admit you're wrong about Paul," she demanded. "He'll forgive you. And then he can help Finn."

"I'm not wrong."

She studied my face. "Then are you right?"

Right in the head? Right in the definitive without-a-doubt sense? I had no good answer to that, so I asked, "Have you been talking to Paul when you bring him meals?"

She peered down at her claws. "Boss said not to."

In other words, yes. "Lark, I believe that my grandmother was warning me against him—so he murdered her."

She slapped her palm against her forehead. "That's really freaking stupid, unclean one. Who the hell would kill the dying?"

Sometimes I wanted to strangle Lark. She was like an annoying little sister. And like siblings, we fought and made up.

"Got a joke for you," Finn said between bites. "What do you call sixty-nining between two cannibals?"

I took my milk and dry toast to the table. "An exercise in trust?"

"No." His lips curved. "The first course. But I like where your head's at, blondie."

"That's really awful, Finn," I said, though I had to fight a grin.

Looking pleased, he said, "The world might be different, but we've still got to find the humor. I've been working on Death. Talked to him today."

"Did you?" Though Aric didn't consider Finn a friend and likely never would, he'd gone so far as to say that the Magician's heart was in the right place. "What'd you talk about?" I nibbled the toast, trying to decide if it'd stay down. *Fifty-fifty chance.*

"Guy stuff. I can't betray the code. But the more I get to know the Reaper, the more I like him. You've got stout taste in dudes." At my expression, he said, "Sorry. Boneheaded thing to say."

"Don't worry about it." I considered asking Finn his opinion about Matthew's message. No, he'd tell Lark, and she'd tell Aric.

"So, are you amped about becoming a mom?" Everyone seemed excited but me. Even Lark had said, "Maybe this could end the game. Finn and I might actually have a shot at a normal existence together!"

I gave him the look his question deserved. "I'm *seventeen.*"

"Maybe in this life. Lark said you've clocked more than a century between your incarnations. We all have, right?"

Technically, I was well over a hundred. I guessed I couldn't view Aric as two thousand years old unless I copped to being a centenarian.

Taking another bite, Finn said, "Even though you're hella old, I think you'll make a great mom. Mothering is what Empresses are supposed to do, right?"

As a little girl, I'd played with baby farm animals—not baby dolls. I'd never even liked kids. "As the Empress, I think I'm supposed to kill."

"But you're the Arcana who pushed hardest to *end* the killing. I thought about you a lot when I was on the road with Selena. If you could ally with her after she tricked you, I figured I could forgive her for targeting us for elimination and all." In a softer tone, he said, "I think that's the most important thing to do as a parent—forgive."

Finn's parents hadn't forgiven him for his involuntary pranks. They'd shipped him across the country, booting him from his beloved California.

"Speaking of forgiveness," he continued, "Joules and Gabe are out there, starving. Lark's falcon spotted them, and they're looking rough."

If Jack lived, was *he* starving?

And yet here I was again, holed up in this castle, not helping, not doing anything but biding my time.

Finn laid aside the remains of his sandwich. "Death hasn't changed his mind about throwing them a bone?"

"It's still a solid no-go." When I'd broached it a while back, Aric had said, "If we feed the strays, they will never move on, and a larger convergence of cards could lead Richter here sooner. Plus, I make it a rule not to extend a hand to those plotting against me."

I told Finn, "Maybe if Joules wasn't so bent on electrocuting Aric."

"True. I had to give it a try."

"I'll keep working on him," I said, even though my influence on Death was negligible these days. I couldn't even get him to jettison my grandmother's killer until the weather turned. "What was it like being on the road with Joules and Gabriel?" The three of them had teamed up after the catastrophe at Fort Arcana and targeted Richter. To no avail.

"Besides feeling like a third wheel to their epic bromance? It was cool. Sometimes they'd open up about their pre-Flash lives. Get this: Patrick Joules, the great and powerful Tower, was a choirboy."

"Brash, foulmouthed Joules?" Every other word out of his mouth was *feck*. "You lie."

"I swear! Self-described goody-goody. At least, before he met Calanthe." The Temperance Card had been the love of Joules's life. Unfortunately, Death had killed her in self-defense.

While I struggled to picture Joules as a choirboy, I asked, "Wasn't Gabriel born into a cult?"

"Kidnapped by one when he was a baby."

"Jesus, how awful."

"They worshipped him as an angel." In the history of the games, Gabriel had been a righteous guardian, a protector of good. "Funny thing: Gabe wasn't born with wings. On Day Zero, he had to leap off a mountain into nothing and hope those wings shot out of his back on the way down."

"Holy shit." That reminded me of one of my escapes from Aric, when I'd made a blind leap off a bridge, with no idea if I might hit debris in the water. He'd ditched his armor to dive in and save me—just in time for cannibals to fire on us.

Shot twice, Aric had ducked behind a boulder. I'd never forget the way he'd looked when he'd peered up at the sky, gaze stark. Had he been thinking that the Empress would always bring him misery? That she'd forever ruin his life?

I cleared my throat to say, "Um, Gabriel must be a big believer to jump without wings."

Finn shook his head. "Not at all. If he hadn't, he would've had some 'help' from the cult members. He was scared shitless, but he had no choice."

"Not a leap of faith? And here I thought you were telling me this story to give me perspective with this baby."

"I think you're like Gabe—you got no choice but to leap." Finn winked at me and said, "Might as well make it a swan dive, blondie."

Would I ever get my wings? I forced a smile. "So, you and Lark are hitting it off like a house on fire. You guys barely left her room today."

He blushed. "Taking advantage of the storm, since her guard duties are lessened. Eves, I dig her." He pulled at his pajama collar. "To the point of, like, love and all."

When I couldn't stop a silly grin, he gruffly said, "Shut it."

I chuckled. "I didn't say anything! I'm happy for you two." My smile faded. "What *are* you using for contraception?"

His face reddened even more. "Jeez, Mom. If you must know, I stored up on condoms when I was out on the road." *Relief.* "When I arrived here, my worldly possessions consisted of one crutch, the clothes on my back, and a metric ass-ton of rubbers. Death would freak balls if we spawned, wouldn't he? Hey, if we had a son and you had a daughter—"

"Don't even go there."

He held up his hands with a mischievous look.

"Finn, can I give you some advice?" At his eager nod, I said, "Try not to push it with Aric. He might seem like a normal, okay guy, but at heart, he's still a knight from another era, still an assassin." He'd made a fortune killing kings and toppling governments with just a handshake.

"I feel for the dude."

I blinked. "For *Aric*?" The hypnotically handsome, supernatural billionaire? The man with the *I have power over all I survey* vibe?

"Sure. He's got to be feeling stressed. He's supposed to prep our defenses, manage our resources, guard you and the kid on the way and everybody under this roof. And he knows how unhappy you are. It's got to be weighing on him."

Then why wouldn't Aric relent? I'd caught him staring at me, as if willing me to understand his position with Paul. He truly didn't believe the man deserved banishment.

"I try to fly under the radar," Finn said. "For instance, I didn't tell Death that I ramble around his digs invisible and naked whenever the fancy strikes me." Irrepressible Finn. "But sometimes Lark gets a little . . . aggressive." *Red of tooth and claw?* "You mind if I pass on your advice to her?"

I nodded. "Please, try to get through to her. Aric's patience has a limit."

Yesterday, Lark had gotten snarky with him for the first time in, like, ever.

Aric had summed up the incident: "As her arsenal grows, so too does her attitude." At times, I heard animal sounds on the mountainside that I couldn't place—sounds that filled me with fear.

Just as they had Gran.

Now that Circe was weakening, Lark grew braver, especially after she'd used her faunagenesis to revive a sparrow a few days ago.

Amidst all the Arcana powers I'd witnessed, Lark's resurrection ability was crazy even for me. I'd watched that bird's first twitching movements in awe, only to shudder at the chilling blankness in its eyes.

She'd told me that she planned to send her wolves out to raid a Flash-fried zoo, scavenging for assorted bones: "I'm thinking about cooking up a bear. Wouldn't a grizzly be wicked? Or maybe something for the moat to keep that water witch on her toes."

But I'd also gotten the strangest feeling that Lark had already been doing this feat in secret.

Finn said, "So I'll talk to Lark, and you can dialogue with Death about things. He hates that you're hurting."

Then maybe Aric should do something about it? I'd ask him again the next time we were together.

"You wanna hear something weird, blondie? I know we're in a messed-up situation, but I've never been more stoked about life than I have been over the last two weeks."

"Not even when you were living in Cali before the Flash? I know you dream about surfing."

With a sappy look on his face, he said, "I dream about Lark a gazillion times more."

A gust rocked the castle, rattling the windowpanes. A deep, percussive sound thundered from what was left of the river. Ice cracked, but no *SLOSH* came after it.

I swallowed. Circe's domain here had frozen solid. Maybe we were all headed for a coffin of ice. What had Matthew once called the changing weather? *Snowmageddon.* "Finn, what if the world doesn't come back? How will we explain the sun to this kid? Or what a *day* used to look like?"

"That's what I'm here for. Follow me." He rose, then hobbled into the adjoining den. Pointing at the couch, he said, "Pop a squat." When I did, he channeled his inner ringmaster to cry, "Prepare to be astounded! And dazzled! By the greatest illusionist *ever to live!*" He waved his hand, and a new scene surrounded us.

Suddenly we were on a beach under the sizzling sun. "Malibu?"

Sly grin. "You know it."

"This is amazing." My greedy gaze took in all the details—the gulls, the foam on the waves, the haze rising off the shifting sands. "I could stare forever."

Finn dropped down on the love seat, resting his crutch between his legs, but the scene continued. "Lark and I are gonna be your kid's favorites. After pony rides and illusion-filled bedtime stories, we'll fill 'em up with sugar then hand 'em a kazoo."

As if he'd conjured her, Lark padded down the stairs in fluffy bunny slippers and flannel pj's that matched Finn's. A train of woodland animals followed her. She sat beside Finn, gazing at the spectacle. "Whoa. The details are unreal. Bigger waves, baby!"

"My girl wants bigger waves? Then we're gonna get totally tubular here."

Not long after, Aric entered. His eyes began to glitter when he saw me. He wore his chain mail, looking glorious. Once he took in the scene, he said, "Make us *feel* it, Magician."

"Can I do that?"

"You know how the incantation begins, and you know what you want."

The Magician closed his eyes and muttered some chant. Soon the crashing surf began to shake the room, drowning out the sounds of the blizzard. A balmy breeze carried the salty mist over our sun-warmed faces.

Careful not to get too close to the others, Aric sat on my other side. He took my hand in his, threading our fingers together, his lids going heavy from the mere touch.

As we gazed at a fiery red Pacific sunset, peace settled over the four of us, a rare sense of harmony among Arcana. I only wished Circe could have experienced it. If a breakfast had made her envious, what would this missed experience do to her?

I finally understood how I'd been able to lure her to land in the past. . . .

At my ear, Aric said, "Some wonders still await us, love."

Hope was a sprout reaching for the light. Once Paul was gone, we could regain all we'd lost.

Finn slipped his arm around Lark, looking like he was about to burst from happiness. He sighed, "I freaking love you guys."

6

As I got back into bed, Aric stood by one of the windows, gazing out at the lightning-lit night.

He wore only low-slung leather pants, his tattooed chest bare. He looked like a god in the silvery flashes.

Still searching for Kentarch?

He turned to me. "I need to talk to you about something."

I sat up against the headboard. "Me too." I waved him on. "You go first."

"I realized something tonight." He sat beside me. "There are no wonders I wish to see without you by my side. Yet I feel like I'm losing you. I can't . . . I cannot lose you."

"This future has been forced on me. But I can let go of my resentment"—*where are my wings?*—"once Paul is gone. And once there are no longer any trust issues between us."

He nodded, as if he'd expected me to say exactly that. "I spoke to him today, even reviewed your patient file."

My lips thinned. "That so? Was it a good read?"

"His notes are meticulously detailed and thorough, his explanation of events logical. In short, Paul's account makes sense to me." Aric took my hand in his. "But I don't care. He will leave this mountain tomorrow, no matter the weather. I'll carry him away if I have to."

My heart sped up. "What's brought about this change?" Then I frowned. "Because you realize you're losing me?"

Nod. "I will trust you blindly, even against my better sense. If you say these things happened, then I will believe they did. *Sievā*, I'll follow where you lead."

In a perfect world, he would have said that he trusted me because I was trust*worthy*. Or because Paul *wasn't*. Aric had all but said he was choking down my version—so as not to risk a breakup.

Still, I'd take what I could get.

Holding my gaze, he murmured, "I look into your eyes and wonder why I haven't already done this."

At last! All my tension was poised to melt away—as soon as Paul left. Only then would I confide to Aric my hopes about Jack's survival.

He cupped my face. "Can we start anew? Will you come back to me?"

Could I? *Yes.* "I will." With a wry smile, I said, "And I've even brought company with me."

"So you have." He reached for my still-flat belly. This time, I took his hand and placed it. His palm was warm through my nightgown.

Pinpoints of light glowed in his starry eyes as he said, "You asked me what I wanted most. My dreams are all of you—spending a lifetime with you. I want this child because it will come *from you*." His hand shook. "I can never forget that I was your second choice." Before I could protest, he said, "But we could share a bond neither of us has ever shared. *That* is what I want most. Will you accept it?"

Back at Fort Arcana, I'd chosen Jack over him. Since then, I'd made a commitment to Aric. Looking at his noble face, I knew I would honor it—even if Jack lived. "Do you truly think this kid will be okay? Bagger funk and all?"

"I'm telling you that our child will be amazing. And I've never lied to you."

As with Gabriel and his involuntary leap into the unknown, I was already falling. Maybe I should laugh all the way down? If I could get up and walk with ten swords in my back—the vision Matthew had shown me—I could survive a pregnancy.

"Do you accept this bond?" Aric was holding his breath.

The night felt momentous, that hope tendril sprouting into a white rose. "Hold on a sec." When I pulled away and climbed out of the bed, he gave a disheartened sigh.

I headed to my armoire and retrieved the ring I'd crafted for him. The red ribbon beside it brought on a pang of longing, but I'd made my decision. I returned to take Aric's hand and place the jet-black band on his palm. "I'll take the leap."

"You made this for me?" His expression was adoring.

I nodded. "From lignum vitae."

He rasped, "Wood of life." He slipped on the ring, his eyes gone starry once more. He murmured something in Latvian. The quiet intensity and urgency of those words affected me, even if I didn't grasp their meaning.

"What did you say?" I turned the syllables over in my mind, wishing I could understand his first language.

"By all the gods, I love you as my life. I've trusted you with my survival, and I've trusted you with my heart—which, for me, is far more vulnerable. I asked you to have a care with it." He kissed me reverently, then leaned down to press his lips to my belly. "And you have."

7

DEATH

I eased away from my wife's sleeping embrace, my heart pounding with anticipation.

She had accepted this unshakable bond between us. My thumb spun the new band on my ring finger. She'd taken such care to fashion it. I beheld the craftmanship with immense pride.

Soon we would have a child together. Over these weeks, I hadn't allowed myself to accept this fully—not until I'd sensed that *she* had.

All it had taken was my blind trust.

The thought of her feeling trapped was unbearable to me. I knew all too well what that was like. I'd been trapped in this deadly body for two millennia. Confined in my isolating armor.

But with her, I could be free.

At the window, I surveyed the wintry landscape. This mountain that had once been so lonely, so steeped in death, was budding with life.

Had the Fool foreseen this pregnancy?

He'd once given me a prediction—*one part heaven, one part hell*— that I'd never shared with my wife. The heaven part had already come true. I'd wanted to warn her about what might follow, but she needed no more worries.

The Empress is as fragile as she is strong.

I cast my mind back to the last few weeks I'd had with my parents, when my mother was with child. My father had treated her as if she were made of gossamer, shielding her from any harshness. I would endeavor to do the same with my wife.

Besides, no fate is fixed. I refused to believe what the Fool had told me.

I made my way into the bathroom to splash water on my face. After drying my skin, I gazed at myself in the mirror.

Stubble. Hair too long. Eyes brimming with satisfaction.

I murmured in disbelief, "I'm going to be *a father.*"

She'd once told me I treated my books like my children. I'd replied, "The closest I'll ever come to having them." No longer.

Me, a father.

How would I protect my family? How would I feed them for a lifetime? *It falls to me.* In my wildest dreams, I'd never considered the possibility of a child when sourcing for the future.

Paul had prepared a list of items critical for this pregnancy and a newborn. Only one place would have them all—the Sick House, a settlement of sorts to the east. I would set out once the storm broke.

Guilt over my servant's fate arose, but I shoved it away.

After drying my hands, I stared at them. Death's touch. My touch. *What if I can't hold my own child?*

My wedding ring glinted, drawing my focus. Calm suffused me. With her by my side, we could weather anything.

"Aric?" she sleepily called from the bed. Her softly amorous voice made my muscles tense and my pulse race. I could see it so clearly: she had reached for me in need and found only my pillow.

"Coming, love," I called back. I would be a good father to our child, but first and foremost, I would always be her devoted husband.

Tomorrow we would have myriad cares and worries—an exile and the fallout from that. Tonight I would count my blessings: a loving wife and a baby on the way.

I took one last look at the mirror to gaze upon the most fortunate man I'd ever known.

8

THE EMPRESS
DAY 529 A.F.

"You might as well put a bullet in his skull," Lark sniped at me when we'd all gathered in the courtyard to jettison Paul.

The blizzard had ended on this very day. The winds had died down to silence, and the snow no longer fell. But the black sky and thick cloud deck glowed intermittently from unseen lightning bolts. The river, a gleaming expanse of solid ice, reflected them.

Finn patted Lark's gloved hand, muttering, "'S cool, babe. Everything's chill."

I received no such gesture of support from Aric. He stood stiffly beside me, dressed in armor, as if Paul deserved a uniformed send-off.

The medic lingered at the perimeter gate with his shoulders hunched. He wore snow gear and a backpack—kindnesses from Aric.

I hugged my own ski jacket around me. "No one's killing anybody," I told Lark, though Aric's words filtered through my mind: *Exile equals execution.*

When she and I had prepared breakfast earlier, her bearing had been frostier than the landscape. The meal had been just as strained. None of us had eaten much except for Finn, who'd merrily chomped down everything, including the frozen ham I'd burned.

He must've made himself sick. His color was off, and sweat beaded on his forehead, even in the frigid air.

When he loosened his scarf, I said, "You okay?"

"Let's get this show *on the road*, huh." His impatience surprised me. His only hope for walking without a crutch was about to walk away.

"Call it what you want," Lark told me. "If Joules and Gabe are on the verge of biting it out there, you know this means certain death for a lone mortal."

Good. He was a murderer.

Paul cleared his throat. With his brows drawn, he said, "I'm to head out into the Ash, then? Where will I go?"

I was more convinced than ever that his whole demeanor was an act. "Not our concern. Leave. Now."

His voice broke as he told Aric, "Sir, I . . . I'm scared."

Damn it, that admission tugged even at my sympathy. What if I was wrong about him?

I'd been wrong before—epically. I'd tried to run away from the game: *wrong*. I hadn't listened to wise cards like Aric and Circe when I'd gone to rescue Selena from the Lovers: *wrong*. Richter had burned her anyway, laying waste to Jack's army in the process.

Though I hated and mistrusted Paul, the responsibility for killing a mortal weighed on me.

I needed Aric to take my hand and offer support. Instead, I could feel his disappointment in me. After last night, I'd thought we'd be united in this.

Finally, he spoke: "This isn't right."

"Seriously, Aric?" He rarely reversed himself. "What happened to trusting me? What happened to following where I lead?"

"Then choose the correct path! Will you show no mercy, Empress?"

"Empress?" I couldn't remember the last time he'd addressed me like that. "What is wrong with you?"

Paul called, "Please don't fight over me. I'm sure I'll be fine. Thank you, sir, for over a year of protection. It's more than most received." He turned to go, heading down the drive.

He took one step farther away. Another. With a last look, he strode out of sight.

Finally! *Good riddance.*

But Aric said, "No, no, this is all wrong."

"Let him go." With Paul out of our lives, I'd be able to lower my guard; I would take the leap. "Please, Aric!"

Finn said, "I know I'm the new kid on the block, and my vote doesn't really count"—Lark's gaze whipped to the Magician's sweating face—"and I know I'm about to be in the doghouse with the missus 'cause she's a fan of Paul's. But I got real bad vibes about him."

Someone else felt the same way! *I'm not crazy.*

Lark's lips parted. "How can you say that? He's my friend."

Finn ran his coat sleeve over his face. "Babe, when he examined me and offered to do the surgery, I turned him down flat. Maybe it's the Magician in me, but I sense something's not right with that dude. Figure he's as trustworthy as gas station sushi."

"God, thank you, Finn." I crossed to him and took his hand. "You don't know how much better this makes me feel."

With his eyes on Lark, he said, "Just calling it like I see it." Had he tottered on his feet? "And hoping my girl can . . . my girl can . . ."—he cleared his throat—"understand." Sweat was dripping down his face now. "Whoa. Something's off." He coughed, then again.

I turned to Aric. His gaze remained on the road, even though Paul was no longer visible. "Aric! We need to get him inside."

A gurgling sound came from Finn's throat. His face was turning purple! Wait, this had to be an illusion. He'd told me they were involuntary to a degree, and the stress of this situation must be affecting him. "Is this a trick?"

When Finn collapsed to his knees, Lark shoved me away. "He's choking!"

Aric sped into action, pulling him up to deliver the Heimlich maneuver. Nothing happened. He tried again.

Frantic, Lark sprinted to the gate. "Paul, we need help!" No answer. "I don't see him on the road!" He couldn't already be down that long mountain drive.

Aric said, "Fauna, send your animals to find him."

She gave a jerky nod, and her eyes turned red as she ran back to us.

When a line of white foam dribbled from Finn's mouth, Aric laid him on the snowy ground. "The Magician isn't choking. This is a toxin of some kind. Maybe venom or a poison."

Finn clutched his throat. Had he eaten something bad? Or . . . "Oh, God, Paul did this." Gran had accused the medic of poisoning her.

Lark dropped down beside Finn. "Enough about Paul! If he was here, he could fix this!"

The Magician's eyes were wide with fear.

"Don't leave me, Finn! I love you."

He released his throat to grasp Lark's hands. *He believes he's about to die, is trying to comfort her.*

Lark must've concluded the same. A high-pitched whine left her lips. Chaos erupted. The animals spread over the property went berserk, yips and howls filling the air.

Finn's illusions flashed all around the courtyard. Waves . . . a sunset . . . a middle-aged woman with a stern expression . . . how Lark had looked the first time we'd all met her.

Those animal screams rang out louder and louder. I was about to howl right beside them.

"Shut them up so I can think!" I concentrated, trying to sense if some plant-based toxin was inside him. *Sensing* . . . Not a plant. I couldn't produce an antidote. But some toxin was killing him. *Think!* Our only hope was for him to vomit whatever he'd ingested. He needed an emetic!

I yanked off my gloves, then flared my thorn claws. In my chronicles, I'd learned that I could deliver more than poison through them.

"You're going to claw him?" Lark bared her fangs, hovering protectively over Finn. "Oh, hell no!"

"I'm going to give him something to make him throw up. Let me try to save him."

She finally relented. "If he doesn't pull through . . ."

I sank my claws into his neck, injecting him. *Please let this work.*

Withdrawing them, I waited, gaze flitting over his face for any sign.

Yet Finn's wide eyes grew sightless.

Lark cried, "I don't hear his heartbeat!"

I turned to Aric. "You know CPR!"

He knelt beside Finn, beginning chest compressions with his gloved hands. One compression after another after another.

Teardrops spilled down Lark's cheeks. "Finn can't be gone. He can't be. I-I just got him back."

Aric was sweating by the time he drew back. "The Magician's passed on. There's nothing I can do."

Finn was . . . dead.

Tears blinded me. Shock numbed my brain. There was something I needed to remember, but all I could do was stare at my friend's terrified face.

Lark wailed, a bloodcurdling sound. *"Who did this to my Finn?"* Would she still not believe it was Paul?

I didn't know how he'd gotten out of a locked room to poison Finn, but I knew why he'd done it.

The Magician had been on to him.

I barely noticed when Aric stood. "Do you feel that, *sievā?"* He surveyed the area. "Something is coming."

"Richter?" Was the end here for all of us?

Aric shook his head. "This is more like what the Moon Card might've done—a feeling. An ominous feeling. Some power is amongst us."

My gaze darted. "Where? How do we fight it?" The air shimmered, and a dome of hazy yellow light appeared above.

When it enveloped us, Aric's eyes glittered. "A pall falls over us."

Pall. Paul. Where was the medic?

The ice in the river cracked more loudly than usual, the sound echoing over the mountain like cannon blasts.

Lark rose up from Finn's body, her eyes turning an even darker red, her fangs sharp. "I know what happened here." Her tableau wavered over her. Then the image began to rotate until it had turned upside down. Reversed. Her animal gaze landed on me, her expression promising revenge. "You killed Finn. You poisoned him."

I gawked. "Me? Paul did this!"

"You made the ham. Finn was the only one who ate it, to be polite to you. And you touched him right before he got sick. You clawed him, and he died."

"Are you high?" How could she doubt me after all I'd done to reunite them? "Why would I ever hurt Finn?"

"You murdered him in the past!" I hated that she had a point. She stalked closer, her movements predatory. "My creatures will fang you apart."

"Easy, Lark, think about what you're doing." Unable to manage so much as a vine, I hurried to Aric's side. "She's losing it!" I glanced up at him.

His Grim Reaper tableau appeared as well, turning, reversing. Just before it locked into an upside-down position, he held my gaze and bit out, "Run to the castle." Seeming to fight some inner battle, he drew his swords. "Run—*from me.*"

9

Reacting purely by reflex, I leapt away and raced across the snow.

The fortress was on lockdown, only the front door open. I careened through the entrance, then slammed the blast-proof door closed. I turned the lock, but even this weighty barrier wouldn't keep Aric out for long.

"There's nowhere for you to go, Empress," he said outside the door. "For the first time since I met you, my thoughts are clear. I know I can never have peace while you live."

"WHAT???"

"You mesmerized me. Made me believe you loved me. Just as you've done before."

"Have you lost your mind—I do love you!"

"Lies!" He pounded on the door with his unnatural strength.

What was I going to do? "Something is happening to you! Your tableau is turned upside-down."

"Everything you say is a lie. Nothing changes. You killed the Magician—another of your allies—just as you do in each game! We trust; you betray." He kept pounding on the door: *boom . . . boom . . . boom.*

I was trapped on this mountain with two Arcana who wanted to murder me. I had dead vines climbing the ceilings, but even if I managed to revive them, Aric would easily slice them away. My only real hope was to get to the nursery, to the sunlamps—

A spine-tingling growl sounded from behind me. I slowly turned; Cyclops crouched in the foyer, saliva dripping from his knifelike fangs. More animals filed into the chamber beyond. The creatures I passed by every day now looked rabid. Under Lark's control, they were all predators.

"No, Cyclops. Don't do this." I raised my palms in front of me, struggling to revive nearby vines. Would Lark truly make him attack? "I didn't hurt Finn!"

From outside, she screamed, "You poisoned him! Cyclops, disembowel her!"

The giant war wolf sprang for me. I squeezed my eyes shut. Vines shot from the ceiling, jabbing like wooden spears, out of my control.

YELP. When I looked again, the beast was skewered throughout his body, pinned to the floor. Unable to move, he cast me a heartbreaking look of confusion—my onetime bedmate and favorite pet.

"Cyclops, I'm so sorry." Reminding myself that he'd heal, I edged around the whimpering wolf.

A trio of badgers, a Komodo dragon, and two snarling hyenas blocked my way to the nursery. As they advanced on me, I screamed, "Stop this, Lark!" I revived more vines to knock the beasts out of my way, but twice as many took their place. My powers were already sputtering.

BOOM...BOOM...BOOM.

I'd never reach the nursery before Aric leveled that door. Lark's arsenal was preventing me from reaching *mine.*

No choice but to flee up the stairs. I'd barely made two steps when a wave of small forest creatures descended. I booted a couple, dodging the worst of the onslaught.

Racing upward, I tripped on two foxes. Falling forward ... My forehead banged the edge of a step. "Ah!" Blood streamed into my eyes. Sprouts shot from the crimson drops, coiling around the creatures.

Gritting my teeth, I pushed on, managing to reach the second-floor landing. I drew up short, swiping my eyes. Paul stood off to the side, guarded by Scarface and Maneater.

"How in the hell did you get inside?"

"I know every secret chamber and passageway in this castle. I grew up here, was the caretaker's son." My lips parted. "I can get in anywhere, have had access to every inch of the place." He smirked as he said, "Even after I was 'locked up.'"

A hazy light glowed behind his head, the same color as that dome outside. It seemed to be strengthening, spreading.

Then an image flickered over him. *A tableau.* I'd seen it before: a man dangling upside-down from a rope looped around his ankle and tied to a tree limb. A jagged burst of yellow light haloed the man's head.

The Hanged Man. Paul was the inactivated card.

His tableau was reversed as well. Which meant the Hanged Man appeared to nimbly stand on his toes. No dangling—because he was in full control.

"You killed Finn." I looked for an icon, but he wore gloves. "You poisoned him, and now your powers have been activated." I tried to recall anything I'd read about this card. He was called Our Lord Uncanny—because so little was known about him.

"We both know that *you* poisoned him. Just as you did in past games. *You* are the princess of poison, remember?"

Had I murdered Finn in this game? I did clearly recall doing it before.

I sliced him to ribbons and choked him in vine. My God, I'd said that aloud! I shook my head hard. "Finn was my friend. I didn't hurt him—you did."

Paul tilted his head. "Interesting. Even as my sphere of clarity spreads, you're able to resist me."

He'd generated that yellow dome. Whereas Sol could emit a pure white light of illumination, Paul's was a bewildering haze. He must have the power to brainwash Arcana, which explained why Lark and Aric currently wanted me dead.

So how *had* I resisted?

BOOM . . . BOOM . . . BOOM. That door wouldn't hold much longer.

Once I killed Paul, the haze would surely lift, and then my husband and friend would return to normal. As I struggled to build poison in my claws, I called on the vines I'd revived downstairs to creep up the steps. Buying myself time to strike, I asked Paul, "Have you always known you're an Arcana?"

Outside, Circe's river continued to crack ominously. I knew she couldn't hear past the ice. Was she sensing Paul's activation?

He leaned a shoulder against the wall, fully relaxed. "When I first spied Domīnija, the mysterious businessman who'd purchased my childhood home, I sensed I had some kind of mystical connection with him. So I figured out how to get into his household and make myself indispensable." Paul cast me the smile I used to think was charming. "I've read everything here I could lay hands on, including your chronicles. After talking to your grandmother for hours on end, I suspected I might actually be an Arcana, the inactivated card. After all, fate likes us to converge, and I'd long dreamed I had supernatural abilities. But how to activate myself?"

"By killing an Arcana."

"It's not so easy a feat! I didn't want to arouse suspicion with an unexplained death, so I decided to kill someone connected to the game—your Tarasova grandmother. The right meds accelerated her decline."

"I knew it!" Everything Gran had said or written toward the end became clear. *A rat on my table gnaws the threads . . . the serpent coils around the tree and chokes its roots.*

Paul was the rat, the threads coming from a hangman's noose. Like a serpent, he'd been coiled around me while choking her—my roots.

But Gran had been too far gone by that time to make me understand. "She discovered what you are."

"Eventually. I feared someone would catch on when she kept blabbering about midnight and noon."

Comprehension. "Twelve is your card number."

"Evie gets a star!" He grinned, crinkles forming around his wide blue eyes. "When I gave her that last injection, she experienced a small window of lucidity. She stared me down and said, 'Evie will figure out I was murdered, but she'll blame Death. She'll avenge me. I want this.'"

Gran had written in my chronicles, *I have put the end into motion.*

"As soon as your dear ol' gran kicked it, I felt the stirrings of my abilities, and I reached out telepathically."

Aric had said "errant thoughts" kept hitting him. Was Paul's telepathy similar to Matthew's, working like a two-way radio? Arcana powers often overlapped—because the gods' powers did.

Could the Hanged Man hear thoughts? I mentally screamed, *LOOK OUT BEHIND YOU, PAUL!*

Yet he droned on: "The Reaper and Lark were easy to reach. But you and Finn... not so much. The Magician was immune to me—I dreamed his card was a foil to mine—but you're not naturally immune." He narrowed his eyes, as if trying to see *inside* me.

"Brainwashing has no effect on me, not since I freed myself from the Hierophant's mind control." Cracking ice still sounded outside. Had Paul reached Circe as well? Was she trying to break free to help me? Or to end me?

Irritation stamped his features. "I'm no brainwasher."

"Then what are your powers?" Would he tell me? After so many months of taking orders and skulking in the shadows, this smug man must be all too ready to crow about himself.

"What do *you* think they are?"

"Aside from telepathy? I think you possess guile and concealment." His forgettable appearance was a power in itself. I'd rarely noticed him in the beginning of my stay here. "Definitely trust manipulation."

"The power to lie and always be believed? That's the same as brainwashing." Huffing with indignation, he said, "I'm not like the Hierophant! From what I've read, he used eye contact to turn his followers into unthinking drones. My sphere brings *clarity*. When I reverse an Arcana's card, they're in no way mindless. They still have free will. They're simply enhanced. Whereas the Hierophant lied, I mentally relay truths."

"Not seeing much of a difference from where I'm standing, Paul."

"Oh, Evie, a card reversal means that I can only work with *what's available.*"

So he couldn't manipulate Aric and Lark to hurt me—unless they were already inclined to do so?

As if to illustrate, Lark shrieked from outside, "I'll kill you, Empress! Why him?"

Paul tsked. "She can't decide whether to end you or herself." Then her most marked Arcana trait—her single-minded determination—was gone. "Of one thing I've recently convinced her: the need to protect me at all costs." He petted Scarface.

BOOM . . . BOOM . . . BOOM. The hinges screamed as the door bowed.

Poison finally welled in my claws, my vines slithering higher. Would I get to Paul before Aric got to me? "And Death?" His card was all about embracing change, letting go of the past and bitter resentment. The reverse of that meant he'd be mired in the past, and our history was filled with mistrust, hatred, and murder.

The present that we'd built for ourselves would be destroyed.

Paul grinned again. "Hating you is the knight's factory setting, if you will. Which works for me."

"Lark will hear everything you've said through her wolves."

He glanced at the slavering beasts. "And she'll thank me for plotting against you. She despised your grandmother, was happy to see her go. I've been of service to Lark, to everyone here but you."

"Plotting? Like with that contraceptive. Now I know why you screwed me over."

He raised his brows in challenge: *Do you?*

"The Hanged Man is also known as the Traitor." His eyes grew heavy-lidded with pleasure, convincing me that he was like every other evil Arcana I'd tangled with—devious killers who liked to play with their prey. "I entrusted only two things to you: my grandmother's care and my birth control, giving you just two opportunities for betrayal. You stabbed me in the back both times." Actually, he was worse than the others; I never trusted them!

"Ah-ah, Evie, your hair's turning red. Since you can't be controlled, you must be destroyed." The wolves snarled, baring those lethal fangs. "I'll just nudge Lark into action." The light around his head flared.

A split-second later, the wolves vaulted toward me. My vines shot upwards to twine around them. Green barbs muzzled their snouts, then slammed their heads to the floor.

Claws bared, I lunged at Paul. I slashed the arm he raised in defense, my thorns hitting home. My poison would lay him out in seconds.

Through the slices in his shirt, I looked for injuries.

Not a mark on him.

How? How was that possible? "You heal like me?" But this had been instantaneous.

As the wolves struggled against my faltering vines, he tilted his head at his arm. "Damnedest thing, Evie. I can't be injured, can't die. I suppose the Hanged Man is already dead in a way. I transcend death."

A crash sounded as Aric broke down the door. "Come to me, Empress. Let's end this once and for all." I heard the rhythmic ringing of his spurs heading up the stairs.

I debated trying to stall him with more vines, but I wanted him to see Paul's tableau. "He's the Hanged Man. Come *look* at him." I glanced down at the stairwell.

Aric was ascending, his swords drawn, black armor glinting. "I know this. He's shown me the truth about you."

"The sphere is Paul's. You're brainwashed within it!"

"I see his sphere. I feel and welcome it. It protects me from your mesmerizing and gives me clarity such as I've never known." Yet his eyes were blank with fury.

I didn't want to hurt him—even if I could. The only place left to flee was the third floor. "Fine; hate me, but don't harm our child."

Raw grief flooded his gaze, and he thundered, "There is no baby!"

"Everybody in this castle knows I'm pregnant!" I'd been convinced of it when I'd gazed at that white rose. After days of my constant vomiting, there was no way anyone else could doubt it.

Paul chuckled, his smugness palpable. "Just now, while Death was breaking down the door, I mentally informed him about your plot—how you forced me to fake a pregnancy test, so he would sacrifice his life to protect you and your made-up kid. Now that he knows the truth, he's going to protect *me* and kill you for tricking him."

"You couldn't force him to hurt his child, so you're pulling a bogus pregnancy test out of your ass?"

Before I could claw the smirk off Paul's face, Aric leapt to the landing, his swords flashing out to slice my vines.

I screamed in pain, stumbling backward toward the next set of stairs.

Aric followed. "You're just as you've always been. Forever a temptress. Forever a liar. I knew you could never be trusted, but I wanted you so much. I was weak."

"Your mind is being manipulated." The Hanged Man was *this* powerful? Able to control the reigning Arcana victor? An immortal who'd lived for millennia? "Paul's wearing Finn's icon—I'm not!" I raised my hands.

Aric didn't even glance at them, didn't seem to hear me. "Throughout our history, you've sought to end me, but you've never connived quite like this. A pregnancy, Empress?"

"*You* are the one who had to convince *me* I was knocked up! I didn't want to believe. But I accepted it. We both did."

"A lie is a curse you place on yourself. Now it's time for you to pay for yours."

Nothing I could say would sway Aric. I whirled around, running full-out. Desperation spurred my powers, and I put up wall after wall of thorns, like rows of barbed wire.

His swords slashed through the blockade as he forced his way forward. He knew how much that would hurt me, but still he cut.

A nightmare greeted me on the next flight of stairs. Hissing snakes coiled around the banister and poured down the steps. With a shudder, I charged into that gauntlet.

Fangs jabbed my boots as I leapt and dodged. From the handrail, snakes struck my arms, ripping my thick jacket. Tufts of down wafted in the air. "Lark, enough!" Pain shot through my hand. Oh, shit! One had gotten me. *Was it venomous?*

I'd be immune, but would this kid?

On the third-floor landing, I chanced a look back at Death. I saw no hesitation in him as he annihilated my defenses.

Where to run? There was a tower similar to mine in this wing. Maybe I could reinforce the door with vines.

I staggered up the last flight of stairs, then locked the door behind me.

Struggling to concentrate over all the sounds—Death's spurs, the animal calls, Lark's wails, that ominous cracking of ice—I managed a couple of vines to create another barricade.

The windows in this room had latches, unlike the sealed ones in my tower. But then, Aric had never intended to imprison anyone in here.

I opened a window, wincing against a gust. I gazed out with watering eyes. The mass of river ice had buckled into gigantic white shards. It looked like the earth had fangs.

Paul's yellow dome had spread down the mountain to capture Circe's river and my thorns. Maybe the Priestess wouldn't be touched by his influence. Her mind and body weren't actually here.

I peered down at the long drop. Normally, I wouldn't even think— would just jump. If I could regenerate from a fall out of a helicopter while Bagman contagion fouled my blood, I could regenerate from anything.

But the kid . . .

Ice coated the slippery shale roof, the tiles glistening in the continual lightning. I'd grown rose vines on the other side of the castle, but they'd been frozen in the storm. I called on them to spread across the roof. Sluggish to respond, they needed me to rejuvenate them.

But I had nothing left in me, no way to fuel them.

Aric gave a yell; I whirled around to see a sword tip breach my vines. He was slicing through the door and my barricade as though through paper. "You will pay, Empress." He kicked the remains of the door open. "Pay for making me believe."

Heart pounding, I climbed up onto the windowsill. Another gust nearly knocked me back into the room. "We love each other, Aric! Shake off Paul's power."

Swords raised, he stalked closer—an assassin in black, with one target. The eerie sound of those spurs was about to drive me crazy!

I swallowed and stepped outside. Balancing my boots on the slick roof, I inched away from the window. Despite my coat, the cold punched the breath from my lungs.

Dizziness surged as I craned my head up. The only place left for me to climb was to the pinnacle of the castle.

I looked back over my shoulder. Aric leaned out the window, eyes enraged. He offered a hand to coax me closer, so he could strike.

I'd experienced his fury in the past, but this was different. Before, even when I'd been his prisoner, his gaze had betrayed longing. Now there was nothing but rage. He looked crazed with it.

Tears welled. "Please, come back to me, Aric. I'm wearing your mother's ring."

"And I will rip it off your cold dead finger—just as I collected that choker off your headless neck."

I nearly vomited. "You will regret this for eternity. You killed your mother when she was pregnant. Now you'll kill your wife and child."

He hesitated for a split second. Battling Paul's influence?

"Yes, Aric, fight him! Paul's the Traitor."

But the reversal was too strong. Aric's mistrust and bitterness won out. "Speaking of rings." He sheathed his swords, then removed one gauntlet. He tore off the wedding band I'd made him. "I forsake you, Empress." He raised his fist.

I whispered, "Don't do it."

He used his ungodly strength to crush that ring. When he opened his hand, black dust scattered on the wind. His hatred was stronger even than the wood of life. "You're next, Empress. You've got nowhere to go."

A raven dive-bombed right for me! "No!" A vine shot from my palm to deflect it. The bird crashed beside me, breaking the shale tile, its head exploding. Brain and skull bits spattered my face. "Damn it, Lark!"

A second bird dove for me. I blocked with vines, but another followed it. *This can't be happening.* By the staccato glow of lightning, I saw a black swarm closing in. *Bats.*

They teemed around me, tearing at my hair, clawing at my face. "Oh, God, oh, God!" My footing shifted, sending me off balance.

I pinwheeled my arms. Teetering, teetering . . .

Over the winds, I heard a shrill whistle. A figure swooped down from the clouds. *"Gabriel!"* He was heading for me—right into Paul's yellow haze.

The tile cracked. I slipped.

To the sound of Aric's laughter, I plummeted.

10

My feet . . . floated.

The Archangel had snagged me in midair! He gripped me under my arms, his razor-sharp talons poking through the ends of his gloves.

"Empress, are you all right?" Frost covered his long black hair and gaunt face. His lips had a bluish tint.

"Get us out of the yellow sphere. Hurry, Gabriel!"

He didn't ask, just sped higher and higher. Old bullet holes in his black wings funneled little blasts of arctic air at my face.

When Aric roared with frustration, Gabriel tossed me upward, catching me against his side. "Hold on."

I clung to his billowing coat as he banked sharply to the left. Then right. Two swords zoomed past us. Aric had hurled his precious weapons at me.

Birds and bats kept coming. Gabriel dodged them, bobbing and twirling. Winds gusted, flinging the other winged creatures away.

We were free. We were . . . falling?

More gusts sent Gabriel spinning in the air like a mimosa bloom. We were heading right for Circe's ice shards! He groaned as he flared his bullet-riddled wings. I squeezed my eyes closed, bracing for impact.

Our trajectory shifted.

I peeked open my eyes. We'd missed the tips of those shards by *inches.* "That was close!"

"What is happening, Empress? Joules and I heard you screaming and the animals behaving erratically. Why would Fauna and the Reaper target you?"

"Our medic is the inactivated Arcana card. He's brainwashed the others. Where's Joules?" The Tower was never far from Gabriel and rarely out of the fray.

"I left him on the next mountain...." He trailed off. "How... what...? Ah, my mind. My mind is so clear."

Paul's influence was affecting him. "Get out of the yellow haze. Fly past the boundary!"

The Archangel's tableau flickered, then turned, like a slow roulette wheel. It clicked into place—in the reversed position.

Movement out of the corner of my watering eyes. Gabriel's hand crept toward his dagger sheath.

"Don't do this, Gabe. The Hanged Man is using his powers on you. You made a vow never to hurt me."

He flashed his fangs. "Vows mean *nothing* to me." Gabriel was usually forthright, principled, and loyal. The reverse of those traits didn't bode well for me. "I was taught that you are one of my three archenemies, but I ignored my teachings to become your friend. Now I shall make good on a kill that should have happened months ago." He yanked his blade free.

"No!" I somehow managed a vine to bind his wrist. "Snap out of this." How could I fight him in the air? I thrashed to get loose. I might have a chance on the ground.

With a yell, Gabriel twisted free from the vine.

"Stop! I'm pregnant."

His blade hesitated. What if Paul's influence was limited by distance? Like a phone signal? We were closing in on the edge of that hazy yellow. "With this baby, we can end the game."

Gabriel blinked his green eyes. Then narrowed them. "Memories arise in my mind. You once cut off my wings." Paul must be feeding him information he'd stolen from my chronicles. "You decorated your home with them, displaying them over your mantel. Oh, Empress, I am going to make this last."

I swiped my thorn claws at him. Couldn't bring myself to use poison on him. Five blades sliced his layered clothing to reach his flesh. Blood gushed. He yelled, releasing me.

I plummeted again. Falling!

I landed . . . in a snowbank. My teeth clattered, but I was uninjured. The yellow haze ended just feet from me. I tripped forward, clearing the boundary. Would Gabriel pursue me? Paul might lose his power over the Angel.

Gabriel hovered in the air but wouldn't cross the edge.

"I did cut off your wings, Angel. Come punish me for it."

He remained in place, as if he were a tethered kite—with Paul pulling the string. "I want my mind clear. I need the Hanged Man's knowledge, and he needs us to fuel his sphere." Even now it was growing.

I backed up several steps. "You're afraid of me," I taunted. "I must've cut off your balls as well."

"Classic Empress. You think to lure me away from my new alliance? Your time shall come."

Howls sounded from the castle. The wolves readied to hunt.

Gabriel grinned, exposing his fangs. "That time is now."

Lark's animals would probably be able to leave Paul's sphere. If so, my only shot at survival was getting to the Tower on the next mountain over. I turned—

Sparking blinded me.

Joules! Not surprisingly, he'd made a beeline for the action. He was weighed down with winter gear, only his glittery face visible. "What the feck is happening over there?"

I'd never thought I'd be so happy to see his scrawny Irish self.

Gabriel called, "She attacked me when I tried to save her." He drew aside his coat, revealing the bloody gashes I'd given him.

Joules's eyes went wide. "You hurt my boyo?" He raised one of his silver lightning javelins.

Between breaths, I said, "Listen, Gabriel's been brainwashed by a new card, the inactivated one. Any Arcana within that yellow sphere is under the Hanged Man's control." Wolves howled. "Joules, we don't have time. Lark and Death are coming for me."

Joules was confused—which meant he was spitting mad. "As if the Reaper would take out the one female he can get with!"

"They are after her for good reason, Patrick," Gabriel said. "She poisoned the Magician."

Joules sparked like a reactor. "Finn's done for?"

"Yes, and the Empress has targeted us next. In the past, she killed us. She cut off my wings for a trophy."

Joules gave me a disbelieving look that faded when I couldn't deny anything. "That's right fecked up."

"But I didn't kill Finn." If I possessed any mesmerizing power at all, I called on it now, telling Joules, "I swear I didn't." Grasping for the most compelling vow I could make, I said, "I swear on Jack's life."

"Jack's dead! We all know Richter got him." *Maybe not?*

The howling wolves neared. I faced Gabriel. "Prove me a liar, then. Just come out from that sphere."

Joules told his friend, "I'm about to fry this one. So put me mind at ease and step out from the haze."

Gabriel offered his hand. "Come stand behind me. I will protect you."

I said, "Joules, if you go in there, you'll get brainwashed too. Those beasts are closing in fast. He's not going to help us."

Finally, doubt crossed the Tower's expression. "C'mere, mate. Meet me halfway."

"Come stand with me, Patrick. You shall be enlightened. You shall know all the secrets of the game. If you side with my new alliance, I guarantee you will be safe from Fauna and the Reaper."

"Side with the bastard who killed my Cally? Now I know you're barmy. All the same, I'll take my chances with this tart." He hiked a thumb at me.

Thanks?

"Join us." Gabriel's face took on a macabre cast. "And then you will be safe from *me*."

Joules raised his pointy chin. "I'd rather die."

Gabriel waved a wing behind him in the direction of the wolves. "That is being arranged."

Joules's jaw dropped. "You're goin' to kick back and watch me get eaten?"

I grabbed his bony arm. "We need to run!" I yanked him away from his best friend.

He staggered along, eyes wide. "What the bloody hell? Tell me you got a plan to undo this."

"I do," I lied. "We can save them. But only if we survive."

Joules nodded, determination overwhelming his shock. He yelled over his shoulder, "We'll be back for you, Gabe." With one last look, he sped forward, taking the lead. "We need a vantage." He pointed toward the next hill, a steep snow-covered rise. "If I get to higher ground, I can light this place up." His javelin glimmered reassuringly. "We're talking dead mutts all over the place."

"Three of those wolves are her familiars. They can't be killed." Roars sounded. "Besides, she's sending far more than mutts."

As we ran, Joules hurled spears blindly behind us, explosions sounding in the distance. He launched one after another, beginning to sweat.

"Save some bolts. We're going to need them."

He looked like I'd insulted his manhood. "I can do this all night." He twirled one spear. "And I got a special one for your man Death. Oh, wait—the Reaper's not your man anymore. Christ, Empress, you move through 'em fast. Jack, Sol, and Death. Three blokes in as many months."

"I wasn't with Sol. Can we focus on current freaking events?"

When we reached the hill, we fell silent as we trudged up the incline. Hunger had clearly sapped him, and my legs were Jell-O. How could I make it to the top?

Struggling . . . struggling . . . For the last dozen feet, I had to crawl in Joules's path.

Made it! I lumbered to stand. We both put our hands on our knees and caught our breath.

Below us, the hillside teemed with beasts. Dark fur against white snow.

I glanced behind me. The hill dropped off in a sheer slope on its other side.

Joules opened his palm to produce yet another javelin. Had it been sluggish to appear? He bellowed, "Get ready for a light show, arseholes. *THE LORD O' LIGHTNING IS IN THE—*"

The ground disappeared from beneath us. In a cloud of snow, we tumbled down the steeper side. An avalanche! It swept us along like one of Circe's currents.

My scream was cut off by a searing pain. Joules's spear had stabbed my shoulder. We plunged lower and lower. *Feet over my head. Dizziness. Lurching.*

Abrupt—STOP.

For a moment I was relieved just to be still, until I realized all I could see was blackness. Cocooned in snow. No *air.*

Panic surged. Which way was out? Where was up? Head spinning, I dug frantically....

A javelin pierced the cocoon beside me. Frenzied, I changed direction and dug toward that spear.

Joules hauled me out. Sprawled on my back, I sucked in greedy breaths. Air never tasted so good.

Coated in powder, Joules said, "You were digging the wrong way."

Then he'd just saved my life. My sense of direction never failed to fail.

He motioned toward my shoulder. "Sorry about stabbing you."

Blood had stained the snow, but I didn't feel the numbed injury. Cold and adrenaline were great painkillers. Making it to my knees, I surveyed our new surroundings. We must've traveled a mile down that mountain, landing in what looked like a ravine. Was this an old road?

My stomach lurched again. *Oh, no, not now.*

I wobbled to the side and threw up.

"Do that on your own time. We've got to move."

I vomited till my stomach was empty. Wiped my mouth. Took three tries to get to my feet.

The sound of howls spurred me. The wolves were well beyond Paul's boundary, which meant they'd never stop until they'd caught us.

Crunch, crunch. Wolves gotta eat. Now it would be *my* bones.

Joules and I staggered along the ravine. "Any ideas, Tower?"

"Yeah. Avoid them." He pointed in front of us. Large eyes glowed in the darkness. Scarface was blocking our exit.

In rapid succession, Joules launched three javelins. When the wolf beat a hasty retreat, Joules yanked me around in the other direction.

"Running out of juice here." He must have burned through a hundred javelins. His skin no longer sparked. "Anytime you want to throw in some vines, Empress."

"I'm tapped out from fighting the others."

"Come on, you've got to be sandbagging. You canna manage one bloody petal?"

"I'm pregnant, okay?"

He gave a mad bark of laughter. "Who's the unlucky father? Death? You're takin' the piss."

"Just shut up and run, you fucking leprechaun! Scarface will be back. And there are hundreds more . . ." I trailed off.

Up ahead, eyes glowed from another animal blockade. Maneater and company were in front of us. Scarface's growl sounded from behind us.

We were trapped.

As Maneater licked her drooling chops, Cyclops limped forward to join her. Again I spied something like confusion in his eye. The wounds I'd given him earlier still poured blood.

"We're surrounded." Joules opened his palm, but nothing appeared. He stared down at his hand in bafflement. "Tapped out? Never happened in me life."

"Where's the fecking Lord o' Lightning?"

"I've never been starving before!" He made a fist. With a yell, he opened his hand again. Nothing.

As the wolves on both sides closed in, Joules and I stared at each other.

I needed the red witch; I needed rage. All I could manage were exhaustion and resignation.

Aric would never forgive himself for this. Never. He would somehow win the game—he always won—and he'd live as penance till we could be together again.

"Any last words, Empress?"

"Look on the bright side, Joules. You're so prickly, they'll choke on you."

His lips curled into a gallows grin. "And you'll poison 'em—"

Headlights beamed into our eyes.

11

A huge truck barreled along the ravine floor. Scarface whirled around, snarling at the new threat.

IMPACT. A deafening yelp sounded as he went somersaulting through the air. Joules and I dropped to the ground, dodging his claws.

The wolf collided with Maneater and Cyclops, a gigantic wrecking ball. They tangled into a heap of limbs.

The truck window rolled down. As my eyes adjusted to the brightness, I spied a man with intense eyes, a beret, and sigh-worthy cheekbones.

Kentarch! His tableau shimmered over him, a helmeted warrior driving a horse-drawn chariot—and it was right-side up. "Get in the back," he commanded in a deep, accented voice.

Joules and I scrambled to the passenger door. I yanked on the handle. Locked.

"The *far back*," he enunciated.

The Tower and I shared a look, then headed for the truck bed. He was still hauling me over the tailgate when Kentarch floored it, spraying snow. Ahead, the wolves leapt to their paws and darted out of his way.

The lights mounted on the cab roof illuminated a mass of animals swarming behind us. Kentarch raced the truck like a chariot, and the ride was just as smooth—in other words, not at all. We bounced along, the large tires airborne more often than not.

Canvas netting covered crates in the back; Joules and I clung to the net for dear life. Sweat and blood on my face began to freeze.

Joules muttered curses as he wrestled to hold on. "He's the Chariot?"

I nodded. Aric called Kentarch the Centurion because of past games. But our cards *did* evolve—if we survived this wild ride, I'd never think of Kentarch as anything other than the Chariot.

"You know this bloke? Trust him?"

"I know of him. Never met him before. He allies with Aric."

"And the Reaper wants you dead."

I bit out, "Any suggestions?"

The back window whirred open. "What is happening at the castle?" Kentarch asked, sounding as calm as Aric had when chased by missiles. "I was invited there, yet a war zone greeted me."

I released my handhold and crawled toward the window. "Death and the others have been brainwashed by the Hanged Man. I'll tell you all about it. You mind if we climb inside?"

"Yes." The window closed, leaving a slender gap.

Dick! It wasn't as if I'd killed him in the past. *Oh, wait.*

Joules yelled, "We've got company!"

I jerked my head around. The wolves had regrouped, were tearing over the landscape. Scarface led the pack, closing in fast. He tensed like he was about to lunge for us. I cried, "Punch it!"

Kentarch gunned the engine; the wolf missed by inches, jaws slamming shut around air. *SNAP.*

As we sped faster, birds and bats dive-bombed the truck, splattering themselves across the windshield.

What was that up ahead? My foggy mind registered the sight: A *bear* had just tromped onto the narrow road through the ravine.

This was no normal bear—Lark must've fed it her blood when it was a cub. Which meant the thing had grown to be gargantuan, nearly as tall as Ogen.

She'd already *had* a bear. What else had she raised that she hadn't told us about?

The beast reared up on its hind legs, stretching its arms wide, claws gouging both ravine walls. No way around it. No way to reverse.

Joules opened his free hand, willing another javelin to appear. "Bloody feck, mother, bloody feck." When he came up empty, he yelled to Kentarch, "Ram it! If we can get past it, the road opens up."

"Are you crazy?" I cried. "It's way bigger than a wolf. It'll crumble this truck." Even if we survived the collision, the other beasts would just descend on us.

"I'd rather die in a crash than from fangs."

Through the crack in the window, I thought I heard Kentarch calmly say, "This will hurt."

I clutched the side of the truck, bracing for impact yet again. Sooner or later, my luck would run out. I was betting on *now*.

Even the birds must have sensed the impending collision—they eased off their assault, circling above the roadway.

Joules began reciting the Lord's Prayer, then broke off to do a countdown: "Five . . . four . . . three . . . two . . . FECK!"

But the crash I expected didn't happen. Shivers raced over me. Time seemed to slow. Suddenly we were surrounded by the bear—we were . . . inside the bear.

Its mighty heart thundered right before my eyes. *Tha-thud. Tha-thud.* Real or unreal? We moved past as if in slow motion.

Just as we started to clear the massive body, those shivers returned, and the truck solidified—while the tailgate was still in the bear.

It exploded from the pressure. Gore and chunks of fur spewed into the air. Blood splashed the back of the truck.

"Wh-what happened?"

"Boyo up there teleported this entire truck *through* the bear. And there's a sentence I never thought I'd say."

I'd seen . . . its heart. Kentarch had moved the mass of this vehicle—through the mass of that bear. No wonder Aric had been so excited to have this ally joining him.

"Are we clear of them?" I asked.

"Nothin' can catch us now."

In front of us: a desolate road. Behind us: thwarted wolves. Maneater snapped at Scarface, and a scuffle broke out between them.

Joules bellowed into the night, "Get fecked, Fauna!"

I gazed away, my attention drawn to the top of a mountain in the distance. *Aric.* He was astride his warhorse Thanatos, illuminated by the yellow haze.

I drew back my whipping hair. He sheathed his swords.

The bastard had already retrieved them. *Way to prioritize, Reaper.*

For my own survival, I was being separated from my husband, the father of my kid. My only hope was for him to leave that sphere. I somehow managed to yell, "Come and get me, Death!" While inside, I was pleading, *Please, Aric, please come and get me. . . .*

12

When I could no longer stand the cold, I knocked on the icy rear window, wincing as pain stabbed through my bare knuckles. My teeth were chattering. "C-can we come inside?"

Kentarch glanced at the rearview mirror.

"Chariot, *please.* I'm freezing, injured, and powerless."

"Why should I trust you?"

"Because if I had any of my abilities, I wouldn't have needed you to save our lives back there."

Joules added, "We'd both accepted that we were wolf chow. Not by choice."

Noting his camo jacket, I said, "Come on, soldier. We're what you'd call neutralized threats."

Kentarch slowed to a stop. "Try to harm me, and I'll put you inside another animal. Or a boulder."

Talk about an awful way to die. "Understood."

Joules and I hopped down from the back. Hastening to the passenger door, I climbed into the front, sliding over the wide bench, Joules right behind me. Kentarch gunned it again.

"Cheers, Chariot." Joules gazed around the roomy cab in awe. "Talk about tricked-out."

Electronics covered the dash—everything from an outdoor thermometer display to a CB box, to a small monitor with GPS coordinates plugged in. Did GPS still work? Aric had said most satellites were untouched.

Storage pouches abounded. The sun visor had sleeves for even more gear: a penlight, a couple of unrecognizable hand tools, and a picture of a gorgeous, smiling woman about Kentarch's age. A rifle was mounted to the ceiling, within his easy reach.

"You got a name for this beast?"

With a shrug, Kentarch turned up the heater. His jacket billowed, revealing a holstered pistol. He also had a pair of blades strapped to a thigh.

I raised my hands to the warmth. "Thanks." My fingertips were discolored, and that snakebite was swollen. I should've already regenerated from two tiny puncture wounds—*so, definitely venomous.*

Kentarch's gaze took in the icons on my hand before he faced the snowy road again. "You said the Hanged Man brainwashed Death. Who is this new player?"

According to Paul, *brainwashed* wasn't the right word, but I didn't have a better one right now. Once my teeth stopped chattering, I said, "The Hanged Man, a.k.a. the Traitor, is a medic who lived in the castle. Goes by Paul. We had no idea he was the inactivated card."

Joules said, "I thought that player had to drop another one to get juiced up." His face fell. "Oh, yeah. The Magician."

"Paul killed my grandmother, a Tarasova, priming his powers. Today he took out Finn. The Magician was immune to his influence, so Paul poisoned him, then blamed me."

Joules punched the passenger window. "I'm goin' to fry him."

I folded my arms over my chest. "Get in line."

Kentarch glanced at his side mirror, clocking the area. "What is that yellow haze?"

"Paul calls it his *sphere of clarity.* It reverses cards, changing their personalities. You can actually see their tableaux turning upside down."

Joules raked his thin fingers through his brown hair. "No wonder Gabe was such an arsehole to me."

Kentarch cursed under his breath. "I finally reached that place to recruit help, and there's none to be found."

Would he jettison us now? The Chariot had one mission, and neither the Empress nor the Tower could assist him. "But there *will* be help. If we free everyone in the castle, Lark can locate your wife as planned." If Issa still lived. "Fauna's animals found the Magician out in the Ash."

And now I wished they hadn't.

Joules asked Kentarch, "So you're really an ally of Death's?" Demonstrating his lack of a filter, he added, "Know that I plot his downfall most minutes of every day."

I turned to him. "Enough!" *Don't give Kentarch another reason to ditch us.* "If you want Gabriel back, we're all going to have to work together to defeat the Hanged Man."

"All of us, is it?" Joules gave a harsh laugh. "We're just a trio, and you're up the duff. Up the flue. Up the pole."

"Pardon?"

"You're pregnant! What are you goin' to defeat that card with? Your swollen ankles?"

I glanced at Kentarch to see if he was surprised by this news.

He shrugged. "Death told me about the baby. You're almost three months along?"

"Two and a half or so." Would this pregnancy survive snake venom, an avalanche, a spearing, and a truck ride from hell?

"I canna believe Gabe and me have been out here starving, while you got knocked up with another mouth to feed. Much less the Reaper's bastard."

"First of all, my baby isn't a bastard. Technically, Aric and I are married." At least before he crushed his ring and forsook me. "And secondly, I didn't do this on purpose. Paul gave me a shot, telling me it was a contraceptive. He knew how much I didn't want to have a kid. He knew Aric would. Paul was trying to drive a wedge between us."

"Death wants a tyke?" Joules asked. "Mind blown."

Kentarch said, "The Reaper believes a child between two Arcana can upend the game."

Joules grew uncharacteristically grave. "*Can* it?" His best friend was an Arcana; Joules wanted to play this screwed-up game as much as I did. *Not at all.*

I exhaled. "Look, I just work here. But maybe? Circe thinks this kid will ring in a new world. If the entire planet is Tar Ro, our playing field, then the gods might bring it back. All I know for certain is that nothing like this has ever happened. Aric has lived through three games, and he's never heard of it."

Joules grudgingly said, "It wasn't in Cally's chronicles either."

My brows rose with my interest. "You have them?" *Want them.*

Joules jutted his pointy chin. "I might."

"What's your plan now?" Kentarch asked.

I let the subject of chronicles drop. "I doubt Paul will ever leave the castle, so we've got to get inside to kill him." Easier said than done. Probably best to hold off telling them how invincible he was. "Which means you two will need some kind of protection against his influence."

"Gabe likes to roam," Joules said. "He might fly the coop and leave that sphere. Then my problems are over."

I shook my head. "They don't want to leave." On that mountain, Aric had been poised at the very edge, but he hadn't crossed to pursue us. "I think that's part of Paul's hold over them."

Kentarch narrowed his gaze. "Why couldn't the Hanged Man control you? Were you immune like the Magician?"

In general, some cards were unaffected by specific Arcana powers. I vividly recalled poisoning Ogen to no effect. But according to the Hanged Man, I didn't possess an innate immunity to his abilities. Though I trusted little of what he'd said, I hadn't *felt* as if I were a foil to him, a secret weakness. And at first, I had been swayed a touch. "I don't think brainwashing affects me anymore, not after I shucked off the Hierophant's mind control."

Joules said, "Oh, yeah, you ganked him."

Kentarch glanced at my icons again, and I felt my cheeks heating.

Joules pointed at his scrawny chest. "Maybe *I'm* immune like Finn."

"There's only one way to find out. Are either of you willing to bet your life?"

That got Joules to shut up.

Kentarch checked the mirrors again. "Then how do we fight this new enemy?"

"The Priestess. Circe is a witch, so I'm hoping she can do a spell." I recalled the sight of those towering ice shards. She'd been trying to get to me—but I wasn't sure *why*. I took a steadying breath, deciding to believe in her. "She's probably unaffected by the Hanged Man since she's still safe in her abyss. I think she was trying to help with my escape."

Kentarch's demeanor turned contemplative. "Strange that she and I were allies throughout the games, but I have no memories of her."

"She was always loyal to you." To me as well. I just hadn't returned that loyalty until this game. "We can try to contact her. She's a friend of mine." Surely she'd know how to defeat Paul, a player I hadn't even been able to scratch.

"Friend?" Joules snorted. "We heard she attacked you outside of Fort Arcana."

"Only a little. She didn't commit to it."

Joules rolled his eyes. "Oh, well, in that case . . ."

"If anyone has any better ideas, I'm open to hearing them."

"How will we summon this witch?" Kentarch asked, making it sound like we were summoning the kraken.

Circe would get a kick out of that. I imagined us chuckling together. Then reality returned. My husband wanted to murder me, and Finn was dead. Laughter was a long way away, not even a glimmer on the horizon. "I usually just make a lot of noise and bat at the water. Doesn't often work."

Kentarch raised his brows. "I'd anticipated something more . . . formal."

"We'll have to find a body of water not trapped in ice. The larger the better. Preferably as close to the Bermuda Triangle as possible."

"I can only teleport to places I've already been, and this is as far south as I've traveled in this country. We could drive to the nearest coast."

"That would put us in the Outer Banks." Right where my grandmother had been locked up. Seemed I'd always been fated to go there—except Jack was supposed to have taken me; that had been our plan. "We'll contact Circe from the Atlantic."

The idea of even more distance between me and Aric made my chest ache, but my MacGuffin awaited. What would I find? Probably something I'd been meant to discover since the beginning.

Glancing from the road to the GPS map, Kentarch said, "If our way is clear, we should make it in less than a week."

"That long?" The man I loved was under the sway of an Arcana killer who betrayed for kicks.

"Yes, we must be vigilant against threats."

"Whoa, hold up on our route," Joules said. "We suspected that one of Richter's lairs is between these mountains and the coast. And if Circe *is* under the influence, she could use the ocean to swamp us."

I turned to Kentarch. "Not if the Chariot can teleport us out of the way."

He nodded. "I will need time to recuperate."

Impatience hammered at me. "Paul's influence will probably keep spreading. And Aric and the others will be sitting ducks against Richter if we're not all united."

Joules asked, "Won't Richter just get brainwashed too?"

"He might know what that yellow haze is and avoid it entirely. Plus, he and Zara don't have to get close; they can strike the castle from afar. We need to get moving on this."

Kentarch shrugged his broad shoulders. "Without food, I tire very easily."

"You and me both." Joules investigated a camo pouch. "You got any scraps in this truck?"

"Nothing. I haven't eaten in days. With luck, we will meet other travelers. My hearing is acute, so I will know of anyone's approach in advance."

"To roll them?" To steal whatever supplies were keeping them alive?

"That's right, Empress," Joules said. "Some of us haven't been living in that warm and holy castle. Out here, it's dog eat dog. Survival of the fittest."

"Don't lecture me, choirboy. After Richter's massacre, I was out on the road alone—with one freaking arm—rolling folks." Of course, I'd reasoned that my robbing the innocent hadn't counted, because I'd intended to go back in time and change the future. My thefts would never have occurred. *The best-laid plans and all that. . . .*

Kentarch said, "I prefer not to harm others, but I will do anything to reunite with Issa."

I had to sigh. "You really love her."

His voice dropped an octave. "Unreservedly."

Without reservations. Aric had loved me, but he'd clearly had reservations.

"I feel as if time is running out." Kentarch gripped the steering wheel harder. "The pressure to find her has been immense."

Sooner or later, would Kentarch ditch us for Paul's alliance?

As if reading my mind, Joules said, "If you returned to the castle, they could still help you. Brainwashed or not, Lark *or* Gabriel could pick up your wife's scent."

I shot Joules a look. *Stop putting ideas into his head!* I hastily told Kentarch, "If you joined them, Paul wouldn't allow you or anyone else to leave his sphere in order to look for her. He'd probably make you believe that he saw her dead body or that she no longer wanted you."

Kentarch said, "All my life I've strived for absolute mastery over myself and my fate. Again and again, I've wrenched victory from certain defeat." *Woe to the bloody vanquished.* "The idea of surrendering my free will to another man, especially a craven murderer, strikes me as a descent into hell."

"Then we're on the same page," I said. "Understand me: there's no scenario where Paul helps you above himself."

Joules's stomach growled loudly. "I'm dying here." He elbowed me. "You can make fruit. How about something for the road?"

"I'd expend as many calories as it would provide. If not more. And I don't have a lot of reserves."

He eyed me. "How come you're skinny? You're pregnant, and you've had all the food in the world."

I shrugged. Ah, now the pain in my shoulder returned. "Can't keep it down."

"So what happens when we kill the Hanged Man? Gabe and I are still screwed. Death will never let us live in his lair. I say we gank Paul and the Reaper, then take over the whole place."

"Really, Joules?"

"How're you goin' to get back together with Death after what he did?"

"Because I've felt how consuming Arcana mind control can be. The Hierophant nearly made me *eat* part of a man I'd just met. I can't even explain how strong the pull was. Paul's influence turned Aric's card."

Voicing my worst fear, Joules said, "I canna help but think the Reaper was reverting to form."

According to Paul, that was exactly what'd happened. The look in Aric's eyes . . . the way he'd crushed his ring . . . Could hatred that strong be manufactured by another?

If not, then Aric's rage had always been there, simmering. *The factory setting.* Had he been conscious of it?

Even if I saved him, what kind of future would we have if a part of him harbored such animosity?

I inhaled for calm. "Aric is a good man." When free of Paul. "I hope one day you can see that. But no matter what, we're going to need every Arcana we can round up to fight Richter."

Kentarch said, "She's right about the Emperor. Besides, I will protect the Reaper as long as I'm able. He helped me after the Flash hit."

"Fine." Joules grumbled. "But I vow to you, Empress—once Richter's gone, all bets are off with Death."

I'd have to handle this later. *Kick the can down the road.* Jack used to say that. With each mile, was I getting closer to him or farther away? Of course, he might be dead.

"What's all this gear?" Joules pointed to the dash.

"Equipment I've sourced since Issa and I first came to this continent and found this truck."

Joules reached for a sort of joystick control, fiddling with it. A roof-mounted spotlight beamed over our surroundings. "Get the hell out!" He was like a kid with a toy, shooting that beam all around. "What is this? A thousand lumens?"

"It's three thousand lumens. And it is critical equipment."

"I'll use it critically."

Kentarch seemed obsessive about his chariot, so I was surprised Joules didn't get his mouthy mouth popped.

"Folks must try to boost this rig all the time."

Kentarch said, "I have an ignition sequence that must be entered to start the engine." I'd noticed a row of tiny rocker switches under the steering wheel. "Also a hidden lever locks the axles, making it impossible to move. So if either of you thought to overwhelm me and take the truck, you wouldn't get very far."

I frowned. "Overwhelm you?"

"It's difficult to imagine someone like you killing." *You haven't met the red witch.* "But your icons remind me."

"I acted in self-defense in both cases. This guy"—I pointed out the Hermit's lantern icon—"liked to kidnap girls for sadistic experiments. I found the remains of a previous subject congealing in the chains he'd made her wear. This guy"—I tapped the Hierophant's two-finger icon—"was the leader of a horde of cannibal miners. He kept victims in his belowground 'pantry,' carving on them bit by bit while they were still alive to keep the 'meat' fresh." I met Kentarch's gaze with my chin up. "How you like me now?"

"It makes me wonder what I did to merit your wrath. Right after the Flash, Death told me to beware of you, that you'd killed me before."

"I did. But I'm different now." As long as I could keep a leash on the red witch. That no longer seemed much of a concern—she hadn't so much as stirred when I'd been on the wolves' meal plan. "Aric just hadn't realized it yet."

Kentarch looked unconvinced.

Joules asked him, "How'd you and the Reaper hook up?"

"He sent me a sat phone before the Flash. After the apocalypse, I contacted him. He answered many questions about my abilities and invited us to this country."

Joules spotlighted a bridge. Then a burned-out car. "You teleported over?"

"Yes. The plains in Africa had little protection from the Flash. I knew our only shot at survival was to find the mysterious Death. But I'd been to the United States just once, for a tech seminar in Washington, DC."

I said, "And you can only teleport to places you've been."

"Precisely. I can ghost anytime—"

"Ghost?" Each Arcana seemed to have his or her own lingo. The glowing markings on my skin were *glyphs*. Vines and trees were my *soldiers*.

"Make myself and other objects intangible, walking through walls and such."

Joules said, "Or exploding bears. Too grand, that was."

Kentarch shrugged modestly. "But teleportation must have an endpoint. Though we had no idea what we would find on a different continent, I gathered as much strength as I could, then we took a leap of faith."

Joules murmured, "Jumping off into nothing."

I added, "With no wings." The Tower and I shared a look. Both imagining Gabriel's leap?

Kentarch nodded. "We materialized to Washington. Barely. Long distances and great weights are equally difficult to teleport or ghost." So what had ghosting this ginormous truck done to him tonight? "Once we arrived, finding enough fuel and water for the trip from DC to the mountains proved nearly impossible. Then I got separated from Issa. She must have been taken from me."

Joules said, "Seems to me that no one could take a damned thing from you."

Kentarch merely stared out at the road. Lost in memories?

I nudged him. "What happened?"

He blinked. "Keeping her safe from Bagmen and marauders as I sourced strained the limits of my ability. Finally I took her to an empty penthouse. I cleared the building of threats, then teleported debris to block the stairwell—after all, we'd never need the steps. Once I felt she was protected in her refuge above the city, I went farther afield for supplies. Water was our most pressing concern back then. One day, I located a well. I returned to her, intending to celebrate. But she was gone."

"Who could have gotten to her?" I asked.

"That's what has tormented me. *Who?* I've questioned survivors for months but have hit a true dead end."

"Maybe your old lady dumped you." Prickly, prickly Joules.

"Never. And even if she had decided to leave me, how could she have? My impenetrable barricade remained in place."

"It sounds like a magic trick," I said, reminded of Finn. My God, I was going to miss him. Even during the apocalypse, he'd retained his happy-go-lucky attitude. His words drifted through my mind: *I've never been more stoked about life than I have been over the last two weeks.*

They'd literally been his last two weeks. At Fort Arcana, he'd told me he was convinced he would die young, that he'd made peace with it. He'd thought we all should. . . .

Kentarch tapped the GPS map to zoom in on our current location; then he turned onto a new road. "There was a military force that mobilized not far outside the city. Maybe a helicopter landed on the roof and forced her away at gunpoint." More to himself, he said, "Though I blocked the roof access as well. Perhaps they rappelled." Shaking his head hard, he said, "Not knowing has all but maddened me."

"If anyone can find her, it'll be Lark," I said, hastily adding, "once Paul is defeated and she's fully recovered. So our first step is Circe."

As the game wanted, we were following a MacGuffin, which meant we would surely cross paths with other Arcana.

But would we find Circe—before Richter found us?

13

"Stop the truck!" I cried. We were a few hours into our drive, and Joules had just spotlighted a legless Bagger eeling its way across the road up ahead. "I need to get close to it."

Kentarch barely let off the gas. "Pardon? I always run them over."

I quickly told him about the Sol and Empress shit show, relaying how the Sun had betrayed me but ultimately redeemed himself. And how we'd communicated through his Baggers.

The Chariot looked disbelieving. *About which part?* "If he can command Bagmen, why allow them to harm humans?"

"He can't command all of them at one time. No more than Circe can affect all bodies of water or Lark all creatures. We wouldn't blame Fauna for every animal attack."

"But the Sun Card *did* control the Baggers who fed on your blood. How were you able to forgive him for that?"

"I've also had to do things I hope can be forgiven by others, and I believe in karma." Kentarch still hadn't made up his mind about me, and that was okay—as long as he pulled over. "Look, Sol's got eyes everywhere. We can ask him to search for Issa."

The Chariot slammed on the brakes, maneuvering the truck onto the shoulder. He jammed the gearshift into park. Off went the engine. With a knife at the ready, he exited the cab.

The night was freezing, snow blowing inside.

Joules opened his door and stepped down as well. Lightning flared above him in the low cloud deck.

With all that electricity about us, I'd thought the Tower would get stronger. Even he'd admitted, "Those bolts are calling my name. I'd be unstoppable if I could eat." Still, he'd already recovered enough to produce a javelin for this foray.

I slid across the seat toward the door, feeling less pain in my shoulder. My offensive abilities might be stifled, but my regeneration eked on. My fingertips had regained their normal color, and the bite in my hand had oozed out venom.

I hopped down from the height of the cab. The truck was a behemoth, so big Joules had dubbed it the Beast. Would Kentarch have enough fuel to get us to the Atlantic?

As we'd covered miles through the eternal darkness, I'd swept my gaze along the road for slaver spike strips, telling Joules and Kentarch: "The threat is real." We'd chugged along through towns with the same striped pattern of destruction that Jack and I had seen when we'd left Louisiana.

On one street, the buildings had been incinerated by the Flash. On the next one over, they would be intact. All stripped by now, of course; zero resources left behind.

Nearing the Bagger, I studied its appearance. It'd been a grown man—all that remained of its clothing was a ragged necktie. It moaned, grappling to reach me, milky eyes gone wide.

Other than this zombie, we hadn't spotted any animals or a single other soul. This area seemed to be a death zone. Lowercase *d*.

So why did I experience that all-too-familiar sense of being watched? I rubbed my nape. Was it another Bagger? Or had Lark's creatures caught up with us? I told the guys, "Keep an eye out for animal sentries."

Kentarch nodded. I'd learned the Chariot was a man of few words. Joules had filled the silence with nonstop chatter. "I'm Irish," he'd said early on, "so it's in me genes to dole out nicknames. Can I call you Kenny?"

Kentarch had demonstrated endless patience with him. "No, you may not."

"Sounds better than Tarch. Still, Tarch it is!"

I'd asked, "What's my nickname?"

"I only give nicknames to folks I like. But if I did, I'd call you *tart*. Tarch and the tart!" Ugh!

Once we reached the Bagger, the putrid stench nearly overwhelmed me.

Joules rocked from his heels to his toes, looking uneasy. "You think the Sun Card'll hear you?"

"He probably won't be monitoring one lone Bagger, but maybe I can get his attention. I've got to try." I asked Kentarch, "Can you hold it still?"

He placed his boot on the creature's head, forcing it to face me.

I knelt just out of its reach, my breaths shallowing. "Sol, can you hear me? Sol?" Zero recognition sparked in those disintegrating eyes. "Come on, Sol!" Choking back my fear, I leaned in and yelled, "SOL! WE NEED HELP!" No answer but for the mindless moans of the creature.

"Call it, Empress." Joules pulled his coat tighter. "This undead doesn't feel like gabbing, and the truck is warm."

I stood. "Fine."

In a pissy tone, Joules said, "Are you just goin' to leave it? Are Baggers off limits now?"

"They're still a danger to our species. Even Sol couldn't begrudge us taking out random zombies. Will one of you do the honors?"

At once, Kentarch let his knife fall, skewering the Bagman's brain. Its body went limp.

Collecting the blade, Kentarch wiped it along the sole of his combat boot, then sheathed it at his thigh. "We might as well stop here for the night." *Night* was relative these days, but his eyes were bloodshot with fatigue.

Once we climbed back in the truck, Joules wadded up his threadbare scarf, making a pillow against the window. "Is somebody gonna take watch? We're deep in cannibal country."

I should have been exhausted, but my nerves were wired. "I've got first shift."

"Hey, Chariot, watch out for this one"—Joules pointed at me—"she's a temptress."

I rolled my eyes at him. When we'd stopped the truck earlier to winch a car out of the road, I'd taken Joules aside to get his impression of our new companion, wondering if we could trust him. Kentarch certainly didn't trust us. He'd concealed his movements when he'd entered the ignition sequence. Insurance so we didn't kill him in his sleep?

Joules had smirked at me. "You got me alone 'cause you want to seduce me, eh? One among your string of doomed men? Tough luck, Empress—I'm faithful to Cally's memory." Sometimes I more than slightly wanted to strangle the Tower.

He swiftly nodded off, his soft snores competing with the sounds of his empty stomach.

Kentarch drummed his fingers on the wheel, clearly wanting to voice a question.

"Just say it, Chariot."

"Do *you* believe the game can be stopped?"

"I used to work toward that very goal." Until my grandmother had gotten hold of me. She'd been right about so many other things.

She'd advised me to stash seeds all over the castle for protection, but I'd felt safe there. The plants I'd grown inside had been more for decoration, and I'd let them wither. She'd told me Death and all my friends would turn on me.

Bingo. Guilt weighed heavily on me. Toward the end, I'd dreaded being around her. Part of me had . . . hated her. Recalling the excuses I'd made not to see her cut me deep.

Yet all she'd wanted to do was warn me—protect me. Her only living relative. She'd wanted me to be deadly because I was immersed in a deadly game. How shocked she must've been when she realized I was in love with my age-old enemy.

I'd told Aric we'd rewrite history. Wasn't that the same as defying fate? If fates couldn't be changed . . .

No, I refused to believe that. If I ever accepted that, then I would lie down and never get back up.

Kentarch quietly said, "You no longer think we can end it."

"Maybe it's possible. But probably not before the world is beyond salvage. The gods like their games, and we're all pawns." *Why me?* Why had I gotten tapped for this bullshit?

"Then we need to figure out how to fight the gods instead of each other—to take control of the deck." He leaned against the driver's side door. "What a splendid battle that would be." In time, he drifted off as well.

I believed the Chariot was a decent-minded, disciplined guy. But I also suspected he would slit my throat with a song in his heart if it meant saving his wife.

Still, he'd gotten me thinking. What if we Arcana had all banded together to fight our shitty fates?

Each of us had myriad weaknesses and strengths. Ogen had been immune to my poison but suffered from hydrophobia. Though Joules didn't have great physical strength, he could electrify his body in defense. Gabriel's black-feathered wings were awing, but they were also a huge target. All-powerful Aric had succumbed to Paul's influence, yet hapless Finn had been unaffected.

What could we all have accomplished if we'd pooled the resources of twenty-two Arcana?

Would even the gods have trembled?

I leaned my head back and stared at the ceiling, thoughts racing. This was my first night away from Aric in months. I tried to call up a memory of his unguarded smile, but all I saw was that rage in his eyes.

The image of him in the window had been seared into my brain forever. I'd learned something in that moment: *Rage is a type of madness.*

Would he ever come back from it? Did some deep-down part of him understand what he'd done? No matter what, he must be hurting.

How was Lark dealing with her grief? A new worry emerged. What would happen if she tried her faunagenesis—on Finn?

No, Paul would never allow it. The Hanged Man's powers had been activated with that kill.

Closing my eyes, I replayed Finn's beach illusion. That last bit of harmony had been the calm before the storm. Years seemed to have passed, but less than a day had gone by.

Finn's voice echoed in my head. *I freaking love you guys.*

Tears spilled down my cheeks.

Though I cried silently, Joules woke. In a rough voice, he said, "Finn was my friend too."

14

"I say we rent her out at the Sick House."

"No way. The Stix will pay more for her."

"But they'll be wantin' her untouched. And dang it, we should acknowledge our own limitations."

"Excuse me, gentlemen," I told my two would-be pimps as they debated what to do with me. *Stix? Sick House?* I had no idea what they were talking about and didn't care. I just wanted to be absolutely certain they deserved what was coming to them: their executions. "Look, I don't want any trouble with either of you." My damsel-in-distress act was getting old.

One guy's halitosis smelled like radioactive waste. I'd deemed him Hal. The other had a handlebar moustache littered with food debris. He was Stache.

"Please let me go." I wasn't managing a believable level of panic. "I'm trying to make it home to my husband." Not a lie.

After parking their serial-killer van, they'd approached me with raised weapons—a bat and what was probably an empty pistol. They'd asked me if I was alone, and I'd said I was.

Definitely a lie. Kentarch and Joules crouched nearby behind an overturned tractor trailer.

I still hesitated to steal from innocent folks, so whenever Kentarch heard a vehicle coming, he and Joules got scarce, and I trotted out to the road to do my damsel routine. If anyone tried to hurt me, the boys stepped in, and the non-innocent forfeited everything. Including their lives.

All I had to do was give the signal. Kentarch would easily pick them off with his rifle, pistol, or throwing blades. Joules normally held off using his spears in close quarters. His javelins tended to go boom in a big way.

My powers remained fritzed.

"You ain't ever gonna see your husband again, peach," Hal told me from way too up-close. His mouth smelled like someone had told him to eat shit, and he'd complied. He kept licking his chapped lips as he leered at me. "But soon you're gonna have plenty of fellas to keep you company."

I was so over this. For the last week, we'd encountered a surprising number of survivors; I supposed they tended to converge like Arcana did.

Not as surprising—they'd all been bad guys. We'd scored twenty-three gallons of gasoline, a bug-out bag for me, half a bottle of gin, and a case of Sheba canned cat food.

I'd declined my share of kitty chow, fearing I'd just throw it up anyway. When Joules had first dug his fingers into a can to scoop chunks to his mouth, I'd gone running to vomit.

My perilous escape from the castle seemed to have done nothing to interrupt my pregnancy. Fatigue was taking its toll. My hunger pangs were constant, the pain like an old, untended wound.

Maybe Hal and Stache had food, something to keep me from daydreaming about hush puppies and ice cream and mashed potatoes and cheeseburgers with extra, gooey cheese.

I turned my thoughts from food, my bleary mind wandering over the last few days. As Kentarch, Joules, and I had descended from the mountains, the temperatures rose, and snow cover grew sparser.

The rivers and ponds had been only partially iced over. I'd hailed

Circe at the larger ones. No answer. Nor had I heard from Matthew. *Jack, are you out here?*

Though I trusted my new traveling companions to a degree, I never told them about the Fool's last message. As time passed, Jack's survival seemed less and less believable, even to me.

I'd also never given them all the details of Aric's attack at the castle—even when I'd woken up screaming. My nightmares of Richter now alternated with those about Aric. . . .

We should've been able to pick up our pace to the coast, but so many roads had been washed out or blocked with vehicles. Whenever the Beast couldn't winch or bulldoze its way through, Kentarch had to teleport us.

He was also using his teleportation each night to measure the spread of the Hanged Man's influence. Kentarch's last report: *It's unpredictable and sporadic.*

Hunger and overuse had weakened the Chariot's abilities overall. Earlier today, he'd tried to teleport the truck across a wreck-choked bridge. We'd flashed from tangible to quavery and back as he'd gritted his teeth. He hadn't been able to move us an inch, so we'd had to backtrack and go around.

Afterward, his outline had wavered, making him look like a ghost, then a man, then a ghost.

At this point, I could have walked faster, but I never complained when I slept in the Beast's toasty cab. I'd once asked Kentarch, "Why don't you carry a bug-out bag?" His answer: "This truck *is* my bug-out bag." Several times an hour, his gaze would stray to Issa's picture on his visor.

His chariot was a weapon and a roving safe house rolled into one, but it was a demanding tool, requiring ever more fuel. As my own resource-suck did.

"Right on!" Stache said, waking me from my daze. "Then we're in agreement." He started forcing me toward their van.

"Guys, if you want to live past the next few seconds, then release me and keep moving."

Stache tightened his grip on my arm. "Another word out of you, and I'll cut out your tongue and feed it to you."

"Literally? Or is that just a saying? These days you have to wonder."

Stache raised his hand to backhand me. Before I could stop him, Hal grabbed his wrist. "Don't mark her up. I want her pretty. No reason not to enjoy her till we reach the Sick House."

Aaaaaand, we're done here. "Your lifetime's over." I gave the signal. "Come, touch," I told these men, "but you'll pay a price."

A knife flew past me, end over end. The blade plugged Hal in the face. He reeled before he collapsed.

Eyes gone wide, Stache released me and fled. He didn't get five steps before another knife sank into his back. *THUNK.* A kill shot.

Kentarch jogged over to retrieve his blades. The first time he'd made a throw like that, I'd gawked. His aim was so uncanny, even Joules—no slouch himself—had been impressed.

"Let's make quick work of this." Kentarch remained as reserved as Joules was mouthy. He mostly liked to talk about tactical things, or about mind over matter, and he never volunteered information about his life in Africa.

As Kentarch siphoned fuel, Joules investigated the men's van, tossing me their bags to root through. They had pictures of family, probably stolen from other victims. I snagged a flashlight and two flints to put in my bug-out bag. Not exactly winning Lotto.

I raised my head, suddenly feeling as if we were being watched. "Kentarch, do you see or hear anyone else around us?"

He assessed the area. "No, Empress."

"Probably nothing then."

"Food!" Joules cried from the van. "They've got food. A container full of soup."

I'd bet I could keep that down! I hurried over.

Joules held up a clear takeout container filled with a dark broth. He ripped off the lid and inhaled. "Take a whiff of that!"

Though the soup was cool, the delicious aroma reached me. My stomach was on board! My first real meal in days.

"Looks like we're goin' to vary our cat-food diet—"

A pinky finger floated to the surface. Mushy skin. With a long, dirty nail.

Joules yelled and hurled the container.

Then he puked right beside me.

Enough. The cannibal soup had marked a turning point for me. Resolve gave way under the weight of depression. My eyes watered, my bottom lip trembling.

As we continued onward, Kentarch kept glancing from the road to my face. "We had a minor setback foodwise, but we gained valuable fuel. Overall, our mission was a success."

I gave him a watery glare. "A minor setback? Do you ever lose your cool?" The closest I'd seen him get was when Joules had nearly opened a bottle of Tusker beer he'd found somewhere in the truck. Kentarch had yelled, "Place that down *slowly*. As if your life depends on it." Later, he'd admitted, "That is my wife's favorite. I found the bottle on the day I lost her, and I've protected it ever since. I believe we will drink it together when we're reunited."

Now he said, "You need to eat from the supplies we have, Empress. If not for yourself, then for your baby."

"I'll never keep it down." The only thing worse than eating Sheba would be experiencing it on the way back up.

Joules rested his head against the window. "Canna stop thinking about real food. Gabe and me used to smell bacon cooking in the castle. About drove us barmy. Sizzling, juicy rashers . . ."

We each fell silent, lost in our own thoughts.

I missed Aric. I missed the life we'd had together. I missed Jack. I missed food meant for humans without bits of humans in it.

As ever, I wondered what Aric was doing in his lonely castle and how Lark was coping. Had they had a funeral for Finn? Maybe they'd buried him on the hill close to Gran.

I wondered if Aric had left my painting on the wall of our bedroom. Would he water the rose bloom he'd grown from a seed—or destroy it?

I frowned. I could simply *ask* Aric. I turned to Kentarch. "Can I borrow your phone?"

15

DEATH

How much longer could I remain in this castle without going mad? I sat in my study, gazing out at the night, sharpening my swords.

This task used to soothe me, but inside, I was chaos.

Kentarch, my long-time ally, had betrayed me, spiriting my duplicitous wife away into the Ash.

I kept replaying the image of her, wounded, in the back of that truck, traveling farther and farther from my reach.

As long as she lived, I would be at risk of falling for her beauty and charms, because I was weak when it came to my nemesis.

I scraped a whetstone along one sword edge. Evidently, there was no end to what I'd believe from her lips. The Grim Reaper, a father? The back of my neck heated, and I cringed at my idiocy.

The Hanged Man's sphere of clarity protected me from her spellbinding, which she'd known. As Paul had explained: "The Empress wanted me dead because I can defend you and the others from her powers. I'm the only one she can't mesmerize."

But his sphere wasn't spreading fast enough. We Arcana had fueled it in the beginning, causing it to overrun this mountain. Now it grew in fitful spurts.

I couldn't reach the Empress without leaving it. Not an option.

A shadow passed by my window, the Archangel flying by on his watch. He and Fauna split those duties.

After losing the Magician, she was proving to be less of an asset than ever. Though she'd sent creatures to scout for the Empress, her usual drive had disappeared.

She'd moved into the menagerie, sleeping continually, seeming dazed whenever awake. And she kept close her wolves, as if she'd sensed a threat from me.

She should. I raised my sword to eye the edge. Along with my new mental clarity, my murderous impulses grew stronger every day. I was returning to the Grim Reaper of old—

My phone rang. I stared at it on my desk.

Her. I knew it was the Empress calling from Kentarch's phone. My chest constricted, every inch of my skin feeling feverish. I set aside my sword and whetstone to reach for the phone. Paul entered just as I answered, "Empress."

"Aric."

She was the only person who'd called me by my given name in more than two millennia. One soft word from her had sent chills racing over me.

I'd gotten used to touch. I'd gotten used to bedding her. To loving her. What if, by some miracle, she could have been true?

Paul studied my expression. Though I masked my reaction to her, he noticed, was clearly disappointed.

Would I spit in the face of his enlightenment? How could her effect on me still linger? "Why have you called?"

"I miss my husband."

My gods. "I miss . . . the idea of you." I'd caught myself debating whether I could ignore everything she'd done to me and take her back to my bed. *Such is her power.*

No. Never. Eventually she would try to poison me. That was her MO. "But I always knew you would turn on me."

"I haven't. You're being influenced by Paul."

"He's shown me the truth. Because of him, I escaped the Magician's fate."

"*Paul* killed Finn—not me!" Then she seemed to make an effort to control her emotions. "He ended the life of my friend, a sweet teenager who respected and looked up to you."

"Ah, my beautiful poisoness, *you* dispatched the Magician—just as you usually do."

"Then how did an inactivated card like Paul get activated? Why does *he* wear Finn's icon? Check his hand."

"He wagered you would bring that up again as 'proof.'"

With a grin, Paul displayed the Magician's mark to me—an ouroboros symbol. The snake eating its own tail symbolized the eternal power of transformation.

"Then how do you explain it, Aric?"

"By the time Paul returned to the castle, your poison had ravaged the Magician's organs and mind, but his body still clung to life. Paul delivered a tonic to put the boy out of his misery."

"You did CPR on Finn. You can sense death, and you told us he was dead. So if I'm guilty, *I* should have gotten the icon."

"I was mistaken. The Magician still lived. The boy's own powers must have altered my perception."

"An answer for everything, huh? Paul told me he wasn't a monster like the ones I've faced, but the Traitor's worse. I never trusted the Lovers, the Hermit, or the Hierophant. I never depended on the Devil."

"Ah, but I once did. Ogen was the only one who could refashion my armor with his demonic grip." The metal was invulnerable to pressure and heat, unless wielded by the Devil Card. And now my suit would be forever compromised because I'd cut out a piece for her cilice. The Empress was responsible for the single chink in my armor. *So too in life.* "I regret killing Ogen to save you." Was that a hitched breath? I'd shocked her.

Paul had broached the subject of retrieving the Empress alive, using the cilice on her. Though she was too evil to benefit from his clarity, she could fuel the sphere. Still, I wanted her *dead* for what she'd made me believe.

In the background, I heard the Tower mutter, "Ask him about Gabe."

I told her, "The Archangel has joined our new alliance and looks forward to facing the Tower."

She made a sound of frustration. "If you have a reason for hating me, then fine, I can almost see it. We were enemies longer than allies. But Gabe and Joules have always been best friends. So why would Gabe turn against Joules, if not for Paul?"

"The Archangel discovered that the Tower and his lover, Calanthe, had intended to electrocute him as soon as he'd outlived his usefulness. Three's a crowd, is it not?"

"Lemme guess: Paul told you guys that? And you're buying it? Joules loves Gabe like a brother."

"And yet . . ."

She didn't relay this to the Tower. What was she thinking? What new strategy would she employ?

Several moments passed before she said, "I'm about three months along now. I should be showing soon."

"Still you continue with this pregnancy nonsense." What was worse? Her conniving? Or the fact that even now *I craved this family*? I hated her the most for that.

"Aric, we're going to have a kid together, but only if I survive for the next six months. Think what you will about me. Punish me, but don't punish our child."

I squeezed my eyes closed. When I opened them, light glittered from my gaze. "You want me to believe not only that I impregnated you, but also that your pregnancy continues?"

Fauna had landed at least one venomous bite. The Archangel had reported that the Empress and the Tower had been swept up in an avalanche and that she'd been bleeding profusely.

"Believe it. As of now, this is our reality."

"You can sound convincing, I'll give you that." So godsdamned convincing. My gaze flickered toward Paul. Almost at once, a memory arose of when she'd first seduced me into bed. "Just as you did centuries ago. As if it were yesterday, I can recall the look in your eyes—right before you delivered your poisoned kiss to me. This is why

I never call you by your given name. While *it* might change, *you* do not."

"I told you I couldn't feel guilty any longer for things I did as another incarnation. I told you that I wouldn't keep paying for the past. You said you understood and that we'd start anew. But we didn't, did we?"

"I was ready; you weren't."

Silence answered me. What trick would she try now? "We'll talk about this after I take Paul down. Understand me, Reaper, I'm going to get you fixed."

"Such bravado, poisoness. How will you defeat a player who's invulnerable to harm?" Paul had demonstrated how a blade drawn over his flesh made no slice, his skin as protected as if he wore my armor. *My hated bane.* Alas, the Hanged Man possessed no offensive powers, was utterly dependent on me and our alliance.

Brimming with confidence, the Empress said, "If he's invulnerable, why hasn't he won every game? Somehow, someway, other cards have taken him out."

"Good point. Paul must have a weakness, but if it's unknown by the Arcana who remain, then he might as well not have one at all." The Hanged Man smiled at me.

"Maybe your touch of Death can kill him."

A glance at Paul. "Perhaps that's true, but unlike you, I don't betray my alliances."

"Aric, you will return to normal one day. But I have to wonder if *we* can come back from this. The guilt will torture you."

"Torture? I dream of delivering pain to you." To equal my own. "Cross my path, and you will know more agony than any other living creature has ever suffered. I give you fair warning."

"Save it, Reaper. I'm pretty sure there's little worse than starving while pregnant. And to think, you'd gotten on my case about taking my vitamins."

"My Empress is hungry. That gladdens me. Remember: exile equals execution."

"There's no reasoning with you," she said with a long-suffering exhalation. "I'd like to speak to the Hanged Man."

This should be good. "Of course." I handed over the phone.

Paul grinned as he said, "Evie, it's been too long."

With my heightened senses, I could easily hear her side of the conversation: "What's your plan for the future?"

"Ride out the apocalypse with my allies. Spread my influence until all Arcana are safe from you. Then we'll hunt you down and pluck that pretty head of yours from your body."

Paul's words grated on me. Despite my hatred toward the Empress, she was still my wife. Though *I* could threaten her . . . *others may not.*

"This kid might save the world, and you plan to off us?" she asked, and I considered for a moment if *she* believed she was pregnant. Caught up in her own lies? "What's in it for you, Traitor? Just plain evilness?"

"I do get a certain satisfaction that you are enjoying the sentence you'd intended for me." His smile was smug.

The Empress was a liar, a temptress, and a killer. But over all our histories, she had also been a formidable foe. Respect was due to her from this upstart card. "Enough."

Picking up on my annoyance, Paul quickly said, "Gotta run, Evie. Let's keep in touch."

"Oh, Paul"—her voice dropped to the breathy whisper of her Arcana call—"we'll see each other real soon."

THE EMPRESS

As I hung up, I struggled to bite back my helpless rage and hopelessness. The call had only worsened my depression.

Aric, come back to me.

At Joules's and Kentarch's questioning looks, I said, "Gabe's still there. The three are all still under Paul's thrall. We're still out here starving. My husband is being controlled by pure evil."

Kentarch's hands clenched the wheel. "Which means the Hanged Man is *winning.*"

16

For the last week, I'd hailed Circe with more and more desperation. Not so much as a ripple from her. Nor a flicker from Matthew.

Each time I tried to communicate with him, I wondered anew if I'd imagined Jack's voice. As ever, I didn't feel like I had a firm grasp on what was real/unreal.

Replaying Aric's tone on the phone didn't help my mental state. It'd reminded me of his hostility when he'd first captured me in this game. He'd threatened me constantly, taunting me with my demise: *Is this the day I decapitate the creature?*

Since then, I'd come to depend on him, counting on his love. He was my soul mate; we belonged together. So how could he say those hateful things to me?

If my mind was as screwed up as everyone kept thinking, then maybe the months I'd had with Aric in his castle were the dream. Maybe I'd been asleep this entire time and would wake up tied to Thanatos, a captive walking barefoot across a punishing terrain.

I'd probably prefer that to being pregnant.

DAY 545 A.F.

Still no sign of Circe.

We'd started going stir-crazy in the Beast. Truck cabin fever. So whenever we found a decent-looking shelter, we'd overnight inside, starting a fire. Kentarch was handy at sourcing precious wood. A door. A chair. A cradle.

But nothing to eat. Cat food was beginning to look good.

DAY 546 A.F.

I was right. Cat food tasted worse on the way up. As my best friend Mel would've said in my situation: "Somebody better get some mothertrucking filet mignon up in this bitch, or I will MUTINY."

DAY 548 A.F.

The big, bad Empress sobbed when we got down to our last cans of Sheba.

Aric, you bastard, come back to me.

17

DAY 550 A.F.

"What can I do for you, Empress?" Death asked me in a pleasant tone.

Half delirious, I'd filched Kentarch's phone from the truck, then sneaked back into our current accommodations—a firelit cave—to place a call. "Aric, I need to come home." I'd feared that Kentarch would leave our fragile alliance, but here I was, breaking ranks first.

"Home?" God, how could he sound so snide? "Do you mean *my* castle?"

"You have to come get me." I knelt beside the cave's trash pile, picking up an empty cat-food can. Tears welling, I ran my finger along the edge for another crumb. Nothing. I'd already licked it clean.

At that moment, I despised Aric.

When I tossed the can away, my ring caught the firelight, the amber stone drawing my eye. The band hung so loosely on my finger I'd had to coat it with sap to keep it on.

"I burn to come *get you*, Empress. Alas, I can't leave just now." His voice was a perfect mix of good humor and callousness. "You see, I have a particular susceptibility to your charms."

As he spoke, my gaze darted around the large cavern. No one was in here with me, and yet I again got that feeling of being watched. I told him, "I feel their eyes on me all the time." It was driving me crazy!

"Whose eyes?"

"I-I don't know. I feel them." Matthew had told me to beware of

Bagmen, slavers, militia, cannibals, and Minors. I'd fought every group except for the last. He'd said they watched us, plotting against us.

Could they be following us?

I'd asked Joules if Cally's chronicles had mentioned the Minors. He'd said, "In parts. Basically the only way you'll know they exist is if something goes really wrong with the game. They're not allowed to hurt us, and we can't hurt them."

Aric said, "Your stint out in the Ash has taken a toll on you, Empress. You're not making sense."

"Not just the Ash. Against all odds, I'm still pregnant." Dizziness was my new companion; sleep was all I wanted to do. "I can't go on much longer."

Late last night as I'd tossed and turned in my sleeping bag, Kentarch had murmured, "Enough is enough." He'd sat beside me and unsheathed his knife. I'd felt a flare of fear until he'd rolled up his sleeve.

"You must have nourishment." He raised the blade above his forearm. *"Come, Empress, you are supposed to be bloodthirsty."*

"Uh-uh," I said weakly. *"Maybe this is the gateway drug to cannibalism. I don't want to be a cannibal."* I'd only throw it up anyway. *The thought of vomiting warm blood made me retch.*

"My people would often drink the blood of cattle. And the Maasai were no cannibals."

I told him, *"You need it."* Kentarch's enviable cheekbones had taken on a grotesque cast.

"If she doesn't want it"—Joules looked sunken-eyed and skeletal himself—*"I'll toss my hat in the ring."*

Now I told Aric, "You promised me you wouldn't stop until I was yours forever. That you wouldn't ever rest. I *am* yours. But you're throwing me away. *Us* away." Tears spilled. "Take me back, and use the cilice to control my abilities until our kid is born. Then kill me if you still want to."

"Ah, the cilice." His tone held a grin. "I found it down in the rubble of the nursery after our battle with Ogen, with your flesh still attached to it."

I'd forced Lark to carve it off me so I could fight. At the memory of that pain, I heaved, but had nothing in my belly to throw up.

"If you only knew the story behind it. . . . Come to my castle, and we will discuss your proposition."

"I can't *get* th-there!" I scarcely recognized my defeated voice. *Hunger* was reversing my personality. These days, my emotions barreled back and forth between weepiness and seething anger.

I felt like a drunk ex, sobbing in one breath to get back together and railing in the next. *Come pick me up at the bar I hate you.*

"Are you crying?" he asked with a laugh. "By all the gods, your tears cheer me. Of course, they'll dry as soon as you hang up the phone. You always were a talented deceiver."

"Aric, *Es tevi mīlu.* I love you." He'd said I kept his soul within me, right next to mine.

"The sentiment is no longer returned."

"Do you want me to beg?" The red witch would *never* beg; she still seemed to be enjoying her nap.

"Yes, Empress. I would like that very much. Beg me, and I'll consider the cilice."

Biting back my pride, I parted my lips to say—

"Oi, bait, c'mere!" Joules called from the cave entrance. "You're on deck. We've got a live one, so leg it down to the road."

Was I relieved to be interrupted or pissed? *Both.*

Aric said, "You're in a cave, near a road. Not even out of the foothills yet? I'll be sure to direct Fauna's most vicious predators to your vicinity."

"Whatever, Death." My emotions catapulted to the seething anger side of the drunk-ex spectrum. "You could have had everything you've ever wanted. But you're letting *your fucking cook* control you. Remember that." I disconnected the call and pocketed the phone in my coat just before Joules came into view.

"Were you talking to the Reaper?" His skin sparked with irritation.

"Moment of weakness. Won't happen again."

"How come you can call him, but I can't talk to Gabe?" Joules probably missed him as much as I missed Aric. Or, rather, the *old* Aric.

"Because you have a temper that Gabriel will know how to needle. He could get you to spill our plans." Such as they were: find Circe before we starved.

"I don't have a bloody feckin' temper!" Our gazes darted as his voice echoed off the cave walls. Lowering his tone, he said, "Just come on with you. Tarch heard an engine a ways down the road. I got a good feeling about this one."

I rose, then reeled on my feet. Joules grabbed my arm and squired me out of the cave.

Not far in the distance stretched the lightning-lit road. Tendrils of fog floated a dozen or so feet above the pavement. Kentarch already lay in wait behind the truck, his knife ready. He took one look at me and said, "You should have drunk the blood."

I nearly stumbled when Joules released me to hide.

"For feck's sake, this'll only work if you can stand up straight. Otherwise they'll think you've got the plague." He himself leaned on his javelin as if it were a walking stick.

Kentarch said, "Mentally will yourself to remain upright for five more minutes. Remember: Your mind has dominion over your body."

I flipped him off. Sometimes I wanted to strangle Tarch too.

I blundered out onto the road. As I waited, I replayed my call with Aric. Back in the golden days of our relationship, that bastard had said we should communicate. Maybe he should have divulged that he was carrying some mega-baggage from our past!

Instead, he'd told me he was a planet off axis. Apparently he'd found his two-thousand-year-old groove again and was spinning right along.

Screw him. Screw. Him. I gazed down at my wedding ring. He'd destroyed the one I'd given him; I would trash the one he'd given me. I yanked it off and tossed it away. "How about that, Reaper?"

Joules cried, "Finally!"

Pling.

The faint sound of it hitting the pavement was earsplitting to me. "Nooo!" How could I have? I dropped to my knees, scrabbling through Flash-fried asphalt and patches of snow. "Where is it?" I closed my eyes to sense the sap, my hand moving. . . .

There! Sucking in breaths, I slipped it back on. If I truly decided to take it off, I knew Aric would be lost to me forever.

Kentarch cocked his head. "A motorcycle approaches. The rider won't have many stores or much fuel. Let's allow this one to pass."

"A *motorcycle*?" The rumbling sound reached me—reminding me of Jack's arrival at Haven all those months ago. A lifetime ago.

"She probably thinks it's the hunter," Joules told Kentarch. "He drove a bike."

"Who's the hunter?"

"A human who went by the name of Jack." Joules, that ass, added, "He was boyfriend number one before the Reaper and Sol. The timeline goes like this: She was boffing Death in a past life, then Jack in this one. Then Death. Then Jack. Then Sol, then Death."

"Damn it, I was never with Sol! I told you we were just friends."

As if I hadn't spoken, Joules said, "Jack was a good bloke. Brave as hell and hardworking. But he died in Richter's massacre."

Kentarch frowned at me. "I thought you witnessed that attack, Empress. Did you not see him perish?"

"I did."

But I'd heard him through Matthew.

But Jack was undefeatable.

The bike's rumble grew louder. *What if? What if? What if?*

Kentarch was studying me, as though I were settling some internal wager he'd made about me. *Yes, Chariot, I'm crazy. Trouble with the promise of rubble.*

I'd just been crawling on the ground to find the Reaper's wedding ring, and now I was imagining another man returning from the dead.

The motorcycle neared, sounding like it was racing toward some emergency destination. Jack would be racing to find me. "I know it can't be him, but . . ."

"Hope is a funny thing," Kentarch finished for me. "When I was once pinned down by poacher gunfire, they called out that they would let me live if I surrendered. I knew they wouldn't, but I was filled with desperation to see Issa again. My hope lied to me, whispering in my ear, 'Believe these men, and you will reunite with your wife.' Tell me, Empress, do you trust the whisper of your hope?"

Did I? I wanted to believe anything that told me Jack lived. But maybe I was too scarred from all the heartache I'd endured to trust my hope. Maybe my hope was slowly dying.

The bike was just around the bend. That creeping fog fanned out in slo-mo, like a blanket in one of those old dryer-sheet commercials.

Joules's tone grew exasperated. "The hunter's dead. Finn told us Jack and Selena rode out with the army. We know for a fact that Selena's toast, and she was always by Jack's side." I knew this. "Gabe and me saw that valley. Or what used to be a valley. No one could have survived that. Especially not a mortal. And since this isn't the second coming of Jack, get ready to face a bogey."

I tried to stand. Failed. Tried again.

A helmeted rider with a tinted visor emerged from the mist. I squinted to make out his build.

He was tall, muscular. Roughly the same size as Jack.

First instinct? Flag him down. Second instinct? Stay where I was and glare at what was surely a bad guy.

I managed to make it to my feet, and the man turned to me. I tugged my hood down, and we stared at each other as he passed me—

The bike's front wheel plunged into a pothole. He flew over the handlebars, his body rocketing down the road, the bike skidding along behind him.

I ran for the crash site. The motorcycle was on its side, still running, its front wheel mangled. The rider was laid out nearby.

Kentarch and Joules flanked me, weapons raised.

I dropped down beside the biker, my flickering glyphs reflecting in his visor. My heart beat erratically, my breaths panting bursts. "Please be him, please be him, please be him." No, my hope hadn't yet died. Was it about to?

I reached for the visor with shaking hands. I flipped it up.

Jackson Daniel Deveaux.

My Jack was *here*. "A-alive." I clutched his shoulders as my gaze greedily took in his face, those broad cheekbones, that rugged jaw, his stubborn chin. "Ah, God, are you okay?" He wore his customary bug-out bag and crossbow.

He opened his gray eyes and blinked at me, then slowly lifted his hand to my face. *"Peekôn?"* he said. "What the hell are you doing out here?" He yanked off his helmet.

My heart thundered. Dizziness swarmed my head. "Jack? Is it really you?" My balance shifted. With all the grace of a boulder, I toppled forward and sprawled over his chest.

18

I didn't lose consciousness—I had to stay awake to make sure Jack didn't disappear again—but my brain seemed to short out.

I felt him lifting me. I heard Joules directing him to our cave, introducing him to Kentarch on the way.

Inside, Jack gently laid me down next to the fire. "When's the last time you guys ate?"

Joules said, "'Bout to ask if you had any grub."

"*Non.* The leather of my belt's starting to look good."

Need to see him! I blinked open my eyes. "You...you're alive. H-how? I saw you... I watched you die." Tears streamed down my cheeks, blurring my vision. I swiped angrily at them. Nothing could mar the sight of Jack.

He'd lost weight—was as leanly muscled as Aric now. "I'm here." Sitting beside me, he took my hand and brought it to his lips. "Selena saved my life. She sensed the Emperor seconds before he struck and shoved me into an abandoned mine."

My God. "She protected you till the end."

"*Ouais.* She did." Jack pulled a canteen from his bug-out bag. "Here, *bébé.*" Unscrewing the top, he lifted it to my lips. "Why're you out in the Ash? You're supposed to be safe in Domīnija's castle."

I drank. "How did you know that?"

"*Coo-yôn* told me."

"Where is he?" No longer could I blame Matthew for letting Jack die.

"We were on the road together for a spell, but he split."

"Then why didn't he tell me you were alive?"

"Richter was in the area, so *coo-yôn* didn't want to turn on the Arcana radio to contact you. Didn't want to give anyone's location away. Plus, it wasn't a sure thing that I would pull through."

"That close?"

Stoic nod. "He told me that Death saved you from Richter. So where's Domīnija?" Jack's gaze slid over my wedding ring. His brows drew together, and raw pain filled his gray eyes.

I'd betrayed him with Aric. I should've believed Jack would somehow come for me. But then I wouldn't know what it was like to love Aric.

Of course, I also wouldn't be knocked up and stranded in the Ash.

What should I say? Damn this dizziness and shock! I couldn't concentrate, couldn't sort my chaotic thoughts.

"If the Reaper isn't here, I know he's on his way."

I shook my head.

In a voice that might have been just shy of hopeful, Jack said, "Dead?"

Joules sat on the other side of the fire. "I wish. That fecker tried to off her. Chased her right out of the castle."

Jack's jaw slackened. *"Bébé?"*

"It's complicated. He's been brainwashed. Lark and Gabriel too."

"Like the Hierophant did?"

"In the same vein." I wasn't ready to tell him that Aric might have succumbed to buried hatred, a murderous rage, and the inability to let go of the past.

Joules said, "Paul, their medic, was the inactivated Arcana, the Hanged Man. No one inside that big, warm, food-filled stronghold knew. So Paul poisoned Finn to activate his powers. Offed the Magician straight out of existence."

"Not Finn." Jack swore under his breath, his expression shaken.

"I'm goan to gut this *fils de pute.*" Jack had spent more time with the Magician than anyone still alive.

Joules tossed more wood on the fire. "The Hanged Man's got this yellow sphere that spread over Death's castle, surrounding the entire mountain. If an Arcana crosses the boundary, he gets brainwashed. When Gabe heard the Empress screaming, he flew off to save her. Then he got nabbed like the rest of 'em. No good deed . . ."

I said, "Paul convinced Aric, Gabriel, and Lark that *I* killed Finn. Her wolves had me and Joules surrounded. We'd be dead if the Chariot hadn't arrived." I waved toward Kentarch, standing off to the side.

Joules added, "He teleported us—or ghosted more like—*through* a giant grizzly. Then he materialized the truck and exploded that bear's arse."

Kentarch looked uncomfortable with this praise, but he did take a seat by the fire.

"Teleporting, huh? My sincere thanks." Jack gave him a nod, taking this new Arcana craziness in stride. Then he turned to me. "What happened to your *grand-mère*? *Coo-yôn* told me she was at the castle."

"Paul killed her. She would've died of natural causes, but he accelerated it."

"He got her too? *Condoléances*, Evie." He brushed the backs of his busted-up knuckles across my cheek. "You guys got a plan to fight this Hanged Man?"

I nodded. "Circe, the Priestess Card, is a witch. She might be able to cast a spell to neutralize Paul's power. We've been trying to contact her in rivers and ponds on our way to the coast." As Jack seemed to let everything percolate, I said, "Where have you been all this time? Why didn't you return to the fort?"

"I got knocked unconscious in the floodwaters down in the mine. When I woke, I was in slaver chains."

I had so many questions. How had he escaped from them? Where had Matthew been going when they split up? But first . . . "I'm so sorry about your army."

That muscle in Jack's jaw ticked, his tell. Whenever I saw that, I knew he was barely keeping his emotions in check—the levee about to be overrun. "I'm goan to make Richter pay for that. Somehow, someway."

He sounded like Jack, looked like Jack. But he seemed changed. Older. Even more hardened. How could he not be?

"I've been saying the same thing. I thought he'd annihilated the army, Selena, *and* you." Another wave of lightheadedness hit me. "Where were you going just now?"

"I'll tell you all about it. But first, we have to get you some food. I'll head west and see if I can scare up something."

"You actually think I will let you out of my sight. Adorable."

Kentarch said, "We came from the west. There's nothing."

"*Merde.* For days, I haven't passed anyone to roll. I can sometimes bag a snake or a rat"—he patted the crossbow over his shoulder—"but I came up empty."

"So you earned your name of hunter?" Kentarch tilted his head. "I could teleport you to a place thick with game. More meat than we could possibly eat."

Huh?

"That so?" Jack asked suspiciously. "You look pretty handy. How come *you* haven't gone and . . . ?" He trailed off with a look of comprehension. "You're talking about the animals at Death's castle. Lark's creatures."

Kentarch nodded. "*I* can't go within that sphere."

"But a civvie could." Jack's eyes lit up. "Oh, hell yeah, Chariot."

"Oh, hell no, Chariot!" I clung to Jack's hand. "Did you not hear the part about the giant grizzly? It's too dangerous." I'd just gotten him back!

"You think I'm goan to let you starve when there's game to be had? Joules will stay with you, keep you company. Kentarch and I'll be right back."

"This isn't like poaching an alligator from a Louisiana state park. This is Death, Lark, and Gabriel. They won't let you just walk in there, fill up your shopping cart, and stroll out. She has thousands of creatures now, and under her influence, they're all killers."

Jack grinned. "Then she woan miss a measly pheasant or two."

"Lark's much stronger now than when you last saw her. She'll do anything to hurt me—which means hurting you."

He pried his hand from my weak grip. "It's the only way." He stood. When I reached for him, he seemed to force himself to back away. "You woan sway me in this."

Was he risking his life because he planned on a future with me? He didn't know everything. "There's something I need to tell you—"

"His mind's made up, Empress," Joules interrupted. "You'll have plenty of time to catch up later. But for now, you don't want anything to banjax his motivation or his *focus*. You don't want to get him killed, do you?"

I glared at the Tower. Selfish much? "This hunt is not happening. Jack, you're not leaving."

Holding his ground, he said, "I know this is tough, but I swear to you I'm coming back." He turned to Joules. "Anything happens to her . . ."

The Tower created a javelin. "I got this."

Jack squared his shoulders and faced Kentarch. "Come on, Chariot. Never teleported before, but by God, I'm ready to poach Domīnija's lands."

"Do you require a rifle? Something more than a compact crossbow?"

"Goan in quiet, me. Slip in, bag some birds, slip out. They'll never know we were there."

If I could manage a vine, I'd tie Jack to me. "I can't lose you again." I raised my hand to use my powers, but nothing happened.

"Evie, I promise you I'll be back."

"No time to dawdle." Kentarch took his arm.

A spindly vine finally shot from my palm. It lashed only air. They'd already disappeared.

19

THE HUNTER

"Mère de Dieu," I muttered when we touched down in a new snowy landscape. I'd officially teleported. One thing I could say since meeting Evangeline: life was never dull.

When I'd first seen her face out on that road, everything inside me had lit up—the way I always felt around her. This time I hadn't *nearly* gone over my handlebars.

I told Kentarch, "You could've let me give her a proper good-bye, finessing that situation a touch more. Remember, I just came back from the dead." And now she'd had to watch me leave yet again.

The last time she'd lost me, it'd broken her. I couldn't imagine what she was going through back in that cave. It had taken sheer will to leave her.

A million other thoughts swirled in my overloaded brain.

Evie's hurting. Got to feed my girl. Not my girl—she's wearing Death's ring. God, the sight of that . . . like I been stabbed. What'd I expect, me? I left her with Domīnija, left her to think I died. When she finds out the truth of that, she'll have my ass. Did I really just teleport?

One thought stood out: *What will happen between me and Evie now?* I'd have to confess that I'd decided to let her go. Because of Matthew, I'd abandoned her to a man who'd then tried to kill her.

Kentarch said, "Trust me when I tell you she has an acute need for food. We have no time to spare."

He was right. I pictured her back there, looking so fragile. When I returned, Evie and I would have a long talk.

Tugging my ragged coat closer, I surveyed the snowscape. Kentarch had brought me to the top of a large hill. From this vantage, I could see a castle sprawled over the neighboring mountain. A frozen moat with huge shards of ice circled it. A dirty yellow haze cloaked the entire rise like a bell jar.

"That place is creepy as hell." And I'd thought Haven House had looked spooky?

On this side of the moat, a line of thornbushes as big as trees trailed over the countryside. Evie must've created that fortification.

"Creepy as it may be, that fortress is stocked for an extended nuclear winter."

Yeah, Domīnija had told me about all the luxuries within. That was part of the reason I'd let Evie go.

I pulled binoculars from my bug-out bag to scope the building. Electric lights shone from windows, while torches lit the grounds. Smoke curled from three chimneys. I caught the scent of cooking meat, and my mouth watered. On one of the many eaves, Gabriel crouched like a gargoyle.

I could even make out Domīnija pacing a room. He'd had everything. *Everything.* Did some part of him comprehend what he'd lost? What he'd done to the woman he loved? She must've been so confused.

I stowed my binoculars, and Kentarch and I started down the hill toward the dome. "I gotta get her back inside that castle."

"Will you kill the Reaper to do it?"

"I'll kill any threat to her. The rest is up to Domīnija." I was conflicted. On the one hand, I hated him for what he'd done to her under the influence. But then I remembered when the Hierophant had brainwashed Evie right out of her head. Could Death be held responsible for his actions when he wasn't in his right mind?

Plus, I felt a deep gratitude to him for saving Evie from Richter's attack.

"You must want her back," Kentarch said. "Will you pursue her?"

She haunted me more than ever. Seeing her again just made it all the worse. But she expected to get Domīnija cured—which meant she expected to return to him. I told Kentarch, "I'll end up doing whatever's best for her. Story of my life with that one. You ever been in love?"

He gave a humorless laugh. "You could say that. My wife, Issa, and I were separated months ago. I've been searching for her ever since. I came to this castle for assistance in finding her."

Bonne chance, Kentarch. Good luck, because his Issa was most likely long dead.

As we neared the dome, I unstrapped my crossbow. Just beyond the boundary, Evie's fortification loomed, a frozen forest of towering thorn plants. The foreboding branches seemed to move under the wavering yellow light.

This place reminded me of tales my mother used to read to me, of enchanted winter forests filled with magic and evil villains.

Only this was real.

Snow trails meandered throughout, forged by what had to be large animals. Another grizzly? I checked my bolt-action clip of arrows, knowing it'd take more than this to bring down something so big.

In a hushed tone, Kentarch said, "If Fauna is awake, she will be able to scent you. Should her beasts give chase, your only hope is to make it back here to me."

I nodded, not looking forward to an encounter with overgrown wolves—or worse. "No pressure." More snow started to fall. *Merde.* This wasn't exactly my preferred hunting environment, and the cold was making my bad leg stiffen up. "I'm heading in." In case something happened to me, I turned to give him a last message for Evie but decided against it.

If I died on her twice, no message was going to fix that wound.

"Be wary, hunter," Kentarch murmured. "All manner of creatures prowl within."

I crossed the boundary, heading into the thorn forest. Vertigo seized me and sweat started to bead my skin. I felt almost drunk. Not surprising. I hadn't eaten in days.

I shook my head hard. A successful take could mean the difference between my girl living or not. *Stay sharp, Jack.* I'd done this all my life. Even before the Flash, my survival had always depended on my ability to hunt. Clotile's survival and *ma mère's* as well.

As I eased deeper into the thorns, I began to hear bird calls. Dozens of them nested on high branches. A jackpot of animals!

We're goan to eat good today. I raised my crossbow. Took aim—

WHOOSH. They scattered in a frenzy of feathers, squawking a retreat. I stilled. What had spooked them? Was Lark on to me?

An unsettling quiet fell over the forest. All my senses told me danger lurked, but I continued forward anyway. Those fowl would have to set down somewhere.

I sucked in a breath when I saw large tracks ahead. Wait . . . my own footprints? I'd gone in a circle, me? I swiped sweat from my brow. *Jack Deveaux doan get lost.*

Not even in enchanted forests.

I peered closer and spotted a second set of prints, almost as large as my own. Those tracks followed alongside mine. Some animal I didn't recognize, something with size to it, was stalking *me.*

Chills skittered up my back. I straightened, muscles tensed. Finger on the crossbow trigger. *I ain't the hunter here anymore—*

A roar sounded in the branches above me. I pivoted, swinging my bow up.

Golden eyes gleamed in the dark. A flash of fangs as a beast sprang for me. I fired.

Before I could shoot again, a weighty body crashed into the snow, not inches from my boots. My arrow jutted from one of its eyes.

A lioness! She looked to be a couple hundred pounds. No wonder all the other game had scattered.

My gaze darted as I shouldered my bow. How to get my prize back to Kentarch?

I *would* be getting it back. We could feed on it for days.

A shriek sounded from the castle. Lark! She must've sensed the kill. Adrenaline spiked my veins. No way I was leaving this lion. I bent down and grasped the carcass under its front legs, maneuvering it for a fireman's carry.

Now to rise. Damn it, I could haul this beast from here. I'd lifted Matthew. But that had been before my injury.

Come on, legs, doan fail me. With a yell, I hoisted it up and across my shoulders. My knees knocked, my bad leg screaming. But I took a step forward.

One foot in front of the other . . . for Evie . . . one foot . . . Lungs squeezing for air, head spinning, I pushed on.

Halfway there. I hoped.

Behind me, creatures gave chase. Their roars and howls were spurs to my back. Another surge of adrenaline. *One foot . . . one foot . . .*

Just outside of the hazy sphere, I caught sight of Kentarch. His jaw was slack. "You took down a lion? With a crossbow?"

A whistle sounded in the air behind me. I knew that pitch. Gabriel was gunning for me.

Closer to the boundary, closer.

"The Angel is diving for you!" Kentarch held out his hand, even as his gaze was focused on the sky behind me. "Drop the dead weight, you madman!"

No way. Digging into the last of my reserves, I forced my burning muscles to keep going. *For Evie. For Evie. Faster, Jack! Boy, doan you know how to run?*

From far too close, Gabe yelled, "You're mine!"

I vaulted the last few feet past the border, collapsing forward into the snow. Kentarch dragged the lion off me, then lugged me several more feet away from the dome.

"*Ahhhh!*" Gabe bellowed his fury. His wings swirled snowdrifts as he reversed direction.

Heaving breaths, I scrambled around to face him.

The Archangel hovered at the edge, fangs and talons bared. "Greet me properly, hunter. Come shake my hand." His wings were much larger than before, and now a lethal-looking claw jutted from each joint.

I croaked out, "Pass."

Eyes crazed and hair wild, he looked like a psycho version of himself. If this shocked me, how stunned had Evie been when Domīnija turned on her? She was lucky to be alive.

Gabe turned to the Chariot. "Join us, and we shall find your wife for you."

Was Kentarch tempted by that offer? I called, "Doan you want to know how Joules—your loyal ally—is doing out in the Ash? I'll tell the Tower you asked after him."

Gabe barely glanced at me, attention on Kentarch. "You do not have to join our alliance. Simply bring us the Empress, and we shall unleash all of Fauna's creatures to locate Issa."

I didn't like that a bit. I rose with difficulty and slapped Kentarch's shoulder. "We got to go, podna." A chorus of howls sounded. "He's just stalling for Lark."

"You're correct." Kentarch clamped my arm and the lion's neck. "I still can't believe you bagged a lion."

Between breaths, I wheezed, "What? Like it's hard?"

His lips twitched. "Come, hunter."

As he began to teleport us, I glanced back at Gabe—just as his wing claw lashed out from behind the sphere.

Air whistled across my throat as we disappeared. The Archangel had missed my jugular by millimeters.

20

THE EMPRESS

I paced the cave, using calories I didn't have. I'd started hyperventilating, imagining all the things Arcana could do to Jack.

Snarling wolves, Gabriel's talons, Aric's unnatural strength and speed. If Jack faced the Endless Knight, he would die. With one sword strike, I would lose both of them forever.

Joules sat by the fire. "How do you plan to tell ol' Jackie boy you're in the family way?"

"That will be a good problem to have." I pinched my temples. "I can't do this again."

"You're still in love with the Cajun."

My eyes watered. "Of course I am! We didn't *break up*, Joules. He was stolen from me."

"So now what are you goin' to do? You got Death's unholy spawn in you."

No matter what had happened, I would still try to save Aric, just as I'd endeavored to save Jack. Both had earned my loyalty.

As long as one didn't harm the other.

"In case you were wondering, my vote goes to the hunter."

"Maybe Jack found someone else out there. We haven't seen each other in months." How long had he been enslaved?

"Come on, Empress. It's not like females grow on nonexistent trees these days. Even if they did, Jack's a goner for you. Gabe, Tess, and me were in and out when he built Fort Arcana. Every day, he was praying he'd get you back and keep you safe inside it."

My tears fell.

"Of course, whichever one you choose, you got to get back into the castle. Why don't you go with the Cajun, and then we take over the place? Jack's good with strategy."

I stopped in my tracks. "I can't believe you're using my heartache to pitch me an overthrow of Aric's home—"

"Heads up!" Joules cried as shapes materialized in the cave.

Kentarch and Jack appeared, dragging something with them.

I stumbled to Jack, wrapping my arms around him. Relief flooded me, until I registered blood. "You're hurt!" My hands flew over him, checking for injuries, brushing away crimson snow.

"Not my blood, *peekôn*. I'm fine." He looked wiped out, but in good spirits.

Kentarch certainly was. "Your hunter deserves the name. He took down a lion with merely a crossbow."

Joules crouched beside the creature. Its lifeless eyes stared at nothing. "Fauna's got a lion on her card."

In the previous games, they'd surrounded her. I'd once asked her why she now favored wolves. All business, she'd said, "Better suited for the terrain here."

Lark would be furious at this loss. "Jack, I thought you were going to snare a hedgehog or something." When he reeled against me, I said, "You need to sit and rest."

"*Bonne idée.*" Good idea. He all but collapsed by the fire.

Sitting beside him, I stroked damp hair from his forehead. "Are you sure you're not hurt?"

Kentarch answered for him. "He carried this game through the snow—what should have been an impossible feat—while the Archangel bore down on him."

Joules's head whipped up. "You saw my boyo?"

Jack nodded. "Since when did he grow wing claws?"

"One of his cult elders said that he'd grow 'em eventually, along with his wings getting bigger and tougher. Must be all the food he's tucking away at the castle." Joules bit out a curse. "I canna believe he's still under the influence."

"Gabe was twisted." Jack looked at me. "Is that what Domīnija was like?"

"Worse. Gabriel doesn't have a history with you or a reason to hate you. And you're not an Arcana."

Joules poked the lion carcass with his javelin. "Is this one of her familiars?" *Poke. Poke.* "What if it comes back to life?"

Kentarch assessed the animal. "Aren't her familiars giant like those wolves?"

I shook my head. "No, the wolves grew so big because they drank her blood when they were pups. Her falcon is a normal size. This lion could be connected to her."

Joules stumbled back. "Can we *eat* a familiar?"

Jack said, "After what I just did to bring that back, we're goan to clean its goddamned bones."

At this point, I had no qualms about dining on one of Lark's creatures, but what would lion taste like? Would I be able to keep it down? "We probably want to cut its head off as quickly as possible." We? Right now, I couldn't cut butter with a hot knife.

Kentarch gestured toward Joules. "You and I will take it outside to butcher."

"Tarch, I'm more on the consumption end of things. Less production, you understand? But I'm an ace baster."

"*Now*, Tower."

As the two hauled up the lion, Jack started to rise, but Kentarch waved him down. "Stay and rest." Catching my gaze, he said, "I'm sure you have much to tell each other." So he hadn't revealed my secret.

Perfect. I'd get to.

At the cave entrance, Kentarch turned back and told Jack, "A lion marked me when I was young, nearly taking my life"—he'd never volunteered anything about his childhood to me and Joules—"but now one will save us from starving. Good work, hunter."

Jack gave him solemn nod. "Thanks for the ride, podna."

This exchange reminded me of how people responded to Jack. He commanded loyalty because folks genuinely liked him. Aric commanded loyalty out of fear.

Once we were alone, Jack pulled off his bow and bug-out bag. "Adrenaline's wearing off." He snagged a flask from his coat pocket.

When he offered me a drink, I held up a hand. "All good." Just seeing his face was a luxury for me. He was safe. Warm. Larger than life. I leaned in closer to him.

One of my biggest regrets was never telling him that I loved him. How would he react to those three words? And to my news?

He took a swig, then stared into the flames. Was he remembering his harrowing escape from Richter?

Needing to comfort him, I took his hand in mine.

He turned to me, and a marked longing lit his gaze. Then he tapped my ring. "So, you and Domīnija, huh?"

Voice soft, I said, "I thought you were dead. We all did."

"That's all that needs to be said, then." He took another drink. "You get hitched?"

"Not officially in this life. Kind of a leftover from the last game." Aric had never considered us *not* hitched. Not even when he'd been trying to behead me.

"I'd love to see the look on the Reaper's face when Gabe tells him I'm alive." I could only imagine Aric's fury. "Still can't believe he attacked you."

"Paul reverses a card, bringing out an Arcana's worst traits. You can actually see a tableau turning upside down. Aric's resistance to change and his rage were brought to the fore. His unresolved anger over the past spilled into the present, and he hated me. He truly would've killed me."

"Tell me everything that happened."

Staring at Jack's beloved face, rememorizing every feature, I told him about the Hanged Man and his powers. About Finn's poisoning and Lark and Aric's attack. About Gabriel and Joules rescuing me, and Kentarch saving the day.

Jack took it all in. He was silent for a moment, then asked, "Why weren't you affected by the Hanged Man?"

"Aric once told me I'm immune to brainwashing after my run-in with the Hierophant." But I didn't know why I'd escaped a reversal. After recounting everything to Jack, I began to see how distinct those powers were.

His fists clenched as he said, "I'm goan to kill the Hanged Man for what he's done to you. And Finn too."

"The problem is *how*. I didn't tell the others this"—I glanced at the cave entrance and lowered my voice—"but I clawed him and nothing happened."

"He regenerates like you?"

"It's hard to explain. His skin was simply unaffected. Aric told me he's invulnerable to harm."

Jack muttered a curse. "You think there's any way to lure the Reaper out of that dome? Gabe didn't seem keen to leave it."

"Nor Aric. He believes it protects him from *my* spellbinding, bringing him much-needed clarity. Since my escape, I've tried to goad him into leaving, but he refuses."

"How'd you talk to him?"

"Kentarch has a satellite phone that still works. I called Aric a couple of times. He's cruel. Jack, you can't believe how cruel." He'd been about to make me beg, had enjoyed my tears. Before I went down that rabbit hole, I said, "Let's talk about something else, okay?" I still needed to tell Jack about the baby, but he looked so whipped with exhaustion. "How did you escape from those slavers?"

"The Fool showed up and rescued me."

I raised my brows. "*Matthew* saved you?"

"In the nick of time too. I'd injured my leg really bad and wasn't long for the world—about to be served up as breakfast for the other slaves. Fucking hate slavers, me." Jack explained the carnage Matthew had caused, and how he'd felt like he hadn't known the Fool at all.

I shuddered. "Where do you think he went?"

"Doan know. And I didn't look for him after he left. Even though he saved my life, we got sideways on some things."

"Like why he allowed all those people to be killed by Richter?"

"*Coo-yôn* said he had a reason. Said he 'sees far.'"

Sounded familiar. Would that be his excuse for letting Finn die?

"I tell myself something worse must've been in store for them." Again, Jack stared into the flames. "Cannibals attacking or the plague. I tell myself his reasoning was pure. Some days I even believe it." Could Finn's fate have been worse?

Yes. Definitely yes.

Jack cleared his throat and faced me. "So, what're the details on Circe?" He didn't want to talk about the massacre any more than I wanted to discuss Aric. "She's the one you fought outside of Fort Arcana?"

"Yes, but she and I have come to an understanding since then. If free of Paul's influence, she'll try to help us. We just need to find her."

"Okay. We got a plan, at least." After a hesitation, he said, "There's something I need to tell you—"

A commotion at the mouth of the cave announced the return of Kentarch and Joules, with the butchered lion in hand.

"It can wait," Jack murmured to me.

"We wanted to give you more time to talk"—Kentarch set up a spit over the fire—"but hunger calls." Once the lion started to cook, he handed us each a skewer with a slice of raw meat the color of pork.

As we roasted them over the flames, my attention shifted back and forth from Jack—*Is he truly here with me?*—to the broiling meat. My mouth watered.

Joules inhaled deeply. "Smell that, would you? Hope we don't draw company. This is Richter territory, after all."

Jack rotated his skewer. "When's the last time anyone saw him?"

I said, "A few weeks ago, we encountered him and Zara. She's the Fortune Card, a chopper pilot. I've tangled with her before."

"What's her power?"

"Freakish luck. She can steal it through touch. She was just about to steal mine when Lark and Aric rescued me."

"Richter's targeting food depots," Joules said. "Anything they canna carry back to their lair, he incinerates. No one knows why."

Jack said, "I'd wondered why supplies had dried up even more lately."

"Empress, tell him about Richter's other ally! Ol' Jackie boy will get a kick out of this. And by *kick*, I mean *stroke*."

As I reluctantly relayed the highlights of my partnership with Sol, the muscle in Jack's jaw ticked overtime. "Lemme get this straight: he made Baggers *dine* on you?"

"He also saved our lives from Zara and Richter."

Joules said, "We were in Death's truck, running from quakes. Didn't know we were headed right for a blown-out bridge and would've eaten it for certain. But Sol had his Baggers show us a safer route. You haven't lived till you've seen a Bagger hitchhiking with his thumb out."

True. "Sol's sense of humor is one of the reasons I liked him."

Jack's expression darkened. "And I bet he liked you too."

"Not in that way. He's a big flirt, but his heart is taken." By two. The tragedy of his love life rivaled mine. "Besides, I was so frantic to save you, I was on my worst Empress behavior with him. I'm surprised he could forgive me."

Jack asked, "How do you know which Baggers are . . . helpful? Which ones are under Sol's control?"

"I don't. Odds are against it. He can only sense through a limited number of them at a time, and only when he's awake."

"Like Lark with her animal sentries."

"Exactly," I said, even as I wished Jack didn't have to be versed in this deadly world I'd dragged him into. *Arcana insanity.*

Joules nodded at the cooking meat. "Looks ready. Let's see if the Empress can keep this down—"

"Because it's really exotic food," I quickly added.

Kentarch cocked his head at me, probably wondering why I hadn't confessed about the baby.

Jack took my skewer from me to blow on it before handing it back. "This'll be good. Good for you too."

I took my first exploratory bite. Lion meat tasted like a cross between pork and beef. "Not bad." Even as Joules and Kentarch chowed down, they kept their eyes on me, as if expecting me to hurl.

But my stomach welcomed this meal like a long-lost love. I dug in, ravenous.

We all did. Jack rolled his eyes with pleasure. Joules had grease smeared over his cheek.

Regeneration fired throughout my body. Aches and pains dwindled as I healed. Energy filled me. *Lion meat; who knew?*

"Another round of skewers?" Joules asked.

"Absolutely," Kentarch said. "We'll save the rest. If we ration it, we'll have meat for a few days."

After our third helping, I grew sated and warm for the first time in weeks. Jack was here with me, and the future wasn't nearly so bleak.

"Your color's returning, *peekôn*. Amazing what one meal can do. How're your powers? Come on, flex for me."

Joules laughed. "Yeah, Empress, show us some vines." *Asshole.* "Maybe some after-dinner strawberries?"

"My powers have been a little wonky lately." Changing the subject, I said, "Did Matthew tell you where to find me?"

"*Non.* I knew you were at Domīnija's castle, but he refused to come off the location before he ditched. He did leave me a message though, wrote it in soot. I figured if he took the trouble to write it, I should memorize it." Clearing his throat, Jack said, "*The Flash taught them that all dreams are nightmares. They became bad dreamers. All hail the bad dreamers as good.*"

"What does that mean? Who's he talking about?"

"You're asking me?" Jack sipped his flask.

"So where had you been heading?"

"Up to Azey North."

"To lead them?" That would make sense. As their general once more, he would've been able to recruit scouts to help search for me.

Yet he shook his head. "I just wanted to show my face, me. Not slink away like some coward."

"Wait a minute. You weren't trying to find me?"

Jack scrubbed a palm over his nape. "Matthew told me you were safe with Domīnija and your *grand-mère*. I wanted you to move on with your life."

I couldn't get enough air. "You were going to let me believe that . . . that you were dead?"

Kentarch stood. "We will allow you two to speak in private."

"Feck that!" Joules said. "We're just getting to the popcorn moment."

Kentarch collared him and escorted him out.

Once we were alone again, Jack said, "I was goan to let you live in peace in that stronghold, the one Domīnija made sure to describe to me, the one with all the comforts I could never give you."

"Remember how you and I talked about being a team? I asked you not to make decisions all on your own for both of us. But that's what you did!"

"Matthew showed me visions of you in the aftermath of the massacre. I saw—no, I experienced—what you went through to bring me back. I felt you breaking for me, and I couldn't let that happen again."

Had he seen me rocking Tess's skeletal corpse? "It wasn't your decision to make."

"I wanted food and warmth and safety for you. I could only give you more Ash. Hell, I figured I'd be dead soon anyway, so why upset you more? Evie, you looked like you were dancing on a razor's edge."

I had been.

"*Coo-yôn* took me to the graves you made for me and *pauvre défunte* Selena." *Dearly departed.* "He told me you were goan to make your way with Domīnija. I wanted that for you, no matter how much the idea twisted me up inside me."

Jack loved me more than he loved his own life. I'd known that, but it'd never been so apparent as now.

"I told Matthew to keep my survival secret and let me stay buried."

"Well, he *didn't*. More than a month ago, he sent me a message of your voice. I thought you might . . . I prayed you'd survived."

"What the hell's he playing at?" Then, seeming to steel himself, he said, "Knowing what I did then, I'd still make the same choice."

My lips parted. "How can you say that?"

"Before the Hanged Man, you had to have been happy with the Reaper. You wear his ring."

"I walled off part of my heart." I'd loved Aric, but it must've been muted by my pain, by the tourniquet I'd used to keep from bleeding out. *Twist, tighten, constrict.* "I could never give him all of my heart—and he knew that. He thought my powers were suffering because I never fully grieved you." Holding Jack's gaze, I said, "I chose *you.*"

"And you shouldn't have!" He threw a rock into the fire. "Doan you get it? You were goan to have Death either way—either you'd be with the Reaper or you'd die out here with me."

"I'm out here with you now. Of course, you're probably just passing by. At least I'll get to say good-bye this time."

Jack looked at me like I'd just blasphemed. "I woan rest until you're safely out of the Ash. Which means I'll do whatever it takes to get you back into that castle."

"Even try to defeat Death?"

Hesitation. "Matthew told me the Reaper saved your life when Richter struck. That true?"

I nodded.

"When I was in that slaver hellhole, fearing I'd gotten you killed, I told myself that Domīnija is fast with strong senses. I told myself that he would have ridden out and rescued you from Richter. I think that was the only reason I didn't lose my mind down there."

"He did save me. I was running into the fire when he caught me and yanked me back at the edge."

Jack flinched. "I'm torn. I want to kill Domīnija for hurting you. But how can I when he saved your life?"

I'm torn too. I was pissed that Jack continued to make unilateral decisions, but I also realized that Matthew had manipulated him for his own reasons. Jack would've been sick and exhausted—his confidence rocked to the core by the massacre—when Matthew had struck a blow as well. Still . . . "You were really going to let me believe you died. You were never going to see me again."

"Noble cuts like a blade to the heart." He raked his fingers through his thick black hair. "I wanted to do right by you, but all I did was put you back in the Ash. I left you with a man who would try to murder you just months later."

One who'd knocked me up—*then* tried to murder me. "The things I did to bring you back . . ."

"I couldn't have stopped you, no, couldn't have communicated with you. I was trapped in that mine."

He was right. I exhaled, unable to maintain my anger over Jack's choice. It was a sacrifice born from love. Matthew's actions, however—

Riiiinnnnngggg. The phone sounded from outside.

Kentarch jogged back in. "It's him."

Joules was on his heels, sparking angrily. "I got some choice words to say to that fecker. And to the Hanged Man."

Surprised to feel my claws tingling, I snapped, "Let it ring." *Beg, Aric? Beg?*

Kentarch raised his brows. The phone eventually fell silent.

Then . . . *Riiiinnnnngggg.* Aric wasn't going to stop.

"Oh, fine. I'll get it." I accepted the phone and connected the call. "This is Evie speaking. How can I help you?"

Aric's raspy voice carried over the line: "How long have you known he lived?"

"I got my first wave of hope on the night we picked up Finn. Matthew contacted me. My nose bled from his message."

"And you felt no need to reveal that to your husband? Yet more evidence that our relationship was not what you pretended it to be."

"I'd planned to tell you everything after Paul's banishment. But that doesn't matter. What matters is that Jack is alive, and he brought us a feast."

"Such a change in your demeanor from earlier."

My cheeks burned as I replayed that call. Aric had once called me a goddess, had said I'd felled armies. Yet, I'd sniveled like a child: *I-I wanna come home.* "Disregard everything that I said before."

"Enjoyed your dinner, then?"

"Did I ever! And the company too."

"Fauna was proud of that lion. You ate her symbolic creature, the beast that marks her card, her very tableau."

"And it was *mm, mm* good! Please give her our compliments. I just don't know what she did to raise such a tender lion, but the meat was exceptional." Joules snickered. "Food on the road can be a wonderful surprise. You should get out more."

In the background I heard wolves howling. *Lark* howling.

"You enrage the Queen of Beasts at your peril. She's hunting you even now."

"She'd already been hunting me. She believes—wrongly—that I killed Finn."

"Still in denial, poisoness?"

"I'd love to chat and receive some more servings of your hatred, but I'd rather catch up with Jack."

"Have you told him about our fictitious offspring?" His dry laugh gave me goose bumps.

"I plan to."

Jack called, "Tell him I'm about to get real cozy with his wife. If he doan like that, then he should come do something about it. Tell him to quit hiding behind that sphere *comme un lâche.*" Like a coward.

I could hear Aric crushing something. *Could* he be lured out from that castle? "Oh, Death doesn't care what I do. He forsook me. Destroyed the ring I made for him. Guess I'm single now."

"The mortal courts his doom," Aric grated. "You want him so much, I'll take both of your heads with one strike."

"You'll have to come find us first."

"Which is just what you want. You won't taunt me into action, Empress."

Then why even make that comment? Was he worried he might be goaded into doing something rash? Silence stretched between us. As I wondered what he was thinking, my temper began to fade. Though I'd eaten and regenerated, my emotions still seemed to be all over the place. Pregnancy emotions were supposed to be crazy, right?

Thanks, kid. The gift that kept on giving.

I told the guys, "I'll be back in a minute." Ignoring Jack's frown, I walked out of the cave into the freezing dark.

"Listen, Aric." I kept my voice low. "You once told me that you wished for the impossible: for me to have chosen you. If you come for me now"—I squeezed my eyes closed—"I'll choose you." Somehow I said those words, even as my chest ached at the thought of having to say good-bye again to Jack.

But I'd made a commitment to Aric. We were having a kid, for God's sake.

If Aric could grapple against the Hanged Man's influence long enough to give us a chance, I'd honor my commitment. If he couldn't, I'd still fight to free him. "We began a life together, and I'll return to it, despite the fact that Jack saved me and our kid. Despite the fact that you tried to end us."

"Do you recall when I told you that Death was all I'd ever be to you? You used your powers to mesmerize me, but I now have control of my faculties once more. All of your lies will fall away, like slings against my armor."

"I could have killed you, but I didn't. Remember when I clawed you but didn't inject poison? And when I knocked you unconscious but didn't hurt you?"

"All a ploy. As your grandmother advised, you kept me on as your protector. Yet now I'll be your downfall, Empress. As I've been twice before."

Fury surged so swiftly it took me off guard. I feared that just as I'd fallen in love with him, I could fall back into hate. "Not unless you come to me. Oh, but you're too scared to face me. Pity." Borrowing his words, I said, "Our game is no fun—if you're weak." *Click.*

Collecting myself, I returned to the cave. Three questioning glances greeted me. "I had to hang up on him."

Joules laughed. "He's goin' to be stewing now."

Enough to come find me? "Today Paul's alliance is winning a little less. Let's continue our streak and get to the shore."

21

"*That* is how you hail Circe?" Jack asked with a chuckle. I'd been kicking waves and yelling along the shore of a medium-size lake. "Thought there'd be some kind of priestess summoning ritual or something."

My throat was hoarse, and I was out of breath. All I'd done was make ripples across the still surface. "Common misconception."

We'd been driving late into the night when Joules had spotlighted water not far off the road. Though we were making better time, we remained in the foothills. The lake was in a bowl of rock, a crater with three high sides.

Bleary-eyed Kentarch had been all too ready to stop. Snow had fallen on and off, and he'd had to teleport the truck past several gridlocked wrecks, which always weakened him.

Jack had offered to take the wheel earlier, but Kentarch politely declined. As Joules put it, "Nobody drives the Chariot's chariot but the Chariot."

He and Kentarch were currently in the cab, catching up on sleep.

I was glad for this time alone with Jack—but now I could no longer put off telling him about the baby.

"How about we head up to that bluff and drop some big rocks in?" Jack asked. The light snow had tapered off, and a white-dusted trail wound up the rise.

"Hike?" Even with all the lion I'd eaten—and kept down—my energy level had ebbed from the initial high I'd felt. This resource-suck kept my body weak.

"Unless you want to rest up some in the truck?"

I needed a time-out from the Beast. "No, let's go."

As we started along the trail, I peered up at Jack's tall form beside me. Would I ever get used to the sight of him? All day I'd fought the urge to pinch myself. Whenever he'd caught me staring, he would wink at me or grab my hand just to squeeze.

He was alive. He was back with me. As ever, I wondered how he would react to my news. I kept replaying that night in Finn's cabin when he'd told me, "There is nothing that can happen to you that we can't get past."

We'd proved that again and again.

When Jack and I reached the bluff, we sat at the edge with our legs hanging over, just as we had at the old mill the night of my sixteenth birthday party. The lake was beautiful, ringed with ice, mirroring the lightning-lit sky. How long before it froze over completely?

"Feel like I haven't seen you in hours." He took my hand in his, and that easy compatibility flowed between us.

God, how I'd missed this.

"Smell that honeysuckle, would you?" He cast me his rakish grin, sexy as ever. "I'm a happy man, me."

It shouldn't feel this right. I was married. In a way. I loved Aric. Yes, my husband wanted me dead and had decapitated me twice, but all relationships had issues, right?

On the other hand, my breath hitched every time I looked at Jack's face. How could I so desperately want to be reunited with Aric, and at the same time yearn to run away with Jack?

Gazing down at my face, he asked, "What's goan on behind those pretty eyes?"

I cleared my throat to reveal all but chickened out. "You, um, seem to be hitting it off with the Chariot."

Earlier, Joules and I had rested in the back of the truck while Jack and Kentarch sat up front, talking with a relaxed camaraderie about weapons and hunting and potential modifications for the Beast.

Just before I'd dozed off, Kentarch had told him, "I know what everyone thinks—that it's futile to hope my wife still lives. But you came back from the dead. It makes me believe even more strongly that I will reunite with her."

"I came back to a different situation." Jack had no idea just how different. "Are you prepared for whatever you get?" They'd grown quiet, both lost in thought.

Now Jack said, "I like Kentarch, but I doan want you alone with him. Gabe offered him a deal: you for Issa."

Oh, shit. "Do they have his wife?"

"*Non,* but I'd be surprised if they aren't searching for her, in addition to you."

"Kentarch would never willingly submit to mind control."

"He doan have to join the alliance; just has to make the exchange. I respect him, but I also understand his motives. In his situation, I'd hand over an Arcana I barely knew for you. Do it in a heartbeat."

Because Jack was steadfastly loyal—even to a fault. And yet I was keeping a huge secret from him. "I'll be careful around Kentarch."

Satisfied nod. "So did your *grand-mère* teach you about the game?"

"She did. She had the Empress chronicles." Which I had completely forgotten about from my early childhood. "I learned that Matthew killed me in the first game. I was in an alliance with him, and he betrayed me."

"*Coo-yôn?* You kidding me?" When I shook my head, he said, "I told you I barely recognized him when he came to rescue me. My vision was blurred, but when I looked at him, I thought I was seeing another person. He was like a *sosie,* an evil double."

"That's how it was with Aric! There was so much hatred in his eyes. Though, to be fair, I deserved a lot of that hatred. In the past, *I* was the *sosie;* I was as bad as they come. Jack, what if I turn that way again?" I recalled when I'd once thought, *I AM the red witch! Evie is a sliver of ME!* "What if I'm evil to the bone?"

I'd asked Aric this same question. Instead of answering me, he'd told me he'd had an errant thought.

Jack shook his head firmly. "In this life, you fight hard and ruthlessly for the people you love. No blame in that."

"Unfortunately, it doesn't matter how I am in this game. Paul read every word of my chronicles, so now he gets to telepathically inform everyone how I screwed them over in the past. You know, my grandmother was unstable toward the end, but she predicted that Aric would turn on me, that they all would. How prophetic was that?"

"But they didn't *want* to turn on you. They didn't make a choice to betray you. The Reaper would normally die for you, which I can always hope for."

I raised a brow. "Jack, Aric might not truly be brainwashed. Well, not *only* brainwashed." I explained what Paul had told me, about working with what was already there. "I don't believe the Hanged Man can manufacture that much bitterness and mistrust. Aric's resentment must have always been there."

Latent, like a seed with terrible potential.

"As much as I doan want to say this, I know Death loves you."

"Not enough to overcome Paul's reach."

"Did *coo-yôn* not warn you about an Arcana this powerful? One you couldn't kill?"

"When we talked about how to identify the inactivated card, he told me, 'Don't ask, if you ever want to know.' Maybe he meant never to ask the card himself, considering that Paul has the power of trust manipulation. Sterling advice." I really didn't miss Matthew's decoder-ring talk.

Jack tilted his head. "What did you do in the next game after *coo-yôn* killed you?"

"He deeply regretted his actions and vowed never to win again, so I allied with him, telling myself I'd dispose of him in time. But that never really worked out for me." Since I kept dying. "I've always felt close to Matthew, but maybe he steered me toward that." Though he didn't possess emotion manipulation—at least, I didn't think so—he could've affected my memories of the past. "I don't know how I feel about him. I can't decide."

"You doan have to decide, doan have to know how you feel. *Peekôn*, how about we just kick that can down the road?"

I couldn't help but smile. "I missed you, Jack."

His answering grin faded when he asked, "How was married life? With Domīnija?" He glanced away and tossed a rock.

"He really tried to be a good husband and make me happy, and in some ways, I was." Strangely, Jack's return made my feelings for Aric even keener. *Everything* felt keener, my emotions brimming. At last, I could loosen the tourniquet. "But I was also devastated from losing you."

"I saw your reaction in Matthew's vision." His voice grew rumbly with emotion. "I always wanted to make a difference, to *matter*. When you crafted that tombstone, I felt important, me. In a way I never had before."

"Even with your army and your leadership?"

"Even then." He tossed another stone. "Before the Flash, I never much thought that I'd be . . .missed."

"God, you were." I swallowed. "When Aric first learned all I'd done to bring you back, he was gutted. Not only had I chosen you, I'd refused to surrender you and accept him, even after you'd 'died.'"

"But eventually, you did."

"Eventually."

"How'd that work with the game? Was I right when I predicted Death had a patsy?"

"Yes." Arcana intrigues: one of the reasons I'd initially chosen Jack over Aric. "He was going to let Lark win after he and I had lived a long life together. But with Richter closing in, we reevaluated our chances of survival and decided to get a memory spell so we wouldn't kill each other in future games. Now everything's changed. Gran said that the earth won't come back until the game is over. And she believed the only way to end it is for all of us to die, save one. If that's true . . ." Death and I truly shouldn't be together. I rubbed my temples. "Richter will probably win anyway."

"We can't let that happen, *bébé*."

"Aric and I planned to go out in a blaze of glory to stop him. And I can finally admit that kind of thinking on my part came about because I'd lost *you*." Now I was pregnant. Now nothing made sense. "A few weeks ago, Aric wanted me to talk all about you. To grieve. I worried I would hurt him with my tears, so I put it off."

He'd wanted to know why the snow made me sad and what the red ribbon meant. I'd left it in my drawer at the castle. Was it gone forever?

Jack looped his arm around me. "I'm back. I'm right here."

I leaned into him, and for long moments, we just enjoyed the sweet stillness. Then cold kissed my cheek. A snowflake. The first of many.

Jack and I raised our faces to watch the flurries. For once, I had no reason to be sad.

The night I'd lost him, I'd been a heartbeat away from expressing my feelings for him. *No more regrets.* I drew back to face him. "When I was riding after you from Fort Arcana, I'd just raised that walkie-talkie to tell you something when all hell broke loose."

"What was it?"

I swallowed. "I love you, Jack. I never got to say those three words to you."

His eyes briefly slid shut, as if he wanted to savor this moment. "Waited a long time to hear that."

"I thought I'd never get the chance to tell you."

Holding my gaze, he cupped my face. "I knew. I heard it in your voice on that recording of your life story. I felt it when we slept together. The tombstone you made me removed any doubt."

Oh, yeah. I'd engraved *I love you* at the end of the epitaph. "So this is old news, huh?"

"You saying those words gives me a thrill down to my soul. I wish I could hear them for the rest of my life—because I am gone for you, Evie. *Je t'aimerai toujours.*" Brows drawn, he eased down to kiss me, and I wanted him to.

I wanted his warmth and reassurance. I wanted my heart to thunder from something other than dread.

His lips pressed against mine, and that fire between us burned hot as ever. I channeled all my emotions—my fear, my missing him, my elation that he was still alive—into that kiss.

He gripped my nape, pulling me closer, until we shared breaths. He caught my moans with his lips. His deep-chested groans made my toes curl in my boots.

Gods, he feels so good. Missed him so much. My Jack is alive. I tunneled my fingers into his hair, frowning as some nagging worry intruded on our kiss. *What is it? Something's not right.*

The ring.

I was wearing a wedding ring that had belonged to Aric's mother. I pulled back. "Wait. I can't."

Between breaths, Jack said, "Listen to me. I know you love Domīnija too. I know you were with him. Doan care. We still got a connection."

Would it survive my revelation? "Jack, I have to tell you something."

"I need to tell you something too."

As I gathered my courage, I waved him on.

"After escaping the slavers, I was in a bad way, me. I thought the fever was goan to take me for true. Matthew dragged me out into a snowbank to bring my temperature down. I was delirious, but Evie, I swear I could touch you, see you, smell you. I was talking to you. Reaching for you."

My eyes widened. "When was this? I broke down one night, lying in the snow, and I imagined kissing you!"

Surprise lit his face. "I imagined every snowflake was your lips." His gaze took in my thunderstruck expression. "We're connected, Evangeline. We can't deny it."

I shook my head. "I don't. So what do we do now?"

"I still believe we've got to get you into that castle. But what if we can't cure Domīnija of the Hanged Man's influence? He might not ever return to normal."

"What are you saying? Are we talking about killing Aric? Because if so, this conversation ends now."

"The Hierophant's brainwashed followers still want revenge against you—even after the bastard died."

I hadn't considered that.

"Death might always want your head, might always carry that hatred toward you. I'm saying that I'll take out any threat to you."

"It's more complicated than that." *How to put this?* "Jack, you need to know something."

"You can tell me anything." His steady gaze reassured me. "Nothing you say can change how I feel about you."

Here goes freaking everything. "I'm . . . the thing is . . . when I thought you were—"

"Hold on." He held a finger over his lips.

I whispered, "What is it?"

"I think I hear a Bagger." He shot to his feet, then pulled me to mine. His gaze darted as he readied his bow. "Over there." He pointed out a pile of rocks a short distance away on the same bluff.

"Did it bury itself?" We knew from experience that they liked to burrow.

"It kind of looks like a makeshift grave."

The rock pile rose and shifted, stones sliding off into the lake. A skeletal hand jutted up. Then another.

"Let's go, Jack!"

He took aim with his bow. "Not till I kill it." Naturally. *Jack and Baggers.*

Wait, was the creature waving at us? Almost like it was shooing us away. When its decomposed head poked up, ash-covered skin peeled from exposed bone. Couldn't tell if it was male or female.

Was it my imagination, or did the Bagger's one remaining eye look frantic? *Wait.* Sol was trying to communicate with us through this creature! "Don't—" I slapped Jack's arm just as he pulled the trigger. The arrow missed the Bagger's forehead, hitting its throat.

"What the hell, Evie?"

I skirted past Jack, addressing the zombie: "Um, Sol?"

Loud groan and a nod.

"Are we in trouble?"

Nodding. Shooing. *"Ohhhhhh. Oh. Oh."*

"Go?"

NOD.

I whirled around. "We've got to run, Jack!"

He grabbed my hand, and we tore off down the path.

"Kentarch!" I screamed. "Wake up!"

Halfway to the ground, Jack skidded to a stop, cocking his head. Eyes gone wide, he yelled, *"INCOMING!"*

22

A shrill whistle rent the night as a trail of light and smoke sped through the sky. A missile zoomed directly for the truck. Kentarch and Joules were still in the cab!

"WAKE UP!" I screamed again. No time left to run. I needed to close my eyes but couldn't look away.

Just before impact, the truck *vanished.* "Yes! Go, Kentarch!"

The missile exploded into the side of the mountain. "Down, Evie!" Jack tossed me to the ground, shielding me. He grunted when rocks landed on his back.

"Jack! Are you okay?"

"Been better. Think my bowstring's snapped."

"Stop covering me," I bit out from underneath him, my ears ringing. "Regenerate here, remember?" But would my kid?

Jack managed to get free of the rocks, shouldering his busted bow. As he helped me stand, a chopper came into view in the distance.

There was no mistaking that helicopter; the nose was painted to look like a dragon's roaring mouth. "Zara's here." The earth rumbled beneath our feet. "And Richter." Quakes always announced his presence.

"We've got to get through the pass before they block it." Jack pointed out the narrow gap by the lake's edge. "Can you run?"

I nodded, and we hurried down the stony path. Though Jack had a limp, he dragged me along, all but carrying me.

We'd just made it down to the lake's edge when I spied a fiery light coming up through that pass. I slowed. "Oh, dear God."

Richter. The King of Hell.

Not even a hundred feet away, he rode a wave of lava right toward us, blocking our only way out. Even taller than Jack, he was a no-neck bruiser, just as Circe had described. Fire wrapped around his naked body, shrouding him. His beady eyes were flame red.

Why hadn't he simply bombed us or flooded this rock bowl with lava? As he continued closer, I made out two icons on his right hand: a moon for Selena and the Lovers' overlapping triangles. He'd harvested their icon from the Archer—when he'd turned my friend to cinder.

Fury engulfed me, but I didn't feel the quickening of my powers. I'd vowed to replace Richter's laughter with screams. I'd dreamed about torturing him. Where were my powers?

"I finally get to meet the Empress of Arcana," he said, his voice booming in the echoing crater.

Sweating from the heat, I raised my hands, managing a few scraggly vines. Once they reached Richter, they turned to ash. With a cry, I yanked my hands back. My spores and thorn tornado would simply disintegrate.

Richter smirked. "Is that all you've got, Empress? No wonder you hide behind Death's coattails. Zara was right—you are the weakest of us all."

Jack shoved me behind him. *"Richter,"* he bit out. "You destroyed my army. You murdered Selena. I'm goan to kill you slow." He reached for his bow . . . only to drop his hand; must've remembered the broken string right as I did.

"Kill me, eh? How would you ever get close enough? I'm too strong and hot to die."

Unless someone struck from afar. Where had Kentarch and Joules teleported to? This was a perfect opportunity to attack!

Jack had the same idea. He muttered in French, "Stall. Give them time to return."

I demanded, "Why are you here, Richter?" Zara's chopper had circled back. Was she looking for a place to land?

"Sol said you were pretty. Pretty doesn't do you justice." Those beady eyes roamed over me. "And you regenerate? Maybe you could live through my special *brand* of attention. Some last longer than others."

Vomit rose in my throat. "Sol?" I had to act like I hated the Sun Card. "Where is that coward? Too scared to face us?"

"He's back guarding our lair with his Bagger horde. When you own as much as we do, it's best to keep watch." He gazed past us. "And where's your ally Death? Trouble in paradise?"

"On his way here to meet us. He defeated you once before, and he will again. You better hurry along."

"He's not coming," Richter said, sounding so confident I wondered if he knew about Paul. "In our last shoot out, you needed four Arcana to rescue you. Who's going to save you now?"

"What do you want, Richter?" Circe had said he craved cataclysm, but there had to be more. "Why are you destroying food stores?"

He shrugged, and a wisp of flame rose from each of his shoulders, taking to the air. "Why does fire burn? Because it consumes to live. *I* consume to live. Empress, my hunger is never-ending, but there's not much in the world that the Flash didn't consume first."

He incinerated things to harvest strength? "Why hurt people?"

A repulsive smile creased his meaty face. "Nothing ever satisfies me, but roasted bodies come the closest."

My fists clenched. I was facing yet another Arcana who wouldn't respond to reason, who'd just keep killing unless we stopped him. "You don't strike me as a deep thinker, so let me lay this out for you. Sooner or later, you'll have nothing left to burn. Then what?"

"I'll win the Arcana game. Because that's what I am—a winner. When the world comes back, I'll fry anything new that grows."

"Then why are we still alive?"

Richter waved in Zara's direction. Her spotlight swept the ground. She *was* trying to land. "Right before Zara got to steal your luck,

Fauna's creatures arrived. Zara gets pissed when luck doesn't flow her way. She's going to fix that now."

Jack grated, "So she'll steal our luck, then you'll torch us?" Just as in my dreams.

"I'll keep the Empress alive for a time. Let her recover between my visits."

Two games ago, he'd tortured me for months, searing away my regenerating limbs, until he'd finally taken my head. My stomach roiled. "Now I understand what hell is."

How could I stop him? I kept hearing my grandmother's words: *Until you fully embrace your viciousness, you have no chance against the Emperor.*

What else had she taught me? Desperate, I mentally plumbed the earth for buried seeds.

I could dispatch plants underground. If I made them thick enough, maybe they could reach Richter before burning away.

There! My eyes widened. I detected seeds deep in the ground, even below the rock—what must be hundreds and hundreds of thousands of potential soldiers. They were ancient. How to fuel them?

"Hell?" Richter flared brighter, the heat making me lightheaded. "You shouldn't anger me. My temper is truly explosive—"

"Oi, this is for Selena and Tess!" From the top of the crater wall, Joules hurled javelins at Richter.

His arm moved like a blur as he launched five—no, ten—no, *fifteen* spears. They rained down on the Emperor.

Yet Richter just bowed his chest. We braced for explosions that never came; the spears *melted* like hot ore. Over and over, silver goop merged with his lava.

"Show your face, Tower!" Richter produced an ominous fireball in his hand. As he scouted for Joules's location, he bellowed, "Stop being a pussy!" Taking aim, Richter tensed, about to lob that fireball. . . .

A rifle boomed from the opposite side of the crater. Kentarch! Three thunderous shots rang out.

Please, God, let this work.

A few feet from Richter's skin, those bullets turned into a trio of smoke puffs. The bullets had crumbled into nothing.

Jack muttered, *"Jesus."*

Suddenly, I spied Kentarch in the air *above* the crater. He was teleporting from one side to the other—with a boulder as big as a car. Could the Emperor be crushed? Halfway across, Kentarch dropped it on him.

I held my breath.

Flames radiated from Richter's body. Even more smoke erupted around him as the rock turned to lava. He saluted Kentarch. "Thanks for the top-off, asshole."

The heat . . . too much. Why wasn't the Emperor weakening? Gasping for air, I stared at the lava bubbling all around us. Time seemed to slow as my mind struggled to process this scene.

For once, *I* could see the future. When Richter won, he would usher in hell on earth. Fire and brimstone. Lava and smoke. The entire world would look like this.

A hellscape.

Jack stumbled, barely keeping me on my feet.

I told him, "We've got to get in the water."

"Non. It'll boil."

The ice was long gone; steam wafted off the surface.

Through the haze, I spotted Kentarch and Joules on the crater rim. Kentarch was soaked with sweat, his outline wavering. Moving his truck and that boulder had weakened him.

Even the Arcana able to strike from afar weren't threats anymore.

The chopper dusted off in a hurry. In a blaze of muzzle flashes, one of Zara's machine guns spat bullets, eating the stone in a path to Kentarch and Joules.

They had no choice but to run. As they fled, Joules flung four javelins at her. They sped through the air.

She banked, but she could never avoid a direct hit—

Lightning bolts shot down from the sky, striking the javelins, sending each one off course. The Tower's weapons flew harmlessly past her chopper.

Strokes of freakish luck.

He howled with disbelief. Before he could launch another javelin, Zara engaged a second machine gun, firing both at him and Kentarch. They had nowhere to run, only a sheer drop-off.

Kentarch clamped Joules's arm and attempted to teleport, but they didn't budge. Zara unleashed a torrent of bullets at them. Just before the first wave hit, Kentarch went intangible, ghosting him and Joules.

One second passed. Another. How long could he keep that up?

Click, click, click. She'd run out of ammo!

But the last bullet ricocheted rock. Kentarch wavered; the rock caught him right at that instant.

He yelled, and they tumbled over the crater's edge, out of sight. Would they survive the drop?

I turned back to Richter, threats dying on my tongue. He'd slithered closer during Zara's attack.

Waves of dizziness hit me. Sweat stung my eyes. I begged for the red witch to stir. *"Jack . . ."* He squeezed my hand as hellfire surrounded us. *Stay conscious, stay conscious.*

This monster had taken Jack from me once before. Was I about to let him again?

"Now, where were we?" Richter said. "Oh, yeah, I was telling you how every Emperor gets an Empress. Which means your ass is mine."

I expected Jack to tell me that this wasn't the end. That we'd somehow prevail. Instead, he reached for his bowie knife and murmured in French, "I won't let him take you alive."

23

"Time to lose the dead weight." As Richter faced off against Jack, he made a mistake.

The Emperor ... laughed.

I jolted upright, staying Jack's hand. That hateful sound had pervaded my nightmares. It was a trigger, activating something dark and primal within me.

Rage unfurled like a blossom, soon as towering as an oak. My vision blurred. My glyphs blazed. The red witch awakened. *Embrace my viciousness, Gran?*

Acid laced my veins.

I called out to those ancient seeds, my body shaking with readiness. New petals tumbled from my reddened hair.

Keep laughing. When the red witch bayed for blood, I fueled the legions of seeds from within me, power on tap as it hadn't been since I'd made Jack's gravestone.

Recognition hit me. The tourniquet around my heart hadn't been *muting* my rage and pain; it'd been *damming them up.*

As my legions grew and began to force their way to the surface, a deep rumble shook the ground, as if the earth had growled. A quake of my own. "Come, Richter." My voice turned breathy. "Touch—"

I never finished the sentence, because I caught a glimpse of something so horrifying that my lungs seized up.

The true depths of my power.

A yawning black hole of rage existed inside me. An endless well of wrath.

Another quake hit. *Mine.*

Richter's laughter faltered as he shifted to keep his balance. His eyes briefly widened, then narrowed on me, as if to ask, *Was that you?*

Jack muttered, "Evie?"

Power is my burden. It overflows a bottomless pit.

If I ever came close to tapping into that well, would I leave collateral damage all around—like Richter with his firestorms? Would I curse the world like Demeter?

A show of power always took a toll on an Arcana. If I unleashed the full measure of my abilities, would my body give out?

Like Tess's?

Richter shook his head, as if he'd just imagined those quakes. After all, I was only a weak little girl. That force couldn't have originated from inside me. "Come peacefully with us, Empress, and live for a time."

Just as I had a well of rage, so did Richter. Those seeds had been entombed beneath rock; maybe the Emperor and I had already played out this battle centuries ago, or the gods we represented had.

If I ever matched Richter rage for rage . . . *we're the nuclear option. No one wins.*

In all of my battles, I'd never been more terrified than now. Not for Richter.

I fear myself.

I'd just recoiled from my connection to those seeds when something skittered up my spine. Hissing sounded, like a giant serpent.

Had Richter's attention skewed behind us? His sleazy smile faded as he craned his head up. And up.

A drop of scalding water hit my neck. I glanced over my shoulder at the rising wall of water. *"Circe."*

Jack cursed under his breath.

"No, she'll protect us." I hoped.

Richter's fireball hovered above his palm. "You want some of this, water bitch?"

Circe's voice sounded from the wave: "That's *Ms.* Water Bitch to you." Her tone would sound coolly mocking to others, but I could detect her fatigue. "Run along now, fire starter. I'm in no mood for your infantile antics tonight."

"You don't wanna tangle with me? Too scared to?"

She gave a bored sigh. "Hmm. I probably should drown you. But then, my fun would be cut short. You start your fires for enjoyment—I delight in extinguishing them. Just as I did when you slaughtered that army."

"I boiled half of your wave away."

"And I turned *all* of your lava back to rock." The water wall crested over our heads toward him, as if she were getting up in the Emperor's face. "Do you know that I can *feel* my victims' screams in the deep? They always scream, right before I replace the air in their lungs—with *me.* Tell me, little boy, who will you scream for?"

His red eyes scanned her wall again, sizing her up. "You'll get what's coming to you, Priestess. My enemies always do." Signaling Zara, he turned to ride away on that lava flow. It undulated snakelike over the ground, leaving a charred scar.

The chopper drifted for a menacing moment before banking to follow Richter's direction.

Over his shoulder, he called, "I'm coming for you, Empress." His laughter echoed. "Soon it'll be your turn!"

Once they'd gone, I cried, "Why didn't you kill him, Circe?"

Her wave drew back, wobbled, then sloshed over the lake bed. A surge of hot backwash slapped me and Jack, toppling us. He had to hang on to me until the water settled.

As he helped me to my feet, I sputtered and cursed. "With allies like these . . ."

Circe sniffed, "You're welcome for saving your lives." A small column of water arose, then shakily morphed into a flat expanse, a window into her temple where she sat on a coral throne.

On the few occasions I'd seen her through the window, she'd always been perfectly coifed and calm. Now her long black hair was tangled, her fawn-colored eyes harried. Her sea-foam garments looked askew, and she held her trident in a trembling hand.

Jack blinked at the sight of her, then said, "You might've saved us tonight, but he's got Evie in his crosshairs now." If he was shocked by Circe's water window, he got over it. More Arcana insanity he should never have to deal with.

"Well, if it isn't the hunter, General Jackson Deveaux." Her island accent was thicker than usual. "I watched over your fort for some time."

"Not for long enough."

"I was busy avenging your army. Speaking of which—aren't you supposed to be dead among them?"

Tick, tick, tick went his jaw muscle.

"Easy, Jack."

"To answer your question, Evie Greene, I didn't try to kill Richter because I'm weak, which means my control is suffering. I didn't want you to boil or drown. Well, not *you*, especially. Your baby."

My head whipped around to Jack.

His lips parted. "You're *pregnant*?"

"He didn't know about my godson?" Circe's titter turned into a cough.

"I-I was about to tell him." I twined my fingers. *What to say?* "Jack . . ."

Anguish and bafflement warred in his gray eyes.

"You two discuss this later," Circe said. "The Emperor might return, and I only have so long." To Jack, she said, "I'd like to talk with the Empress alone. You should go check on the others anyway."

Jack blinked rapidly, as if regaining his senses. He looked from me to Circe and back. "You safe with her?"

"Relax, hunter," Circe said. "If I wanted the Empress dead, she would be so. For months, I had her trapped within my watery noose, but I never struck."

He peered at my face, then in the direction of my belly. "I'll be back, me."

"Be careful," I called as he started through the pass.

Shock hammered me. We'd just faced Richter—smoke still oozed up from doused lava—and now Jack knew my secret.

But I'd learned about another one: my devastating full potential. I'd been playing host to unlimited wrath this entire time.

Had I actually worried about the lack of sun or Bagger contagion undermining my power? Nothing could undermine it.

Nothing but *me.* Aric had been right: I'd bottled up my feelings so totally that I'd weakened my abilities.

"Oops," Circe said. "You really ought to have told him."

I was still staring in his direction. "I'm going to get him killed before all is said and done."

"With villains like Richter around, yes. Unless the Emperor weakens as well. Eventually, that little fire starter will run out of fuel."

Such as roasted bodies. I shuddered.

In the past, Death had waited to attack until the Emperor had drained himself. Yet just now Richter had looked like he was only warming up.

"But you weren't summoning the great Priestess for help with Richter. Not yet. You want to defeat the Hanged Man. I sensed his activation at the castle."

My gaze shifted toward Circe. I needed my eyes on Jack, but I'd waited weeks to talk to this woman. She was the key to my future, the ally who'd just saved our lives. "Yes. He poisoned Finn and reversed the others' cards."

"The *dark calling.*"

I frowned. "My grandmother spoke of that."

"We're all at risk for our card turning. Any uncontrollable emotion can reverse an Arcana. Fury, pain, sorrow. Remember, the Lovers' tableau was reversed."

Matthew had described them as *reverse, perverse.* "I've felt fury before, but I didn't succumb to the dark calling." So what would happen if I tapped into my well of wrath? Every time I called on my Empress gifts, I played with a primal force—and I had no idea of the cost. "After Richter's massacre, I nearly lost my mind."

"Yet you *didn't*. The reverse comes when you *do*. Or else the Hanged Man can turn a card with just a thought." At my exasperated look, she said, "The dark calling exists without the Hanged Man, but the Hanged Man doesn't exist without the dark calling."

Now that we're all clear on that . . . "Why couldn't Paul reverse me? I might be immune to brainwashing, but that's not his only power."

She glanced at my belly. "The Hanged Man can't control mortals. Perhaps your child shielded you."

A breath escaped me. My thoughts about this baby were as conflicted as ever. I hadn't felt much protectiveness toward it. But maybe it'd already protected me? "Paul told me he couldn't make Aric and Lark hate me unless they were predisposed to it. Is that true?"

"What you want to know is whether the Hanged Man can plant a tree where there is no soil. I can't say for certain."

"Aric's rage over the past *was* real." Again, what kind of future would we have?

"Clearly." She hiked one slim shoulder. "Since mine is."

My lips thinned. "Can he be saved or not?" What if Paul's influence did last even after I killed him? Aric might *already* be lost forever.

"So little is known about the Hanged Man, but I believe his demise will end his sphere. Without it, he has no influence."

"His demise? One problem: he's invincible, as far as I know."

"True. He can't be harmed by most weapons. To trump a card like that will take more than bullets or blades." Or claws. "I recall that he has a weakness to a specific weapon, but I don't remember what it is. I have been researching."

I swept wet hair from my face. "Maybe you could use a spell of some sort to locate it?"

"Perhaps. This temple is my spell book, the walls covered with incantations, all written in tiny letters. I haven't eaten or slept, too busy reading every word."

"How big is your temple?"

She rose from her throne. "Vast." The water window followed her as she meandered down a torchlit passageway. I could hear tentacles slithering but couldn't see below her waist. When she entered another chamber, a stone slab ground closed behind her.

Impatience gnawed at me—why hadn't Jack returned yet?—but I sensed I was on the verge of some revelation with Circe.

She paused beside a wall to trace her fingers along a section of foreign text, and firelight glimmered over one arm fin. Was she becoming more sirenlike, just as Lark had become more animalistic?

I'd seen Circe in my memories of past games. She'd looked like a normal girl, with a few scaly body mods. Now she might have tentacles for legs. "Circe, what's happening *to you*? Are you changing?"

"Maybe I'm more myself in my temple. Maybe I become more myself every day I remain down here."

"What does that mean?"

"I feel so tired, Evie Greene. The cold makes my bones ache. Trespassers claim my domain as their own. They pollute every last atom of me. I hear *much* of what they say. *Some* of what you say. *None* of what my currents sigh. The trespassers don't make the proper gifts to me."

"What do you mean? What gifts?" Decoder-ring talk from Circe? But hadn't I done the same on the phone with Aric? He'd told me, "You're not making sense, Empress."

"If I received a proper sacrifice—one that would be dearly missed— I could see farther, could regain my strength and control over my element." Revealing more of her domain than ever before, she headed into another chamber. Inside was a stone table carved with trident symbols, stained with blood. Was that a sacrificial altar?

No freaking way. "Ogen used to demand sacrifices."

"The Devil Card wanted power. Just as I crave it." Those tentacles slithered anew. "I *am* a priestess, you know. Didn't expect me to have blood rites?"

So much for making her my kid's godmother. Or godsmother. Which reminded me . . . "Earlier, you said your god*son*. Why do you think I'm carrying a boy?"

"Because I'm a powerful witch, and I know things."

Ah. So Aric would have a son. My hand drifted to my belly, but all I felt was conflict.

"By the way, Empress, I did eat Fauna's tiger—one she would dearly miss—and it tasted delicious."

I muttered, "We ate her lion."

"Bravo! And my ally Kentarch killed her bear. Lions, and tigers, and—"

"Don't. Just don't."

"Fine," she grumbled. "You were more fun in previous lives."

I gazed past her. Mosaics covered the walls, depictions of tidal waves destroying ports and monsters devouring ships. "Did you once control those monsters?"

She chuckled. "Of course not, Empress. I *was* the monster. The terror from the abyss."

How delightful.

"All who hear my call will fear my catastrophal powers."

Why did that sound so familiar? "Did we talk about that in a past game?"

"Hmm." Her gaze grew unfocused, and she swayed. "Much activity at the shore. I've been away too long. The suit I've been missing is right there."

"A suit? I don't understand." I was freaked out and exhausted, and I needed to know that Jack and our friends were okay. "Damn it, just tell me what to do."

No answer.

"Circe, give me some idea how long it'll be before I can face Paul. He's already killed one of our allies. What's to stop him from taking more of them out?"

"I don't know. I too have limited time. All my bodies are freezing. I'm starving down here. Maybe I can figure something out. But if this continues, I will perish. Coming to land might be my only hope."

"What kind of hope is that? You always *die* when you come to land."

Circe faced me with a wry half-smile. "Such worry, Evie Greene. It warms the cockles of my ice-cold heart."

Jack called from a distance, "We need some help here."

Her smile dimmed. "Go to them."

"How will I find you again?"

"As with all things, you'll find the answers you need on the shore. Wait for me there."

"Where specifically?"

"Go to the nearest coast. Then keep going." Her voice faded away, and her water window subsided into the lake.

"Ugh. That makes no sense!" I hurried through the pass, then around to the other side of the crater. Over here, fires still burned, the smoke needling my eyes.

Joules stumbled into view. "Goin' to get bandages out of the truck." He had blood all over him and a shell-shocked expression.

"Whose blood is that?"

"Tarch's hurt. Bad."

I rushed past him and found Jack kneeling beside Kentarch. The Chariot sat propped against a rock, cradling his arm. Staring at nothing, he demonstrated zero emotion.

Blood covered the ground, had splattered Jack's face. He'd used his belt to make a tourniquet around Kentarch's forearm. "Evie, can you give him something for the pain?"

"Of course. What happened?" I rubbed my gritty eyes, trying to make out the injury amidst all the smoke.

Jack rose, then crossed to a small fire. His knife was heating in the flames, the blade red-hot. "We're goan to need to cauterize his wound."

I turned back to the Chariot and finally saw. Breath left me.

His right hand was gone.

24

Jack drove the Beast at a furious pace.

Kentarch was passed out in the back, mumbling in his sleep.

Before Jack had sealed his wound, the Chariot had roused long enough to teach Jack the Beast's security measures and to *decline* my medicinal plants.

No matter. I'd injected him with a generous dose, telling him, "Think of Issa. Think of better times to come."

He'd peered up at me with soulful eyes. "Did you kill me? As you did before?" Even after all the shit we'd been through together, he still considered me cold enough to poison him. . . .

I gazed over at Jack's strong profile. My emotions were going haywire, tangling up inside me. I was appalled by what had happened to Kentarch and spooked to my marrow by what I'd glimpsed.

Jack clutched the steering wheel with white knuckles. What must he be thinking about everything? I dreaded his reaction to my pregnancy.

Joules asked, "What did you give Tarch?"

"A sedative-slash-painkiller. Want some?"

He looked interested-slash-skeptical. "Why didn't the Priestess tsunami Richter's arse?"

I debated whether to reveal the truth. But what was the point of pretending? "She's weak. She could barely put up enough of a front to scare the Emperor off." I wondered how a well of wrath would affect her.

"That's just bloody great! How can we fight them? The Emperor's immune to—to *everything*. And Zara? What are the chances that lightning—me own element—would end up saving her?"

"Freak coincidences are her power. But she's got to be depleted now." Unfortunately, they'd just go hunt survivors for a top-off.

"Depleted? Not before her power did *that*." Joules waved at Kentarch's arm. "What are the feckin' odds that a flat shard of rock could sever his gun hand clean?"

Jack said, "Right now, I'm more concerned with them finding us again. The Sun must've been the one to tip them off."

Joules snorted. "So much for a man on the inside, Empress."

"Hey, he used a Bagger to warn us about Richter's approach, okay? And then we warned you. So if not for Sol, you'd have one of Zara's missiles up your *arse*. In any case, I'm sure he has to help them. They're only keeping him alive as long as he's useful to them, which he must know."

Joules asked, "What did Circe tell you about the Hanged Man?"

How to put this without crushing all their hope? "She's researching a weapon to kill him. She told me to go to the coast and wait for word." Kind of. "We'll be safer there from Richter too, closer to big water. As soon as she comes up with a plan, she'll contact us." But with her rate of deterioration, would she be less and less help?

"Where on the coast?" Joules wanted to know.

Have no idea. I thought we should continue our heading for the Outer Banks. "I'll know more when we get there."

"Grand directions, Empress. You'd best plug that into the GPS." He laughed without humor. "Maybe I shouldn't be working to rescue anyone from the Hanged Man. If Jack and me save Death, then we sacrifice ourselves to the Ash—and Gabe too. The Reaper will never share his resources with us."

"Joules, I vow to you that if you help me, Aric will reward you. He'll give you a freaking medal."

"Canna eat a medal. Just want in on that bacon we smelled. Hell, at least Gabe's got food and warm shelter right now. He's thriving there."

Jack said, "Gabe's living with a sword over his neck. He only survives as long as the Hanged Man says. And who is Paul goan to take out first when the food supplies dwindle?" Jack's gaze slid to me. We both knew Aric had set up the castle to sustain people for decades.

As long as the generators had fuel, the Reaper could use those sunlamps to grow crops to feed humans and livestock. Centuries of planning had gone into his home. It was everything to him.

I said, "Look, the bottom line is that Aric's the only Arcana alive who knows how to kill Richter. Understand me: saving Death could mean saving the world."

Joules's gaze darkened until I could all but hear his thoughts: *Nothing good comes from Death.* "Worst road trip I've ever been on," he muttered, leaning against the door. "Grabbin' a kip. Wake me up when there's even more fun to be had."

How could he sleep at a time like this? Soon his soft snores sounded from the back, effectively leaving me and Jack alone.

I touched his arm. "I know this is all . . . a lot."

When Jack's muscles tensed under my palm, I pulled my hand back.

"Please, talk to me. I need to hear how you're feeling about all this."

Quick glance from the road. "Doan know, me. Confused. I pictured *us* having a kid together, down the line when we were older. Now it's you and Domīnija." He briefly squeezed his eyes closed, as if the thought brought on fresh pain. "You two do this on purpose?"

"Never! Paul gave me a contraceptive shot—or so I thought. I told him I didn't want to have a child in a world like this. And I'd already told Aric that I was way too young."

"Domīnija *wanted* you to have his baby?"

"Yes. *No.* He did at first, but then he changed his mind. Still, after we found this out, he was happy. He thinks it could derail the game. Plus, he simply wants a family. To this day, he misses his."

"Tell me about it." Jack would always miss his beloved mother and his sister Clotile. "What if the Reaper plotted with the Hanged Man? What if they set you up?"

"No, I don't believe so. I trust Aric. Or I *did* trust him." Death's look of fury plagued my memories. "I'm really confused too."

"How could he attack you and his kid?"

"Paul convinced him I lied about the pregnancy. Now Aric hates me for 'tricking' him into believing it for a time."

"I'm goan to kill that medic."

"Not if I get to him first. I've wanted him dead since I learned I was pregnant."

Jack's gaze dropped to my stomach before returning to the road. "How far along are you? Women sometimes lose pregnancies."

"More than three months, I think. I get the feeling this one is here to stay."

"You doan sound overjoyed by that."

"I think having a baby is the craziest thing anyone could do during an apocalypse, much less during a deadly game. At best, I'm no longer bulletproof. At worst, it's draining my body."

All of my bottled-up thoughts spilled out: "And how could this kid be normal? Just weeks before I got pregnant, zombies dined on me. Since then, I've been bitten by a viper, caught in an avalanche, stabbed, starved, and nearly parboiled by Richter. And it's not like I can run out and get a sonogram. Not to mention that my grandmother warned me that Life and Death would become something dire. I'm probably carrying the Antichrist. Of course, she was half-crazed when she told me that—which reminds me: great genes I'm passing on."

"Wait. Circe said her god*son*. If you haven't had a sonogram, how'd she know it's a boy?"

"She sensed it, because she's a witch."

"Then couldn't she sense if anything was wrong?"

Huh. Good point. But then, Circe's judgment might be off. Aside from her mental decline, her likes included an occasional bloody sacrifice and being a sea monster.

"What'd the Priestess say about your pregnancy?"

I admitted, "She made it sound like the kid had shielded me from Paul's reversal power, his *dark calling*. It doesn't work on humans, and the baby might be a regular mortal."

"That's something, *non?*"

"Circe's probably biased. She thinks this baby could usher in a new era—the key to saving the world. She called me Mother Earth and reminded me that my powers and history were all about birth and rebirth."

"A new era?" Jack said, a wistful note underscoring his words. "You believe something like that could happen?"

I sighed. "Could this development affect future games? Yes. But I don't think my having a kid will make the sun shine again. I'm coming to accept that only the natural conclusion of the game can do that." This subject always made my head hurt. "Jack, I understand if you want to bow out of this mission. I mean, this is really messed up."

"I woan stop until you're safe. Being out in the Ash is a certain death-sentence. Being out here when pregnant? You might as well have a target on your back."

"Which means you'll have one as long as you're close to me."

"I was never goan to live long anyway. I figure the average survival time out here is a year. I'm not average, so maybe I can eke out three more years. If I make it to twenty-three, I'll do a jig, me."

So how could I bear ever to be separated from him again? If Aric returned to normal, and I returned to him, Jack would leave. I'd never see him again.

"We've got to get you safe in that castle, now more than ever. That stronghold is your only hope. Come hell or high water"—we'd experienced both recently—"you're goan to be there when you give birth."

I nibbled my bottom lip. "How can you want to help me when I'm knocked up by another man?"

"You think I'm goan to abandon you, just 'cause you're pregnant? That's something my father might've done, but I ain't him." Emotion simmered in Jack's gray eyes. "I'll help you no matter what, Evangeline. I always will."

I couldn't accept this. There was no upside for him—only more Arcana madness, Death, and death. When Jack had decided to let me make a future with Aric, he'd been free for a time. "We aren't . . . together anymore. How can you risk your life for mine?"

He shot me a look like I'd gone crazy. "How can you ask that? You got my heart in your hand. I told you—I'm not ever getting it back."

I had his heart in my hand, and he had my thorn in his paw. I almost felt like I'd . . . doomed him somehow along the way.

Never meaning to, but done all the same. I rubbed my aching brow. "What will happen now?"

"I doan want to put pressure on you with another choice, so let me tell you how this is goan to go. If Domīnija can be saved, and I trust that he woan give in to that rage again, then I'll let you two get back to your life. If we can't save him, we'll defeat him and take that castle. You and me'll live there and raise this kid for as long as we can hold on."

My breath caught. Jack was offering to raise Aric's son?

From the back, Joules said, "I know what I'm hoping for."

I shot him a look. He shrugged and closed his eyes again.

Facing Jack, I said, "There's something else you need to know. I can't win this game. I'd rather die than become immortal."

"Look on the bright side, *peekôn.*" He stared out into the night. "You probably woan get a choice about that either."

25

THE HUNTER
DAY 553 A.F.

I'd just opened a gas can when Joules climbed down from the truck to join me. "This rig's a right beauty, huh?" he said.

"That she is." Though the extended-range tank held thousands of miles' worth of fuel, we'd hit empty. Luckily, Kentarch had spare cans in the back. *Time to feed the Beast.*

For the last two days, we'd been making slow progress, catching naps in the cab.

I'd left Evie asleep in the front seat. She'd looked exhausted, her lashes fanning out against the purple smudges under her eyes. I'd brushed her hair from her forehead and murmured, *"À moi."* But she wasn't mine. Not anymore.

"Sooo," Joules began, "your girl's up the duff with the Reaper's spawn. How're you taking that news?"

Conflicted as ever. Evie was going to be a mother, would soon have another man's son.

I told myself this over and over. Still, I needed to draw her to me every time I caught a thread of her honeysuckle scent. And that kiss at the lake? She'd been telling me something with that kiss, something I was desperate to hear.

She loved me just as much as she ever had, maybe even more. But

knowing that only made this situation harder. "I've heard better news."
Elle me hante. She haunts me.

"What's your play now, hunter?"

The last thing she needed after all she'd been through—and in her condition—was me putting pressure on her. The weird part about it: I got the feeling she *expected* me to. "Stay the course," I said, no matter how badly I wanted to tell her that we'd run away together.

My old issues remained. I had *nothing* to give her. She needed food and safety more than ever. She needed to be back in Death's castle.

Our dream of Haven would never have worked without food and supplies.

"You really believe Circe's goin' to save the day with some kind of weapon?"

I emptied one can, then grabbed another. "Got to."

"Then let's think about how we'll use it. Instead of a Reaper rescue mission, let's plan a hostile takeover. We sack the castle, you and the Empress set up house, and we all ride out the apocalypse."

So unbelievably tempting. But . . . "A kid belongs with his father."

And damn it, I owed Domīnija for Evie's life. For mine as well.

Joules leaned against the side of the truck. "Evie can make promises for him all she wants to, but we both know Death'll never share his resources with us. Especially now that there's a little Reaper on the way."

"I'm not eager to sing the praises of the man who married the only woman I'll ever love—"

"And knocked her up."

"—but Domīnija's honorable. You help reunite him with his wife and kid, then he's goan to reward you."

I had to admit that I'd actually *liked* the man. Take away the drama around us, and I could almost imagine us being podnas. We'd emptied more than one bottle of whiskey together, and I'd found him to be honest, smart, and brave as the night is long.

Evie might think that her and Domīnija's baby would be a mix of the worst in the world; I didn't see that at all.

In fact, I probably cared more about the kid than she seemed to. Mixed up with all my jealousy and confusion, I felt a strange sense of protectiveness.

If I was this conflicted, I couldn't imagine how she must feel.

She'd admitted that the kid could've shielded her from the Hanged Man, but in the same breath, she'd blamed the baby for draining her. . . .

"Just think about my idea," Joules said. "Goin' to take a slash." He ambled off.

A what? And folks thought *I* talked funny?

Kentarch exited the truck, looking damned hale for a man who'd lost a body part just days ago.

Cauterizing was a great way to stop blood loss, but it left the door wide open to infection—especially since he'd stopped eating. Evie's plant-based drugs must be helping him out, because he hadn't developed a fever, and his wrist was healing without issue.

When I'd seared his skin, the smell had reminded me of branding myself to get rid of the Lovers' mark on my chest. And then when I'd done it for Selena.

I rubbed my scar. Burning off that hateful mark had been Death's idea. Another thing I owed him for.

I told Kentarch, "You need to eat something." We still had some lion left. I'd been hoarding my share for Evie and the baby. Apparently she'd thrown up everything before this meat. She hadn't lost her stomach since.

Kentarch blinked at me, as if I'd just uttered nonsense. "Taking from our supply when I can no longer contribute?"

"Contribute?"

"I can deploy no offensive weaponry, and my teleportation power is nonfunctioning." He'd strained it so bad against Richter that he still couldn't manage so much as waver. He hadn't been able to return to Death's to check on that sphere.

Okay by me. I'd rather Kentarch not know if that alliance located his wife. Evie was safer that way.

He continued, "My father taught me that there is power in excellence.

Does the opposite not follow then? That without excellence, there is only weakness? What use will I be to Issa like this?" He held up his stump.

"Well, ole Jack Deveaux is here to teach you something too: *anything is better than nothing*. If you ate, you'd replenish your power faster. As for shooting, can't you aim with your left hand?"

He raised his chin, bitterness in his eyes. "No. Not at all."

"Then learn the hell how to." I tossed the empty gas can into the truck bed. "I taught myself to shoot with either hand in no time." I patted the trusty bow over my shoulder. First thing I'd done was restring it.

"You did?"

"*Ouais.* You can too." I saw a spark in his gaze battling that bitterness. "Look, Kentarch, your wife might be alive. She might not be. But if she is, she's goan to need whatever you can bring to the table." I clamped his shoulder. "It's mind over matter, podna."

Accent thick, he said, "I believe very much in the strength of the mind."

"*Bien.* You got work to do. We'll train every day."

He nodded, his posture straighter than before.

Evie opened the cab door then and hopped down before I could help her. She ambled over to sit on a nearby rock. Looking lost in thought, she began braiding her hair.

My fingers itched to thread through that silken length. Her sweater rode up, revealing her barely rounded belly. On her steady diet of lion, she was putting on flesh, looking as curvy as when I'd first met her.

Lust was a punch to my gut. Fantasies ran riot in my head. I shouldn't crave her this way. But God, I *did*.

Kentarch must've read my thoughts. In a lower voice, he said, "You want her that badly, and yet you'll fight to get her back into the arms of your rival?"

Inner shake. "I'll fight to get her to safety. She needs inside that castle. If that means back with him . . ."

Kentarch seemed to be considering this. "I could find myself in the same situation as you. What if Issa is carrying another man's child?"

"What would you do?" I respected Kentarch's opinions.

"Celebrate that she was alive. I hold so much love for her that it would spill over to any babe she bore. Our connection is so strong that I would become a father—just by virtue of her becoming a mother."

Is that what's happening to me?

"The longer you provide for and protect the one you love and her babe, the more you'll think of both as your own."

"That so?" Then how would I take losing them when Domīnija went back to normal and wanted them back?

"Hunter, whatever we're going to do with this mission, we need to be quick about it."

I gazed at Evie's belly. Blasting past all my reservations was that strange protectiveness—a feeling so strong it scared me. *"Ouais,"* I told Kentarch. "We got to move damned fast."

26

THE EMPRESS
DAY 556 A.F.

"I've never been on dunes this high," I told Jack as we climbed a mound of blackened sand under a lightning-streaked sky. He'd insisted on going before me, making me follow in his tracks.

"Me neither." He paused, and I caught up with him. Gazing down at me, he said, "This is just like we planned all those months ago."

"Yeah." Somehow we'd made it to the Outer Banks. *Together.* It'd been our mission, the reason we'd banded together in the beginning.

Back then I'd had no idea what Aric would come to mean to me—or how strong my feelings for Jack would become.

For the last few days, I'd felt his eyes on me constantly. I'd see him reach for me, only to lower his hand, as if he no longer had the right to touch me. Or maybe he was trying to keep his distance. To protect his heart.

But whenever he finally pulled over to sleep, I'd curl up next to him, yearning for the physical contact, the comfort of his strength.

After a hesitation, he'd always pull me close. He'd needed the contact too.

"Let's take a breather." He opened his canteen and handed it over. All we had left was water, a few rations of lion, and Kentarch's sacred bottle of Tusker beer.

I accepted the canteen, but said, "I'm fine."

"Not stopping for you." He jerked his chin at my midriff.

Jack had shown more concern for my kid than I'd managed to. His loyalty was so strong, he would even protect another man's child.

As I took a drink, I gazed down at the truck. Joules and Kentarch had stayed with the Beast. Joules laughed as he balanced a sparking javelin on his forefinger, while Kentarch practiced throwing his blade. He now holstered his pistol and knives in reach of his left hand.

We were fortunate that the Chariot was healing up well; the one place we could get help wasn't an option.

We'd started picking up a recorded radio message from the very place Hal and Stache had spoken of—*the Sick House*: "Do you or a loved one need medical assistance? At the Sick House, we can help. Our doctors are on standby to save lives. Come to us with goods to trade and get treated today!" The spokesman had sounded like a smarmy lawyer: *Have you been in an accident?*

Jack had heard on the road that the Sick House was a military base commandeered by a gang that traded drugs, medical care, and *women*.

His pensive gaze took in our surroundings. Here on the coast, the snow had dissipated. We'd gone from pristine blankets of white to the ash we all hated—like ripping off a clean bandage to reveal a festering wound. "I always thought it was my job to get you here. *Non*. My job was to get you to safety, to a place you could call home. I haven't succeeded yet."

"We'll find that place, Jack. Somehow." Would it be the castle? Everything depended on Circe.

"So this is where your *grand-mère* rode out the end of the world?"

"Yep." I surveyed the coastal town. *Apocalypse: Beach-Style!* How had she survived here for so long? The towns we'd driven through had once been filled with seashells, sun umbrellas, and beach towels—not canned goods.

"How'd Domīnija find her?"

"Like you, there's little he can't find." Both men had an innate talent for sourcing.

"He'd had her at the castle the whole time the three of us were on the road together?" I nodded. "Why didn't he play that card when you were about to make your decision between us? Seems that would've made him a shoo-in."

"He realized how much I would resent the coercion." I admitted, "He said he'd felt so strongly about me that he believed I must have felt the same." At Jack's troubled expression, I changed the subject. "I told Gran about you. She said she would've liked to see me with a bayou boy."

That muscle ticked in his jaw. "Why you tell me something like that?" he grated. "You've never been more out of my reach."

"Jack?" He looked exasperated with me, like I'd forgotten my bug-out bag or something.

"Sorry." He ran his fingers through his hair. "I told you how the future would play out, and I'm not liking my odds."

"You said you had to be convinced that Aric would return to normal and keep his rage in check. I've been replaying my escape from him, and maybe I'm not liking *his* odds." If the trust Aric and I shared had vanished like a desert mirage, I wasn't eager to trudge across scorching sand in that direction again. "And don't forget, when I accepted him as my own, I believed you were dead. It's like I explained to Joules—you and I didn't break up. We were planning a future together. Now . . ." I bit my lip.

"Now we doan have enough information to make a decision. So we live in limbo."

Which wasn't fair to Jack. "I don't know what else to do." At present, my missions were to meet up with Circe, plan a takedown, and rescue Aric.

After that? *Beats me.*

"Your kid's goan to need his father."

"I didn't have mine for long. And look how mentally well-adjusted I turned out."

"I'm serious, I know this better than anyone." Being abandoned by his father had shaped Jackson. But I'd come to realize that all his hardships before the Flash had strengthened him, preparing him for ever more challenging trials.

He and I were alive because of his hardships.

He studied my face. "What you thinking about, *ma belle?*"

"Remember how much envy there was in high school? I envied Mel because she had two parents. Grace Anne envied me because I lived in a big house. I wish I could go back and tell everyone: the more perfect your life is, the less prepared you'll be for the future. If you don't have bullshit to deal with, you're about to get hosed."

"You believe that?"

I held his gaze. "My mother once told me that diamonds were born of pressure, but I never understood what she meant until I met you."

His brows drew together, and his voice roughened. "For true?"

"Jack, your past—and how you handled it—is why we're both still breathing."

A flush tinged his broad cheekbones. Uncomfortable with the praise, he coughed into his fist, then said, "Let's get goan. Like a shadow, you." He pointed to the sand. "Doan want you to step on a surprise."

"*Bagmines,*" I muttered, and we began to climb.

When we crested the dune to take in the lightning-lit view, my heart sank. There was *nothing.* Not a drop of water. "Jack?"

"It's okay. I didn't figure the ocean had risen to its normal levels yet."

"Circe told me to go to the coast and then keep going. But I'd assumed there'd be another target to shoot for. Not this"—I waved at the horizon—"nothingness."

"Guess the question is: how much do you trust her?"

"With my life, now that I'm pregnant. But she's been unwell." Who *hadn't* been? *Hello, bottomless pit.* "Maybe she got things confused."

"One of Kentarch's maps showed a shelf of land that used to be under the sea, dozens of miles wide. It drops off into a trench. My bet? We got ourselves a new coastline."

I tried to wrap my head around that.

"The Beast has enough gas to get us to the edge of that shelf, but not back. So do we try to scare up some more fuel and food?" We'd found nothing on the way here. "Or do we take our chances out there?"

I thought of Aric, pacing his lonely castle. I pictured Finn's grin on his last night alive. I thought of how vulnerable Lark was under Paul's rule.

I might not blindly trust that Aric and I could regain what we'd lost, but I would still fight to free him. "Let's take the leap."

27

DAY 557 A.F.

"Would you look at that?" Jack murmured at our surroundings.

We'd driven miles and miles past the last of the burned-out high-rise condos into an undersea landscape that was no longer under the sea.

The going was slow, the shelf teeming with debris—anchors, traps, sunken wrecks, and even crashed planes. Enormous whale skeletons stood as big as houses. Every now and then we would pass a Bagger, emerging from the sand, scrambling to catch us.

According to Kentarch's elevation gauge, we should've been well beneath the surface. I wished Aric could witness this surreal scene with me. How would I ever describe it to him?

The fog thickened the further we descended, slowing us even more. Lightning illuminated the gray cloud deck. I rotated the spotlight, picking out wrecks through the eerie mist.

From the back, Joules said, "This place makes me bollocks shrivel."

Kentarch made a sound of agreement, his gaze alert.

Jack tapped the fuel gauge. "We just passed the point of no return."

I swallowed. "Are you sure we're going the right way?"

He pointed to the map screen. "Due east."

We continued on in anxious silence, descending another hill, chugging around a pair of whale skeletons. . . .

Suddenly a flare lit up the sky over the horizon.

"Who could've shot that?" And why? Matthew had warned me to beware of lures, like *a light in darkness.*

"It's coming from the direction of the trench." Jack rolled down his window and slowed the Beast to a stop. An engine revved somewhere in the night. Another followed, and another. He killed the headlights. "Company from the northwest." For my benefit, he added, "North of where we first hit the shelf."

The darkened mist grew brighter. Bouncing beams of light shot into the sky. "Are those headlights?"

"No way," Joules said. "There's too many of 'em."

Jack eased the Beast over a rise of sand. Stunned quiet reigned.

Finally I said, "Am I seeing what I think I'm seeing?"

Jack nodded. *"Traffic."*

Not far in the distance, dozens of trucks and dune buggies hauled ass past us on what looked like a cleared sand road. Whereas we'd spent a day inching our way around debris, they were charging across the shelf. "Why are they racing?"

"No idea, me. They're heading toward that light."

Joules slapped Jack's shoulder. "Back in Oirland, me ole mam said, 'Whenever you see a mysterious line, Patty, you best hie your arse into it.'"

"Even with what you guys are packing, that many survivors could pose a threat to Evie and *Tee.*" His new nickname for my kid, short for *p'tee garçon.* Baby boy.

"No choice but to push on," Joules said. "We're skint—out of grub and running on fumes."

What else could we do? Despite the lure, my instinct told me to head toward the light. "Jack, that must be where Circe wanted us to go." And she was our only lead to save Aric.

Jack read me so well. "So to spring Domīnija, I'm supposed to risk you and Tee? No way."

Kentarch said, "If we get into trouble, I believe I've conserved enough strength to teleport us back to the mainland."

Jack and I jerked our gazes at him.

"Eating does, in fact, fuel an Arcana's replenishment."

"Well, then, that changes things, *non*? I doan like to be last in line, me. What do you say, Kentarch? Want to see what this chariot can do?"

"Open it up, hunter."

Jack glanced at me. "I know how you like to go fast."

"Then kick her in the guts, Cajun."

He slid a grin over at me, and I spied the resemblance between him and Brandon, his dead half brother. For a moment, I was transported a million years back to before the Flash. *A sunny morning over a Louisiana road . . .*

Jack floored it, kicking up rooster-tails of sand, bouncing our way into the rush. What prize were we all chasing?

After cutting off two drivers at once, he veered aggressively toward a third, who flinched away. He swerved around a stalled-out truck nearly as big as ours, then charged straight up a narrowing slot between two vehicles. We gained on the lead car, a souped-up buggy with oversize exhaust pipes.

Jack feinted left, then gunned it to the right, maneuvering around the buggy. We'd just passed it when our headlights illuminated a hand-painted sign: *JUBILEE. All good things flow to us.*

Joules leaned forward. "What's that coming up?"

Through the fog, I spied a structure. I worked the spotlight higher and higher over a looming crush of shipping containers. In between them, sailboat masts jutted threateningly.

"It's a giant wall," Jack said. Torches lit a wide opening, with a pair of huge gates. "Guess we're heading inside."

With no idea what we'd find. As we neared the entrance, I muttered, "Please don't let this be a cannibal trap."

We zoomed through the gates. Ahead of us was a line of men, dressed in hazmat suits and aiming rifles at us.

"Jack!"

He slammed on the brakes. The vehicle skidded in the sand, stopping mere feet in front of the men. Yet they made no move, seemed more concerned with holding the line—against us. Each one wore a red armband. Designating a unit or something?

Another two dozen or so vehicles careened inside behind us as the gates began to swing closed. They slammed shut, blocking several other cars.

My anxiety ratcheted up. "This *is* some kind of trap."

Yet the other new arrivals were celebrating, yelling. "We did it!" "We're in!" "We beat the rush!"

Outside the wall, the excluded drivers honked and cursed. What would happen to them?

Everyone else began turning off their engines, so we did as well.

I squinted, trying to make out what lay beyond the cordon of guards through the drifting fog. "What do you think is back there?"

Jack rubbed his chin. "Something worth guarding. Check out those rifles. They're fitted with bayonets. Saves bullets." He gazed around, admiring the battlements. "We must be right at the trench. They built this stronghold on the edge of a drop-off, just like I built Fort Arcana."

I jumped when a PA system crackled to life. A male announcer said, "Please remain in your vehicle. Quarantine begins now."

My heart sank. "Quarantine?"

"We'll be fine." Jack said. "Any car carrying a plague victim probably would've been heading for the Sick House. Not here." He patted my knee. "This is a good sign, *peekôn*. First place I've seen with an active containment zone. Maybe life is still possible out here. We're in an actual *settlement.*"

Like the one we'd dreamed of building at Haven—at least, before the threat of snowmageddon. "How long will a quarantine last?"

"I'd guess a day or so."

"And you think it'll be safe and good inside this place?" What sort of leader would they have? A monster like the Lovers' father? Or a militia man along the lines of Cou Rouge? A freak like the Hierophant with his cannibal miners?

All I knew about Jubilee's leader? He likely wouldn't be a great one.

"*Non.* I doan necessarily think that. But what if?"

A half dozen more hazmat men passed through the line of guards, heading toward the vehicles. They carried what looked like medical gear.

I frowned at them. "Do you think they'll test for plague?"

Jack tensed in his seat. "Kentarch, nobody takes her blood, no."

The Chariot put his hand on the truck, readying to teleport. "Understood."

The men approached us, then walked right on by. I swiveled my head around to watch them stop at other vehicles, apparently at random, to take blood samples.

Joules huffed. "No one's interested in us? Careful that I don't feel slighted."

"What good would random samples do?" Kentarch wondered. "Perhaps they possess some kind of new technology."

As we waited, I tried to block out the reverberating clangs of the people outside banging on Jubilee's metal wall, their frantic calls: *"Please let us in!" "We'll starve out here!" "There must be room!"*

I asked, "What will happen to them?"

Jack shrugged. "They could be second string, in case some of us doan make the cut."

Not twenty minutes later, the PA announcer said, "Leave your vehicle and enter the settlement. Welcome to Jubilee!"

When the guards lowered their rifles and left their posts, folks scrambled out of their cars, hurrying to get inside.

Joules snorted. "So much for a quarantine."

I worried my bottom lip. "Maybe there's another staging place."

"I'll go in with Joules." Jack collected his crossbow, strapping it over his shoulder. "Kentarch, you stay here with Evie. Be ready to bug out."

"Look." I pointed out a woman with a kid among the newcomers. "They might know something we don't." I wasn't confident on that score, but I didn't want Jack going anywhere without me. "I'm coming with."

He scrubbed a hand over his mouth, clearly weighing the risks. "Fine. Hood on. Bag on your back. And try to keep your head down."

He turned to Kentarch. "You keep ahold of her at all times. If we get separated, try to get back to the cave where we met up. That'll be our BOL." Bug-out location.

The Chariot nodded.

Once I'd covered my hair and donned my bug-out bag, Jack cast me a wary look. "Let's all stay sharp in there." He engaged the Beast's security measures, and we hopped out onto the sandy shelf.

With Jack in the lead, Kentarch and me next in line, and Joules bringing up the rear, we entered Jubilee.

28

The other newcomers chattered and jostled excitedly, acting like they'd just won the lottery. As the fog shifted and the settlement came into view, I began to see why.

Lights and music greeted us inside the walls of a sprawling, sea-floor town. Along what looked like the main thoroughfare, ships sat on rusted cradles, some connected by metal rope bridges.

Shipping containers had been stacked high, with ladders clinging to the sides like climbing ivy. Laundry hung out to dry beside makeshift doors and windows. People lived in those tin cans?

At the foot of one container building was an open-air restaurant with sails for a roof. Food scents made me salivate.

Kentarch's watchful gaze swept the area. "They've got fuel here. Lots of it."

Jack nodded. "They must be working a derelict cruise ship or something. All the boats we passed on the shelf probably had supplies just for the taking."

He'd once told me that folks often forgot to roll ships in dry dock. But these Jubileans had been savvy enough to head to this desolate place and hit all these wrecked vessels. A ballsy move.

Among the hundreds of residents we saw, many were smiling as they went about their business, and they waved when they passed each other.

I even spied a few females. I nudged Jack. "Women walk freely."

"Means they got order here."

Kentarch asked, "How are they enforcing it?"

"Good question." Something was off with the residents, something I couldn't put my finger on.

Then it hit me. Aside from the hazmat guys, no one was armed. No machetes or rifles or pistol holsters. Jack and Kentarch looked overaccessorized.

When we followed the main street to what must be a central square, vendors swarmed us. "Hot rice! Fresh off the *Queen Mary!*" "Spaghetti from the *Carnival Sunshine!*" "Canned tuna! The chicken of the sea from the *Princess of the Seas.*" "MREs from the USS *Stryker.*" One merchant had nothing but peach preserves and jars of olives. Another peddled liters of liquor.

Joules spun in a circle. "I haven't seen this much grub in one place since the world went tits up."

Jack raised a brow at a half-gallon bottle of Jack Daniels. "Mercy me." Seeming to shake off his thirst, he asked a spaghetti vendor, "Who's the boss around here?"

I pictured a militia type. With a big belly, jowls, and leering eyes.

"The Ciborium rules Jubilee and all the oceans." He winked as he said, "One Ciborium in particular. You'll see."

One *what*? I raised a finger to correct this guy—*Actually, Circe rules the oceans*—but thought better of it.

The PA announcer chimed in once more: "Orientation begins now. Make your way toward the *MSY Calices* and gather in the square off the bow."

Twelve or so official-looking men, all wearing red armbands, waved us forward along the main drag, past more container buildings. The men carried rifles with those wicked looking bayonets. I suspected the hazmat guys had done a wardrobe change.

At the end of the street a gigantic yacht sat on a cradle.

Kentarch said, "It must be lined up parallel to the very edge of the trench."

Elevated platforms had been attached all around it. Ground spotlights lovingly illuminated the exterior.

The pristine vessel looked totally out of place among the other Flash-fried wrecks.

Jack narrowed his gaze. "Looks like something my father would've wanted."

Even Mr. Radcliffe couldn't have afforded a rock-star megayacht like that.

On the spacious front deck was a seashell throne worthy of the Priestess herself. Colorful pennants snapped in the breeze.

In addition to all of us new arrivals, a crowd was gathering. As we waited for the "orientation," Kentarch kept close to my side, Jack standing on my other.

The armband guys filed out onto the deck. Were they the Ciborium? Of varying ages, they flanked the throne, but none of them sat in it.

A petite brunette in a fancy silver ball gown exited from the yacht's interior, seeming to glide across the bow. She wore seahorse earrings and a seashell belt and had an unfocused, blissed-out look in her eyes. She was attractive in a soft way, like a stoned fashion model.

She gracefully took the throne. The leader of Jubilee was a she? A young she? The girl couldn't have been much older than Jack.

When cheers broke out, I peered around. Most of the men in the audience looked as if they were in love with her.

She waved a fragile hand, and everyone fell silent. "Welcome, new Jubileans," she said in a scarcely raised voice. Even the winds seemed to die down for her.

I wished Sol were here to experience the spectacle. The master of self-expression would've appreciated her themes. As would Circe.

"As many of you know, I am Lorraine Ciborium. My guards"—she indicated the armband guys—"are all Ciborium as well. Our family welcomes you to our settlement, a place of dreams. Whenever we have more bounty than we have hands to harvest, we signal to the old coast, to the faithful awaiting, and open our gates. You are the latest to receive the fortune of entry. Here there is no slavery, plague, or cannibalism. Here we salvage everything we could ever want. All good things flow to us."

The armband guys and most of the crowd repeated, "All good things flow to us."

Which sounded a little creepy. Still, I was psyched to see a woman leader. She'd *have* to be better than the ones we'd crossed swords with before.

Right?

Lorraine continued, "The Ciborium are on hand to help newcomers acclimate to life in Jubilee. Our currency is food and fuel. Aside from plenty to eat and warm fires for all, we have a restaurant to prepare feasts, tailors for new clothes, and machinists. We have religious officiants and a physician."

Jack gave me a meaningful look. "Maybe somebody to deliver Tee?"

I gazed away. How long did he think we'd be here?

Lorraine said, "Jubilee has been made possible because of creativity, ingenuity, and dreams." She seemed distant, almost detached—nothing like the charismatic leader Jack had been—but the people here seemed to revere her.

Maybe a girl leader was exactly what the world needed.

"Use your imaginations and follow your hearts," she said grandly, then added in a darker tone, "along with the *rules*. If you break the laws of Jubilee, you will walk the plank." A ground spotlight flared to life, directing our attention to the trench side of the ship.

Two sailboat masts had been soldered to the side deck, jutting out at forty-five-degree angles over the trench, a plank attached between them. Like a suspension bridge to nowhere.

A pair of armband guards with bayonets shoved a bound man toward that plank.

"Please! No!" the battered-looking prisoner begged. "I didn't do anything wrong! They set me up!"

Lorraine spoke over him: "Though all good things flow to us, this thief tried to smuggle out three cans of tuna, valuable protein, from the trench."

All around us, the crowd chanted, *"Plank! Plank! Plank!"*

She nodded to the guards. They jabbed those bayonets at their prisoner, forcing him onto the plank.

Halfway out, he yelled, "Please, no! I didn't do what they said—" The plank pivoted at its midpoint like a seesaw, dumping the man.

He screamed all the way down—what seemed like an entire minute of horror. How deep was that trench?

I gazed around at the Jubileans' satisfied expressions and whispered, "Did the theft of three cans merit death?"

Kentarch answered, "There are strict laws and swift justice. Considering the alternatives . . ."

Widespread kidnapping, rape, murder.

Lorraine stood, the breeze ruffling her dress. She seemed frail, no match for an apocalypse—or for a settlement mainly composed of men. How did she keep power?

"Obey the rules, my dear ones, and dream of bounty. My heart is with you." She turned to go, followed by more cheers.

"We love you, Lorraine!" "All good things!" "Long live the Ciborium." I heard one woman yell, *"Our queen of hearts!"*

As the crowd dispersed, Kentarch said, "Time for recon." He jerked his chin toward what looked like a raised observation deck at the edge of the trench.

Jack nodded. "Let's go."

We climbed the slippery metal steps, then eased toward the cobbled-together guardrail to peer below us.

Covering the trench wall were old nets and dangling debris. Milky-white shells clung against gravity. Oversize spotlights shone like movie premiere lights in reverse, illuminating the crevasse.

"Jaysus," Joules breathed. "Take a gander at that."

What must have been hundreds of feet down, wrecks littered the trench—tankers, cruise liners, submarines. The recovering ocean lapped among them and had reclaimed some, but ships were still visible as far as the eye could see.

Jack said, "When the Flash struck, they must've all got sucked down there, piling up."

Swells sloshed between the walls of the vessels, a giant wave machine. Winds howled in the confines of those artificial cliffs. Flecks of foam wafted upward like blowing snow.

With rhythmic banging and welding sparks, scores of men worked on the wrecks. A spiderweb of pulley systems stretched down to the ship graveyard.

Jack's gray eyes glimmered. "For true, they've got more bounty than they know what to do with."

I asked him, "How much could there possibly be?"

"One of those subs"—he indicated an enormous one balanced precariously on top—"might've been provisioned for a months-long mission under an ice cap. Lots of cans and freeze-dried packs. And we're talking three full meals a day."

Joules said, "That cruise ship over yonder would've been outfitted for thousands of Yanks to stuff themselves."

Jack pointed to the zigzagging stairway attached to the trench wall. "See those steps leading to that ocean liner? It's gotta be the gateway for the entire operation." Metal wires and ladders led from the liner to other vessels. "Connecting them for access is clever. I'd bet they even cut out sections from the hull to reach ships beneath. Must be like a maze to work." The possibility of navigating it clearly had him stoked.

I couldn't summon the same enthusiasm. "Sounds dangerous to me." I didn't see any women heading down to salvage, but I wasn't surprised. There were so few of us left; I doubted Jubilee would've allowed it.

Kentarch said, "Great risk, great reward."

When a sudden spray of welding sparks cascaded below, Jack flashed me a grin. "Sourcing in wrecks? This is my goddamned dream job. Sign me up." He loved all things inventive. Jubilee was like an altar to inventiveness. He all but vibrated with excitement.

"How cool will this be?" With his skin nearly sparking, Joules said, "Never been on a ship before! Much less a submarine."

"I like it here," Jack said. "Feels like industry. Like *possibility*."

At that moment, he and the Tower looked like teenage boys.

Kentarch remained reserved. "How long will we remain here? I need to return to the mission."

Joules flushed, as if he'd briefly forgotten about Gabriel and now felt guilty. "Me too."

I thought, *Me three*, but said nothing.

Jack cast me an appraising look. "You got a clock on your interests as well. So do we set a time limit?"

"How can we?" I wiped sea mist from my face. "It all depends on Circe."

Kentarch gestured to the trench. "As you said, this must be where the Priestess wanted you to go. And now we've arrived. Can you sense her nearby, Empress?"

Not at all. Yes, my instincts had told me to come here; were they as wonky as my sense of direction? "Um, not as of right now." In fact, the ocean felt dead. I had no special connection to the sea or its creatures, but I could sense life. This water had none—as if the ocean had gone numb.

No wonder Circe sounded increasingly exhausted. Maybe she suffered from more than the bitter cold. Maybe she suffered because there were no more mysteries of the deep.

Joules crossed his arms over his chest. "Say the Priestess finds a weapon to kill the Hanged Man. Me and Kentarch canna help Evie wield it, or we risk getting caught by the sphere." He looked at Jack. "Are you goin' to let the Empress storm the castle to fight Arcana by herself?"

"While she's pregnant and powerless? *Non*. No way in hell." Reading my expression, he said, "You show me some oaks or some big powers, and we'll talk. Until then, you need to hole up somewhere safe. If a weapon comes our way, then *I* will be heading in."

Joules turned to me. "Are you goin' to let Jack go up against four Arcana, including the three-time winner?"

Against Death? "Never."

Jack and I exchanged determined looks.

"Then what're we doing?" Joules threw up his hands. "Any weapon's useless without a hero to wield it."

"That's for Circe to figure out," I said. "Our job is to stay alive long enough to use whatever she comes up with. Look, she might figure out how to short-circuit the sphere. In which case, we can all ride in, full-force. Let's give the lady a chance. It's only been a few days." I turned to Kentarch. "While we wait, you could continue your search for Issa. I've been hearing all kinds of accents, which means people have come here from across the country. Question them. Show them her picture. Someone might have seen her. With good nutrition, you could teleport from here each night."

Kentarch tilted his head. "Very well. But once my leads are exhausted, I will be forced to move on. Issa awaits me. . . ."

29

Later that night, I lay on a lumpy pallet listening to the gusting winds that rocked our new home: the highest shipping container in a stack of them.

We'd gotten the worst accommodations because the Chariot had refused to sell his chariot, and we had nothing to barter besides weapons.

"You got a hide-a-key," Jack had said. "If we need the truck, you can just steal it back from the parking yard." They were already planning to ghost through the wall of Jubilee's arsenal and reclaim their weapons—probably the only reason Jack had given up his crossbow, with great reluctance.

Kentarch had shaken his head firmly. "I need to own it, so I can offer it as a reward for information leading me to Issa."

Jack had opened his mouth to argue, but surprisingly, he'd backed off.

Another gust hit. I squeezed my eyes shut. Would we be blown right into the trench?

Think of something else. I laid my hands on my belly, but quickly drew them away. This pregnancy was no comfort. The opposite of.

Even over the winds, I heard Joules's soft snores. Were Jack and Kentarch asleep as well? The guys had cots on the other end of the container, giving me the pallet behind a curtain on this end.

When the tin-can salesman—a Ciborium guard—had shown us this place, he'd asked the guys, "Is she with all of you?" We'd learned that four usually lived in one of these containers, a wife and husbands—plural. Because Jubilee encouraged females to marry a minimum of three.

While Jack had been momentarily stumped by the man's question and Kentarch incredulous, Joules had snorted. "Sounds right." *Dick.*

Before leaving, our salesman had advanced the guys gear for the trench—waterproof coveralls, performance boots and gloves, neon quilted parkas, and miners' helmets—against their future finds.

The Ciborium company store demanded eighty percent of everything workers salvaged.

We'd also received a few boxes of macaroni and cheese, since Lorraine insisted that all newcomers got a meal advance. This was the first time since the Flash that any stranger had offered up food—other than human flesh or the poisoned fare the Hermit had plied me with.

I'd been suspicious—was this a *feast when our stomachs cleave?*—but nothing bad had happened.

The tin can came with some cookware and a potbellied stove with enough busted-up wooden crates to start a fire for boiling water. Jack had helped me prepare the food, giving me more from his share. As usual. I'd been about to protest, but he'd glanced at my stomach and said, "Tee needs it more than I do."

Another gust rocked the container. I turned on my side, then to my other. Anxiety bubbled up inside me. Finally, I whispered, "Jack?"

The curtain drew back at once. "I'm here." He'd just been waiting there? "I'd hoped you were sleeping through this." Shirtless and barefoot, he wore only a low-slung pair of jeans and his rosary.

I held out my hand for him. He closed the curtain behind him, then lay beside me on the pallet. Even in the low firelight of the stove, I could make out the new scar on his chest. The last time I'd seen him without a shirt, he'd just taken Aric's advice to sear the Lovers' mark, obscuring it.

I reached forward to touch the scar. "This healed well."

"Put it with my collection." He sighed. "Might as well get this over with." He turned to reveal raised scars across his back.

I stifled a gasp, unable to imagine that pain. *Don't cry, don't cry.*

"What happened?" I traced one, making him shiver.

"I was a disobedient slave."

Those slavers had whipped my Jack. I balled my fists, my claws sharpening.

"They made a mess of me, *non*?" In a gruff tone, he said, "Not like you're used to with perfect Death?"

"He has scars as well. He's not perfect. Besides, do you think I give a damn about scars when you're *alive*?"

The winds howled, shifting the container stack once more. Jack faced me, noting my wary gaze. "I'm goan to get us a better place soon." In Jubilee, you didn't work your way up, but down.

"I'm grateful to have a roof over our heads and food. Thank you for getting us here."

"You deserve more." Shadows crossed his expression as he said, "When Domīnija told me how you were 'indulged' in every way at that castle, I wanted to throat-punch him—because we all knew I could never provide the life that he could. I'll never be able to spoil you like you were used to. You were raised to expect better."

"Jack, that's not me anymore. That's not anyone now," I said, though I thought Lorraine was doing pretty well for herself inside her megayacht. "Let's focus on what we've got right now."

"Not my nature, me. I need to be thinking about the long game. Need to be working toward something. At least we could kill it at salvage here."

When Lorraine had explained that they had more bounty than hands to harvest it, she'd been a *touch* disingenuous. We'd found out there'd been a Rift, what the locals called mass deaths when the pile of ships moved, trapping salvagers beneath the surface. That was why the Ciborium had sent a flare to call others to the new coast.

Jack was heading into danger tomorrow, and nothing I'd said could dissuade him.

I tried to look on the bright side of Jubilee. No one forced folks into the trench. Lorraine's armband patrol kept order. With her plank, she was a ruthlessly effective leader.

So why did my intuition tell me she was a threat? Or was that my paranoia, born from bitter experience?

Echoing my misgivings, the wind blasted over this metal box, sounding like the scream of that condemned man.

When I shuddered, Jack pulled the blanket up higher around me. "Doan be scared. I've got you."

I loved it when he said that, but . . . "I can't help it. Even if it's not the wind and this strange place, it's the future." I burrowed into the blanket. "Though I wish I was fearless, I'm not. I still get afraid."

"But you do brave things. That's what matters."

"Only when I have no other choice." Anything "brave" I'd ever done had been because the alternative was unthinkable.

Storm the Lovers' camp to save Jack from torture? Of course.

Draw down on that bottomless pit? No thank you. If uncontrollable emotion could turn a card, would that well reverse me?

"Doan matter *why* you do something. Just that you *do.*" His hand absently strayed to his rosary. It'd belonged to his mother, but he'd never revealed to me how she'd died.

"I just wish I had a better handle on what was coming my way. I'm afraid of the unknown. Of labor. Of having a kid when there's no sun. We're all on borrowed time. Why would I ever put someone else in that situation?"

"Mark my words, Evangeline, there'll be sun again one day for Tee."

I wished I could believe that. "This limbo is about to drive me crazy." Was I married? Would Aric ever be in my life again? A memory arose of him saying, *I was called Aric. It means a ruler, forever alone.* But, for a time, he hadn't been alone. He'd been happy with me. Or I'd thought he had been.

Real? Unreal?

"Maybe we doan have to be in limbo." Jack hesitated, gazing past me with his brows drawn. "I told you how things were goan to go down. But now, I got new information."

"What are you thinking?"

He faced me. "We might have another option besides the castle.

There's work here and a doctor for the baby. You're safer from Richter on the coast. Jubilee's better than the Ash, and it beats dying at the hands of other Arcana."

"*Is* Jubilee better? I didn't get the greatest feeling about Lorraine."

"I thought she was okay. She's got this place running smooth."

I quirked a brow.

"Look, if you doan like it here, then let me build up enough of a stash to last us for a few months. We get twenty percent of whatever we find. With Kentarch, we could smuggle out even more. Once we're outfitted, we'll head south. The Fool hinted that I could do some good down there." He held my gaze. "Bottom line: Death ain't your only option."

"We can't just leave him under Paul's control." I still burned to fight for him. But I didn't know if I burned to *be with* him. Could I ever move past his attack and my nightmares? "Aric once told me that you were the closest thing he's had to a friend since his father died. Would you abandon him to his fate?"

Jack's jaw muscle ticked. How did he feel about that admission?

"I thought you felt gratitude toward him for saving me."

"Exactly! You and I both know Domīnija wouldn't want you anywhere near that castle. He'd want me to keep you and Tee safe. Here with me. That arrogant bastard would beg me to keep you."

Normally, Aric would. "How can I leave him behind? I wouldn't abandon you."

"You're not hearing me—I would want you to, would pray you abandoned me."

When I remained unmoved, Jack turned on his back, staring at the ceiling. "Logic flies out the window when you're in love, *non?*"

What to say to that? Of course, I still loved Aric, but my need to save him was based on more than love. I couldn't stand the thought of him, Lark, and Gabriel vulnerable to Paul.

Jack exhaled a long breath. "I thought I was cursed because the people of my blood only love once. But you got it worse. You're cursed to love two men."

"Cursed." I could think of worse ways to describe my conflicted situation. When Aric and I had spent the night at that slave boss's house together, I'd realized that whenever I was with him, things reminded me of Jack, with the opposite true as well. Which meant I was forever screwed. If I chose one, I'd never stop thinking about the other. I'd concluded that pain awaited me, no matter what I did.

"If life with one of them isn't possible, *peekôn*, then you're goan to have to make do." Jack took my hand. "Now, that's all I'll say on the subject, me. You got to figure out your fate, take charge of it. Just like I need to take control of mine."

He'd once told me he could handle all of this apocalyptic bullshit better than he could handle life before the Flash, because at least now he had more control over his fate.

But taking charge of mine would mean cutting out the variables I couldn't affect—such as all the uncertainty surrounding Aric.

I wouldn't rush a decision, despite the emotions I felt for Jack.

Despite the hopelessness I felt over Aric.

"Tomorrow me and the guys are goan to head out early. While we're out, you can relax here."

"You want me to stay inside? By myself?" I'd go stir-crazy in this tin can. I might grudgingly accept why women didn't get to salvage, but I could do *something*.

"Not saying forever. Just till we get the lay of the land. A week or two at most." He cut off my protest: "If you're running around in the settlement, I'll be too worried about you to concentrate on the job at hand."

"On the *dangerous* job at hand." Kentarch had mentioned that the water in the trench was so cold, it'd kill in moments.

Shrug. "It is what it is."

"What about announcing ourselves as Arcana? You used to tell everyone what we are."

"That was . . . damn it, Evie, our situation has changed. The last thing I want to do is bring attention to you."

Oh. "Because I have no jaw-dropping abilities." He'd witnessed my paltry defense against the Emperor and didn't disagree. "Jack, what if I don't have *too little* power? What if I have *too much*? In our last skirmish with Richter, I detected seeds in the earth—hundreds of thousands of them. When I called on them, the ground quaked."

His eyes widened. "That was you? You actually spooked Richter! I thought he'd sensed Circe. Why didn't you attack?"

"Because I glimpsed what I'm truly capable of, and it terrified me. I can't control a force that primal. No one could." At his frown, I said, "You know my powers are fueled by emotion, but rage burns hottest." Like rocket fuel. Easy to burn but polluting. "And now I've got a huge toxic well on tap."

My tourniquet had helped me survive tragedy. But with no outlet, my wrath had just burgeoned inside me.

"You always worried about turning into the red witch and never coming back. Give me the worst-case scenario. What would happen then?"

"I don't even want to consider the possibility." I lowered my voice. "She loves to kill Arcana—like my friends. I didn't tell you this, but in some ways, my grandmother was hateful. She told me that to become the Empress I was meant to be, I needed to draw on my hatred and pain. She pressured me to kill Aric, Lark, and Circe in cold blood."

Jack winced. "But what if you doan unleash the witch and you die? Though we got lucky with Richter, the monsters are just goan to keep coming. Somehow you've got to learn to turn your power on and off."

"*On* is a problem—because *off* is a problem."

"You got a kid to think about now. If that toxic well saves your life, then you drink it, you guzzle it, you dive in. You got no choice."

I held his gaze. "I think there will come a time when I've sunk so deep that I can never resurface." Then I'd become the red witch forever. My grandmother had actually been surprised that my hair wasn't red nor my eyes green.

Uneasiness swept over me, because that future was beginning to seem . . . inevitable.

"On that recording, you said I helped you."

I nodded. "You're my reminder that I want to be good. You're my link to humanity."

"Then I can be there to pull you back to safety." He took in my anxious expression and said, "Just think about it. We'll keep talking it out, okay? In the meantime, if you're not ready to draw on that well, then you've got to stay out of sight here."

"That's a big ask."

"I know it is. I hate even the idea of it. But again, we doan have a choice." When another gust rocked the container, he looked whipped with guilt, which wouldn't do.

"Fine. I'll stay inside until you think it's safe." I'd spend the days practicing with my abilities and trying to communicate with Matthew and Circe. Maybe I'd call Aric again, just to make sure he was still safe. "You win, okay?" I put my hand on Jack's cheek.

He inhaled deeply, and his lids grew heavy. I expected him to kiss me, would welcome it, but he made no move to. Jack could still love me; didn't mean he was as attracted to me.

I was beginning to fear he didn't want me that way anymore. Which really sucked. Not that I was DTF, as Mel used to say, but I still wanted to be wanted.

He seemed to give himself a shake. "So much is goan on behind those eyes of yours. But you need to rest."

"Will you stay with me?"

"*Ouais.* I'll be here, watching over you and Tee."

"You need sleep, to be ready for tomorrow—" I tensed, my stomach suddenly feeling strange. *Flutter, flutter.* "Something's off." *Flutter, flutter.* I took his hand and put it over my belly. "Can you feel that quiver? Oh, God, they probably poisoned our dinner!"

He grinned. "Or it could be your kid moving."

"Oh. Ohh." We stared at each other. "Can you feel it?" He hadn't removed his big, warm hand. I relaxed under his comforting touch, sleepiness washing over me.

"Might be too early for me to, *non?*"

"You're asking me?" We both knew so little about this subject. Once the feeling had gone, I said, "How weird."

"Maybe Tee's telling us everything's goan to be okay."

"Maybe." I started to nod off. My last thought before sleep took me: *Jack never removed his protective hand.*

30

THE HANGED MAN
DAY 582 A.F.

I walked a fine line with Death.

As Gabe and I sat before the man's desk in his firelit study, my gaze roamed over the great Grim Reaper.

He wore no armor, and blond stubble covered his jawline. He stared out the window at the falling snow, having little interest in our game of Tarot trumps.

Gabe sorted his hand with talon-tipped fingers. "'Tis a boring life with no battle to flavor our days," he said, his speech as outdated as ever.

"Sometimes boring is good." My own hand looked promising.

Death made no remark. His cards lay facedown on the desk, ignored.

Yes, a fine line. On the one hand, I needed the Reaper to despise Evie, so I sent him reminders to stoke his animosity. On the other hand, the more he hated her, the more he hungered to go end her.

I wished I could read his thoughts. Unfortunately, my telepathy was one-way, my ability limited to hints, suggestions, *commands.*

I'd told Evie that I couldn't brainwash. Long story short: I lied. Why did everyone always assume villains told the truth? *I'm the TRAITOR, for fuck's sake.*

I could imagine what the Reaper would write in his notes about me. *Hanged Man: card reversal, absolute invulnerability, concealment,*

205

telepathy, emotion and trust manipulation. Plus, my handy sphere, a.k.a. an evil aura.

But I couldn't read minds. Luckily, I was adept at reading moods. Under his desk, Death ran his fingers along a red ribbon. From what I could gather, that ribbon reminded him of when the Empress had first taken up with Jack Deveaux.

More than three weeks had passed since Death had learned of their reunion—weeks of his roiling jealousy.

Gabe played a card: the three of swords. "How goes Fauna's search for the Empress?"

I answered, "She told me it's as if they'd disappeared." *No kidding, Lark.* I'd wanted to strike her baffled face. "Which, of course, they *did.*"

The Mistress of Fauna scoured the Ash, howling for revenge against the girl she believed had poisoned her mate. At least, Lark did so whenever she was awake.

For most hours of the day, she slept among her creatures, as if she were going into hibernation, shutting down from grief. What I'd urged her to do to Finn's body seemed to have been the breaking point for her mental health.

Gabe said, "They could be back in Kentarch's home country by now."

Death deigned to reply: "He would never return to Kenya without his wife. Besides, the game will force us to converge."

The Reaper craved that convergence. He was so strong, growing more so every day, and he *burned* to go out and punish his age-old foe. To keep him here, I was draining myself.

What a paradox. I garnered strength with each Arcana I trapped in my sphere; but keeping an unwilling one sapped me.

My sphere suffered as well, not expanding as fast as I'd hoped. But it did continue to spread in unexpected bursts. I'd almost captured Kentarch when he'd finally returned to spy on my progress.

I played the five of pentacles. "Lark also searches for Issa. The woman's scent would've been helpful, but then, there are only so many females left in the Ash."

Gabe laid down the knight of swords. "Would Kentarch turn over the Empress for her?"

Death pocketed the ribbon, taking an interest in this subject. "Easily."

Then Evie assumed a huge risk by keeping her new ally around.

Gabe frowned. "And if this exchange should occur? What would happen then? I suppose it would only be fair for Death to finish her."

I said, "I've been thinking about that eventuality." Since Evie's escape, I'd changed my mind about her future. I didn't plan on killing her; I planned on keeping her for a time. My powers would only continue to grow with another Arcana in the sphere.

I'd already broached the subject of the cilice with Death, would ask again: "Wouldn't you rather make her a prisoner, Reaper? We have the cilice; we should use it."

"The Empress recently suggested that very thing." The conflict inside him was palpable. "She probably knows how close I came to freeing her last time. You underestimate her charms."

And you underestimate my influence, Reaper. Was I conceited? Yes, but I had every reason to be. Who was more powerful? The great Grim Reaper? Or the man who controlled Death?

I let the cilice subject go—for now. "Speaking of the Empress . . ." I played her Tarot card, winning the round.

Death narrowed his eyes with hatred.

"If looks could reap." Gabe laughed. "How many times has she endeavored to murder you anyway?"

"She nearly succeeded twice. She's as vicious as she is seductive. I can never forget that again."

"Aren't we all vicious at our core?" Gabe asked. "Aren't all Arcana made to kill?" He'd certainly been enraged to miss Jack Deveaux's throat with his wing claw. While Lark had been howling over the loss of her lion, Gabe had used his growing wings to destroy his room in the castle. Splinters and black feathers everywhere.

The Archangel had once been known as enlightened and forthright, the most fair-minded of all the cards. With his reversal, he'd turned hostile, underhanded, and petty.

Depending on how our resources fared over the years, I'd eventually be forced to cull my herd. I'd start with Lark. Then him.

Richter and Zara would be drawn here soon enough, and then I'd command them and their ungodly powers. What use would I have for Fauna when I had the King of Hell in my thrall?

"Of course we were built to kill," Death said. "The gods selected us for a game with but one end. They didn't choose peaceable individuals to represent them. I believe the heat of battle we all feel is our innate need to win. But I mastered mine for centuries." He frowned, no doubt wondering why he'd lost control against the Empress.

I placed thoughts in his head: *She's taken even that from you. What more can she steal? Your honor. Your faith in others. Your hope of a line to come after you.*

Clenching his fists, he turned his unsettling gaze toward the window again, all but bristling to go hunt her down. Who needed mind-reading when I could read faces so well?

Using ever more power to keep him in line, I daubed the perspiration dotting my upper lip. This study was warm—even formal Gabe had removed his coat—but using my abilities fatigued me.

The Angel turned to me. "What about you, Hanged Man? Are you a killer at heart? Perhaps you took lives even before the game began?"

"Never." *Often.* From an early age, I'd recognized the power of treachery. To me betrayal was, I imagined, like flight was to Gabriel.

I soared.

And ending a life was the ultimate betrayal. My lips curled into an irrepressible grin. "I cared only about sacrifice and duty. I helped others," I said, picturing my first serious girlfriend, a champion athlete. I'd *helped* her get hooked on opiates, even injecting her as she slept.

By the time she realized what I'd done to her, it was too late. The once-proud girl had lost everything, reduced to selling herself for her next fix. After my first year in medical school, I'd located her, offering my assistance with rehabilitation. By showering her with condescending pity, I helped her turn another corner.

She'd OD'd that same night.

I shuddered with pleasure to recall the betrayed look in her eyes. There was a point at which resentment became poisonous to the body and mind, when bitterness became lethal.

I enabled people to find that point. With my medical background, I'd been like a virus that spread suicide and "accidental" death.

Whenever my victims had gazed up at me with realization in their glazed-over eyes, I'd told them, *Never fear me, for I mean no harm.*

"Helping others is my calling." Assuming a troubled expression, I said, "I tried to be there for Evie, but she betrayed me. And yet she walks free, with no repercussions." Actually, she was knocked up out in the Ash. A special kind of hell, I'd imagine.

Death's lean frame tensed, his gaze on the window once more.

I wanted him in my alliance, my immortal henchman. Even should I lose him, I would eventually reclaim him—I was certain of it.

These Arcana coveted my guidance. They needed it. Life was better with me. Considering how Death, Gabe, and Lark reacted within my sphere, they would hate it outside.

After the safety and order of this place, how could they not find the Ash jarring and incomprehensible? Much less without my clarity.

If the Reaper didn't go mad outright, he'd be drawn back. Once I set my hooks, I set them for life.

Still, I had no intention of simply allowing him to walk away. I'd taken precautions to keep them all here.

One night the Reaper had told me, "I will join Lark's hunt for the Empress."

"No," I'd said. "That's not a good idea."

In a flash of his old arrogant self, he'd said, "Do you really think you can contain Death, little man?"

Yes, Reaper. Yes, I do.

31

DEATH

The Hanged Man's face was clammy, the yellow light behind his head flaring. He was probably straining the limits of his abilities to keep me here.

Amusing. Did he not understand that I remained here by choice? As strategy?

The need to ride out and slay my wife clawed at me inside—I still seethed over her words: *our game is no fun if you're weak*—but I leaned on the Hanged Man. I used his power like a tool.

Some might say like a drug.

As the Archangel dealt more cards, I wondered why I had allowed them into my private sanctuary. Perhaps because I'd felt weak when I'd run a hand over this desk—where I'd taken the Empress. Or when I'd gazed at the couch where we'd often read together. Her gentle affection . . .

My gods, I missed her touch. Sex with her had been stratospheric, but her mere touch coupled with a soft look had *felled* me.

I ran my fingers along the red ribbon in my pocket, some memento from Deveaux that I'd retrieved from her drawer. *What does it mean to her?* Before I claimed the Empress's life, I would force her to tell me the significance of this crimson length.

No doubt she and the mortal had resumed their liaison. Though jealousy choked me, I pitied Deveaux. He believed the Empress was kindhearted and good.

I knew the truth.

A week ago, she'd phoned me again, informing me that they'd found a shelter out in the Ash. She'd been alone at the time of the call. She'd sounded at once healthy and *lonely*, seeming in need of someone to talk to.

"I, uh, don't get out much here," she'd admitted.

I'd bitten back the worst of my rancor to keep her on the line, attempting to discover her whereabouts. She'd been calling from some kind of echoing, enclosed area, but I'd also heard waves, wind, music, and people. A settlement on the coast?

In a casual tone, she'd told me Circe had contacted her and revealed the sex of our child. A boy.

What a brilliant ploy on the Empress's part. Though I wouldn't have cared whether I'd fathered a boy or a girl—either would have been a delight—her revelation made me imagine scenarios, such as teaching a son all that my father had taught me about being a man.

It made the lie more real.

It made the pain cut deeper.

Finally, I'd been unable to stand it any longer. . . .

"Must you carry on with this charade?"

"Charade? Oh, Aric, if only it were."

"Why do you continue to call? You're giving me clues about your location, which makes Fauna's job easier. Be on the lookout for giant predators."

"You won't tell her where I am."

"Will I not?" I asked, begrudgingly amused.

"You want to claim my icon yourself."

True, *I thought, but I said,* "Care to bet your life on that, beautiful?"

Silence for several seconds. Then: "There's no reaching you, is there? I can't goad you into coming after me. I can't make you remember what we had. And we can't take on you and all the others to mount a rescue." *Before she abruptly hung up, she said,* "I have all the information I need to make a decision."

What decision? Again and again, I'd turned those words over in my head.

The Archangel rose. "'Tis exceedingly hot in here." As he headed toward one of the windows, my gaze fell on his molting wings.

When inside, he folded them up, but his wingspan was mind-boggling. They seemed to grow with each hearty meal he enjoyed, the bullet holes healing with new feathers.

Like him, I was becoming stronger. Perhaps all the deaths across the land fueled my own transformation. Soon my power and speed would be unmatched among the Arcana.

When the Archangel opened the window, chill air entered. I drew in a cleansing breath, even as I regretted the waste of precious heat. Both he and Paul kept their rooms like saunas. When I'd said something to Paul, he'd reminded me that we no longer had to hoard our resources for a fictitious child and superfluous Arcana like the Empress.

The Archangel turned back, muttering, "Better."

No sooner had the words left his lips than a gust blew in and sent the cards on my desk flying.

I stared at the disarray, my thoughts veering in strange directions. An Arcana had allowed in the frigid cold, displacing all the cards—as if this very room were Tar Ro, an arena manipulated by a mysterious entity. Like the gods, we controlled the weather, the play of the cards. We wreaked havoc on them.

My suspicion that the earth was a tilted stage had strengthened.

With surprising insight, the Archangel said, "So too do the gods play with us. I sense their return."

"I as well," I said, recalling the tumultuous night when I'd claimed the Empress as my own. So what would that mean for Arcana?

Paul gazed from me to the Archangel. He had read enough of the chronicles to follow along.

Only one card remained on my desk. The Empress. I snatched it up, hatred and lust warring inside me. I crumpled her card and threw it into the fireplace. Flames licked the image, immolating her.

Suddenly I sensed we were being watched. Had Fauna dispatched some creature to spy on us? Doubtful; she slept all day, hay in her unkempt hair.

No, this was another Arcana. I mentally murmured, *You. I always know your unblinking gaze.*

—*Tredici. Tredici.*— a familiar voice echoed in my mind. Tredici, the Fool's name for me, meant *thirteen* in Italian. He materialized by my side. Or a projection of him did. He wore earmuffs, a thick jacket, and fingerless gloves.

From Gabe and Paul's lack of reaction, I gathered they couldn't see or hear him.

I rose to pour a vodka, giving them my back as I collected my thoughts. *What do you want?* How had the Empress ever viewed this player as anything but malevolent?

—*You must see the future too, Tredici.*—

My sight dimmed, replaced by a scene from some distance away. Salt water. Waves. Rain. Cold.

I relaxed into the vision, easing the way for the Fool's delivery. I saw the Empress. Her face was pale, her wet hair whipping in the wind.

A mob of humans with bayonets were yelling, "Plank, plank, plank!"

She gazed up at me with a stricken expression and whispered, *"Jack."*

I felt a jolt, then realized I must be experiencing this vision through Deveaux's perspective, his senses becoming mine, his thoughts known to me.

The humans were forcing him and the Empress out onto a walkway of some sort that was positioned above a vast trench.

The men wielded bayonets. Deveaux tried to evade their strikes, to ward them off, but he could only hold out for so long.

Completely immersed, I let the scene unspool in my mind.

"You can't take another stab!" Evie inched back, yanking on my hand. We were already past the midpoint.

When the plank teetered like a seesaw, I said, "Just hang on, you!

Not another step." Braving the bayonets, I leaned forward, but I waged a losing battle. The plank joggled again. *"Putain!"* We were going into the drink!

We started sliding backward, were looking up at the opposite end of the plank, about to be dumped. I clenched her hand hard.

She cried, *"Jack!"*

The plank pivoted; we plummeted—

Weightless.

Stomach lurching. Wind whipping over us. Falling, falling. FALLING . . .

COLD. We hurtled into the deep, the temperature snatching the breath from my lungs. I snatched Evie, and we struggled to the surface. We breached a wave, gasping for air.

Shock had me by the throat. Towering waves battered us, but we clung together.

My frantic gaze darted. Sheer wall. Jagged. Dark. *"Doan kn-know where to climb!"* My numb limbs were barely keeping us afloat.

Her lids grew heavier, her lips already blue. Her face was as pale as snow. *"C-Circe will come."*

When? The cold would take us in moments. I pleaded, *"You hold on! You're a t-terror in the pool, remember?"*

A swirling wave—a vortex in reverse—began to rise beneath us. My eyes widened. Seeing this right? A column of water, like a slow-moving geyser, lifted us.

"Circe?" she called weakly.

We continued to rise. *"It's her, Evie! Just hang on. Faster, Priestess! We've got to get her to land."*

Evie bit out, *"T-too c-cold, Circe. Jack c-can't take much more."*

"I can't?" I was losing her!

A watery voice sounded from the column. *"It's not your time, Evie Greene!"*

"Circe, she's fading!" I yelled. *"Ah, God, you stay with me, Evie."* Desperation strangled me. I burned to fight. To save her. I needed to give my life for hers.

Couldn't do a goddamned thing.

Circe's column wavered, her voice garbled. "I can't hold this! The ocean demands its due. It always wins!"

"Then fight back, Priestess!" But we were out of time. Knew it, me.

Circe screamed, her control lost. Her waves began annihilating the side of the trench, devouring it.

We're done for.

Evie's heavy-lidded gaze grew vacant. "L-love you, Jack. So much . . ." Her head lolled, body gone limp.

Agony ripped through me. "No, Evie! NOOOOOOO!" I clutched her shoulders and shook her in the water. "You come back to me, bébé, PLEASE!" When my eyes met her sightless ones, comprehension took hold: She's gone. My Evie's dead.

A roar burst from my chest as my mind turned over.

When her body started to sink, I kissed her lips. "It'll always be Evie and Jack."

Then I joined her in the deep.

I cracked open my eyes, emerging from the vision. The Fool's projection stood to the right of me.

I mentally demanded, *What was that?* Deveaux's pain was worse than even I had felt over her demise in previous games—because I'd never loved her in the past. Not like I loved her now. Or *had* loved.

I pinched the bridge of my nose. *Has it . . . occurred?* Was the Empress lifeless even now? Had mere humans been her downfall?

—*Not yet. Soon.*—

I swallowed. Her death was about to be stolen from me. Would Circe harvest her icon? Unacceptable.

You gave me her location. From the Fool's vision, I knew where to find the Empress—she was in a settlement at the edge of a trench, due east of where I'd located her grandmother. *Why let me see that? Because she can mesmerize me if I leave the sphere?*

He blinked, as if waiting for me to get up to speed with him. —*Can she?*—

I regarded my drink. Shouldn't she have been able to sway the mortals who'd doomed her and Deveaux? Her powers must still be muted, would be no match for the scalding animosity I'd stoked every day.

She'd once recounted to me her brutal attack against Ogen, Fauna, and myself. She'd said she'd felt like a marionette with hatred pulling the strings. I felt the same now.

Hatred would inoculate me against her floundering abilities as much as Paul did.

Blood began to run from the Fool's nose, his eyes vacant. —*Tredici, know this: the only way you'll win this game is to claim her icon yourself.*—

Otherwise, I would lose? Had I actually once decided to bow out of this Arcana game? To choke on defeat? Yes, because of *her* influence!

If I lost, I would reincarnate with no knowledge of her evil. Ignorant and vulnerable, I would fall for her machinations yet again.

—*Last chance. She will die in the deep. Her torn heart will stop.*—

When will this occur? How long did I have? Urgency lashed at me.

—*How badly do you want her?*— With that, he disappeared.

No longer did I have a choice but to leave. Making my expression blank, I turned to my allies. In a casual tone, I asked them, "Care for a vodka?"

Should they catch wind of my plans, they would try to stop me. Already Paul had disabled the vehicles. I recalled being outraged, until he'd explained that Fauna or the Archangel might be tempted to sneak away, weakening the sphere, and therefore our entire alliance.

Within the hour, I would steal out on a pale horse—as Death had done so many times over the last two thousand years.

Once I'd collected the Empress's icon, I would return to my castle and settle into my new alliance.

Though I would be traveling beyond Paul's sphere of clarity, his powers against the Empress might hold. If not . . .

Hatred pulls the strings.

32

THE EMPRESS

"Hi, honey, your husbands are home," Joules called, as the three walked into our new digs.

I glared at him from the stove. "That never gets old, Tower. Truly."

For weeks, he'd made that crack whenever they returned from their shifts. For just as long, I'd bitten back retorts, feeling like one of Richter's volcanoes set to blow.

Yet now things were finally going to change. . . .

My roomies always looked exhausted after spending sixteen hours at a time in the trench. Sometimes Joules fell asleep at the table. Kentarch's outline would waver, his powers sapped from getting them out of whatever wormhole they'd crawled into that day. But tonight, the guys seemed even more fatigued than usual.

Jack crossed to me, leaning in to give me a quick kiss. "Missed this pretty face."

I mustered a smile. His lingering looks and stray comments had finally convinced me that he was still attracted to me.

He wanted me; I wanted him. But we had a ghost between us.

Though he and I shared that pallet, we never touched as we both needed. The tension between us filled this tin can.

As we'd lain together, we'd talked for hours. One night, wondering if he'd ever make a move, I'd teased him.

"Aren't you strung tight? Remember telling me that out on the road?" Imitating his voice, I said, *"I been strung tight for days, bébé."*

He exhaled. *"I've done some growing up since then. You called me selfish, and I was. I would've done anything to sleep with you and make you mine."*

"And now?"

He tucked my hair behind my ear. *"Now I'd give anything for you and Tee to be happy and safe."*

I gazed at him, taking in his proud, tired face, smudged with engine grease, and I sighed. Since I'd first met Jack, he'd not only become a man; he'd become a great one.

After pulling off helmets, coats, and gloves, the three sat at our rickety dining table. I'd served them pasta with a sauce of canned tomatoes. I'd grown fresh ones from the seeds, then chopped them up for garnish.

What had taken me hours to prepare would take them seconds to polish off. We'd all regained weight since our arrival.

"Were you safe down there?" I asked, sitting with them.

Jack and Kentarch had grown even closer, depending on each other in that lethal maze. Even prickly Joules had been bonding with non-Gabriel males.

Jack said, "Always." As predicted, they were killing it at salvage. Despite the danger, he relished the work, considered it one new puzzle after another, and the man loved puzzles.

Already he'd moved us from the worst tin can to the best double one on the ground floor, closer to Jubilee's amenities—which I could never use. He still didn't want me to explore the settlement without him.

I passed my days doing domestic chores, which I sucked at. I did the dishes. In a bucket. I did the laundry. In the same bucket.

And when I wasn't trying to hail Circe and Matthew for help—they never answered—

I spent hours wondering why Aric hadn't loved me enough to break free of Paul.

Every second convinced me: *He isn't coming for you, Evie.* Our last phone call had cemented that realization in my mind.

Between bites of tomato, Jack said, "We went to the BOL today." Bug-out location. They'd been using the Chariot's teleportation to smuggle supplies back to that cave. "It's filling up all right. And we've topped off the Beast's tank too."

Not so easy a feat. All vehicles that hadn't been cannibalized for Ciborium parts were parked in a guarded lot.

As much as Jack liked it here, he still believed in preparing to bug out. The Beast was a bug-out machine.

"'All right'?" Joules snorted. "Jackie boy's got a nose for finding *booty.*" Side-eye at me. "Never seen anything like it. Everybody's talking about the Cajun ace."

Kentarch raised a brow. "His sourcing sense is unparalleled. He's sounded the horn more than anyone."

Whenever a salvager found more than his crew could offload, he'd invite everyone to come take a share. That all-hands-on-deck horn reminded me of the cannibal miners' shift-change signal.

Jack grinned. "I sound it so folks doan suspect we're a bunch of selfish smugglers. Plus, it keeps all the prying eyes in one spot while we go plunder even more."

A total Finn ploy. *Don't look at this hand . . .* God, I missed the Magician. Every day that I sat in here, I had too much time to think about all we'd lost. I wasn't ready to lose more.

"We're closing in on a medical frigate," Jack said. "I got a good feeling about it. Medicine's like gold now."

"Enough about our exciting careers." Joules smirked at me. "What'd *you* get into today? My dirty socks?"

"Yeah. I used them to dry your plate."

His smirk faded.

"Plank! Plank! Plank!" echoed throughout Jubilee. Again? This was the fourth execution since we'd gotten here.

I stiffened in my seat when the victim screamed that he'd been set up. They always said that. *Where there's smoke . . . ?*

The guys kept eating, not even reacting—though they'd been breaking the law routinely.

Joules shoved pasta into his piehole. "Lorraine came by our shift today. Gave us another pep talk." Had he sounded braggy?

If I heard another word about saintly Lorraine . . . My roomies were half infatuated with the ethereal woman. Whenever she spoke to the troops, they'd fanboy for hours.

Apparently she'd been studying to be a psychologist pre-Flash, planning to help the world one case at a time. Now she considered herself a "protectress of the earth."

Evie called, wants her shtick back.

My short-lived excitement over a female leader had waned even more. Yes, I was suspicious of shrinks after my stint in a mental ward—but it was more than that. My current helplessness made it impossible not to envy her power. To resent it.

I was becoming a wreck here—just like the ships all around us. Why were my talents wasted?

Inside this tin can, I relived what it'd felt like to be *aflame* with power. The Empress didn't get collared or contained.

Except for when living in a container? "I'll bet Lorraine pep-talked you. She needs all of you down there, risking your lives." Though the Ciborium refused to share in those risks, they got eighty percent of the salvage! "You're like mice nibbling at cheese in a trap. Sooner or later, you will get caught. You will die. Her house always wins, and she knows it."

Joules's face turned red as he blustered: "She's got a dream of rebuilding society! No one is forcing us down there."

"Something isn't right about her and the Ciborium." Lorraine and her crew might not be cannibals or mad scientists, but greed was a form of evil too. In my mind, that made them my enemies. "We need to be on our guard."

"Stop being an eejit. You're up the duff and barmy to boot, and you're never around her. Why should we listen to you?"

I slitted my eyes. "One day, Joules. One day . . ."

"Hey, now, you two." Jack pushed away his half-eaten plate. "I thought we were managing here. We got a plan. Let's stick to it." Since he'd returned from the dead, his patience seemed to have no end. But his reasonable tone was driving me up the metal walls.

When would he demonstrate frustration? When would he make demands about our relationship? Instead, he'd kept us fed and gotten us a better place. Whenever I had nightmares about my escape from the castle, he would stroke my hair. He'd diligently sourced for baby things.

He slept with his hand over my growing belly, confident he'd feel Tee kicking soon and scared to miss it.

Jack might be controlling his emotions, but mine were about to spill over. I'd figured that if I could keep from screaming when my mom had been dying, I could handle myself in any situation—even this tin-can solitary. But no longer... "Down on this level, I can hear people talking." Today I'd heard a woman's sobs.

After deliberating, I'd pulled a hoodie over my hair and headed out to investigate. I'd gotten attention from male Jubileans, but nothing too bad. No one had nabbed me or anything.

I'd found a crying woman in a black veil and worn snow gear.

"What's happened?" I gently asked.

She sniffled. "My wedding day. To three strange men."

Finally! Proof that Jubilee wasn't utopia. "Is the Ciborium forcing you to marry?"

"Forcing?" The woman scoffed. "I'm a widow with a kid. I lost three husbands in the last Rift."

Now I stared down Joules, Kentarch, and Jack. "Today, gentlemen, I found out how *often* Rifts occur."

Cursing under his breath, Jack shared a look with the others.

"Every twenty-one days on average." *Tick-tock.* Approximately every three weeks, Jubilee suffered mass casualties, and called in an order for more workers to replace them. With one flare, people raced here to die. "Aren't we overdue?"

Joules sputtered. "What do you expect us to do? Not work? I bloody like eating. I don't want to go back to the lean times."

Though my own recent starvation weighed on me, I said, "At the very least, don't take double shifts. Limit the amount of time you're in the trench."

"We're safer than others," Jack assured me. "We got Kentarch to help us out in a pinch."

"Excellent," I said. "He can teleport your body back to me."

"Evie, just be rational about this. After filling up the BOL cave, we're tapped out. You and Tee gotta eat. Which means we work doubles."

Jack continued to show such concern about the kid's future. He'd met with Jubilee's physician to get a sense of the man and came away unimpressed: *The doc likes to be paid in liquor and had vomit on his coat.* So Jack had tracked down a former midwife. He liked her better but wasn't sure if he trusted her to examine me yet: *Maybe this week. We can't be too careful.*

After Paul, neither of us were too eager for me to see a medical professional.

In the meantime, Jack had peppered the woman with questions. He'd learned how bad stress was for a pregnancy and what kind of food to be sourcing for. Based on information I'd given him, the woman had estimated my due date to be around Day 730 A.F., or Year Two.

My own birthday.

She'd provided Jack with a list of supplies we'd need by then, and he'd already unearthed half the items, stockpiling them at the cave—everything from diapers to baby food to a teething ring.

He'd even put together a tiny bug-out bag to go with ours.

One of my mom's favorite sayings had been *The difference between involvement and commitment is like ham and eggs. The chicken is involved; the pig is committed.*

Jack was ready to go all-in.

But if we were going to make this work, I needed to pull my weight. "I'm getting a job," I announced to the table. "The restaurant's got an opening. When I start pulling in salvage gratuities, you can limit your exposure."

Jack leaned back in his chair. "Not happening."

I raised my brows. "I don't remember there being a question mark at the end of my statement, Jackson."

"The men here are dangerous," he said. "We didn't want you to worry, but it's not safe enough for you to walk around, much less mingle. And who knows what they'll do if they see a pregnant woman?"

If I untucked my shirt, I didn't look pregnant yet. "I was out for several hours today."

Jack's expression said, *Dafuq?*

"No one messed with me. Besides, if anyone tried to hurt me, then your adored Lorraine would make him walk the plank."

Jack said, "The plank comes after somebody hurts you. You might regenerate, but will Tee?"

I turned to Kentarch. "If I work, you could search more."

He'd shown around Issa's picture, garnering some new leads. With each one, he would teleport away, often taking Joules with him.

Whenever the Chariot was here, he would pace well into the night. If he did sleep, he would call his wife's name.

I told him, "I could monitor all the gossip, maybe even gather more leads." And information on Lorraine. Damn it, something wasn't right about her. Nobody could be that perfect after the Flash.

Kentarch put down his fork. "Now is as good a time as any to talk about the future. The Empress is right—I'm spending more time searching for food than for my wife." In his quietly intense way, he said, "Everyone at this table has known loss. But I might be able to reverse mine, just as the Empress did with Jack. I don't want to be disloyal or selfish, but you three must understand my situation." He asked Joules, "What would you do to reunite with Calanthe?"

"Bloody anything. No offense, but if frying you blighters could bring her back, you'd be fricassee."

In a dry tone, Kentarch said, "We each have our personal boundaries, no?" He turned to me. "In any case, how much longer can we wait for Circe? I haven't wanted to add to your worries"—quick glance at Jack—"but we can't continue like this indefinitely."

As much as they tried to limit the pregnant chick's stress, I still felt tons of it. "Circe's reading every wall in her temple, all the fine print. That's got to take time." I told myself that over and over, but lately I'd begun to suspect she would never show, that her coffin of ice had closed over her forever.

Shouldn't I start considering the possibility that we might be stuck here? I gazed at Jack. Should he have to live with a ghost between us?

Expression grave, Kentarch said, "How long, Empress?"

"What are our options? Take away the fact that you need Lark's abilities, and I need to free Aric—we all need the resources at the castle."

Kentarch drummed his five fingers on the table, clearly wanting to say more. Yet then he abruptly rose and took his plate to the dish bucket. Letting the subject drop, he said, "I have a lead I want to check out, but it will take some time, perhaps till morning. I will also stop by the castle."

The Hanged Man's influence continued to spread, like the plague. But Kentarch could find no discernible pattern of growth. Some nights Paul would gain an inch, other times a mile.

"I'll come with." Joules hopped up, leaving his plate on the table. *Dick.*

With a nod, Kentarch clasped Joules's shoulder, and they disappeared.

Jack exhaled a breath. "We're on borrowed time with the Chariot. As soon as he runs out of leads, he's goan to head out."

"We can't lose him." Another worry to put on the list.

"I understand where he's coming from. When Matthew got me out of that mine, I would've done anything to see your face. 'Bout went crazy, me."

I rose to put another piece of wood on the fire. Over my shoulder, I asked, "Then how could you decide to leave me behind forever?"

He crossed to stand behind me. "I was trying to protect you from a breakdown." He turned me to face him. "Never doubt that I longed for a life with you."

"And now? More than a month has passed since I found you, Jack.

A month A.F. might as well be a year. We've been in limbo this entire time. You're okay with that?"

"Hell no, I'm not okay. You know I want you for my own." Lowering his voice, he rasped, *"Corps et âme."* Body and soul. That combustible heat between us simmered. "But at the end of the world, the last thing you need is more pressure."

"Maybe I *want* you to put pressure on me. If you believe Jubilee is such a great place—"

"I believe it's a . . . place. It's got possibility. You'll have the midwife to help you with labor. You have food you can keep down. A warm place to sleep." Jack ran his fingers through his hair. "What more do you want from me?"

"Limit your time salvaging." Today when I'd explored Jubilee, I'd headed up to what the weeping bride had called the widow's walk—the observation platform we'd first climbed to view the trench.

I'd stared down into that angry depth, sea foam gathering around my feet. Against the strength of those waves, the Jubileans' network of welded passages and scaffolding had looked like gossamer. A spiderweb quaking before a hurricane.

Would *I* be the widow with the baby, marrying three strangers?

"I can't do that," Jack said. "Having provisions stockpiled could be the difference for us. For Tee."

"Why are you working so hard to provide for us? When you have no idea what will happen between you and me?"

He seemed confounded by my question. "Because that's what I do."

"Circe might never appear again. I need to start accepting that. She wasn't doing well before, and it's only getting colder out there." My eyes began to water. "Convince me to let Aric go."

"You could no more give up on him than you gave up on me. The second you figure out a way to reach him, you'll be saddling up to go."

"Why won't you yell at me? Get mad? Stop being so freaking patient and *fight* for me!" I knew I wasn't being fair, but I was frantic for resolution in at least one area of my life. "Tell me I'm staying with you no matter what happens in the Arcana world."

"And what about the Reaper's son?"

"You said if we couldn't save Aric, then you and I would raise this kid together. Could you love Tee?"

"Your kid?" Jack leaned in and put his forehead against mine. *"Ouais."*

"Then tell me you'll raise him as your own son. Demand to."

"I'm trying to do right by you, Evie. You think this is easy for me?" He drew back, something like panic in his eyes. "I'm scared to hope. Scared to get too attached. I know how this song ends."

The Jubilee all-hands-on-deck horn blared over his words, signaling *LOOT!* More than that shift could carry.

Jack muttered a curse. "I bet they breached our goddamned frigate." He strode over to his gear. "I got to get down there, me, or all the meds'll be picked over."

Wait, what? "You can't go without Kentarch."

With a resigned shrug, he said, "Got to learn to navigate those ships without him." He dragged on his coat and grabbed his helmet. "I give him a couple of days tops." He turned toward the door.

I rushed forward, grabbing his arm. "Don't you dare leave!"

"You just got through telling me you want me to step up and demand to raise Tee as my own. Then you tell me *not* to go out and provide for him? You can't have it both ways. You stay put, you hear me?"

"No." I jutted my chin. "I won't. If you leave, then I will too."

"I'll be so worried about you, I woan be able to focus. You want my concentration divided?"

He knew how much I feared losing him again, and he was using that fear to manipulate me! "Of course not, but—"

"Then *stay put.*" He slammed the door behind him.

"Ugh!" I hadn't felt this helpless since the days right after the Flash when I would primal-scream in my barn.

If he could risk himself in the trench, then I could risk grabby hands and drunken apocalypse survivors in a freaking eatery. Either we trusted saintly Lorraine's laws—or we didn't.

I went to the makeshift sink and washed, then laid out my best outfit: new jeans and a red sweater that Jack had found for me. I had to lie on the bed to zip the fly over my rounding belly.

Suddenly the ground seemed to totter. Metal screeched in the trench, and explosions sounded.

A sob escaped my lips. *"Jack."*

33

DEATH

Just inside the sphere

I gazed over my shoulder at the castle in the distance, then forced my attention back to the road. The edge of the sphere loomed not even half a mile away.

No time for doubt, Domīnija.

Thanatos whickered impatiently, as if reminding me of the stakes: the loss of the entire game. And just as importantly, the loss of revenge.

I would find my wife before she died, in time to collect her head myself, and then I would proudly wear her icon for the next several centuries.

As I always did.

How badly do I want her, Fool? Very badly indeed.

I dropped the visor on my helmet, urging Thanatos into a gallop. His breaths smoked, his hooves crunching the snow.

As we picked up speed, I leaned forward in the saddle, our movements unconscious after all these years together. I'd missed this rhythm, had missed the chill air stealing through my helmet.

We approached the yellow boundary. Nearing... I tensed as we crossed.

Freed.

I took a mental inventory, then exhaled with relief because I felt no different. My hatred of the Empress still seethed. I laughed and ran my gauntlet along Thanatos's neck.

My laughter faded as a hollow feeling grew in the pit of my stomach. Clear of the Hanged Man's influence, my memories began to take shape differently in my mind. I shook my head hard, fighting vertigo.

As emotions shifted, righting themselves, bile rose in my throat. Paul had . . . *reversed* me.

He'd buried anything good in me—as if in a grave.

I spurred Thanatos into a breakneck pace. What had I done to my wife and child? Images of her escape flashed through my mind.

I gnashed my teeth, my insides flayed. *Dear gods, what have I done?*

34

THE EMPRESS

On the widow's walk, I stared down at the mindboggling scene. *"Jack!"* I shrieked, not expecting an answer.

Ships sloshed about, toys in a giant bathtub. The ocean liner had tipped over, its bow underwater and sinking fast. Enormous propellers crept round and round.

Much of the metal framework had crashed down.

Rain-soaked Jubileans gathered on this platform, murmurs carrying through the crowd. *"They're gone. They're just gone." "The Rift took out the entry ship." "Anybody trapped in there is dead."*

All the workers had made it into the first ship and beyond, but then their sole way out had been turned upside down.

Like a reversed tableau.

One by one, Jubileans staggered off the platform, shaking their heads. No citizens mounted a rescue brigade—the crowds that were so quick to call for executions had fallen quiet—because nothing was left to be done.

From my chronicles, I knew that a past Empress had been able to see through her vines. Could I use them to locate Jack amidst that colossal snarl of wreckage? If so, how could I bring him back to the surface?

At my wits' end, I screamed for Circe. No answer as usual. My claws dug into my palms as I fought the urge to pull out my hair.

What can I do? Jack, I can't lose you again!

Mind racing, I scanned the surface. What could I do—?

I spied something out of the corner of my eye. A faint light flickered just above the waterline. I squinted against the foam and stinging rain. A helmet light?

My breath left me. *"Jack!"* He clung to a remnant of scaffolding.

An enormous wave rumbled along the trench, barreling down on him. If I didn't get him out of its path, he'd be washed away forever.

I was transported right back to that night when I thought I saw him burned alive.

Can't lose him again! Glyphs blazing, I slashed my claws over my forearm, bleeding vines. Uncaring that I might be seen, I commanded my soldiers to charge down the face of the trench. They spread like lightning bolts, forking out.

When they reached him, I perceived the vibration of his relieved yell. Coiling around him, my vines began returning him to me.

I sensed him bellow, "Go, Evie, faster!"

That wave raced toward him. In its grip was more lethal wreckage. He'd be crushed, drowned.

"No, no, no!" I clenched my fists. My vines responded in fits and jerks. *Going to be so close.* Why couldn't I control my soldiers? They sputtered—even as that foaming wave crested. . . .

Panic drummed in my chest. Nothing mattered beyond this!

With a scream, I raised my bloody hands. "Obey me, soldiers, or pay!" They shot higher, as if in fear.

The wave roared by just below Jack's feet!

I sagged against the railing, murmuring, "Bring him to me. . . ." Soon he was close enough for us to exchange a look.

His face was pale, but his eyes were intent on me. So incredibly brave.

Even over the tumult, I heard a gasp. I whipped my head around. The widow I'd met earlier stared at me, her eyes wide.

I said, "You can't tell anyone about this." A glance from her to Jack. He was only fifteen or so feet away. Almost to the railing.

Mouth ajar, she backed away, then sped down the platform steps. *Shit!*

I couldn't worry about her right now. Jack was still in danger. Getting him topside was only the first step. I had to get him warm. *Closer to me, closer . . .*

Here. He hauled himself over the railing. Somehow I forced myself to release him from my protective vines.

"*Peekôn?*" He yanked me against his chest, his strong arms locking around me.

Against his coat, I cried, "You almost died!"

"You saved me." He pressed a kiss atop my head, then drew back. "Come on, I'm taking you home. You got to be freezing out here with no jacket."

"Me?" I felt nothing but adrenaline and the tingle of regeneration across my clawed arm. "What happened?" Though the horse might be out of the barn concerning my abilities, I commanded my vines to drop off into the deep. Sacrificed soldiers.

Jack helped me down the stairs. "I was on the scaffold, about to step onto the ship. I watched it break off right before my eyes. The steps above me collapsed."

As we hurried through the town, people milled around in shock, like Baggers without prey.

"Christ." Jack yanked off his helmet. "They're all gone. An entire shift of workers. Dead." Was he reliving the devastation of his army?

One thought was on repeat: *Almost lost him again.*

Almost lost him.

Almost lost him.

To keep from screaming, I bit my lip till it nearly bled. Finally home was in sight.

As soon as our tin can's door closed behind us, I turned on him. "I told you not to go!" I burst into tears as I beat on his chest. "You'll never go down in that cursed place again! Do you hear me, Jack? *Never.*"

"Stop it." He grabbed my wrists. "*Calme-toi!* You got to keep yourself calm."

Tears fell unchecked. "Screw calm! Do you understand what that was like? To see you clinging ... and that wave coming. And if you knew what I went through last time ..." *Twist, tighten, constrict.* "When I thought you died, I imagined a tourniquet around my heart because it was *bleeding out!*"

"Evie, *non.* I'm here." He cupped my face, using his thumbs to brush away my tears. "Not goan anywhere."

He *was* here. But in this world, how long could we possibly have together? "Jack, I love you. I can't ever lose you again." Adrenaline and fear morphed into heat. *Desire.* I turned my head to nuzzle one of his palms, kissing the callused skin.

He sucked in a breath, and his big body tensed against mine. Combustion ignited.

When I faced him, his attention dropped to my lips, so I wetted them. His eyes met mine, his smoldering expression asking, *Do you want this?*

Mine answered: *Try to deny me.*

He bent down; I'd already gone to my toes. When our lips met, logic evaporated like a water drop on a sizzling skillet. I tasted cold and salt on his lips. *Almost lost him.* I deepened the kiss, tugging on his neck as he yanked off his heavy coat.

The tension that had been building between us erupted. I drank in his raw passion, unable to get enough. Between kisses, he tore off his soaked shirt as I snatched at his belt. His strong chest heaved breaths.

Tumbling to the pallet. More kissing. Tongues twirling. *My God, he's a sinful kisser.*

As he helped me shed my wet clothes, he murmured in French how much he'd loved and missed me, how much he'd lusted for me. "Now you're in my arms. I've imagined this so many times."

The winds gusted, reminding me of when I'd first been with Aric. As soon as the thought arose, I felt myself shutting down, my hands settling on Jack's muscled chest.

He sensed the change, drawing back.

My guilty gaze flitted to my wedding ring. *Aric's not coming for*

you; you can't go to him. Circe's MIA. Make a life with Jack, the man
who deserves all the happiness you can give him.

I'd almost lost him tonight.

All I had to do was accept him and revel in the fact that he'd
survived.

He grasped my hand. "Let's take this off." He gently drew the ring
from my finger, like a reverse engagement.

A nullification.

But I let him. He set it beside the pallet.

"Be with me," he said, his accent thickening. "*Stay* with me." He
nipped my bottom lip, as exciting and sexy as he'd ever been. "Let's
stop regretting and start living."

With a breathless nod, I allowed myself to fall under his spell. I gave
myself up to it, to him.

His brows drew together. "If I'm goan to love once, I'm glad it's
you, *peekôn.*"

In answer, I pressed my lips to the cleft in his rugged chin. I
feathered kisses along his jaw, then down his neck. I felt his groan
beneath my lips. Then I kissed the brand on his chest. It was part of our
history, the one we kept making together.

Once we were naked, his heated gaze roamed over me. My body
was changing. What would he think of my new shape?

"*Mère de Dieu.* You're so goddamned beautiful." I'd never felt
more naked, more vulnerable, but he sounded . . . awed. "A *divinité.*"

My glyphs glowed brighter, the light reflecting in his gray eyes.

His head dipped, his mouth trailing down my body, seemingly
everywhere. My eyes widened as he explored me with his wicked lips
and seeking tongue. Between kisses, he'd nip my inner thighs.

I melted for him, my fingers tunneling into his thick hair. "Jack . . .
Jack!"

As his rough hands kneaded and cupped, he groaned his delight.
He teased me till I was at the very edge, till I was panting and writhing
for more. Then he rose up between my legs, threading his fingers with
mine.

He gazed down at my face—as he had when he'd taken my virginity in that suspended moment of time. "I've got you, *bébé*." He'd often told me that, his way of saying *don't be afraid; you're safe.* Now those words held an aggressive undertone. As if he was telling me, "I'm never letting you go. Never."

That tone thrilled me.

His rigid muscles quaked with anticipation. "*À moi,* Evangeline." His hips tilted.

My back arched with pleasure. His sinful kiss stole my screams.

35

DAY 583 A.F.

By what must have been morning, Jack and I lay side by side, catching our breath as the room stopped spinning. We'd had sex four times over the night.

In a dazed tone, I murmured, "It *is* like coming home."

He grinned over at me. "That's what I've been saying. When it's good between us, it's *really* good."

Good? He'd set my nerves on fire.

When we'd slept together months ago, everything had been new for me, our feelings just taking root. This time we'd been different as people, two individuals deeply in love—who'd thought we would never have another chance to express it.

Rising up on an elbow, he peered down at my face, searching my expression. "How're you feeling? Got to know, me."

"I have no regrets, if that's what you're asking." But now reality descended on me with all the finesse of a collapsed ocean liner.

"And guilt?"

I looked away. "Some." *Tons.*

He pinched my chin, forcing me to face him. "None of that, Evie. We got no time for it."

Though I agreed ... "I can't help it." Aric was the ghost between Jack and me. Just as Jack had been the ghost between me and Aric.

Forever screwed, Eves.

Making his tone light, he said, "As long as we're talking about the elephant in the room . . . You've been with two beaux, and one of 'em is a supernatural knight."

I saw where this was going, but a comparison between the two was futile. What I'd shared with each man was different—yet perfect in its own way.

And perfect for me couldn't be bested.

"How'd ole Jack compare?" He was partly teasing, but kind of serious too.

His rare show of insecurity made me want to wrap him in my arms and never let go. "You were amazing, and you know it, you cocky Cajun." I found myself grinning, before I shut down.

"No, doan you dwell. Enjoy this peace with me." In a gruff voice, he said, "Being with you is the only thing that makes me feel this way, but it's no good if you doan feel it too."

"I did. Earlier. Now I'm just confused." I *didn't* regret having sex with him, and surely that made me a bad person. An unfaithful wife. "Jack, I promised Aric forever."

He sat up on the pallet, his scars filling me with equal parts sadness and tenderness. "You made that promise to him when you thought I was dead. And you promised *me* always, long before he was ever in the running."

"I know, I know." At least in this life.

His broad shoulders rose and fell on a breath. "I'm about to feel a heap of guilt myself."

"Why?"

"For taking advantage of you. The only reason last night happened is because I almost went into the drink. You would've gone your whole life faithful to him, but you relived when you lost me last."

That was true. Still . . . "Maybe *I* took advantage of *you*. You were freaked out because you almost died. Didn't you believe you were done?"

He admitted, *"Ouais."*

"Don't forget I'm supposed to be this minxy seductress/mesmerizer. A mere mortal like you stood no chance."

His lips curled. "So what do we do now, *séductrice*?"

Despite Jack's efforts, I couldn't relax. I sighed. "After nearly two months, I need to accept that Aric's not coming for me. And saving him from Paul seems even more impossible when we can barely keep ourselves alive." My eyes went wide. "What if that woman from the platform tells others what she saw?"

"We can't stay here anyway. That first liner has never gone down before. The infrastructure's toast."

"What will we do?"

"When our podnas get back, we'll teleport the truck to the cave to load up. If we can talk Kentarch into searching a new area, the four of us'll head south to the Gulf. There might be a similar situation with ships off the old coast of Louisiana."

"What's taking the guys so long? They've never been gone a whole night before. What if Paul's sphere caught Kentarch?" Another Arcana trapped?

"You're not supposed to be borrowing trouble, supposed to be relaxing for the kid."

"Is that possible A.F.?" No sooner had I made the comment than Jack stilled, cocking his head.

"We got company." We both leapt up, snatching on jeans, dressing in a hurry.

"Is it the guys?"

"Uh-uh." He stomped into his boots.

As I reached for my own, I caught sight of my former wedding ring lying on the floor. With a pang, I pocketed it.

Someone banged on the door. "Open up! It's the Ciborium."

I hissed, "That widow must've ratted me out." I tied my boots. "Do you have any weapons hidden?"

"*Non.* We stole ours back from the arsenal, but then we stashed them in the cave. Look, we'll get through this, Evie. As long as we're together, we can handle anything. Remember?" Once he'd yanked on his coat, he tossed me mine, then marched to the door. A glance back at me. "You ready?"

I nodded, and he opened up.

Five Ciborium guards stood outside with their guns pointed at his face.

36

DEATH

Hundreds of miles from the sphere

My stalwart mount ultimately buckled under the strain. I abandoned him and began to run east.

When I'd first regained my mind, the need to return and slaughter Paul had nearly consumed me, but I could never enter that sphere again.

Besides, time was now more of a threat than the Hanged Man.

I couldn't govern my emotions, chaotic thoughts overwhelming me.

My wife has been vulnerable out in the Ash. Starving. Nearly dying. Now in danger once more—because of Paul. He will die bloody. She and I are going to have a son—if she survives long enough.

I saw her demise. Will the Fool's vision come true before I can reach my beloved wife and child?

I ran into the night. I ran for their lives. . . .

37

THE EMPRESS

Surrounded by Ciborium guards, we entered the *MSY Calices*, heading for an audience with Lorraine herself.

The men hadn't taken their fingers off their triggers. They weren't treating us like suspected criminals—but like convicted ones.

Was the plank in our future?

In French, I muttered to Jack, "What are we going to do?" For weeks, I'd had a bad feeling about Lorraine. Yet after using my powers last night, I could barely manage to sharpen my claws.

He answered in the same, "Kentarch and Joules will be back soon. They'll find us gone and come after us. Just hang on."

News of my vines must've spread; as the guards had escorted us across the settlement, people had begun to gather outside the yacht, whispering and pointing at me. I'd heard the word *witch* a few times.

On board, we passed one stateroom after another, trudging across plush carpet toward the bow. Soft floor lighting guided the way, and warm air blew from the vents. I made out the faint hum of generators. *Must be nice.*

Cleanliness and order marked every inch, which made me doubt my suspicions about the Ciborium. How could villains have a lair like *this*?

I was used to subterranean dens—not rock-star megayachts. I'd descended into the Hermit's laboratory, the Hierophant's pantry, and the Lovers' shrine. Again and again, I'd emerged to the surface and lived. Like a plant.

Would we survive this next trial?

We passed the exit that led to the plank. The two spotlighted masts cast shadows inside. I held my breath as they wavered over us.

The guards forced us into an opulent ballroom, our steps loud. Chandeliers hung from exposed rafters, shimmering light across the empty space. A grand staircase curved from a balcony to the gleaming dance floor.

Atop a dais, Lorraine sat on that seashell-covered throne, more of her guards flanking her. Imperious in another silver dress, she'd braided her long brunette hair over one shoulder. Up this close, I saw her irises were so light a brown, they looked yellowish.

"Welcome to our court, my dear ones," she greeted us in her soft, singsong voice. An ornate gold chalice sat on one throne arm. On the other arm lay a jewel-encrusted blade.

Jack demanded, "What do you want with us?"

Ignoring him, she turned to me. "We had a little time before we send up our next flare to the faithful awaiting on the coast, and I wanted to meet the Empress in person."

I jolted at her casual mention of my title. "How did you know?"

With a dreamy expression, she said, "How could I not? I'm an Arcana."

I shared a shocked look with Jack as comprehension sunk in. Lorraine. *La Reine.* The queen. My gaze flitted to the chalice beside her. "You're the Queen of Cups." One of the two Minor Arcana my grandmother had specifically warned me about.

Why hadn't I put this together before? This ship's name—the *Calices*—was French for *Chalices.*

There were thirteen guards with armbands. Lorraine would make fourteen. "The entire suit of Cups is here."

"Correct, Empress."

Circe had said she'd found a *suit* on the coast. Bingo.

I'd learned that Major Arcana rarely encountered the Minors, but when we did . . . not good news. My grandmother's words: *They can be as dangerous as Major Arcana. Especially the court cards.*

Matthew had told me they watched us, plotting against us. Had that been what I'd sensed out on the road?

So what would Lorraine do now? "How did you recognize me?"

"Not easily. You look nothing like the Empress of old."

For now. "Why have you forced us here? You can't harm a Major Arcana."

She smiled sweetly, but her face resembled a mask. Now that I knew what to look for, I could see the cracks in the surface, the danger lurking beneath—like that trench on a calm day. *Give it time.* "I wouldn't dream of it. Though I do feel I should remind you that you can't aggress against us either. Else risk punishment."

"That depends on whether you'll let us go."

"Oh, we can't harm *you*—but your handsome companion doesn't warrant such consideration." Two of the guards seized Jack's arms. "A shame, since the Cajun is my ace salvager."

As he struggled against them, I said, "You do *not* want to hurt him." I had steel in my tone—as if I were still the great and powerful Empress. In reality, I needed help. Would Kentarch and Joules come for us?

"Relax, Empress. If you cooperate, the Cajun will emerge from this ship unscathed. You *both* will."

At that, Jack stopped resisting.

Wary, I asked her, "Where's the King of Cups? Shouldn't a Major Arcana like myself be negotiating with the man in charge?"

She gave a negligent flick of her hand in one guard's direction. "That's him." An older man with salt-and-pepper hair bowed to her. "But we're the *Queendom.* It works best that way."

Damn. I hate that I like that. "Where have the Minors been?"

"We watch. We endure. We prepare for the future. One day this game will end, and we'll be ready."

"Do you have powers like the Majors?"

"We all have sharply honed instincts. We knew how to survive the Flash and avoid the plague-stricken. And each suit has a specific talent."

"What's yours?" I asked, casting my mind back to some of Gran's mad ramblings. Hadn't she made a strange comment about the Cups and . . . blood?

Lorraine ran her finger over the rim of the chalice. "Soon I will demonstrate it for you."

That sounded ominous.

Jack gave me a subtle nod. Telling me to keep stalling?

Though we hadn't slept and I was still thrown from the events of the night, I would try. "Where are the other suits? Why are you not all living in one settlement?"

"We've been at odds. A little-known secret is that we each favor a Major to win, helping him or her behind the scenes."

"All of you need to band together to support one champion—who can go up against Richter. Otherwise, he's going to usher in hell on earth. I've witnessed his powers in person."

"We've seen them as well. Sometimes an Arcana really *is* his card. He's as immovable as rock. His wrath is as fiery as lava and just as destructive. But then, Major Arcana are born evil."

Many I'd met were. "I'm not evil." Not yet. In this game, I'd done vicious things for pure reasons: protecting my friends and loved ones or preserving my own life against deadly adversaries. I'd never harmed the innocent. At least, not maliciously.

I'd kept the red witch on a tight leash.

The Cups laughed at my statement. Lorraine looked delighted with me, as if I were a precocious child who'd just made a funny. "Are you saying the gods selected you all those eons ago because you were good-hearted? No, they each chose a predator to empower and sponsor."

Doubts flooded in, but then I recalled sweet Tess, who'd destroyed herself trying to undo Richter's carnage. Even Gabriel had dearly wished for the game to end. And Finn? He'd never wanted to hurt a fly.

"As for your concern," Lorraine said, "the Minors *are* banding together. We've been in contact with the Kingdom of Pentacles. They control the Sick House."

"The ones with that smarmy radio message."

"That *successful* message. Their settlement is even larger than Jubilee. They were most interested to know we've been housing three Majors, but not surprised." So the Cups were aware of Kentarch and Joules too. "We've begun talks with the Pentacles to unite, in order to move things along more quickly. We Minors are stewards of the earth. The earth won't return until the game is finished, until all the Major Arcana but one are gone."

"I take it by your attitude that I'm not your dark horse this time around."

"Some believe you'll be needed to reseed the earth." She rolled her eyes. "We can find seeds. Once the sun returns, we can grow whatever you could. In any case, we're associated with water. We favor the Priestess to win. That's what our hearts and dreams tell us to do."

"Yet you've never made her any sacrifices?"

"We make weekly plank offerings." She flashed me a new mask—self-satisfied Lorraine.

"So those men were telling the truth when they screamed their innocence?" All the way down . . .

"Of course." She shared a chuckle with her guards. "As I said, there's no need to steal here. We have a bounty. We even have plenty of offerings."

Jack bit out, "You routinely murdered innocent men?" He looked sorry for doubting me.

"Not innocent. They were agitators who spoke out and threatened our harmony."

The Cups were serial killers. I'd known something wasn't right about them. "I talked to my good friend Circe about this very subject, and she complained that the settlers on the coast weren't making 'proper sacrifices.' Whatever you're doing, you're doing it wrong. It's not a *sacrifice* if you don't *feel* it. Maybe try dumping the King of Cups next time."

A flicker of doubt crossed Lorraine's mask as she gazed at the older man. He pulled at his collar.

Attention back on me, she said, "Your good friend Circe, is it?

And yet you keep betraying her in every game."

Really sick of those reminders. "How do you know that?" Trying to sound cool, I said, "You must have chronicles." *Want them.*

"With our talents, we have no need of them."

Fatigue weighed on me, irritation growing. "What are these talents? You said you'd demonstrate for me."

"What do you want most in the world?" she asked. "I can tell you how to attain it."

Could I risk divulging what I needed? "Out of the goodness of your heart?"

"No. You'll give me other secrets. I'll discover whether you will leave our settlement peacefully. I'll learn whether you speak the truth or tell your Empress lies."

"How?" Out of the corner of my eye, I spied two half-materialized shapes on the balcony. Kentarch and Joules!

"I'll need your blood." She grasped the knife and chalice. "Haven't you noticed our red armbands? They're symbolic of bandages."

Jack thrashed against the guards holding him. "Nobody's drinking her blood."

"Drinking?" Lorraine looked aghast. "Of course not! It seems that would lead the way to cannibalism." Again, she and I agreed on a point. "No, we are clairvoyants. We can see an individual's past, present, and future—"

"In a chalice of blood," I finished for her. Gran had told me that, but I'd thought she was delirious. Had she been teaching me all the way up to the end?

Lorraine nodded. "If the blood is freely offered, we will answer a single question."

Matthew wasn't the only one who could see far. That's why the Cups had taken random samples in the quarantine. They hadn't been testing for contagion; they'd been foreseeing whether those folks had an epidemic in their future.

Kentarch materialized fully up in the balcony. "Clairvoyants?" Joules blipped beside him.

Lorraine turned to them. "Ah, the Chariot and the Tower." Her guards tensed, readying their rifles. "Do you mean the Cups harm?"

Kentarch shook his head, then teleported down to her. "My wife is missing." He was already rolling up the sleeve on his bad arm. "I have searched for her for months. Can you tell me where she is?"

If Lorraine was surprised that he'd lost his hand, she didn't indicate it. "I can tell you whether you'll find her and where." She positioned the knife and chalice.

I quickly said, "Kentarch, watch yourself with her. You weren't here when she bragged about forcing innocent men off the plank. They've been executing a new victim every week."

"Empress, I must know how to find Issa." He said to Lorraine, "Please help me."

She tilted her head. "Where did you last see her?"

He explained the situation at the penthouse, how his wife had disappeared from an impenetrable stronghold.

Lorraine listened intently, then said, "No wonder you're desperate to locate her. All you've known is victory. How frustrating for the eminent Chariot, the card associated with bold excellence, to fail for so long." She tsked. "All you want is a foe to vanquish." *Woe to the bloody vanquished.*

He offered his arm. "I have no care for success or failure, as long as Issa lives." His brows knitted when Lorraine drew the blade above the scarred skin of his wrist, but he didn't make a sound as his blood poured into her chalice.

"There." She smiled at the steaming contents. "That should do it." She gazed into the cup, as if looking through a window. "I can seeeee you," she murmured in an eerie tone. "I've found you here in the blood. You carry around a bottle of her favorite beer. Tusker, is it?"

His eyes went wide. "Yes! Will we share it? Please, tell me."

Taking her time, Lorraine said, "Your modern penthouse still had electricity."

Impatience emanated from him. "Is that where we will reunite? Will Issa return to our home?" How *could* she if he'd blocked all the exits? But then, how could she have left?

"The maddening puzzle of that locked stronghold will call you back there. Frantic for a clue, you'll take a pickax to the very walls."

For the first time, uneasiness crossed Kentarch's expression.

"Behind a façade, you'll uncover a hidden panic room. Had she found it as well?"

He made a sound like a whimper. What was he fearing? What pain was coming his way?

"You'll recall that the redundant power had failed that last day, and you'll fear the outage triggered the door to close on her. You'll imagine her running for the exit, only to be sealed in the darkness. You'll suspect that even with your acute senses, you couldn't have heard her screams through those slabs of blast-proof metal. Shuddering, half-mad, you'll go intangible and walk through the wall. Inside the panic room, you will find . . . her remains."

My breath caught in my throat as I shared a stunned look with Jack. Issa had been dead all along?

"You will read the letter that she wrote for you in the dark," Lorraine said, as if discussing the weather. "You will comprehend that you abandoned your precious wife—*you*, the one person who could easily have rescued her from that tomb." The queen gazed up at Kentarch. "And you, my dear one, will lose your mind."

He shook his head violently *"No. No. No."* He backed away from her, as if he could distance himself from her words.

I cried, "She's got to be lying." But how could Lorraine know those details?

Joules clambered down the balcony steps. "Easy, Tarch!"

Lorraine frowned into the cup, then jerked her head up. Was that a flicker of fear? She snapped her fingers, and two guards rushed in front of her. "This isn't the *future* I'm seeing. This is the *past*. You've already done these things! Have already lost your mind! You returned and discovered Issa's body right before you set out for Death's castle."

My jaw slackened.

Kentarch's strong frame quaked. "That body I found cannot be Issa's. My eyes must have deceived me. Which means this letter"—his voice cracked as he brushed his coat pocket—"cannot be hers. I would never leave her behind; Issa is everything to me."

I tottered on my feet. "Kentarch . . ." He was a friend who needed help, a man broken by the Flash.

He'd asked me if I trusted the whisper of my hope. The Chariot had trusted his too much.

He ran his bloody forearm over his watering eyes. "She is out there. I will keep searching the Ash." His outline began to waver. "I will *never* give up."

Jack thrashed again. "Stay with us, podna!"

Joules lunged for the Chariot, catching his shoulder. "Don't go, mate!" But Kentarch was already disappearing.

The two vanished.

38

The Queen of Cups stared at the spot vacated by Kentarch, looking stunned by the turn of events.

"How could you do that to him?" I demanded.

Regaining her composure, she said, "He asked me a question; I answered it. The problem with being a winner like him is that sooner or later, everyone must lose. He couldn't stomach a defeat like that."

"Who could?" He felt responsible for the death of the one he loved best in the world. Could we locate him and bring him back into the fold? Maybe he was forever lost to us. If so, what would Joules's fate be? "I thought you liked to help people. You were going to be a freaking shrink—you could have helped him."

"A Major we don't favor?" Lorraine snapped her fingers again, and a guard traded her full chalice for an empty one. As if she hadn't just crushed a good man, she said, "Your turn, Empress. Remember: one question only."

I, too, was a Major they didn't favor. Like Kentarch, I wasn't the most psychologically sound individual. What if she told me something that sent me over the edge?

Whatever Jack saw in my expression had him struggling to break free. "Doan do it!" He caught my eyes. "You know what's at stake. Stay with *me*."

He was telling me not to give my blood. Not to risk insanity. Not to reveal my pregnancy. To live out my days with him.

But if Lorraine could divulge so much to Kentarch, surely she could tell me how to kill the Hanged Man. Hadn't Circe said the answer would be on the coast?

I sensed I was only going to get one shot to learn Paul's weaknesses—and this was it.

Decision time. My hand drifted down to my stomach. Aric wouldn't want me to jeopardize his son.

"Fight them, Evie!"

Fighting meant surrendering Aric forever. How would I tell my kid that news? *Yeah, I could've saved your father, but I gave up on him.*

Lorraine said, "What would you like to know? Perhaps how to kill the Hanged Man? He's taken control of your allies, hasn't he?"

That settled it. I crossed to her throne. "Yes."

"Damn it, no!" Jack snapped. "The Cups have got to be the ones *coo-yôn* warned me about—the bad dreamers. The Flash turned them evil. Everyone's been hailing them like they're good, but they're not!"

"We *do* believe in dreams, Empress." With a challenging glint in her light eyes, Lorraine said, "Perhaps you should deny me."

Ignoring Jack's protests, I shoved up my sleeve.

She raised her knife to my bared arm. "Very good, Empress."

I winced from the slice. Lorraine and I both watched my blood pour, like two elevator passengers regarding floor numbers as they lit up. *Almost there . . .*

Once the chalice was full, she didn't even glance at my blood before she said, "There is only one way for an Empress to defeat the Hanged Man: you must strangle him with a noose that has taken the lives of twelve murderous souls, his Arcana number."

This was the weapon Circe had spoken of! All my waiting had paid off.

She gave a dramatic sigh. "Alas, the noose no longer exists. An Old West museum had one in an exhibit, but the Flash burned the rope to ash."

My chest twisted. Then Aric was lost to me forever. "You knew it was gone, yet you still took my blood."

"We know all the Majors' weaknesses. I didn't need to waste a blood offering."

Bitch! "Tell me how to kill Richter."

"Ah-ah." She held up one finger. "A single query only. Now it's my turn." To do what? Lorraine gazed at my collected blood, swirling it like wine. *Top notes of nightmares.* "What secrets does the Empress harbor that I need to know?" She breathed over the rim. "Wait, what is this?"

The Lorraine mask began to slip.

Slipping . . .

Slipping . . .

Gone.

She jerked her gaze up, lips drawn back from her teeth. She threw the chalice against the wall, blood streaking the fancy wallpaper. "You carry *his* child! You're pregnant with Death's spawn!"

I gazed from one Minor to another, gauging their shocked expressions.

"You sought that noose because you want to save Death, so you can return to him as his wife!" Lorraine sputtered, "All but one Major must die or the earth won't revive! Yet you want to live on with your Arcana offspring? Should the earth perish forever because of your selfishness?"

"My kid isn't an Arcana. He'll be a normal mortal." Saying the words out loud almost made me believe it.

One guard said, "A union like that violates the dictates of the gods. We'll all be punished!"

The King of Cups added, "You'll bring down the gods' wrath upon us all!"

Jack yelled, "Or she could save everyone!" One of the guards whaled a punch into his stomach. Jack doubled over, gasping.

The men holding him forced him against a column, cuffing his wrists together behind it.

I advanced on them. "Don't touch him again!"

"Or what?" Lorraine cried. "I saw enough of your blood to know your powers are stifled."

They knew I was a wreck. *But I have a secret. . . .*

Should I try to attack an armed suit of Minors? One bullet could end my kid, and they had Jack as their hostage. I caught his gaze as he grappled to get free of those cuffs.

Lorraine told the King of Cups, "Kill her."

Two words I'd never wanted to hear again. "You're not allowed to harm me."

"We have no choice," Lorraine said. "You're pregnant with an abomination!"

I didn't necessarily disagree. But Tee was *my* abomination.

Squaring her shoulders, she said, "You broke the rules; you no longer deserve to be protected by them."

I had broken the rules. I wasn't supposed to be with Death. Or to defy the gods' dictates. Or love two men at the same time.

The king raised his brows. "Make her a sacrifice?"

Before Lorraine could answer, I said, "You really want to go there?" I might not be the Empress I once was, but I still had powerful friends. "Circe is my child's godmother. If you throw me in the trench, you'll suffer her wrath."

The Cups murmured as one, *"Abysmal."*

"Take her to the mainland," Lorraine told the king. "Quietly. Then return with her head."

My slitted eyes took in the guards' expressions. These men looked excited by the prospect of beheading a pregnant teenager.

My God, it was never going to stop. Just like Jack said—the monsters would keep coming. Richter, Zara, cannibals, the Sick House, another Hal and Stache. And I'd been battling them all with one hand tied behind my back.

Faced with these assholes, I came to a startling realization: I'd rather risk the toxic well.

Jack bit out, "Fight, Evie! You've got no choice."

I agreed. The red witch stirred inside me and blinked open her eyes.

Lorraine commanded, "Shut him up!"

A guard launched another punch, but Jack kept yelling. "Rise up or die! The little doll's got teeth!"

My claws dug into my palms, bloody crescents. My breaths came in shallow bursts. They'd beaten Jack, they'd torpedoed my hopes of saving Aric, and they planned to end me. A disgusting old Cup wanted to behead me on a dark shore.

Tee would be no more. The red witch bristled at the idea. *Protect what's yours. . . .*

"I'll bring you back, *bébé*. I'll always bring you back."

Glyphs sparked across my skin, my hair turning colors. I told Lorraine, "One last warning: let us go—or you'll pay the price."

"And doom the earth for all time? Never!"

Then it's done. Before I could surrender to my rage, she gave some kind of signal.

"Evie, look out!"

I turned in time to catch a rifle butt with my face.

39

Dizziness ... pain ... Jack's yells ...

I couldn't seem to raise my head—or wrap my battered mind around what was happening.

My forehead throbbed, yet my cheek and nose also tickled. Blood running down my face? Yes, my hair was wet with it.

Guards cuffed my wrists in front of me. Another sliced my arm, spilling more blood into an awaiting chalice. Were they replacing the one Lorraine had splashed over the wall or further weakening me for my execution?

As if from a great distance, I heard Jack bellowing that I couldn't lose more blood.

When the King of Cups lifted me into his arms, Jack thrashed like a madman, so the guards beat him some more. He landed a vicious head-butt against one, but without his fists ...

Lorraine glided over to me, her gown swishing. In a soothing tone, she said, "You shouldn't take this personally, dear one. Just consider today a reverie. Surrender to the dream, and it will be over soon."

All you have to do is surrender, Gran had told me, *draw on your hatred and pain. Become her: the Empress you were meant to be.* I twisted against the king's grip.

"Calm yourself." Lorraine's blissed-out voice sharpened as she commanded her guards, "Shoot the Cajun."

Jack suddenly went quiet.

Oh, hell no. I sank my teeth into the king's wrist.

He tossed me away. "You bitch!"

I hit the bloody, wooden floor, and jerked my head up. A guard had his rifle aimed at Jack's forehead.

"Evie." We met gazes as the gun cocked.

Wooden floor. Wooden ... With a shriek, I stabbed my claws into the floor and revived the boards. Shoots exploded upward across the room, impaling the Cups, stabbing limbs.

Shafts of wood immobilized each of them—just as I'd done to Cyclops back at the castle. Had some part of me wanted these Minors alive?

Jack alone was unharmed. He looked dumbfounded by my handiwork; he'd get over it.

Across the dance floor, the Cups were trapped upright like pinned butterflies, unable to raise or reach their weapons. They yelled in agony, struggling to get free, yet only injured themselves worse.

I used my claws to slice the cuffs off my wrists. Swiping blood-drenched hair from my face, I stumbled to my feet and stalked toward Lorraine.

She craned her head around to keep me in view, sniveling at my approach. "No, nooo!"

As I passed the other Cups, they spat blood, hissing that I was carrying an abomination. That I was condemning the world.

Sticks and stones. "Shouldn't you have seen this coming?" I asked Lorraine. If only she'd read the future beyond my pregnancy. *Talk about a buried lead.* "But then, these days I can barely predict what I'll do. You didn't stand a chance."

"Go to hell!" Blood spilled from her lips. "You'll d-dream of this memory forever."

"Oh. You think this is the worst I've ever seen? It doesn't even make the podium. Besides, it's only a reverie, right? But I can turn it into a nightmare. Should I make this wood grow inside you? Replace your every vein?" I thumped the shoot through her right leg, the vibration making her cry out. "Or you can talk. Is there truly no other way to kill the Hanged Man? Were you lying?"

"Vow you'll spare our lives . . . and I'll tell you."

I canted my head. "Fine. I give you my word as the Empress that I'll spare you."

"The rope was destroyed . . . no longer exists! I'm glad of it!"

For some reason, I believed her. After all these weeks of waiting, my mission was over? And Aric was already a casualty of the game?

"How do we kill Richter? How's he supposed to die in this game?"

"The Hanged Man . . . convinces the Emperor to kill himself."

My lips parted. What would stop Paul from doing the same to my friends—and to Aric? The Hanged Man was poised to win the entire game. Evil would rule.

I didn't want Richter to win, but everything in me rebelled against Paul's victory too.

My eyes narrowed as an idea surfaced. I could create hemp. I could always make a noose. Just needed to execute with it.

A whole suit of guilty souls happened to be trapped in this place, offered up to me.

If I defeated Paul and freed Aric, we could put Richter in the crosshairs once more. But first I had to secure the weapon.

Was I strong enough to do what needed to be done here? Callous enough? *I am*, the red witch said. *Give yourself over to me!*

I looked at Jack. His face was bruised and pulpy, one lid swollen shut. *He'll bring me back.*

Proceeding with this noose plan wasn't necessarily the *good-guy* thing to do—but it was the move I wanted to make.

To survive in this new world, I'd need to be deadlier than my violent adversaries. Crazier than the insane ones. More monstrous than them all.

In other words, *mother of the fucking year.* The heat of battle scalded me. "Jack, I think I'm going for a swim."

His smile was bloody. "Not too deep, *bébé.*"

Lorraine and the others kept thrashing to get free. Whatever she saw in my expression made her eyes grow crazed.

"You vowed . . . not to kill us."

I rapped my purple claws together. "As everyone keeps reminding me, the Empress is a known liar." The deviousness of briars was my own. "Put yourself in my position. Basically, I'm weighing your serial killer lives against the future of mankind. Dear one, you shouldn't take this personally. Just surrender to the dream."

Vines erupted from my skin as rage burned. I gazed down at that bottomless pit with a little less horror than before—*it's getting easier, Evie*—because I was becoming the Empress I was meant to be.

"Other Minors . . . will sense our murders. The kingdoms will unite . . . hunt you and your child . . . hunt all Majors."

"You bashed my face in, planning to cut off my head. You threatened the lives of Jack and my kid. The Cups shouldn't have picked a fight they can't win." A thornless rose stalk surfaced from my nape to circle my head, creating a crown. Leaves pointed up, and a dozen red blooms matched my drying blood. In a breathy voice, I said, "Recognize me now? Lorraine, maybe in the next game you'll remember: An Empress always trumps a queen."

Gran would be so proud. For the first time, I gave myself over to the red witch completely.

Do.

Your.

Worst.

40

"PLANK, PLANK, PLANK!"

I blinked open my eyes, found myself kneeling beside Jack. Was he yelling at me? In my clenched fingers was a crimson-spattered noose. I could barely move my heavy limbs, drained by my power outlay.

"Jack?" My throat was on fire. From the red witch's shrieks? Petals and razor-sharp thorns surrounded me like a victim outline.

"Snap out of this, Evie! They're coming for us. Cut me loose."

I leaned around him, slicing through his cuffs.

Jack pulled me close. "You back with me?"

I nodded against him, not sure of anything at all. "What happened?"

"We've got to go." He pried my white-knuckled fingers from my new noose, taking the thin length from me to loop it around his waist. He zipped his coat over it.

I caught a glimpse of the dead Cups before Jack pinched my chin and drew my gaze away. "Doan look at that, *peekôn.*" He helped me stand.

"What did I do?" Everything was a blur.

"What you needed to." We headed toward the exit. On the way, he seized a rifle from a fallen guard.

Outside, Jubileans clamored for the plank. *"Lorraine's dead!"*

"All the Ciborium were murdered by the witch and that Cajun!"

"The criminals are still aboard."

"Jack, what's going on?"

"Somebody came in during... while you were..." As he tried to put my actions into words, I vaguely remembered someone rushing in, vomiting, then fleeing. "Doesn't matter. They've broken into the arsenal. You got any more fight in you?"

A whimper left my lips.

"Afraid of that. Come on, you." Rifle raised, he grabbed my hand and charged out of the ballroom.

We almost made it off the ship, but an armed mob blocked our way. *"Plank! Plank! Plank!"*

Jack aimed his gun from one to another.

I glanced over my shoulder. More Jubileans circled us from behind. "There's too many of them."

A tall, burly man took a step forward. Their new leader? Leveling a bayonet at us, Burly said, "Drop it, Cajun, or we shoot the witch in the face."

"Putain." After a hesitation, Jack laid down the rifle. "You'd kill a rare female?"

"After what she did in there?" Burly's eyes held a mix of animosity—and fear. I was as good as dead in his mind. "For the murder of our queen and guard, you'll both walk the plank. Or you'll get stabbed to death." He motioned with his bayonet. "You know the way."

With frenzied grunts, the men prodded us. We had no choice but to stumble along, closer to our execution.

In French, Jack told me, "If we survive the fall, the cold will kill us in the blink of an eye."

"Circe's our only hope." But how could she adjust the temperature of her element? She'd been unable to fight the ice at the castle.

The mob forced us out onto the foggy deck. In the freezing darkness, the plank loomed.

Both Jack and I stopped in our tracks.

I strained my voice to scream, *"Circe!"* Was she anywhere near us? Could she hear us down in her echoing abyss?

Burly snapped, "Shut up, witch." He swung his bayonet at me, but Jack defended with his arm.

Slice. Blood poured.

"You're goan to pay for that."

"Save it, Cajun."

Would they stab Jack's stomach next? His heart? "I'd rather chance the water." I shuffled out onto the plank, chancing a glance below. My breath caught in my throat. The trench was a hungry beast, awaiting its due.

Jack followed, keeping himself between me and those blades. "Doan go any farther, no." He planted his boots. "If Circe is goan to save us again, now would be a mighty fine time."

"CIRCE!" Fog banks swirled, obscuring my vision at intervals, but I thought I saw the water level rising? My imagination?

Jack peered back at me, and his solemn expression broke my heart. "Another adventure together, *non*?"

Now I knew we were about to die. "At least I'm with you."

A thicker blanket of fog swept in until I could scarcely see Burly and his men. Shouts carried from the crowd below, followed by a sharp scream that ended abruptly. "What's happening down there?"

"Maybe Kentarch and Joules came back."

Burly ordered some men to investigate the commotion. Several hurried away, but he and three others remained focused on us. Bayonets breached that dense fog, slashing at Jack.

Another slice on his upper arm. Then his wrist. He held his ground, refusing to back up.

"You can't take another stab!" I inched back, yanking on his hand. The plank teetered, making my stomach dip.

"Just hang on, you! Not another step." He leaned forward, but it was a losing battle. *"Putain!"* The plank bounced up and down.

Up. Down. Up. Uuupppp—

The bayonets disappeared. Four loud *thuds* sounded. Had bodies just dropped to the deck?

Jack and I started sliding backward. We were looking up at the end of the plank—about to be dumped! *"Jack!"*

Over my scream came a stomping sound.

The plank stabilized! A metal boot was lodged atop the other end. Black metal.

Oh, dear God. I gazed up in dread.

The Grim Reaper loomed in the mist, clad in full armor, with both of his bloody swords drawn. His helmeted head turned, his gaze locked on me. The man who'd decapitated me twice had me in his sights once more.

Death has come to claim me....

41

Maybe this was some kind of nightmare. Maybe I was still unconscious from that earlier rifle blow.

"Come with me." His raspy voice sent chills over my skin.

No nightmare. Was the Reaper cured? Or had Paul somehow dispatched an assassin to kill us?

From behind Jack, I sputtered, "Go with you? So you can drink my blood from your sword? I'd rather Circe have my icon!" I scrambled back a step.

Death hissed in a breath, his eyes glowing behind his helmet visor. "Do not move, *sievā*. The Fool showed me a vision. If you and the mortal go into this water, you will freeze and your heart will stop."

With my free hand, I wiped sea spray and blood from my face. "Why should I believe anything you say?"

"I'm here to help you." He glanced down at the trench. "We must leave this place at once. We're running out of time."

"For Lorraine!" Two more Jubileans attacked with bayonets.

Aric twisted to keep his boot on the plank as he struck the two men down. Their bodies joined the pile with Burly and the others. Aric turned to us. "Come!"

His tableau wavered over him, right-side up. But I barely trusted my own sight. I remained frozen until the entire shelf of land seemed to move. Another Rift?

As I reeled to balance myself, Jack decided for me, pulling on my hand to escape the plank. Back on the deck, he asked, "You got a vehicle, Reaper?"

He shook his head.

"We need to get to Kentarch's truck down in the lot, but more Jubileans will be waiting for us."

"Tell me where it is, and I will lead the way."

"Get to the ground, then head left." Jack squeezed my hand, telling me, "I've got you, *peekôn*. If you doan trust him, trust *me*."

I met his gaze and finally nodded. We hurried back through the yacht, passing body after body. To reach us, Aric had taken down a score of men.

Jack snatched a rifle from the clenched hand of one corpse. Bullets from another's vest.

When Aric stormed outside, shots erupted, hitting his armor. *PING PING PING.*

Jack tucked me close against his body, shadowing Aric as the Reaper covered us.

Down on the ground once more, we ran, water splashing up around our ankles. The sand had always drained quickly; there'd never been standing water before. It seemed to be seeping *up* through the sand.

The shelf rumbled, sloshing the overflow. I asked, "What's happening?"

Aric answered, "The Priestess is losing control." Of her *catastrophal* powers?

More men attacked, stupidly testing out their bayonets against Aric's swords. Death left behind a wake of bodies for Jack and me to blunder through.

Over his shoulder, Aric asked, "Where are the Centurion and the Tower?"

"They left today," Jack said. "Could be for good. Long story . . ."

By the time we reached the Beast, water was up to our knees. Jack released my hand, then located the hide-a-key under a spotlight.

Aric headed toward the other side. "I'll drive."

Jack opened the passenger door, tossing his rifle in. "In you go, Evie!" He helped me up. "Take this key."

I'd just snagged it when more gunshots rained down; like a blur, Aric had covered the distance to us. Stretching out one of his swords, he deflected a bullet about to plug Jack's skull. "Get in, Deveaux!"

Jack dove inside the cab, slamming the door behind him. "Jesus, that was close."

I warily unlocked the door for Death, then handed him the key.

He jammed it into the ignition. When the engine didn't start, his gaze dropped to the row of tiny rocker switches. He yanked off his gauntlet and reached for the switches—just as Jack did.

I slapped away Jack's arm with all my strength. "No!"

"Don't ever come that close to my skin, mortal!"

Jack held his hands up. "Easier if I just enter the ignition sequence."

"Do it." As Aric pulled on his gauntlet, Jack pushed the buttons in the correct order.

"I already unlocked the axles. We're good-to-go."

Once the engine rumbled to life, Aric shoved the Beast into gear. "We've got to get to higher ground." Waves rolled out from the wheels. If this truck hadn't been so high, we'd already be stuck.

Jack said, "Go for the main gates. They'll be reinforced against entry—not against exit. I doubt anyone's manning them."

Aric deftly steered the truck through the outskirts of the settlement, approaching the gates.

I held my breath as he gunned the engine. His straight arm shot out to protect me, just as Jack's did from the other side.

Oh God, oh God . . .

We rammed the metal barrier head-on. *BOOM!* One gate flew off its hinges. We plowed over the other one.

Free of Jubilee! I exhaled a breath, though we weren't safe by any means. Rising water already covered the sand road. We needed to put miles between us and that trench.

I turned to check Jack for injuries. He had bruises on his face and gashes on his arms. The worst one bisected the old scar on his right forearm.

"You need a bandage." I ripped the hem of my sweater, then tied the strip of material over his wound.

"*Ma belle infirmière.* You okay?"

My gaze slid to Aric. "As well as can be expected."

He removed his helmet, swiping his hair off his forehead. His expression remained intent, but I knew him well enough to see how rattled he was. If free of Paul's influence, did he again believe in my pregnancy?

When I turned back to Jack, he said, "Your eye's turning black." He grazed the knot on my forehead. "They popped you good, *non*?"

I was freaked out and on my last stores of energy. My emotions were as up and down as a teetering plank. "I'm sick of assholes attacking me." Through gritted teeth, I added, "Present company *not* excepted." Blinding headlights beamed our sideview mirrors as trucks raced out after us and buggies launched off the dunes. "Are you kidding me? Are they running away from the trench or chasing us?"

When a bullet nailed the tailgate, Jack said, "I think it's a little of both."

Aric whipped the wheel as the Beast's engine roared, sending up a spray of water. "What happened back there? Why are these men so bent on stopping you? And why sentence a female to the plank?"

Jack flipped off his rifle's safety and checked the chamber. "A suit of Minor Arcana wanted to kill her because of Tee."

"Tee?"

Jack rolled down the window. *"P'tee garçon."*

Aric turned to me with his brows drawn. "Little boy?" His gauntlets tightened on the wheel. "Our . . . son."

Guess Death is back to believing.

"Your son—biologically." With that parting shot, Jack hung out of the window, taking aim with the rifle. I snagged his belt, clutching him as he blasted our pursuers.

After taking out a truck tire and a buggy's driver, Jack popped back in to reload. "They planned on beheading Evie. She disagreed with the plan, so she took out the entire suit of 'em."

More trucks and buggies dogged our tracks, trailing plumes of spray. "Can we talk about this later? They're still behind us!"

Aric muttered, "It's not the mortals I'm worried about." Globs of wet sand splattered the windshield. The wipers couldn't keep up.

We launched off a dune, suspended in midair for a long moment; again, two arms crossed over me just before the teeth-rattling landing sent us momentarily airborne a second time. A crack spread out along the windshield.

Aric said, "I didn't think it was that high. Forgive me."

"Forgive?" A hysterical laugh burst from my lips.

A buggy raced closer, the passenger firing on us. Back at the window, Jack took a bead, then squeezed the trigger once. Fire leapt from the vehicle's front. An explosion shot it into the sky. The flames reflected over a sheet of water that seemed to be rising by the second.

"Well aimed," Aric said, with another glance at the rearview mirror.

Jack scowled. "Do what I can."

The remaining vehicles bottomed out, headlights receding behind us. I said, "They're getting stuck!"

Jack twisted around to watch. "Uh, Reaper, you better drop the hammer. I mean, *now.*"

Aric leaned forward against the wheel, squinting at the coated windshield. "Can't see a damned thing." But he floored it, driving blindly. Soon we were hydroplaning across the surface.

"I ain't kidding, Domīnija." Jack holstered his rifle in the rack above us. "Head for that incline." He turned the spotlight to mark a large dune ahead.

At the base of the rise, the wheels bogged down, the engine straining. Aric's leg was straight, the pedal all the way down. "Come on, come on."

The tires gripped at last, and we broke free; the Beast chugged up the dune. Once we reached a higher plateau, I glanced back.

The lights twinkling in Jubilee began to topple. The entire water-drenched shelf was *giving way.*

I watched all that ground get sucked into the trench like a hungry inhalation. As depicted in her temple, Circe had devoured another port.

Terror from the abyss.

42

Jack, Aric, and I rode in stunned silence until we'd reached even higher ground. At every mile, I'd expected that sinister seep to catch us.

"How do you ... fare?" Aric finally asked me with a glance at my stomach. He would have no way of gauging my pregnancy through my coat.

How *did* I fare? Wow, he'd stumped me.

When I didn't answer, Jack said, "She's healthy, all things considered. Been eating good since the lion."

Aric swallowed, his Adam's apple bobbing. "I am pleased to hear that."

I still couldn't believe I was sitting next to him. Couldn't believe what had just happened to Jubilee. "Why did Circe do that?" I asked in a deadened voice.

"She never intended to hurt you—just the opposite. Unfortunately, she lost control of her powers. It's happened in previous games."

"And we can *never* forget what's happened in the past."

He parted his lips to say something, then must've thought better of it. *Smart man.*

But the quiet left me too much time to think. I'd taken down all of the Cups, mainly to save Aric. He'd already been on his way here.

Would a future Empress read about my gory attack with horror? I told myself that all the Cups would've died in Circe's catastrophe anyway.

"Those Minors were clairvoyants," Jack said. "Seems they should've foreseen the loss of their settlement—and their lives."

Aric shook his head. "The future is fluid. Through their own decisions, they altered their fates. Provoking two Major Arcana was ... ill-advised."

Once we reached what remained of the old coastal road, Aric stopped the truck. "Which direction?"

Jack shrugged. "Doan know, me. Where you wanting us to drop you off?"

In a low tone, Aric said, "I know I have no right to ... anything, but I will do whatever it takes to protect her."

"*Merci* for the assist back there, but this isn't your party anymore. Evie and me are heading out together." After last night, Jack must've taken my advice; he was demanding my future. "We made it work for a time in Jubilee. We can again."

"You call that *making it work*, mortal?"

"You're one to talk, Reaper."

Aric exhaled. "You're right." To me, he said, "If you bid me to leave you, I will only follow."

Jack scoffed. "You goan to keep up with this truck on foot?"

"You'd be surprised what I'm capable of. I ran countless leagues to get here."

"Why *run*?" I asked.

"I lost Thanatos on the way." Lost? That tank of a warhorse had survived a scalding tidal wave and the Lovers' carnates. He'd seemed invincible.

Realization hit. Aric had run that mighty steed into the ground. How hard he must have pushed Thanatos.

As if trying to convince himself, Aric rasped, "He could have survived yet."

A pang of sadness pierced me. Aric had shared a mystical bond with Thanatos that I could never understand. They'd ridden together for longer than I'd been alive.

"My point remains," Aric continued. "I will be watching over you from near or afar. My success will be improved with proximity."

Jack said, "And what about her mental health?" Fair question after my behavior with the Cups. "To do right by this kid, she needs to be under as little stress as possible. After the day she just had, she's now sitting tense as a board."

True. Even though I was exhausted.

"I'd rather she be tense than dead," Aric said.

"See now"—Jack tapped his chin—"that's not the way I heard it."

Aric's gauntlets creaked as he clenched his fists. If Jack's tell was his jaw muscle, Aric's hands gave away his emotions. "I've broken free of the Hanged Man's control, which means I will never hurt her again. I can protect her, as I just got through doing."

I finally chimed in. "Why now? After all this time."

"The Fool appeared to me and showed me the future should I not intervene. The end of your life."

"You left Paul's sphere because you wanted to save me?" I hated how hopeful I sounded.

He cast me a pained look. "I left because I didn't want . . . because I ached to take your icon myself."

Honest as ever. "To *behead* me yourself." An involuntary sob escaped my lips.

"*Sievā*, I am so sorry. I was in the grip of his powers." He reached for me.

But I flinched, leaning into Jack. "Right up until you weren't. Which is almost worse."

He lowered his hand. "Yes." He stared straight ahead, seeming like he was crumbling inside. And yet he admitted, "Had the Fool not intervened, I would be there still."

"Gabriel *liked* being in the sphere. Do you not miss it?"

"My thoughts were not my own. Rationality disappeared, replaced by bitter rage. Once I crossed the boundary of the sphere, I comprehended everything. Everything I did to you."

Jack said, "You didn't answer the lady's question."

My gaze flicked over Aric's weary face. "Maybe this isn't your natural reticence. You might feel a lingering loyalty to Paul."

Aric turned to me with his eyes ablaze. "That vile fiend is going to die bloody. I swear this to you."

Well then, my knight was back. Aric had returned to me the day after Jack and I had slept together. Repeatedly.

"How?" Jack demanded. "You know how to kill him?"

"Not yet."

I said, "You smugly told me there's no way to take him out."

"And you were correct when you pointed out that there must be."

Jack said, "Maybe we have the means. And if we do, seems we should keep it to ourselves."

Before we revealed anything, I needed to know: "Aric, do you miss being within that haze?"

"I am grateful to be free, but there are repercussions. It is simpler within. And this guilt I feel over my actions is . . . it's crippling—as is jealousy. I miss . . . not contending with those emotions." For him to admit even that, it must be pure chaos inside him.

Jack muttered, "Nothing less than you deserve."

"Yes. I will gladly take my punishment as long as I can protect my wife and child."

I said, "Obviously things are different now."

"I understand that, *sievā*."

Jack put his arm around my shoulders. "News flash, Domīnija. We've been together."

Everything out in the open? Sure! Why not?

Aric grated, "Do you think I don't know that?"

I had to ask, "How?"

"If possible, the mortal is even more possessive of you." He pinched the bridge of his nose. "I'm not asking for anything other than the privilege of protecting your life. And his as well, then. I saved him twice earlier."

"And I appreciate that," Jack said sincerely. "God knows I do. But even if you've escaped Paul's control, what if you get reversed again?

Evie told me what happened in that castle. How she didn't lose Tee is a miracle. We'd rather face the dangers out in the Ash without you than risk touching gloves with you."

"I will not be taken in by the Hanged Man's power. It cannot happen."

"How can you be so certain?" I asked him. "Your hatred came from our history. Which means there's no reason he can't tap into that and turn you against me. It's like you have a bomb waiting to go off inside you."

Jack pointed out, "Kentarch said the sphere is still growing. It could engulf you."

"I won't get close enough to allow that." Aric's brows drew together. "Where did Kentarch go? We need to find him as soon as possible. I can't believe he's separated from his vehicle."

My eyes watered. I hoped Kentarch didn't teleport himself and Joules back to Jubilee. There'd be nowhere to land.

Jack scrubbed a hand over his face and explained what had happened.

As he spoke, the duality of the Chariot's card struck me anew. Kentarch was so physically strong, yet he'd been damaged down to his soul. He was a warrior vanquished not by violence, but by love.

Aric's expression registered his shock. "Issa was dead all along? Then Kentarch is lost." He cursed in Latvian. "We needed him in the fight against the Emperor."

Jack said, "He wasn't able to help."

Aric did a double take. "You faced Richter?"

I murmured, "And Zara. She cost Kentarch his right hand. The only reason we escaped them is because of Circe. In any case, there's no fighting the Emperor. Bullets melted. Javelins and rock too. No weapon can reach him."

I frowned. Right before I'd killed Lorraine, hadn't the queen whispered something about Richter? What was it?

Jack added, "That *fils de pute* has Evie in his sights now, wants to make her *his* Empress."

Another string of curses from Aric.

"So what's your plan, Reaper?" Jack asked. "You always got one."

"Since I escaped the sphere, my only plan was to reach my wife and prevent her demise. Now I do not know." The infallible knight looked more unsure than I'd ever seen him.

Jack raised his brows. "Never thought those words would come out of your mouth."

Aric's *I have power over all I survey* vibe was shot. "We're going to need food and fuel. I can raid the closest settlement and steal both. If they're disorganized enough, perhaps I can infiltrate and take control, securing a safe shelter."

"What settlement?" I asked.

"The Sick House."

I shook my head. "It's run by the Pentacles. Lorraine—the Queen of Cups—said the Minors were uniting in order to hasten the end of the game and bring back the earth. And that was before I took out an entire suit. Now they're going to be gunning for me and my kid. No place could be more dangerous."

Jack said, "Besides, how do we infiltrate without Finn?"

We all grew quiet. Outside, rain began to fall, dotting the cracked windshield of Kentarch's chariot. Like tears.

I asked Aric, "How is Lark doing?"

"Not well. She grieves the boy she loved."

"Did she attempt to revive him?"

"Paul persuaded her to cremate the body."

Though I'd figured Paul would never risk the Magician's resurrection, some part of me must not have accepted that Finn was gone.

Until now.

I kept replaying his last night when he'd given us that breathtaking illusion of the surf at Malibu. I'd never forget the excitement in his voice and his lively expression. Finn had promised to teach my kid what the sun looked like.

Rage bubbled up from a bottomless well of it. Paul had robbed the world of my friend.

Aric said, "That's an example of the Hanged Man's total control.

He convinced Fauna, a card known for being driven, to blindly follow his dictates. When she gets free . . ."

I was confused on so many scores—Aric had returned, Jack was alive, and my heart was torn apart again—but I knew one thing for certain: Paul needed to pay. "No one will be free or safe until the Hanged Man is dead. Which is why I'm going to face him." Now that Death wasn't defending the castle, I might have a shot against Paul and the others. Or at least, the red witch would. "Aric, we do have the means to kill him."

"How?"

"Lorraine told us that the only weapon capable of ending him was a noose that had executed twelve murderous souls. Unfortunately, it'd been destroyed. Then I realized I could make another noose, and I happened to have an entire suit of serial killers within reach."

Jack reached beneath his coat and untied the length of rope from his waist, tossing it on the dash. "No way, Evie. We doan know if this thing will work."

I needed revenge against Paul. I needed to save my friends. I needed a place to give birth. "I'm facing him. And there's no question mark at the end of that sentence."

"Look, we doan have to decide anything right away." Jack took my hand. "You just hold on. I got food and fuel, me. We can think things through for a spell."

Aric said, "*What* food and fuel?"

"We worked salvage in Jubilee, looting wrecks. With the help of Kentarch and Joules, I set up a bug-out location, filled it up nice and good." Narrowing his gaze, he said, "You bragged about that castle enough, but I bet you're wishing you had a bolt hole right about now."

Instead of arguing, Aric asked, "Can we reach this place with the fuel we have?"

"*Ouais.*" Seeming to make a decision, Jack said, "Head north on this road."

Aric quickly started driving. He hid it well, but I sensed his relief.

"And then what happens when we run through those supplies?" I asked. "We're just delaying the inevitable: my battle against Paul."

"He is protected by Fauna, the Archangel, and his own sphere," Aric said. "*Sievā*, think of the baby."

Sick of hearing that! I whipped my head around so fast, my damp hair slapped my bruised face. "Like you thought of the baby when you threw your swords at me? You don't get to say that to me! You don't get a say in my existence."

The pain in his expression . . .

"Do I?" Jack squeezed my hand. "Tee comes first, Evie. You know this. I'm all for duking it out when there's *no choice*"—he cast me a significant look—"but let's not pick a fight either."

"Lark would rescue me if our situations were reversed. And Gabriel got trapped in the sphere because he saved my life. I won't repay him by doing nothing. At least Aric's not there anymore. I can handle three of them."

"Can you not wait?" Aric asked. "What is the rush?"

"Circe believes this kid is my shield against Paul's powers. Once I give birth, I could fall under his control."

"And will our child be a shield against other Arcana? Gabriel is stronger than ever before. Though Fauna is suffering, her predators would still be deadly."

"Why wouldn't Paul want me alive? Since he lost you, another Arcana would grow his sphere, right? And he has the cilice."

Aric admitted, "The Hanged Man *did* suggest we use it."

When I shuddered, Jack asked Aric, "That came from your armor, right? Neutralized her powers?"

"Yes. I forced her to wear it." A shadow crossed his expression. "Even if Paul wants you alive, Fauna might reach you before you ever get a chance to face him. Her hatred for you is nigh uncontrollable. If the Hanged Man's control slipped, your body would be eviscerated."

Jack said, "Which is why *I* will go in with the noose."

I glared at him. "Not happening. I'm not losing you again."

"Lots of confidence you got in me. I'm a good shot."

"I don't want Lark or Gabriel killed either. If I can manage spores, I can put them to sleep. The creatures too." *Big if, Eves.*

Aric pointed out, "You didn't manage spores when you were escaping the castle."

"I was taken off guard then. You're really going to remind me of that night?"

"If I must."

Jack asked me, "You expect me to sit with the Reaper while you go take care of business?"

"I expect you to keep him away from the sphere. To remind him what's at stake." My head was beginning to ache, fatigue taking its toll. "And I expect Aric to watch your back while I'm gone."

Jack folded his arms over his chest. "This solo plan ain't cutting it. What about Circe?"

Aric said, "The Priestess will be depleted from that show of power, whether she controlled it or not."

I added, "How would we contact her anyway? It took me weeks before she answered at the lake, and we can't return there or risk another face-off against Richter." I worried about Circe's well-being, but I also didn't see how I could help her. "Keep in mind that I only have so long before I . . . give birth." First time I'd ever said those words.

In all the excitement, I hadn't felt Tee flutter once. Had my run-in with the Cups been the final straw for this pregnancy?

No, I refused to believe that. "Look, I'm tired of debating something that's as good as done." The truck's heater blew a constant warm blast over me. Sleep called.

"Maybe the Reaper and I doan *take* you to the castle."

My glyphs began to glow. "Either help me—or get out of my way. I'll find it myself, if I have to. Somehow." To my utter irritation, Jack and Aric shared a look. Yes, I was directionally challenged, but screw them! "Wow. Haven't you two learned by now never to underestimate me? Why don't you ask the Hermit and the Hierophant and the Cups how that worked out for them? Oh—you can't." I stared straight ahead. "Because they're all dead."

43

THE HUNTER

Evie slept with her head against my chest, my arm around her.

As Domīnija drove us in the direction of the cave, he glanced over yet again with that anguished look on his face. The guilt was killing the Grim Reaper.

"She needs more sleep these days," I said, as much to reassure myself as him. "'Specially after what happened to her today." Those assholes had bashed her head in and bled her. Her left eye was still black from the impact, nearly swollen shut.

I'd never forget the sight of her blood pouring, knowing the cost of every drop.

"I can imagine this pregnancy has been very ... difficult for her." Domīnija kept making these stoic understatements, like he didn't trust himself to say anything with emotion.

"Yeah, what with the starvation and danger and all. But things got better when I arrived." I couldn't help but add, "In Jubilee, she looked at me like I hung the moon when I found pickles for her." Pickle craving: not a myth.

I'd known our time there couldn't last forever—she'd been cooped up and I'd had dozens of close calls that she would never hear about—but we'd been out of options. Now she thought she was going to take on the world. Alone.

No chance I'd let that happen. Evie was *ma fille*, my future, my home. And she felt the same way about me.

Memories from last night stole into my mind, until even *I* felt like blushing. Her cries, the way her hair had haloed around her head as I'd ridden between her thighs. The heat of her soft flesh. The trust in those blue eyes as she'd peered up at me, her sweet lips parted.

We'd had each other four times, and all she'd done was whet my appetite for more. Not surprising. When I'd been inside her, that same feeling had come over me: *where I'm supposed to be.* I pulled her even closer.

Under his breath, Domīnija snapped, "Try to control your heart rate, mortal; that's *my wife* you're holding."

I shot him a killing look. The first time I'd been with Evie, the Reaper had stolen her from me. Now he was back in her life once more. How in the hell could I be expected to give her up again? Much less Tee? Kentarch had been right; I'd started thinking of that kid as mine. "I doan see a ring on her finger, Reap." Had she left it in the confusion this morning?

Shuttering his expression, he said, "Was it lost?"

"Are you hoping it slid off her finger when she was caught in an avalanche? Maybe that she had to barter it for food in Jubilee?" Frustration boiled over. "*Non,* I took it off her finger right before I slept with her the first time." Not a lie, though I'd made it sound like we'd been together for a lot longer than we actually were.

Evie stirred but didn't wake.

I expected words of anger from the Reaper, lashing out. I craved a dust-up. But he said nothing, just seemed to be grinding his molars.

After several miles of silence, he asked, "How far is this cave?"

"Took us days to get from there to the coast, but we had to wait for Kentarch to recharge his teleportation power. Vehicles block the way. Doan know how we're goan to get around them now."

No way Evie could go on foot. She didn't have gloves or a thick enough coat. I'd stored bug-out bags for her, me, and even Tee in the cave. But how to reach our gear?

"Leave the obstacles to me. We will drive directly to our destination."

Sure thing, Reaper. "You look whipped." Something told me he'd run farther than *humanly* possible. "I can take a stint at the wheel."

He gave a humorless laugh. "Concerned for me, mortal?"

"Last thing we need is a wreck." The further inland we drove, the more snow blanketed the ground.

"Despite my exhaustion, my reflexes are infinitely faster than yours. I will remain where I am, thank you."

I rolled my eyes, 'cause he had a point. He'd deflected a bullet with the tip of his sword. A bullet meant for the back of my skull.

After another few miles, he said, "How did you survive Richter's massacre?"

I smirked at him. "I told you, I cheat Death."

He didn't respond to that, and goading him was no fun if he refused to go toe-to-toe. "Selena shoved me into a mine. I survived the lava and the flood, but then slavers nabbed me. *Coo-yôn* rescued me from their salt mine right before they butchered me for food."

Domīnija seemed to be assessing me. "The Fool has never showed such interest in a mortal before."

"What can I say? I'm special in every way."

"Didn't he tell you that you should go down to Louisiana?" Domīnija and I had talked about that the last time we'd drunk together back in Fort Arcana. "Have you given up your dream of rebuilding Haven?"

No, but . . . "Kinda hard to think about that since Richter took out my army. Besides, you're not getting rid of me. If you think I'm bowing out again—"

"Again? Are you talking about when you left the fort?"

I'd marched out my troops while Evie slept to make it easier for her to go with Domīnija, all the while praying she would read the letter I'd left her and come running. She had—and almost died in Richter's fire.

"After *coo-yôn* saved me, we were on our way to your castle. He took me to the memorial Evie made for Selena and me. Through a vision, he showed me her grief. When I thought about all the things you could offer her, I told him to let Evie believe I died in those flames. Next thing I know, she's out in the Ash, starving, with little power and a kid on the way. Seems to me that you forfeited any right to her."

He swiped his hand over his face, that spiked gauntlet catching my eye. *Not nearly as dangerous as the skin it covers.* "I know that. I'm not asking you to bow out. All I expect is for you to work with me to make her safe. Then we will figure out the future."

Future? My gaze was drawn to Evie's pale face in the glow of the truck's electronics. *She* is *my future.*

I glanced over at the Reaper. Both of us had just been staring at her. *Saps, one as bad as the other.*

Clearing my throat, I said, "What happened when you shed Paul's control?"

"I believe I was very close to losing my mind. All at once, I went from zero doubt and confusion to more panic than I'd felt in two millennia—combined. I couldn't think. Couldn't reason." In a lower voice, he admitted, "I rode my warhorse into the ground."

While under the power of another Arcana, he'd had no control over himself. Could I continue to blame him? Could Evie?

He said, "If I'd gotten there sooner, I could have spared her that battle with the Cups."

"She did all right by herself."

"I saw the aftermath. I'll bet she was glorious in her wrath."

"Glorious? That's one way of looking at it." Though I'd been the one to egg her on, I'd still been shocked. I'd never seen her so creepy. "They drew first blood, but something tells me that woan matter in the long run."

"The Empress has destroyed an entire suit; there will be consequences. If the other suits unite, danger for her will multiply. And she already had a target on her back." His expression hardened, as if he imagined eliminating all those threats to her. "How much power was the Empress able to expend against the Cups?"

"A fair bit, but she burned out fast. She was . . ."

"What?"

Different, I thought. Like she'd *enjoyed* the violence. When she'd unleashed the witch down in the Lovers' shrine, she'd taken care of business. This time, she'd played with her enemies. No wonder she was worried about heading to the dark side. *And I primed that pump.* "Nothing," I finally said.

He let it slide. "Based on what you saw, do you believe she can defeat Fauna and the Archangel?"

"She was powerful, but so are they." I replayed Gabriel's wing slicing out at me and said, "She can't go up against them. You and I will have to talk her out of that plan. Before we near the castle, we've got to convince her against it."

"I hold zero sway over her. But I will try."

Didn't sound promising. "I doan suppose *coo-yôn* offered up any wisdom when he sent you the vision?"

Domīnija shook his head. "Nothing of consequence to me."

Typical. "I heard he offed Evie in a past life."

"His biggest regret. He was never the same after that."

"From what I understand, if he'd given me directions to the castle, I could've reached Evie before you took her to bed. She would've come back to me. Would've chosen me."

He briefly closed his eyes. *"Yes."* Seeming to give himself an inner shake, he said, "Which means everything that is happening to us is because of the Fool. He must've wanted the Empress to have a child."

Evie curled up closer to me. Before I'd even thought about it, I pressed a kiss to her hair. Death stiffened in his seat.

"The jealousy's about to eat you alive, *non*? I can only imagine what's goan on inside you right now."

"My servant stole all that I'd ever worked for, and you took all that I love."

"You sure did make it easy." Stony stare. "What? You're your own worst enemy."

Clenching the wheel, he said, *"Newsflash, Deveaux,* I was under the thrall of another card."

"You're not now. Here's a hint. Maybe in the future, doan brag that you escaped an Arcana's mind control just so you could behead your wife."

"Should I have lied? As you customarily do?"

"Oh, no, no, I learned my lesson, me. No more lies. But goddamn, man, you could try softly handing her the truth instead of clubbing her with it." I lowered my voice to say, "She's wiped out, scared, and pregnant. Instead of abiding by your sterling sense of morality, consider her and the baby. Think: *buffer.*"

"Buffer?"

He was actually listening to me? Taking advice from a much— much—younger man? "Doan give her anything too heavy to carry." For weeks, I'd been trying to cushion her from the world, and I had. Until today.

"Before Paul struck, I did endeavor to buffer her." He muttered to himself, "The Empress is as fragile as she is strong."

One way to look at her. "Hell, this might be a moot point."

"Why? What are you talking about?"

I met his gaze. "Before she took out the Cups, they bludgeoned her head, threw her on the floor, and bled her. She still might lose Tee."

All light dimmed in the Reaper's eyes. "Then I was too late after all."

"Maybe so," I said, while wondering how much more guilt Domīnija could shoulder before he snapped.

44

THE EMPRESS
DAY 584 A.F.

"Where are we?" I sat up, blinking my bleary eyes.

Aric had just parked the truck. "Outside the cave."

"Really?" I didn't recognize our snowy surroundings.

"I'd like you both to stay here while I clear the area. Allow me to start a fire if possible."

"By all means." Jack turned up the heater in advance of Aric's departure. "The entrance is due north from here. Look for lion bones. Inside, there's a bag for Evie with cold-weather gear."

"I'll return with it." Casting me a last look, Aric dashed from the truck.

As I watched him disappear into the night, I said, "We got here this quickly?"

"*Ouais.* The beauty of no pit stops."

Aric had simply moved the obstacles. The first time we'd come upon a blocked road, Jack had been keen to help. Aric had told him, "Without proper clothing, you'll get frostbite. Besides, I need no assistance."

Jack had started to argue, but Aric had cut him off: "I am asking you not to get in my way, mortal."

"Then knock yourself out, Reaper. I'll be inside keeping my girl warm."

As we'd watched Aric shoving aside the first wreck, Jack's lips had parted. "Has he always been *that* strong?"

I'd shaken my head. "Supernaturally so. But not like this."

Over the night, I would rouse from the shock of cold whenever Aric opened the door to go move another vehicle. But then I would promptly pass out again.

I raised my hands to the air vent. "It's getting colder."

Jack enfolded me in his strong arms, his delicious warmth seeping into me. "'Cause we're heading up into the mountains."

"You know that's not the reason it's *this* cold." The weather continued to deteriorate. The idea of remaining out in the Ash during snowmageddon was laughable. I had no choice but to face Paul. My out-of-options brand of bravery would be forced to rise again.

"I also know the midwife said you shouldn't be worrying about things you can't control."

Ah, but maybe I did have some control over the weather. With the end of the game, the earth should return. Maybe all the united Minors truly would call open season on the Majors, hurrying things along.

Jack stroked my hair behind my ear. "So, we goan to talk about went down with the Cups?"

If we must.

"You didn't have to take that risk, Evie. Letting her have your blood."

"Yes, I did."

"Because you would do anything to save Domīnija? Was the alternative so bad—living out a life with me?"

I drew back from him. "Aric said the same thing when I tried to turn back time to resurrect you. Of all the things I've done to him over the millennia, I think that hurt him the worst."

Jack glanced in Aric's direction, as if trying to imagine how the man must've felt. "What happened with your powers in Jubilee?"

"I barely remember the attack."

"You blanked out?"

"No, not exactly." How to explain what I'd felt? "It was like an out-of-body experience, with the red witch in control." Snippets of memories kept slipping into my consciousness.

The sound of my new noose tightening. Of bones snapping. The smell of their fear mixed with my roses.

Practice for the Hanged Man?

Lorraine had whispered something about Richter right before I'd ended her. *What, what?* "I get scared by what I can recall."

Jack's expression said it'd scared him too. "I goaded you, but it seemed different than it'd been in the past."

"Do you remember when you beat up that man who wanted to hurt your mom? You looked as if some force had overtaken you. I felt the same way. Out of control. Horrified by myself after the fact. But at the time . . ."

"Everything was right in the world?"

"Yeah."

"Evangeline, it ain't ever goan to be easy with you, is it?"

"Nope." He'd asked me that before, and my answer had never wavered.

"No matter what happened, I'm proud of you for taking care of business." He jerked his chin toward the cave. "How're you doing with him around?"

"Conflicted. You?"

"Same. Granted, he's handy to have on our side. But this has got to be messing with your mind. I doan know that I could sit beside someone who'd recently tried to off me."

And who'd succeeded in the past. "The red witch wasn't exactly a fan of Aric's *before* he nearly skewered me, and she's not discerning. If she slips the leash . . ."

"I sure would miss him."

Smartass Cajun. "Part of me wants to hurt him for everything I've been forced to endure. But not like she would. Never like that."

Jack sighed. "Still in love with two."

"I wish I wasn't. I really do."

He gruffly said, "Whenever we get started together, he always rides in and rips us apart. We had a good thing goan before he came along."

Good thing? Jubilee could never have lasted. But the castle was life support, the spaceship on the surface of the moon. And Paul now ruled over it.

Did the Hanged Man sleep in the room I'd shared with Aric? Bile rose in my throat. What if he tried something with Lark? Mind-controlling her into his bed? "Jack, we're going to figure everything out. But first I've got to take Paul down. You won't talk me out of it, and I won't let you go in my place."

"We'll see about that." He brushed his scarred knuckles over my cheek. "I'd kiss you to take your mind off things, but I made you a promise not to pressure you. Considering how you respond to me, well, it wouldn't even be fair to the Reaper."

My lips twitched. "Very big of you."

"If you knew how bad I want more of what we enjoyed . . ." He leaned in to nuzzle my ear, his stubble giving me shivers. "This is a sacrifice without equal. Woman, you turned me inside out."

I sucked in a breath. "Mutual."

Snow crunched outside. Considering how quiet Aric could be, he must be purposely making noise. *Can't stand to see us together? Should've decided to come take my icon sooner.*

Jack pulled back from me, exhaling with disappointment. "Returned already?"

Aric had two bags in hand and Jack's bow slung over his armored shoulder. I braced against the cold as he climbed in the truck. He handed me my bag, then tossed Jack's stuff to him. "Your take is impressive, mortal."

Jack seemed surprised and reluctantly pleased by the praise. "Kentarch made it possible."

I pulled on gloves, a hat, a scarf, and a thicker parka. "But it was Jack's idea." Because of him, I now had a bounty of clothes.

"I doan like to keep all my eggs in one basket." Jack dragged on gear as well, then shouldered his bow. "We'll pack up the Beast before we leave, take some of our windfall with us."

Aric said, "The snow is deep, making the trail treacherous. I can carry her faster than she can hike." He pulled off his gauntlets. In readiness? He wouldn't feel the temperature as we would, and he'd probably take the cold just to have fewer layers between me and him.

Jack didn't like that a bit. "Or I can carry her." With his bad leg and my extra weight?

"Come, *sievā*." Aric offered his hand—as he had when he'd leaned out of the castle window, coaxing me closer.

I stared at his hand, wanting to tell him I didn't need his help. But didn't I? I'd slept for what felt like a dozen hours but was still exhausted, and I was starving again. When I'd trekked from this cave weeks ago, I'd needed Joules's help to make it to the road.

"*Peekôn?*"

"I'll be okay." Lips pursed, I took Aric's hand.

He upped the ante. "I'd like to talk to you inside. Alone. Mortal, you may take your time."

I glanced at Jack. "I might as well get this over with."

Tick, tick, tick.

Before Jack could say anything, Aric drew me into his arms, then swept me from the truck into the freezing night.

I didn't know where to hold on to him. He had no such problems; one of his hands gently grasped my waist, the other palming the back of one thigh. He carried me as if nothing had happened between us, as if he'd just swooped me up to take me to bed.

Was he getting his fix? The thought made me shiver.

He mistook my reaction. "Almost there, love. It will be warm by the fire."

Though I was nervous to be this close to him, my body remembered his. Even with his armor, we fit. I still felt our soul-deep bond, could almost hear that endless wave along the shore.

As soon as the thought arose, I recalled his snide tone as he'd said, "By all the gods your tears cheer me."

On the way inside, we passed those lion bones. I'd never forget the taste of that meat. How desperate I'd been for it . . .

When we entered the firelit cave, my lips parted at the treasure trove of supplies. Food. Full gas cans. Fireplace logs and wood furniture to burn.

Though proud of the guys' haul, my surroundings rattled me. Too many memories lingered here. My gaze darted from one area to the next.

That patch of dirt was where I'd passed out, wondering if I'd ever wake up.

That rock shelf was where I'd contemplated drinking Kentarch's blood. Our friend was missing, aching for his beloved wife, and probably insane.

Beside that fire pit was where I'd eaten *cat food*. A couple of empty cans remained in a trash pile off to the side.

"You can put me down," I said, my tone sharp.

He crossed to the fire, then set me on my feet. "As you wish," he replied, ever gallant.

Pulling off my gloves, I took a seat by the flames and held my hands out to the heat. "You wanted to talk."

His gaze fell on my left hand. "You no longer wear my ring?" I thought he bit the inside of his cheek; regretting his opening line?

I pulled the ring out of my pocket and offered it back. "Maybe I should have destroyed it in retaliation. If you knew how much time and effort I spent crafting yours ..."

"I can only imagine. I *grieve* it." He reached for my hand, closing my fingers around the ring. The contact of our skin made his voice grow raspy as he said, "Please honor me by keeping this for now."

I feigned an uncaring shrug, then pocketed it again.

Clearing his throat, he said, "You haven't made one for Jack?" He probably hated how hopeful he sounded.

"Been a little busy," I lied. I'd had far too much time in the tin can, but a part of me must've held out hope that I'd get Aric back. And a girl couldn't be committed to two guys. Right?

When I thought back over the last few weeks, I felt a fresh wave of sadness. I'd mistrusted Jubilee, hated being confined, but at least I'd had Jack by my side.

Talking every night. The warmth of his arms around me as the storms raged. Tee fluttering under his hand until Jack swore he could *almost* feel him.

My eyes widened. *Tee.* I'd grown so sensitive to his movements that I always woke, but I hadn't awakened for hours and hours in the truck. He still hadn't fluttered at all?

I reached up to touch my head. The knot was gone, but it'd been severe. And I'd bled a lot. *How much can this kid take?*

Aric glanced at the cave entrance and back. Feeling pressured for time? "You told me on the phone that you would choose me if I came for you. Did you mean that?"

"At the time, I did. I know you won't believe this, but Jack and I never got together before two nights ago."

"I do believe you. Why wouldn't I?"

"Because you've considered me a lying 'harlot' for longer than you haven't."

He flinched. "What made you decide to . . . take that step with Deveaux after waiting so long?"

"It doesn't matter why."

"Do you intend to be with him? I know you two had planned a future before Richter's massacre."

I gazed at the fire, couldn't even think about that now. "I don't know what will happen." What had Aric said? *The future is fluid.*

He sat beside me. "Talk to me, please."

Really? Be careful what you wish for. "I hope I didn't overstep when I promised Joules that you would help him and Gabe once we took back the castle—*your* home. If not for the Tower, I would have been eaten alive by wolves before Kentarch ever had a chance to rescue us. You remember that, don't you? When you stood on that rise, ready to watch your pregnant wife be slaughtered."

His eyes were stark.

"But then, you didn't believe I was knocked up. You believed it was just more of my Empress *conniving*."

"When I left the sphere and my thoughts became my own again,

I realized that you were out here, starving, and with child . . . *our* child. . . ." His voice grew ragged. "I relived all I did to you. *Sievā*, there are no words."

Why was I unleashing so much anger on him? Because I'd been hurt? So had he been. Because I didn't want to be in a position of choice again? If I never forgave Aric for what had happened to me over the hellish last two months, then my life would be easier. My heartache would be lessened. "I owe my life to Patrick Joules. Tell me, do you still regret that I spared him back in Requiem, Tennessee? You made me feel foolish, telling me, 'Have you lost your wits, creature?' Paul wasn't controlling you back then."

"You are teaching me, *sievā*. I understand now that players can change. We're not bound by the past. Joules and Gabriel are both welcome within the castle. I owe them both debts that I can never repay."

"More mouths to feed? You were already rationing."

"We still have fifty years. I was greedy for a decade or two more, so our child could live a full life."

"How's Paul going to manage the resources while you're away?"

Aric's expression told me he had concerns.

"That good, huh? I know you and Jack think you're going to talk me out of challenging him, but you won't. We don't have a choice. You feel how cold it is tonight. I don't plan on giving birth in this cave."

"Instead you plan on risking our son in an Arcana battle."

"Those who threaten my kid don't live long." I kept saying *my kid*. It didn't feel right to include Aric by saying *our*. And didn't Jack have as much claim? Without him, there'd be no kid. "If I'm in enough jeopardy"—and enraged enough—"the red witch should rise." The trick was sticking to the shallow end.

"Should? *Should?*" Aric stood, beginning to pace.

"She took me over completely in the battle with the Cups. It was like an out-of-body experience."

He slowed. "Ah, that is what the mortal hesitated to tell me."

"In fact, I don't recommend lowering your guard around me. When

I knocked you out last time, the witch wanted to kill you. What if I lost control again? I could poison you in your sleep."

"You've unleashed her before and returned to normal."

"The return gets dicier each time." Rage *was* a type of madness, and I had enough on tap to lose my mind a thousand times over. "I'm coming to believe I'll eventually turn into her for good, just as I always have before. Only a matter of time. I'm her, and she's me."

"I don't believe that. You've come so far. And you won't harm me. Even in self-defense, you hesitated to strike against me."

My gaze lit on those cursed cat-food cans. The sight ratcheted up my fury even more. "I didn't have this much rage in me before. Facing off against you made me understand it better than I ever have. When you attacked, your eyes were filled with it."

"I had no control of myself!"

"What about when you first abducted me away from Jack all those months ago? Or when you stabbed my picture? You hated me back then, and it had *nothing* to do with Paul!"

"*Sievā*, I am so—"

"*Evie!*" I shot to my feet. "My name is *Evie*. But you don't call me that, because I'm interchangeable with the other Empresses, right? The names change, but the evil bitch remains the same? Then watch this evil bitch go take care of business."

"I call you *wife*. I am proud and humbled to do so."

"And I liked that, but can't I be more than either a wife or an enemy? Because right now I'm not fitting into either box you want to stuff me into!"

"I do not wish to do that." In a voice laden with regret, he said, "I only wish to make amends, to make things right between us once more."

His patience just stoked my fury. My God, pregnancy emotions were *crazy*. I couldn't catch my breath, felt like I was spinning around on Tess's carousel. Faster. *Faster*. Until I'd be flung out into nothing. "Amends? What if you can't make up for what's happened? What if we've lost too much?" Why hadn't Tee moved again? I clutched my stomach. *Damn it, kid, do something*. "I can't handle this! I just can't—"

"Hey, now." Jack hurried inside, striding between us. "Let's save some fight for the days ahead."

"Being in this place makes me remember things. Like licking an empty cat-food can while talking to *him*." I pointed accusingly at Aric. "Or Kentarch trying to feed me his blood. I should've tried to drink it. If not for me, then for . . ." My voice cracked.

Was I even expecting a kid anymore? Just like that, I burst into tears.

Jack pulled me into his arms. I could feel him waving Death away behind my back.

In a rasp, Aric said, "Please forgive me." His spurs were silent as he left the cave.

45

DEATH

I paced outside, sucking in lungfuls of air. The weight of a meteor rested on my chest. It must be that—my heart couldn't pain me this much otherwise.

I could hear my wife sobbing in the mortal's arms. Yet I could do nothing to comfort her. When we'd spoken on the phone, she'd predicted that the guilt would torture me.

It does.

I heard Deveaux murmur, "Shh, I got you."

Fists clenched, I stared at the sky. She'd once told me that he used to say that to her. Jealousy warred with despondency.

"*Bébé*," he continued in a hushed tone, "you might've caught a touch of PTSD. Not surprising, *non*? But remember, there's nothing we can't get through as long as we're together."

I flinched at that, cursing my enhanced hearing.

"Just breathe," he told her. "That's it, *ma bonne fille*."

"I-I can't do this anymore."

"If you can't be here, then let's go. I'll take you anywhere you want." I half expected Deveaux to walk out and tell me the two of them were setting off: *Au revoir, Reaper.*

She cried, "Y-you know where I want to go. To confront Paul. You t-told me if I could show you some powers, you would support me. I killed all the Cups." She cried harder at that.

How much more violence and grief could she be expected to suffer? I'd concluded that she'd been through too much trauma even before the Hanged Man had woven his insidious web.

He was my kill to make. And yet, I *couldn't*. After being in control for millennia, I could do nothing but endure this misery, lest I get taken in by that sphere once more.

The mortal was right—*I* was the biggest threat to them.

"Shh, shh, *calme-toi*. You got to breathe."

After all her trials, being near me while in that cave had pushed her past some limit that I'd never known existed.

She'd sent me awash in the scent of her deadly roses. Maybe she *would* poison me in my sleep. I deserved nothing less.

The day she'd fled the castle, I'd taken all of my rage combined through the ages, and I'd afflicted her with it.

Of my many past sins, that pained me most—and I'd been a murderous son. I put my head in my hands and squeezed.

So many sins. I'd left her unprotected against Ogen, her powers bound by the cilice. She'd nearly died in the grip of that devil—my ally! I'd kept Paul in the castle, despite her doubts, despite her pregnancy. While Deveaux kept trying to shoulder every burden for her, I'd let her grandmother's killer live in our home.

I hadn't trusted my wife's judgment when she'd needed me most.

I gazed back at the cave where she'd nearly starved. On the phone, she'd pleaded with me to come home, and I'd laughed. *Home? Do you mean* my *castle?*

If Deveaux hadn't come along, my wife and son would be dead. The babe might be even now. And how could she weather that? With me as a reminder of our bloody history? Or with Deveaux's understanding?

What right did I have to her? What if this had always been her story with Jackson Deveaux, and *I* truly was the villain?

46

A blur of movement outside of the truck caught my eye just as Jack and Aric both tensed. I straightened in my seat between them. "What was that?"

We'd been riding in silence since we'd left the cave. I was mortified by my breakdown. I usually handled my business better than that. And what was the point of my fury? I couldn't possibly punish Aric more than he was punishing himself.

He frowned, his eyes bloodshot. "A Bagman in a hurry." I wondered when Aric had last slept.

Last night, even the fire hadn't been enough to keep me warm, so Jack had climbed into my sleeping bag. I'd been dozing off when Aric had finally returned, hours after he'd left. Though nothing had happened between me and Jack, Aric had sat on the other side of the fire and met my gaze with pure anguish in his expression.

"Up ahead." Jack grabbed his bow from the backseat. "Three o'clock."

When Aric braked, I squinted into the snowy dark. Dozens of Bagmen swarmed along the roadside. Why had they gathered?

"My gods," Aric muttered, just as I caught sight of their meal.

A white horse. *Thanatos.*

He lay on his side in the bloody snow—but was still moving!

Aric slammed the truck into park, then leaped out. He drew his swords with a yell. Metal flashed in the headlights; Bagger heads and entrails went flying.

Once Aric had cleared the way and we saw what remained, Jack breathed, "Jesus."

I put my hand over my mouth. Thanatos's red eyes were crazed with fear and pain, his legs nothing more than bloody stumps pawing the air. His black armor had been torn away, chunks of skin missing from his flesh. Bite marks told a horror story—hours of torment.

"Is that horse immortal like Domīnija?"

"No. Any horse that he claims as his own is mystically connected to him, but not immortal." Still, Thanatos had survived so much that I'd thought of him as deathless. "Aric's going to have to put him down."

"Stay here." Jack hurried from the truck to join Aric.

Ignoring him, I followed.

Aric had dropped to his knees beside Thanatos. "Whoa, stallion. Rest easy." His gaze held Thanatos's, which seemed to calm the horse, easing its wild-eyed movements. "I'm here. I will make the pain end." As he soothingly stroked a narrow swath of unbitten flesh, Aric clenched his other fist.

I sidled closer to them. "What about Lark? You could use her powers," I said, even as I pictured how vacant-eyed that sparrow had looked.

"Never," he rasped. "Never that. He's earned his rest. He's earned far more than I gave him at this bitter end. I left him half-dead with threats lurking all around."

"Then let me help. I can make it painless. He'll just go to sleep."

"We'll be within striking distance of the castle tomorrow. You can't spare an ounce of your power if you're still bent on the same plan."

"I am."

"Then I will end this." Aric placed the tip of one sword against the steed's chest. To Thanatos, he whispered, "Good-bye, my old friend. Rest well." Aric plunged the sword.

The horse shrieked, and I could have sworn Thanatos looked . . .

betrayed. Was he wondering why his golden-haired knight would forsake him? After all his unending service?

Thanatos's red eyes flickered. Once. Twice.

They closed forever.

Aric's stoic façade never faltered, but I could sense his utter agony. He must be drowning in guilt and grief.

I put my hand on his armored shoulder. "I'm so sorry."

He inclined his head, couldn't seem to find words.

Jack said, "I'll help you bury him. Evie, it's too cold for you out here."

"I'll be fine."

"We doan know if more Baggers will smell the blood."

Aric absently said, "It isn't safe."

Jack squired me back to the truck, then helped me into the cab. Under his breath, he said, "Let him grieve without having to be in protection mode." He was right.

"Okay. I will."

Jack closed the door behind him. After fetching a shovel from the nearly-full truck bed, he secured a burial spot.

From their body language, I could tell Aric insisted on digging the grave, no doubt wanting to punish himself.

As he buried his horse, Jack stowed the tackle, armor, and saddlebags among the many boxes he'd loaded up from the cave. Joining me inside the truck, he pulled his flask from his coat. At the rim, he said, "Thought I'd give the Reaper some space too."

I nodded. "He shared a bond with Thanatos for longer than I've been alive. On his card, Death is astride a stallion. Now he's a knight with no steed." Death was incomplete. "Aric loved that horse, yet he ran him into the ground and didn't even spare a sword strike to euthanize him."

"Which means the Reaper was out of his head to reach you." Another swig. "Damn him."

"Damn him," I echoed.

"So much harder to hate him."

"Welcome to my world."

"What are we goan to do with him?"

"Hell if I know. But I don't want to hurt him anymore." I deeply regretted flying off the handle in the cave. "He must have already been crumbling inside because of what he did to me, and then I piled it on last night. Now this."

"It's not your fault. You've been through a lot. You're doing the best you can in a shit situation."

"It's worse than you think. Jack, when Aric's powers first manifested, he accidentally killed innocent people—including his parents. His mom was pregnant at the time."

Jack swore low.

"For him to have come so close to ending me and Tee . . ." I trailed off when Aric turned toward us, trudging back.

His eyes were dim and glinting, his shoulders heavy.

Jack muttered, "Never thought I'd say this, but *il tombe en botte*. The Reaper is falling to ruin."

When Aric rejoined us, he had a frozen track down his cheek. A tear.

Oh, Aric. The pain I felt convinced me that I was still as deeply in love with him as I'd ever been.

Did that mean I was right back where I'd started with both of them? Without thought, I placed my hand on his cheek and gave him a sympathetic expression.

In a pained tone, he rasped, "A touch and a soft look. I am felled."

Jack tensed beside me, breaking the spell.

47

DAY 586 A.F.

I couldn't believe I'd agreed to come to this place.

As the truck meandered up the snowy drive to the cabin where Aric and I had first had sex, emotions churned inside me.

Yes, it was strategically located with a generator, a small kitchen, and running water. We would be able to grab a shower and cook some of the food we'd transported from the cave. For the first time in months, I'd have a real bed to sleep in.

But the cabin also held way too many memories.

When Aric had first suggested it, I'd said, "It's less than a day's drive from the castle. How close will the sphere be?"

"Some distance away. And that haze might even have contracted with my absence." Over the long drive, Aric had seemed to bury his grief over Thanatos, at one point saying, *You live. That's what matters.* But he was still running on empty.

"Or not. Aric, the risk . . ."

"*Sievā*, I will never be taken by it again."

He and Jack had both looked exhausted, so I'd acquiesced, even while wondering if I could handle what this place meant to me.

Aric parked in front. The cabin was built into the side of a mountain with a nearby stable. The last time I'd ridden here, Thanatos had been inside.

The enormous satellite dish came into view, illuminated by the continual lightning overhead. Were pieces of my clothing still littered around the base?

"Look at that dish!" Jack exclaimed. "Does it work?"

"Alas, it does not." Catching my gaze, Aric murmured, "A hailstorm damaged it beyond repair."

My cheeks heated. His face was flushed as well. So we were both replaying the details of that night?

Tee had probably been conceived here. Had Aric put that together? When his attention dipped to my belly, I had my answer.

Jack climbed out, bow at the ready. As he helped me down, I couldn't meet his gaze. Coming here had been a mistake.

Outside of the cabin, I was about to voice more opposition, but Aric said, "It's safe here. It's comfortable. Battle comes tomorrow, and this is a strategic point of departure. Allow me to enter first and ensure that no one—or thing—has taken up residence."

My wide-eyed look told him: *Ensure it doesn't look like a love nest.*

A couple of minutes later, Aric gestured from the door, and Jack and I followed him inside. I peeked into the back room. Aric had used his supernatural speed to make the bed and straighten up. He could have flaunted what had gone on here, but he was being a gentleman about it.

If the cave had reminded me of my rage toward Aric, this place reminded me of promises. I vividly recalled the way it had felt to stroke the blond stubble on his defined jaw. The way his lips had covered mine, demanding everything from me. The way he'd tried to explain his feelings—clumsily, because he'd had no experience with things like that.

As he tossed wood into the fireplace, Jack explored the radio equipment on the desk. "How'd you find this place, Reaper?"

"I commissioned the dish and the cabin to be constructed before the Flash." In moments, he had a fire going. "I suspected communications would fall with the beginning of the game."

"So you had an alternate site of your own."

"Yet I foolishly didn't provision it."

Jack thumped the copper covering the walls, then turned to inspect the maps of constellations. "How much did something like that dish cost? Millions?" When Aric didn't deny it, Jack said, "So you were a multimillionaire?"

Shrug.

Perceptive Jack narrowed his eyes. "Billionaire, then?"

"For all the good it's doing me now."

"Jesus. Can't even wrap my head around that much money."

Aric leaned his armored shoulder against the wall. "I would have given up every penny not to be immortal."

Jack's smile was bitter. "You can say that 'cause you've never been poor."

"And you can say that because you've never lived forever."

With a contemplative look, Jack gave a nod, and something seemed to pass between them.

As different as the two men were, they had more than me in common. They shared a rapport that they likely both hated. But it was there, all the same.

God, I loved them both.

Jack turned from the desk. "I'm goan to grab some food for us."

Once the door closed behind him, I said, "Aric, I don't like this. Coming here feels underhanded. I hate keeping secrets from Jack."

"I don't like it either. But this made sense."

"Still, I—oh!" My eyes went wide. I felt that fluttering inside, stronger than ever. Relief swamped me, and my eyes pricked with tears. *Decided to stick around, kid?*

"What is it?" Aric hurried beside me.

I peered up at him. "Tee's kicking. I worried he'd been lost. That was part of the reason I freaked out so bad in the cave."

"May I?" He tugged off his gauntlet.

I nodded before I'd thought better of it. Aric swallowed with nervousness, then placed his shaking hand on my belly. His amber eyes turned starry with emotion. "I feel him, *sievā!*" he said in wonder. "I can feel our son. He's strong."

As I stared at Aric's noble face, my glyphs shivered over me, glowing brighter and brighter. That old feeling of unity between us bloomed. I'd missed this so much. I'd missed the life we'd made together. "Strong like his father."

Jack stood in the doorway, a box of supplies in his hands. His troubled gaze took in the scene.

I drew back with guilt. "Tee kicked. Hard." After all those nights Jack had patiently waited to feel that . . .

Where's your head at, Evie?

"Good, good." Before Jack schooled his expression, I saw his disappointment. He wordlessly began unloading food in the small kitchenette.

I hurried to join his side. "Let me help you."

He shook off some of his unease, even managing a smile for me. "You sure? Two cooks, and all that?"

"Over the last few weeks, I've become really proficient at cooking pasta."

In a dry tone, he said, "No, *bébé*, you really haven't."

I slapped his chest. "Dick."

Aric avidly watched this interplay, then excused himself. While Jack and I prepared the meal, he changed from his armor to clothes he'd had in his saddlebags. Customary gloves, of course.

In front of the crackling fire, we three ate in silence. As soon as the warm food hit my stomach, exhaustion set in again. Nagging doubts about tomorrow surfaced. Would I be strong enough to do what needed to be done?

Aric studied my face, reading me so easily. "You should rest a couple of days before this battle. Discretion is the better part of valor."

"I'll be on edge until Paul's dead." I rubbed my nape. "And we're closer to the sphere than I'd like to be. I bet you can see it from atop the satellite dish."

"You would be able to, yes. But we've dozens of miles between us and it."

Jack asked me, "You got a plan for tomorrow?"

"Sure. Smash and grab."

Aric pinched the bridge of his nose.

"I'm kidding." Not at all. "Tell us the lay of the land, Aric. What do I need to know?"

"Lark normally sleeps during what passes for day, so an early incursion would be advisable. As soon as you cross the boundary, the Archangel will likely trail you in. If we are lucky, he'll escort you to Paul, instead of exacting his own revenge for past games."

Jack shook his head. "Too big a risk."

"*Sievā*, if Jack accompanied you with his rifle—"

"He stays. I can't watch him die again. And I can't watch him put a bullet in our friends to protect me." I asked Jack, "Would you shoot Lark if I was in trouble?"

He exhaled, but said, *"Sans doute."* Without a doubt.

"Then I go alone. Once I'm inside, I'll knock everyone out with spores, then strangle Paul with the noose while he's asleep." I sounded confident, though spores could be tricky.

Aric said, "Over the last year, you've asked things of me that I didn't feel capable of. Taking off your cilice. Trusting you not to strike against me. Letting you go. But now you're asking me to endorse your plan to challenge a trio of Arcana—when you're more than four months pregnant with our son. And no matter what happens at the castle, I will not be able to assist you."

"I know it's a big ask. But you'll just have to trust me." Softening my tone, I pointed out, "You didn't trust me about Paul, and look what happened."

"If you tell me you feel one hundred percent confident that you can prevail tomorrow, then I will believe you."

"I feel one hundred percent confident that we have no choice. If you come up with a better plan, I'll listen. But otherwise, my mind is made up...."

After dinner, Jack started gearing up for the cold. "Goan to check out that sphere." He seemed as uncomfortable around it as I was.

"If I fall asleep, will you make sure it doesn't sneak too close tonight?"

He grabbed his bow. "On it. In the meantime, maybe the Reaper can talk some sense into you." They shared a look before Jack left.

I rose and went to the window. As I watched him head out into the wintry landscape, I thought of the little bug-out bag Jack had painstakingly put together for Tee. Damn it, he should've been the first to feel a kick. Instead, he'd witnessed a moment between me and Aric.

In the letter Jack had left for me before the massacre, he'd written: *You and Death have something that I don't understand, and I've got to start trying to get over you. To pull your thorn from my skin.*

Seeing hints of the shaky tie between me and Aric emerging again must be killing him.

He probably sensed my gaze, but he didn't glance back. Was Jack even now trying to pull my thorn from his skin?

Did it pain him? Was he bleeding inside? He didn't understand; we could be separated, but I'd never release my hold on him. Only fair, since I would never get over him.

Like me, Jack Deveaux would bleed for life.

"How are you feeling?" Aric asked hesitantly. He must be recalling how badly our conversation had gone in the cave.

I turned to him, not yet ready to be alone with him. That earlier moment between us had slipped up on me so totally, but now I was on edge. "I'm okay, I guess."

"You don't have to do this tomorrow."

"Agree to disagree." I didn't want to hurt him anymore, but I couldn't just magically forget all I'd been through. It would take time. "I probably need to rest." I grabbed my bag and headed to the back room.

At the doorway, he said, "I would like to watch over you as you sleep."

The idea sent my emotions spiraling. Memories of his attack were too fresh. "Aric, I'm not ready for that. It's too soon." I'd had nightmares of him for months.

The blond tips of his eyelashes glowed in the firelight as he said, "Are you afraid of me?"

I wanted to protect his feelings, but I also needed to be honest with him. Honesty won out. "This close to the sphere? Yes." Maybe I did have PTSD. "Besides, I warned you about the witch."

"Though she isn't partial to me, apparently she's been looking out for our son. If need be tomorrow, let her do so once more."

"And if she doesn't stop at Paul?"

"You won't harm Lark or Gabriel on a whim."

I wished I could be so certain. "Aric, I can't predict what will happen with me. She truly might harm *you*."

"A bridge to cross another time." Aric's way of saying *kick the can down the road*. He opened his mouth to say more, closed it, then tried again. "Over these months, I've made so many mistakes. I should have done a score of things differently. But you know I can learn from my mistakes—if given the chance. You know it can be good between us again, love." He was making it sound like we could pick up right where we'd left off. How could we ever find our way back there? "Even when under the Hanged Man's control, I longed for you. I missed my wife." He took a step closer.

I took one back. "Should I forget everything that's happened and resume life with you at the castle? Should we send Jack back out into the Ash? Could you doom him after he saved me and Tee?"

He exhaled. "I have no solution for this situation. Not one we can all live with."

Neither did I. "Aric, will you please give me some breathing room? I need to think."

His eyes went dark and dim once more. "I will go. To make you more comfortable, I won't return without the mortal."

"Take your time."

Before closing the door, he stopped and said, "I do not want you to go to the castle alone."

I rubbed my temples. "This is my lot." I now had one mission: destroy Paul. If I won the day, I would reevaluate everything else then. "I've accepted it."

He held my gaze as he said, "Our son *is* strong. Like his *mother*."

Oh, Aric. He left me, the door clicking shut behind him.

I released a pent-up breath, wondering when—or if—I'd feel comfortable with him again. Was it PTSD making me so antsy? Or the sphere? Pregnancy?

My vote: all of the above.

What was I going to do about him? Them?

Mulling this conundrum, I used some of the cabin's water stores to shower and get ready for bed. I climbed under the covers, sighing at the softness of the mattress and expensive sheets. Compared to the pallet I'd been sleeping on, this bed should've been heavenly, but it was missing Jack.

I was missing him.

And Death. When I detected Aric's addictive scent on the pillow—sandalwood and pine—memories of our fateful night here overwhelmed me, until I felt like I was cheating on Jack.

I adored his raw passion, yet I craved Aric's seething intensity. One love fated. One love endless. Since perfect for me couldn't be bested, how could I live without either?

Jack, the love of my life, had told me, "*Peekôn*, it'll always be Evie and Jack."

Aric, my soul mate, had told me, "We are forever."

Whom to believe?

I'd come full circle, was right back to that night at Fort Arcana when I'd struggled to decide between them. As I'd done then, I imagined my life as a road. On one side was Jack, on the other Aric.

Even after everything that had happened, I'd covered only a few measly miles.

One thing I knew about tomorrow? Nothing would ever be the same.

48

THE HUNTER

"Where's Evie?" I asked when Death joined me atop the satellite dish. I'd been sipping a bottle of whiskey I'd snagged in Jubilee. From this height, I could see the sphere in the distance.

A constant reminder of the stakes.

"She wanted some time to herself. I'll know if any threats approach."

I already had my eye on the sole cabin door. I handed him the bottle. "Must be nice for her to have a real bed again." I wasn't stupid, me. Knew those two had probably been together in it. Jealousy prickled.

I put my gloved hand in my coat pocket, turning over my most valued possession: the phone I'd stolen from my half brother. I'd stowed it and the tape recording of Evie's life story in my bug-out bag at the cave—*merci mon Dieu*. The way Domīnija and Evie were looking at each other earlier, I'd probably be needing a way to hear her voice soon. Because I'd be on the outs. "I doan suppose you talked her out of her plan?"

"She remains determined."

"I'm not letting her drive off on her own. I'll go without a weapon if I have to."

He drank. "She wants me to keep you out of the fray."

"But you woan?"

"I might." At my scowl, he said, "Perhaps I'd be more supportive of her plan if we could provide a decoy, distracting her foes. I could lure out some of Fauna's animals and put them down. With luck, I could even goad Gabriel into crossing the boundary."

"You? That close to an unpredictable sphere? If you got caught, you'd kill Evie and me. You're a ticking time bomb, remember?"

"I won't get caught. I'm too swift."

"Will speed make a difference? I doan think it's possible for you to stay away from her no matter what you heard. Think about it: if Lark's wolves tore into her, you still couldn't pass that barrier."

"Remaining away would be the hardest thing I've ever done. Battle is easy. Facing my demise is easy. Denying my need to protect her would be grueling. But I would summon the strength." He handed me the bottle.

I tilted it up, then asked, "In past games, has the Empress ever lost herself to the witch? Like permanently?"

"There was no separation between the two, no name for an alter-ego. She was the red witch always. Her hair was forever red, her very eyes green."

And by all accounts, that was a damned bad state. So what had we dredged up in Jubilee? What might she tap into tomorrow?

The wind gusted again, rocking the dish and sending snow blowing across the ground. I pulled my coat tighter and said, "Evie's right about one thing. She's got to get inside that castle."

"If I'd developed an alternative site, that castle wouldn't be all-important. I thought I'd anticipated every possible contingency, but I couldn't. No one could. And now I've left my wife and child so vulnerable that I actually have to consider the prospect of letting her take back that stronghold."

"You never played with the idea of a bolt hole?"

"History told me I had no need. I was raised in a fortification. A strong enough sword meant all was protected. I am the strongest sword alive. So chalk up this failing to arrogance."

"I was raised in a place that couldn't be defended, and I learned early that life was unpredictable. So chalk up my wariness to experience."

"It's served you well, mortal."

Kind of what Evie had said about my pre-Flash hardships. Could all my tough luck in the past be a gift in this future? "Say she can take out Paul. What then?" Would they expect me to let them get back to their marriage? When I needed her like I needed my next breath?

"Regrettably, the advantage is all yours, mortal." He voiced my own thoughts: "You're the only other male alive who knows what it's like to covet her like this."

"I get that you want her back, want your family. But I bowed out before, and you nearly killed her."

In a strangled tone, he said, "Yes."

I'd told Evie that if we could trust that Domīnija wouldn't give in to his rage again, I'd let them get back to it. Which meant I needed to do some digging. "I want to look at this from your point of view, walk a mile in your shoes."

He stared at the sphere. "A mile in my shoes? I wouldn't wish that on you."

I could now see all too clearly what his long life had been like. I had no family left. No close friends. Everyone but Evie had died, and I'd lived on, just as this man had done for two millennia. "How much of your rage was Paul? How much was you? Make me understand what happened."

"How can I, when I hardly comprehend it myself?"

"You must've put some of the past behind you. You two were together and happy, *non*?"

"I knew she was hurting because of you, but I believed that we could overcome any obstacles. Then I got the news that she was expecting. You can't understand my shock. For a time, I thought myself the most fortunate man alive."

"For a time, you were. When I hunted that lion, I saw you through the window. I wondered if you felt what you'd lost. I thought, *Would I rather have everything and lose it—or never know that happiness?*" Too late for me. I hadn't had everything, but I'd tasted enough to ruin me.

"Even then, I did feel the loss." He eyed me. "Astute mortal. Not for the first time, I am reminded of why she fell for you."

I hated that I enjoyed his praise. But he *was* a wise immortal, wise even beyond his endless years.

"Yes, I had everything, but then I forfeited all." He clenched his fists, as if he wanted to punch himself. Or Paul?

"How'd it start?"

"At first, stray thoughts would enter my mind, like an idea with no genesis. Memories of her treachery from long ago would feel more visceral. I began to dwell on our past more than ever before. I know now that Paul was already testing his skills, sowing discord. After activating his full powers, he convinced me that she'd betrayed me again, lying about the baby. I thought she had mesmerized me. And being mind-controlled is as vile a curse as you can imagine."

"I can imagine a lot." Under the Hierophant's control, Evie had nearly become a cannibal.

"In Tarot, my card reversed symbolizes the inability to change—which provides the grounds for resentment to grow. He made me burn with it, as I never have before. Had I once harbored resentment toward her? Yes. But I'd moved past it. I'd grown. It would be like you hating her now because you two had a rocky start."

"Rocky's one way to put it." I turned up the bottle, saying over a gasp, "I considered her a stuck-up bitch." I'd had no idea what she would come to mean to me, calling her *bonne á rien*.

Good for nothing—except making all my dreams come true.

"Under Paul's influence, you would forget all the good. He would force you to dwell only on the negative, magnifying your bitterness." I nudged Domīnija to take the bottle, and he drank. "Even after what I'd done in a far-distant past, the loved ones I'd wronged, I nearly repeated my sins on the one I love above all."

"Evie told me what happened to your folks. You were close to them."

Gazing out at the sphere, he said, "Very. I adored my mother, and my father was my best friend. I'd planned to take a wife, and thought their new babe would grow up with my own. Instead I killed them all in the most painful manner conceivable."

"Wasn't your fault."

"And yet . . ." He still felt the anguish, would forever. I knew this because I'd forever feel it over *ma mère*.

Clearing his throat, he said, "Were you close to your mother?"

"As much as I could be. She didn't make it easy toward the end." Because she'd given up hope. If I couldn't be with Evie, would I? "She told me the people of our family love only once. She loved and lost. Said it felt like something was missing from her chest every second of the day."

"What happened to her?"

My hand went to my rosary. The Reaper had just admitted he'd killed his family. Could I be as forthcoming? Like the man had said: *If you can't speak your deeds, then don't do them.*

I snapped my fingers for the bottle. He handed it over, and I took a chug. "On Day Zero, I got separated from her. She was stuck in our old cabin. No protection from the Flash."

The Reaper's lips parted. "She was turned."

I swallowed thickly. "Not a day later, she attacked Clotile, goan for my sister's throat. *Ma mère* was so goddamned strong, so frenzied to drink. I . . . I struck her down. Me, raising a hand to my own mother. *Chère défunte mère.*"

"You had no choice. In any case, she was dead by the time you acted. The Sun Card might think differently, but these Bagmen will never return to how they were. I can sense death, and once the thirst for blood rises up in them, they are already gone."

I eyed him over the rim of the bottle. "That true?"

"Yes. Deveaux, know this: your mother died in the Flash."

My God, that relieved my mind. Another thing I owed Domīnija for. "Never told Evie that, no."

"You should. She would understand."

"It's why I've killed so many of 'em." I took another swig. "'Cause if I ever got turned, I'd want someone to take me out before I hurt anyone." I handed him the bottle back, and we sat drinking until a few flurries drifted down.

"There's something I'm curious about," he said. "When it first started to snow, she would grow sad. It must have something to do with you."

"The first time I saw snow was right before Richter attacked. She and I were talking on the two-way radio, and she could hear my excitement."

"First time?" This must be odd for a man who hailed from the snowy north. "And what does this mean to her?" He pulled that red ribbon from his pocket.

Couldn't take my eyes off it, me. "I gave it to her when the three of us were on the road to save Selena. Told Evie to return it to me when she'd chosen me for good."

"I see." He shuttered his expression, but I caught the glint of pain. "She'd intended to give it to you before the massacre. I took it from her drawer after she fled the castle, but I will return it to her." He pocketed it.

"Hell, Reaper, she might give it to you. I saw the way the two of you were looking at each other when your kid was kicking away."

"You say that just when I've decided I'm the interloper in her story with you."

Seriously? I mulled that over for a moment, sighed. "We all have our curses. The people of my blood are cursed to love only once. You're cursed never to touch any but one. And Evie? She's cursed to love us both. She really does, you know."

"She did. Before . . ."

"She still does." Unfortunately. "You know, Evie and me were only together for one night. Took me nearly dying in the trench before anything happened between us. She didn't want to give up on you."

He tilted his head at me. "Why tell me this?"

"It proves her feelings for you never died."

"Thank you. It helps."

I gazed at the cabin, picturing her asleep. "She's due on her birthday."

"Just so," Death murmured. "What if I hadn't escaped the Hanged Man? Were you prepared to raise my son?"

"De bon cœur." Wholeheartedly. "I told Evie that you'd rather me keep her and raise your kid as my own than risk them at the castle. Was I wrong?"

He leveled his gaze at me. "You were not."

Why'd he have to be so damned stand-up?

Straightening his shoulders, he said, "You're a good man. I can think of no one better to be a father."

Before I could ask what he'd meant by that, his eyes flickered to the sphere yet again.

"You keep looking at it, Reaper." *Making this Cajun nervous.* "Where's your head at?"

He shrugged.

Not the answer I was looking for. "You made that haze sound like some kind of a drug. Life in there was *simpler*, remember? Being out here is *crippling*. Do you feel a pull to it? What if you just walked right in?"

"If I felt a pull, I would slit my own throat. Hear me, mortal, I will never again be taken by that sphere." Even as he said this for the umpteenth time, his gaze kept straying to the light. His eyes began to glitter. "A thought has just entered my mind. An *idea*."

He turned that starry gaze toward me, and chills raced up my back. "Reaper?"

49

THE HANGED MAN
DAY 587 A.F.

He's mine once more!

Death was back in the fold. My sphere had lured him back in.

Through a frosted windowpane in the study, I watched him exit a truck in the courtyard. He yanked a bound Empress from the cab.

"I hate you!" she screamed at the Reaper. "I knew this would happen!" Her eyes were red, her face pale. She shook uncontrollably in the falling snow.

Was she still pregnant? I couldn't tell with her coat. Despite her fury, her glyphs were dim, and her hair remained blond. She must be tapped out from fighting the armored knight. Not that she'd had much in the way of abilities even months ago.

Death's recapture was so predictable; he must have *wanted* it to happen. His leaving had been a blow to my sizable ego. Without my immortal henchman, I'd felt vulnerable, taking steps to protect myself. But now his card was in my hand once more. I smirked, victorious.

When Gabe landed in front of him, I cracked open the window to eavesdrop.

"Hail, Reaper. I am glad to see you've once again found clarity."

Death gave an arrogant chin jerk in greeting. This time around, I would do more to curb that arrogance. No longer would I tolerate being called a *little man*.

Gabe asked, "Where is your mount?"

"Lost."

"I see. The Chariot and the Tower?"

Ah, yes—where had Kentarch and Joules gotten to? I was greedy for more fuel for my sphere.

"Be on watch for them."

Gabriel nodded. "And the hunter?"

Evie cried, "Jack's dead!" She turned on Death, beating his armored chest with her bound hands. "How could you? He trusted you, and you struck him down!"

So sublimely satisfying. Not only was this a win for my alliance, Death had yet again fed her a dish of betrayal, killing her first love.

Speaking of alliances . . . my gaze shifted past them to the menagerie. Where was Fauna? Probably sleeping, even through this disturbance.

"I'll kill you for what you did!" Evie spat at Death. "I told you we were too close to the sphere—"

"Silence!" he ordered.

Gabriel asked him, "What are you going to do with her?"

He answered, "A gift." *I love gifts.*

"The Hanged Man is in the study."

"Very good." Death yanked on Evie's bonds. With a cry, she went careening along behind him.

Gabriel took flight, beginning his watch. Backdraft from his wings turned the courtyard into a snow globe.

I hurried from the window to the desk I'd commandeered from Death. Taking a seat, I opened a drawer. Beside my new weapon was the Empress's cilice.

Death's spurs clinked in the hallway as he made his way to me. I liked it here in his former office. The temperature was brutal outside; inside, the fire radiated heat. I propped up my feet on *my* desk and ran my fingers over the barbs on the cilice.

Death entered, posture erect, black armor gleaming. A terrifying vision.

I rose, cilice in hand. "Well, well. What do we have here?"

"A gift," he said in his raspy voice.

And what a gift she was! "My thanks, Reaper."

"Aric, what are you going to let him do to me?" Evie clasped her bound hands together. "Snap out of this. I'm begging you."

"Silence!" Death yanked on the rope, causing her to totter, then handed me the end.

With a smile, I accepted it, reeling her closer. With my other hand, I raised the cilice.

She paled even more. "Get that thing away from me, you freak!"

"We'll have to amputate a good part of your arm to get this back into place, but your flesh will regenerate. Cooperate, and Death won't take your head. For now."

Eyes glassy with rage, she said, "I'm warning you, Hanged Man. You don't want to do this to me." Was her hair beginning to turn red? Her glyphs emitted light!

I whipped my head up to the knight. "There's still some fight left in her." She couldn't harm me, but she might be able to poison Death. "Do something!"

"Like what?" he sneered with such contempt that his very voice sounded different.

I scowled. "Knock her out so I can get this cilice on her—"

"That's not the boss!" Lark's scream carried from the menagerie.

My stomach dropped as I gazed upon this armored stranger. Then who was towering over me, drawing his sword . . . ?

50

DEATH

Our ruse was up.

To evade detection, I'd been waiting leagues from the sphere—but I could still hear Fauna's scream echo down the mountain.

No need for me to remain concealed any longer. I began to sprint from where I'd paced a hole into the ground.

Could my wife and Deveaux fend off Fauna's creatures and the Archangel long enough to kill Paul?

Would that noose even work? So many risks.

As I ran, I replayed this morning. Had my plot been a colossal misjudgment?

I waited until she'd awakened and dressed, then said, "I have an idea, sievā, but you will not like it."

She crossed her arms over her chest. "Let's hear it."

"It involves the mortal," I said.

Jack cast me a quizzical look. "Am I finally goan to hear what you refused to tell me on the dish last night?"

I'd needed time to analyze my idea. "You mentioned that you wanted to walk in my shoes. Why stop there? You and I are nearly the same size. You can borrow my armor and swords, then stroll directly into the castle. They will think you're me. Paul's ego is his weakness; he'll assume I came crawling back."

Jack's eyes began to glimmer with anticipation.

But Evie shook her head vehemently. "Even if Jack has a disguise, I won't send him in to face Arcana. Why should he alone have to take such a risk?"

"Because if he succeeds, I will give him the castle."

"WHAT?" she and Jack said at once.

Brows drawn, she asked, "And by extension, you'll give him me?"

I clenched my fists to keep from reaching for her, striving not to reveal how much this prospect gutted me. "I want him particularly motivated to secure the castle. As in olden times, if he wins it; he keeps it."

"You're talking about abandoning your home? You're a freaking homebody. You'd never leave behind all the belongings that you've safeguarded for millennia."

"None of that matters now. I would sacrifice anything to have you and our son safe in that stronghold."

"Including me and Tee?" Her hand went to her rounding belly.

Never to see her? Never to meet my son? My gaze bored into hers as I murmured, "Anything."

"Oh, I'm in," Jack quickly said.

She pointed out, "You'd be going up against three powerful killers."

"I've faced worse odds for a ton less upside. You were worried about me shooting your friends. I woan take a gun, will only be carrying swords and a noose. With that disguise, I can walk in and strangle the Hanged Man. Then Gabe and Lark woan be threats."

She cast a glare from Jack to me. "The plan won't work. If Lark's awake, she'll scent the difference. Gabriel could too."

I said, "Not if they don't get too close, and Jack is wearing my clothing underneath."

"He would have to sound like you. And, Aric, you've already commented on—how should I put this?—his license with the English language."

I'd said he slaughtered the English language anytime he attempted it.

Jack's lips curled. "Now, how hard will it be to sound like an arrogant prick from Russia?"

I narrowed my eyes. "Latvia."

"Come on, peekôn." I loathed it when Deveaux called her that—because she clearly loved it. "I can learn a few short phrases to use and imitate his accent."

She turned to me. "You sweetened the pot too much. He's not going to be thinking straight. I'd rather take the risk myself. I want to reclaim the castle, then think about the future...."

Jack and I both pressed our case to her, and half an hour of arguing ensued.

At length, she said, "Fine! I'll agree to this—if I go as Jack's prisoner. We'll wrap the noose around my wrists, and he'll lead me inside with it."

"Bonne idée," Jack said. I thought he was making a valiant effort not to crow with victory.

"Are you two happy?" A flash of something cunning crossed her blue eyes.

I suspected she had agreed to the battle strategy, but not my terms. No matter; if Jack succeeded, I would keep my word and forfeit my home.

Which meant that regardless of the day's outcome, somehow I would be losing my wife for good.

"No time to waste." Jack started unbuttoning his shirt. "Let's do this."

Though she'd seen both of us unclothed, she turned her back while we traded clothes.

But I hesitated to hand him the first piece of armor. "I have never—in two millennia—allowed another to wear this."

"First time for everything. Come on!" He could barely contain his excitement. And why not? He'd be getting what he wanted most. The castle was icing on the cake.

Wearing Jack's gloves, I helped him strap on the pieces.

"Damn, this metal's light." He pounded his gauntleted fists against

his chest. "Are we pissing off some death deity with this stunt?" Jack knew I'd been divinely led to this suit by my god sponsor.

"Probably."

When he dropped the visor down, I did a double take. I hadn't gazed at my armored self in a mirror in ages. Was this what I looked like to others? No wonder everyone was terrified of me. Add in red-eyed Thanatos . . .

Then I recalled that my steed was dead. Turn your mind from that scene, from the guilt.

Jack asked me, "You never get, uh, claustrophobic in here?"

He had no idea. "Just try not to think about the decomposing corpse I scavenged the suit from."

He muttered, "Beck moi tchew." Bite my ass.

Reminded of his drawl, I said, "The Empress can talk over you, but you'll need an approximation of my accent. Say the word silence *as I might."*

"Saylanss."

I stopped myself from cringing. "Enunciate the syllables, mortal."

She added, "And sound more arrogant. As if you never make mistakes." I stiffened at that, and she noticed. "I'm not giving commentary, but you do usually sound infallible."

"Infallible?" Choking back my frustration, I managed a harsh laugh. "I killed my parents, my unborn sibling, and nearly my wife and son. Infallible and I aren't in the same realm." I regretted the words as soon as I'd uttered them. The Empress wasn't the only one having difficulty governing her emotions.

She softly said, "Aric, don't."

Assuming a brisk demeanor, I said, "We'll spend the next hour practicing some catchphrases. You can get used to the armor and the swords at the same time."

Another mile beneath my boots. Wolves howled from the castle, preparing for a hunt. *Still time!* I powered up a mountain rise, fingers digging into the snow. . . .

Before she and Jack set off, I told him, "I am entrusting everything I love to you, mortal." I would be doing something so much harder than riding in to save the day. I'd be letting go. Depending on another. A rival.

"And I'll handle it, Reaper. But I want it noted that you once told me you'd never need my help."

"I need it more than I've ever needed anything."

With a nod, he continued to the truck, giving me a moment alone with my wife.

I told her, "Be your magnificent self. At any cost."

She gazed up at me from under a shining lock of hair. So beautiful, she pained me. "Aric, if I don't succeed, you'll have to win the game."

"I know I have no right to ask anything of you. But imagine what the next centuries would be like if you do not seize a victory. Could any man withstand such guilt and loss for one lifetime, much less several? I am relying on you to fight hard and prevail. I am expecting you to slay our adversary."

The pulse point in her throat fluttered. Nervousness about the upcoming battle? Or my nearness?

"I believe in you, love." I leaned down and pressed my lips to hers, knowing it would be our last kiss.

She allowed it, which made my heart thunder. . . .

Running headlong, I spied the boundary's glow in the distance.

The need to charge into that fray blistered me inside. I didn't crave the Hanged Man's false sense of clarity—I craved fighting for my family.

I felt as if my entire endless existence had led up to this. As I ran, I clenched my fists impotently. *Please, gods, let her prevail.*

How many times had I clenched my fists because I couldn't touch? Now I couldn't even kill—the one thing I'd been born to do.

51

THE EMPRESS

"Evie, now!" Jack yelled, his voice distorted behind Aric's helmet.

As I slipped from my bindings—the noose—Paul's expression twisted.

That light behind his head flared. "You can't kill me." He still held the other end of the rope.

"This is for Finn, you asshole!" With a wave of my hand, I commanded the noose to strike. Like a serpent, the length shot up his body, coiling around his neck.

"*Nooo!*" His fingers clutched the rope, digging in between the hemp and his skin.

Finn's icon was stark on his right hand. I'd barely kept up my damsel-in-distress act when I'd first seen it.

Wolves howled, answering his scream. They were inside the castle!

When Lark had first blown our cover, Jack had run for the door and slammed it closed, locking it.

What sounded like a stampede headed this way. Our plan depended on Paul's quick demise. Could I take him out before those animals swarmed the study? Before Gabriel returned? I'd been stunned by his menacing new size.

Gritting my teeth, I tightened Paul's noose. His eyes bulged and his glowing light flickered, but he still fought me.

Jack raised one of Aric's borrowed swords, positioning himself between me and the door. "They're coming, Evie!" Wolf claws clattered in the hallway.

Tighter, tighter. But Paul remained on his feet, grappling against my hold. His face was purple. Veins jutted in his neck and forehead.

He made unintelligible sounds, his eyes pleading. Vessels burst across the white. Why wouldn't he die? With each moment, *I* was weakening.

What if the noose didn't work? As I kept up the pressure, I tried to muster spores. . . .

Nothing. I'd only weakened myself.

Growls sounded from the hall just before the door bowed. Surely they couldn't break through—

In a rush of splinters, the wolves tore at the wood, ripping out chunks with their fangs.

Jack jabbed the sword through a hole in the door.

Yelp.

The blade came back bloody, but the wolves kept attacking.

I tightened the rope even more, cutting short Paul's gurgling. "Die already!"

A giant frizzy head breached the door, jaws snapping the air. Cyclops. He snatched his head back just as Jack swung.

"Evie, whatever you're goan to do, do it fast!"

Lark had reached the hall. "Empress, release Paul, and I'll spare you and Deveaux. Otherwise, my wolves will clean your bones—like you did to my lion."

"You think I killed Finn. You'd never spare me."

She screamed, "You don't get to say his name! Gabriel, kick down the door." The Archangel was here as well!

The battered door rocked off its hinges, crashing to the floor. I gaped at Gabriel and Lark in the hall.

His wings flexed ominously, his eyes crazed. She was just as wild-eyed, with her mane tangled, looking more like an animal than ever before. Her wolves crouched beside her, saliva dripping from their bared fangs.

Jack readied his sword, gliding it back and forth.

I scrambled behind Paul, raising my claws to his face, all the while keeping the pressure on the noose. "No closer!"

Lark laughed. "Your glyphs are dark, which means you're out of juice. Besides, he can't be killed, dumbass. You can strangle or poison him all you want, but he won't die." She said to Gabriel, "The Empress is *my* kill."

His eerie green gaze landed on Jack, and his wings flexed again, those talons so sharp.

Realization: *We're done for.*

Gabriel struck, one wing zooming out from the hallway. Before Jack could swing his sword, his body had been launched across the room.

"Ah, God, Jack!"

He unsteadily rose, had somehow managed to keep hold of his weapon.

"Don't touch him again, Gabriel!" *Or what?*

"ARCHANGEL," Aric yelled from a distance. He must be at the edge of the sphere. "Face me! I have no armor. No swords. Come seize my icon."

Would Gabriel take the bait? "Death has no protection," he told Lark. "We will not get another opportunity like this. My wing's reach is long. I can kill him without crossing the boundary."

Then Aric was more vulnerable than he'd ever been. *Need Paul to die before Gabriel reaches the edge!*

Lark nodded. "Go. I can handle one mortal playing dress-up and a powerless Empress." Cyclops slinked inside, Scarface and Maneater behind him. They circled me and Jack.

Gabriel charged away, and Lark focused her chilling red gaze on me. "I'm going to make this hurt." The wolves pounced.

I tossed vines their way, muzzling their snouts. Each ounce of power I used for defense weakened my attack on Paul.

Jack swung at Scarface, landing a sword blow against his flank. The muzzled wolf leapt for him, knocking him onto his back.

"*Putain!*"

"Jack!"

Scarface broke free of his vines and snapped at Jack's raised arm, fangs on metal. *Clang clang.* The sword flashed out again, striking the wolf's other side. Blood poured, but its eyes were demented.

When I threw another vine to protect Jack, Paul stole a few wheezing breaths. His struggles grew stronger.

Maneater pawed her green muzzle off, then charged me. I scrambled back, blocking her way with more vines. All the while, I could feel Paul inching his way out of the noose.

We were losing ground, about to lose our lives! *Anytime, red witch. Here's another monster for you.*

Jack had the same thought. Between breaths, he grated, "Let her loose, Evie!"

Out of the corner of my eye, I spied Paul fumbling with something in the desk drawer. What was he—

A pistol.

He used my moment of shock to yank back from me. I tightened the noose, but he still managed to raise the weapon, aiming it right at my stomach.

The gun fired.

Blinding pain made me scream. Aric's anguished roar carried from the distance.

I gaped down at my body. The bullet had gone in and out of my arm. Paul attempted to steady his shaking hand. Too late; a vine leapt from my skin, knocking the weapon to the floor.

Paul had only given me a flesh wound, but he could have shot my vulnerable belly. The red witch shrieked for vengeance, rising up inside me, a terrible fever. Drawing on my wrath felt good. Surrendering to rage was like living in Paul's sphere: simpler.

Power surged. With every one of his exhalations, I tightened the noose's grip. The scent of roses steeped the air. The heat of battle was an inferno.

The light behind his head dimmed as he fell to his knees. He clawed at his throat, his eyes pleading.

Ah, heavenly. "Come, Paul. Touch." When one eyeball popped out, I laughed with delight. *Just like old times.* "But you'll pay a price." I flicked my wrist.

The noose contracted. *SNAP.*

Paul's limp body collapsed to the floor, and his tongue lolled from his slack mouth. At last!

I laughed again as a shivery feeling tingled on my hand. Then another. *Icons.*

Yanking off my glove, I stared down at the new marks: a noose for the Hanged Man and Finn's ouroboros. *Want more.*

I slowly turned to Lark. I could take her down, just as my grandmother had wanted. Then Gabriel. Four icons in one day!

Why stop there? Death had no armor. . . .

Expression baffled, Lark clambered back against a wall, her wolves staggering toward her. "What the hell?" Her red eyes sparked with realization. Her lips curled back, revealing her fangs. "Paul did it? He killed Finn! He made me burn . . . ah, God, I burned Finn."

The wolves leapt upon the Hanged Man's corpse, snatching at flesh, tearing him apart.

Crunch, crunch. Blood painted the walls, crimson spatter arcing over antiques and book spines. It pooled on the floor around Paul's remains as the beasts fought over pieces.

The violence excited the red witch. As I sized up Lark, her eyes were laser-focused on the gore.

Jack lumbered toward me. "Hey, hey. Come back to me." He pinched my chin and turned my face. "Lark's been through enough. Come on, you can do this."

I thrashed my head away. *Nooo.* Now awakened, the witch had no desire to yield. *Evie a sliver of me! I can protect the baby better than anyone. We're stronger like this.*

"Come back to me, *peekôn.* The fight's over."

But it *wasn't.* The monsters would just keep coming. And I couldn't keep doing this without drowning in the well. "It's better this way, Jack." My voice even sounded different, breathy and evil.

I'd never felt so in line with the red witch, so unified. Maybe my split personality was melding. Maybe it *should*.

"I'm right here, *bébé*. You have to come back to me."

With each second that I clashed against the witch for control, Lark seemed to be emerging from her own inner battle. Eyes lost, she gave a heartbreaking sob.

That sound was like an alarm going off inside me, warning me of danger.

I was the danger.

Damn it, Lark was my friend! I never wanted to hurt her. I peered up at Jack, holding his gaze, taking deep breaths.

The witch finally began to recede.

"*Ma bonne fille*, that's it. You've got this."

In time, I met eyes with Lark. "Are you with us again?" Her tableau appeared—right side up.

She nodded. "Yeah. I'm back now."

I glanced out the window. The sphere had dissipated. The pall was gone, but had I gotten to the Hanged Man in time to stop Gabriel? "Can you see if Death is safe?"

Looking for him through her creatures, she said, "The boss is closing in fast."

Relief overwhelmed me.

"I'm so sorry, Evie," she said, tears welling. "For everything."

"You couldn't help it. It's not your fault."

"Great trick, by the way." Her voice broke as she said, "F-Finn would've loved it." She lurched away.

I hurried after her. "Lark, wait."

Glancing over her shoulder, she held up her claw-tipped fingers to stop me. "Need to go lick my wounds. Alone." Her gaze flitted past me to the blood. Was she staring at it hungrily? *Red of tooth and claw.* Maybe I wasn't the only one wrestling with the heat of battle. "Just give me a t.o." She turned once more. Her wolves followed her, severed limbs dangling from their jaws.

Jack grabbed my shoulder, enfolding me in his arms as much as the armor would allow. "Let her go. Finn's death is probably hitting her for real for the first time."

I couldn't even comprehend how she must be feeling. Oh, wait—yes, I could.

Jack pulled off the helmet, setting it on Aric's desk. "You okay? Can't believe that bastard shot you."

"Yeah." I checked the wound. Regeneration was kicking in slowly. "It's nothing. Already healing."

"If Domīnija had been here, he could've prevented that."

"It was close quarters. Are *you* okay?" Without that armor, he might have died.

"I'm good." Jack drew back and started to remove the onyx pieces, piling them next to the helmet. Breastplate. Left armguard. "But I want this off me." He reached down to unbuckle the last leg guard.

I frowned at the discarded armor. "That suit probably saved your life. Gabriel's strike could've broken your back. At the very least, Scarface would have taken your arm."

"Wearing this made me understand some things." He straightened. "This suit isn't just Death's protection against the world; it's the world's protection against him—a cage. Domīnija told me I'd walk a mile in his shoes. I have. And inside this armor is the loneliest place I've ever been, the most separated from everything I've ever felt."

I thought back to all the times I'd asked Aric to wear it. "He must hate it." But he'd still worn it to allay my fears.

"*Ouais.*" For the first time, Jack's attention strayed from me. Details of the study caught his eye, the books and scrolls, the scepters and crowns on display. His curiosity was clearly redlining. "So this is the Reaper's lair. Mind-blowing, *non?* One thing to hear about it; another to see it inside. I was slack-jawed the whole way in. Almost forgot to act like an asshole to you."

And now, by rights, the castle of lost time was his. Yet as much as I tried to picture living here with Jack, I couldn't see it.

He must've picked up on my shift in mood. "You never intended to send Death packing, did you?"

"I didn't make any decisions about him or you, but it felt wrong to oust him from his home."

"For true." Another glance around the room. A rueful exhalation. "Nice place to visit ..."

Despite everything, Jack made me want to smile. "When Aric brought up his idea, I just kept my mouth shut and went along with it."

At the same time, we both said, "Kick the can down the road."

I gave a weak laugh. "Yeah."

He took my hand in his. "But now we're at the end of the road. Castle or no, ousting or no, how're you feeling?" He took a step closer. "Just so we're clear about how *I'm* feeling ..." He leaned down to press his lips to mine. The tender kiss told me more than words ever could.

I love you. I desire you. I need you. He drew back to gaze down into my eyes, leaving me breathless.

"*Jack* ..."

"Pardon me," Aric said from the doorway, his expression stricken, his lungs heaving. With his hair disheveled and still wearing Jack's careworn clothes, he looked as far from the perfect nobleman as I'd ever seen him. "I heard a gun go off." His brows were drawn, his eyes searching. "And your scream."

I said, "Only got a nick on my arm."

Grave nod. "Very good. I am relieved to hear it." He swallowed hard and his gaze dipped to where Jack clasped my hand. "I will gather some supplies and be on my way."

I hadn't even noticed we were holding hands.

Jack frowned. "What about your armor and swords?"

His eyes flickered over what was left of Paul. "You will need them more than I will. To protect her." With a last glance, he left us.

Jack whistled low. "He would truly give up everything for you. *Everything.*" He muttered, "Fucking stand-up Death."

I said, "That armor belongs with him."

"I sure as hell doan want it."

Gabriel rushed into the room, his gaze frantic. "Empress, I'm so sorry! Your babe? The avalanche! You lost so much blood."

"I'm still pregnant." I needed to reach Aric. I would hear his anguished roar for the rest of my days. What must he have thought? I absently said, "You saved me, Gabe. You saved *us.*"

Gabriel put his head in his talon-tipped hands, then slid down the wall, losing a couple of black feathers. "My God, my God. I would have stabbed you."

Jack released me, hastening to the Angel's side. "Easy, podna. Just breathe."

"And I nearly killed you, Jack. I was a hair's breadth from slitting your throat."

"But you didn't."

He grabbed Jack's arm. "Where is Patrick?"

"With the Chariot. They were okay as of a few days ago. But we got separated. I think they might be in the DC area."

"I threatened him." Gabriel curled his wings around his body, seeming to hug himself. "Would have killed my best friend. How will I find him?"

Jack turned to me. "I got this, Evie. Damn it, go stall Domīnija."

I nodded, then hurried after Death.

52

By the time I caught up with him, Aric had already changed his clothes and was using his supernatural speed to unload all the supplies Jack had transported from the cave. Staples, fuel, and a ton of baby things.

Baby things. Because Jack was committed.

Aric had opened one of the garage doors, was stacking boxes against the wall. I asked him, "Are you in a hurry?"

Curt nod.

"Why?"

"Even my willpower has its limits." He carried another box inside.

"Thinking about reneging?"

His shoulders stiffened, and he slowed. "Before, you would never have asked that, would have known I am a man of my word. If nothing else . . ."

"Oh, I think you'll give up ownership of the castle. I was just hoping you were having second thoughts about leaving me and our kid behind." There. I'd said *our kid*.

He set aside the box and turned to face me. "It's become clear that you and Jack belong together. I saw the emotion between you two when you stared into his eyes."

"And what about my relationship with you?"

He crossed to me. "That's what I'm trying to tell you. I've realized I was wrong about us. I belong with no one. It was always my fate." *A ruler, forever alone.*

"Forever alone, Aric? Too late." I pointed at my stomach. "Too late."

He pulled off a glove and cupped my cheek. His lids went heavy from the contact. *"Es tevi mīlu."* I love you. "But my soul is too tainted to be with another."

"I disagree." I didn't know what I was here to fight for. I just knew I wasn't ready to lose Aric.

Still had no idea where that left me and Jack.

Aric dug into his coat pocket and handed me the red ribbon. "Give this to him."

I stared down at it in shock. Jack must've told him its significance. Seeing it sent my unruly emotions into overdrive, but I needed to be rational about this. I pocketed it, clearing my throat to say, "You can't leave, Aric."

"He's not." Jack strode into the courtyard. "I'm the one heading out."

Gabriel followed him, looking calmer.

Aric drew his head back. "You too think I'll renege on the bargain I made with you?"

"Not at all. Which is why I can't do this."

"I don't understand."

"I made a promise to Evie: if I felt sure you were back to normal and wouldn't give into that rage again, I'd bow out. When I harbored doubts about you, I had no problems imagining myself robbing you blind, taking everything of yours. But now . . ." He waved to indicate me and Aric. When had I gotten so close to him? "Damn you, man, you're back to normal."

"Am I to have no say?" My eyes filled with tears.

"Non, peekôn. For once, *non.* I told Kentarch that in the end, I'd do whatever is best for you. The fact is: Death can protect you better than I can. The man is ready to surrender his wife and kid to his rival just to keep them safe; you think I'm not ready to make the exact same sacrifice? I've got to put you and Tee in the best situation I can. No matter how bad it hurts."

My emotions were all over the place with this pregnancy and from the trauma I'd been through. If they did leave the decision to me, maybe it *would* put me over the edge. Because this was a choice I would never be able to make—perfect for me couldn't be bested. "You're leaving because you get to control the outcome. You need to control your fate."

"Doan matter *why* I'm goan. Just that I *am*," he said, echoing what he'd told me our first night in Jubilee.

I gave Aric a helpless look. *Fix this, like you usually do.* But how could he? I wanted them both.

Squaring his shoulders, he told Jack, "I struck a bargain with you. I will honor it."

"Me and Gabe have been talking. He's coming with me to find Joules and Kentarch. Then the four of us'll all head south to put together another settlement. That might steer Richter away from this place."

"You'll act as bait?" Aric said. "I can just as easily undertake that mission, leaving you here with her. Only two Arcana would remain then."

"Hell, Reaper, how far are you goan to get down the road with *Joules?*"

"I'll manage."

Jack shook his head. "You know this makes the most sense. We agreed that Evie and Tee come first."

Now they were fighting over who got to leave. Confusion swamped me. I'd tried to imagine a life here with Jack. Now I was back to raising a son here with Aric?

"Your boy needs to be with his father." Jack turned to me. "If my father had wanted anything to do with me and another man drove him away, I would've ended up hating that man. I woan be the wedge that separates Domīnija from a son he's desperate to raise."

"I . . . I . . ." Oh, God, I had no argument against that.

To Aric, he said, "You've waited two millennia to meet him, and now you're goan to bug out a few months before he gets here?" Clever

Jack. "Look, we agreed you need a bolt hole for Evie and Tee. If you outfit me with sunlamps, fuel, and food, I can make that happen. Give me a job, Reaper. Put me to work." Holding Aric's gaze, he said, "I woan be moved from my decision. I swear *on my mother's soul* that this is what's happening."

A look passed between them, something that indicated those words were more than a weighty vow. Aric's defiant posture changed. Why?

What would he say? What would *I* say?

Silence stretched out—so many emotions played over Aric's face—until finally he intoned, "As you wish, mortal."

I was too stunned to speak.

Jack said, "Gimme a minute with her, guys."

"Of course." With a last look at me, Aric turned to go.

Gabriel followed, but paused a few steps away to say, "Empress, I once told you that I dearly wished you could end this game, but I don't believe it's possible anymore."

"Why?"

Sadness filled his eyes. "Because we're almost at the end of it." With that, he left Jack and me alone out in the snowy night.

Gabriel would know about the end. He had the senses of both angel and animal. So how could I be separated from Aric when the game was spinning to its conclusion? Not to be able to watch over him?

But then, how could I live without Jack? Tears fell unchecked as I closed the distance between us. "I'm in love with you, and you're going to leave me? What about the night we spent together?"

He swallowed hard. "Makes this all the more difficult."

I waved at all the baby gear. "I think a part of you already loves this kid. Are *you* okay with never meeting him?"

"I'm okay with making sacrifices to keep you two protected." He curled his finger under my chin. "Think about it: getting you safe to your destination was always on me. That was my job. I did it, Evie; you're here. Let me have that."

"Jack . . ."

"Now I'll be goan back to where it all began. I'm goan home, me."

Right when I was about to beg—*Take me with you!*—he said, "Let me go, *bébé*. I got a blade in my heart."

Like a thorn in his skin? "I don't even know if Death and I can come back from everything that's happened." I loved Aric, but we had so much pain between us. I didn't believe he should be forever alone, but I also wasn't optimistic about recovering what we'd shared.

"I know you can. I saw you two together. Your bond's still there, busted up, but still there. Dust it off. Just hold off kicking his ass too bad. He's had a hard time of this, too."

"And the red witch? You're supposed to be here to pull me back to safety."

"If you get into trouble, I'll come running, me," Jack said with a sad smile. "But I trust you not to hurt anyone who doan have it coming—including the Reaper."

I wasn't convinced. Even now, the witch's shrieks still echoed inside me, a bell tolled.

"*Peekôn*, it seems you're forgiving everyone but Domīnija."

"Gabriel and Lark didn't kill me in the past. *Twice.*"

Jack gazed down at my face expectantly, as if waiting for me to realize something. What? I was too overwhelmed to make sense of this. I felt like I was disappointing him. "What am I missing? Just tell me. I've had a day, you know?"

"If you blame the Reaper for previous games, then you're doing the same thing you accused him of: holding on to a bitter past, to unresolved anger."

My lips parted. "Oh, my God." Jack was right. I'd forgiven Lark, Gabriel, even Matthew to an extent. I'd forgiven Selena and Sol.

I'd been asking myself how I could ever repair things with Aric. Had he asked himself the same question about me? Somehow he'd worked past his mistrust—past *my* murder attempts—to love me. If not for a fiend like Paul, Aric never would have stopped.

Just as I'd never stopped loving him. Could *I* let go of my mistrust and our past? Didn't I owe it to this kid to give it a try?

But where would that leave Jack?

"Answer me one question, Evie. You answer no, and you're coming with me."

What would he ask? I didn't breathe.

"Does half your heart still belong to the Reaper?"

Though *all* of my heart was breaking, I whispered, *"Yes."*

53

The truck was running. Jack had his fingers on the door handle.

Gabriel was already inside the cab, wings folded as he waited. The back had a tarp holding down supplies. They'd even hitched a utility trailer for more cargo.

Because this was happening. Jack was leaving me. And I was allowing it?

I'd gone inside out of the cold as they'd packed. After Aric finished helping them, he'd retreated to his study to give me privacy to say good-bye for good.

As I walked out, he'd murmured, "Please, stem your tears. For him. I rode away from you once—I know from experience that he is going through unimaginable pain. Don't make this harder on him."

Somehow I'd stopped my tears, but now they were threatening again. I asked Jack, "Are you going to pull my thorn from your skin?"

He turned back to gaze down at me. "*Jamais*. Never. Not even goan to try."

"You told me you had to feel me with your every step. You *told* me that."

"I will. As long as you're alive and safe." His voice broke lower. "Got to go, me. 'Fore I lose it." That muscle ticked in his jaw, the levee about to collapse.

"How can you leave after what we felt? I told you that being with you was like coming home."

He leaned down and grazed his lips over mine. I reached for him to deepen the kiss, but he pulled back. "That's the thing about home, *bébé.*" Gray eyes glinting, voice hoarse, he said, "It'll always be there waiting for you." He turned and climbed into the truck.

I gasped when he put it into gear and began driving away from me. I could still feel the heat of his lips on mine, yet I was letting him go.

His taillights grew fainter, the snow trying to block my view of him. Tears poured down my cheeks as I willed him to turn around.

I wanted to scream that this was a mistake. He seemed to think so. Halfway down the winding drive, his brake lights pierced the night. Twin beacons in a storm. I wanted to run for them.

The truck came to a stop on the bridge spanning Circe's frozen moat. It sat idle, the exhaust smoking in the crisp air. *Come back to me, Jack.*

Maybe he'd found the gift I'd left tucked behind the truck's sun visor: the red ribbon wrapped around a branch of honeysuckle. He'd once called it his *porte-bonheur,* his good-luck charm, saying it told him we'd be together again.

Had I chosen Jack *over* Aric? No. But the ribbon belonged with him all the same.

Tee began kicking up a storm. Sensing my desperation? I placed my hands on my belly and a strange warmth stole over me.

Jack was heading into danger, so why did I get the feeling that I'd see him again? Even amidst my panic, a glowing, welcome certainty banked inside me.

Jackson Daniel Deveaux and I would meet again.

Eventually, the truck continued on. Maybe Gabriel was telling him the same: *You will see her once more, hunter. Believe in this.*

I watched that truck until it disappeared into the curtain of white. Until the winds muffled the engine sound, wrapping it up.

Until the night stole him from me.

I watched long after there was no sign of him. Of Jack. The love of my life. I watched until my tears had frozen on my cheeks. I tightened the tourniquet once more, knowing that one day it would break, and I would bleed out in the snow.

Or worse.

But if he could sacrifice for Tee, so could I. Stemming my tears, I turned back toward the castle.

My soul mate, the father of my son, awaited me there. I had a relationship to repair, alliances to rebuild, and a home to defend.

As certain as I felt that I'd see Jack again, I was even more sure the game was spinning to a bloody end.

I'd be ready.

—*Empresssss.*— A whisper in my ear like a breath of frost. The Fool was contacting me through our mental link.

I drew up short. *I've been waiting for you to answer me.* I plumbed my emotions. How did I feel about my former ally now?

Conflicted again. I'd missed him, and I owed him for saving Jack from those slavers. I owed him for helping Aric get free from Paul. But Matthew had also allowed awful things to happen to our friends.

To Finn . . .

—*Do you know what you really want? I see far, Empress.*—

Then tell me what's to come.

—*The gods vent their wrath. The Minors unite. Hell on earth. Quakes. They'll all be coming for you.*—

Out loud, I said, "Let them come." My claws budded and sharpened. The scent of roses steeped the frigid air.

—*Empress?*—

"Matthew, I finally understand what you've wanted me to learn all along." I glanced down at my marked hand, then back at the lonely road Jack now travelled. In that breathy, evil voice, I said, "For better or for worse, anyone who touches me pays a price."

I headed inside.

AUTHOR'S NOTE

Dear Reader,

I often get asked if I'm Team Jack or Team Aric. Like Evie, I think each is perfect for her in his own way.

And so writing this book was bittersweet. My eyes water every time I read Jack's farewell or reflect on the pain lingering inside Aric.

The Flash is leaching away hope, and a perilous future lies ahead for the woman they love. But the pieces for the final showdown in the Arcana Chronicles are now in place. Everyone remaining has a part to play in the battle to save the world.

Evie can be a reckoning, but at what price? Has the seed of hope already been planted?

Thank you so much for continuing on this journey and for trusting me to shepherd these characters to a better tomorrow.

Stay tuned; the end is beginning. Warmest wishes,

KC

P.S. The health of this series, of *all* book series, depends on reader support. If you enjoyed this installment, please kindly leave a review at vendor sites and recommend to your friends. Thank you, and Hail Tar Ro!